A NEXT GENERATION NOVEL

AFTER

J.M.
WALKER

IBSN: 978-1-989782-20-0

After Us (Next Generation, #6)

FAMILY TREE

Angel and Geneviève "Jay" Rodriguez
(Grit, King's Harlots #1/Grim, King's Harlots #3)
Angelica "Gigi"
Ryder
Meadow

Asher and Meeka Donovan
(Stain, King's Harlots #2)
Aiden
Ashton

Coby and Brogan Porter
(Rude, King's Harlots #4/For You, King's Harlots #7)
Zachary "Zach"

Dale and Maxine "Max" Michaels
(Numb, King's Harlots #5)
Piper

Vincent "Stone" and Creena Stone
(Rust, King's Harlots #6)
Luna
Vincent Junior

Greyson and Eve Mercer
(Greyson, Hell's Harlem #1)
Jaron

Tray and Zillah Lister
(Tray, Hell's Harlem #2)
Beatrix "Bee"

John and Beatrix "Trixie" Butcher
(Hell's Harlem Series)
Cyrus
Samson "Sammy"

PROLOGUE

JARON

I CRAVED HER SCREAMS, her moans, her eyes telling me everything I needed to know about the woman I was in love with. Even though I had never voiced those words out loud, I didn't need to. Piper Michaels knew exactly how I felt about her.

My baby was currently growing inside of her. A life that both of us created. We had so much shit to talk about but first, every male instinct inside of me wanted to gloat that I was the one who got her pregnant. That I was the one who she would spend her life with. Even though we hadn't discussed our future plans, she was waiting for me. Knowing she had been with several other guys before me, I was proud of the fact that she was carrying my baby. I only wished I could have claimed her long before I slept with anyone else. Not that I would ever call what I did sleeping. I was curbing an itch that I couldn't reach. Piper had been the only one who could ever scratch it. She was the one I needed to satisfy this hunger. This need. This desire.

Or so I thought.

Truth was, it only made this hunger fiercer.

More intense.

She would be about six months pregnant now. I got random updates from my dad whenever he came to see me.

The outside world changed when you were stuck behind bars. People went on with their lives, but prisoners? The only thing that changed was their appearance as they got older. But day in and day out, they followed the same routine. I tried keeping myself busy and out of trouble, but it hadn't worked. Fights started. Lives were lost. Some were even my fault. It messed with my head, knowing I had a family to get home to. But the light I once felt, dimmed the longer I was away from those I loved.

My cousins, Sammy and Cyrus Butcher, would also keep me informed as to how Piper was doing. Thankfully, Sammy didn't beat around the bush as much as my father had.

Bottom line, Piper was hurting.

The pain she felt only made me strive to get out sooner for her. I tried my best to be a good boy and keep my nose clean. But being the vice president and son to the current president of Hell's Harlem, you ended up knowing people.

No matter how many fights I had been in, the memory of Piper's smiling face kept me going.

I didn't want to ask about her, knowing it would just make me miss her that much more. But I couldn't help it. I needed to know. Even though I felt it, I needed to hear the words that she was waiting for me and that I was the one. Her one like she was mine.

"Please tell me how you feel," she begged, her voice shaking on the other end of the phone.

"I can't, baby. I need to see you when I tell you. I need to look into your eyes as I confess how I feel."

A shaky breath left her. "I can't wait for that day."

My chest tightened. "I know."

Truth was, I had fallen for her hard and fast. Even as a kid, I knew from the very beginning that I wanted her. She had been with friends. Both of us were young. Barely sixteen. She was nice to me while at times, I felt like an outcast because I didn't hang out with them often. But much to my dismay, a twin set of boys were always with her. It was like they knew, so Ashton and Aiden made it so we could never be alone.

But no matter how hard they tried to keep me away, it didn't work. No matter where she was on this earth, I would find her.

Take care of her.

AFTER US

Love her.
Piper was mine and I was hers.
Forever.

ONE

Piper

IT WAS FINALLY TIME.
I would be seeing Jaron Mercer again in only a matter of minutes. I had been stewing for the past few weeks. Probably driving everyone I knew absolutely crazy but my excitement got ahold of me.

Every nerve ending in my body came alive at the mere thought of seeing him again. It had been so long since I touched him. Since I had seen his handsome face with the dark scruff on his strong jaw and his slate gray eyes that looked like they were reaching down into the deepest pits of my soul.

It had been a long road between us. Everything was new. Fresh. Fun. Intense. So damn intense, one look from him and I was putty in his hands. He could tell me to jump and I would always give in. He knew it too. There was no sense in denying it. From the first look to the last kiss, I was his. He let the world know as well that I belonged to him. In every sense of the word. But even though that had been the case, we didn't know each other. Not completely. Maybe we never would. But I wanted to at least try.

It had been so long since I had seen him, I wasn't sure where we went from here. Whether we could make it as a family or even a couple. Could we move forward? After everything that had happened in such a short amount of time, could we finally be happy?

Leaning against my car, I waited. I checked the time on my phone, glanced around me. And waited some more.

My eyes flicked to the large sign sitting on the side of the building.

State Penitentiary.

Just the name gave me shivers. I never once in my life thought I would end up picking up a guy here. Let alone the father of my daughter and the man I was in love with.

I sighed, checking my phone again.

Sammy: He out yet?

Me: Do you see him anywhere?

Sammy: Geeze, girl. Just asking.

My cheeks burned.

Me: Sorry.

Cyrus: Ignore him. You can have as much attitude as you want.

Me: I love you guys.

Cyrus: We love you too, kiddo.

I stuffed my phone back into my pocket, ignoring the text coming into the group chat I had with the brothers. Cyrus and Sammy Butcher were twins and a few years older than both Jaron and me. They were his family and now they were automatically mine as well. They were good to me and my daughter. They didn't have families of their own and at times I felt like I was taking them from having their own happiness, but they never complained. I often suggested they go out, have a good time, and not worry about me, but they shot those suggestions down rather quickly.

"Jaron asked us to look after both of you, so that's what we're doing," Cyrus told me.

"Truth." Sammy nodded. "Besides, I'm boycotting pussy at the moment anyway."

I frowned. "What do you mean?"

He scowled but he never responded.

"It means that there's a woman he wants but she doesn't want him back," Cyrus explained.

"She's delaying the inevitable and I don't know why." Sammy shoved to his feet and stormed into the kitchen.

That conversation had been a few months ago and I hadn't heard of this secret woman since, but whoever she was, she clearly got under Sammy's skin. I couldn't wait to meet her.

My phone dinged again, making me jump.

Cyrus: You got this.

I put my cell into my purse and threw the bag in the back seat of my car.

Waiting for Jaron was enough to drive me mad. My body vibrated, my heart raced, my thoughts ran a mile a minute. So many questions bounced around in my head.

Did he change at all?

Did he still look the same?

What if we no longer got along?

Was he still as grumpy or worse?

Did he still love me?

What if we couldn't make this work and had to go our separate ways?

Letting out a hard sigh, I opened the back door and reached for my purse. I was antsy and needed to check my phone to see if there were any updates. When I saw that there weren't, a lump formed in my throat. I just wanted him. I wanted him to come out, smile at seeing me and we could drive off into the sunset and live happily ever after. But I knew none of that would happen.

As soon as I closed the door, the hairs on the back of my neck tingled.

I inhaled a sharp breath, slowly turning around.

Jaron stood just outside the jail, watching me. Waiting for that invitation he never needed. Ever.

My eyes welled, my throat burning over the hard lump that had taken up permanent residence there so long ago.

His dark eyes searched my face, studying me.

I took a step forward.

He did the same.

We continued walking toward one another until we finally stood a foot away from each other. I expected to crash into him, but I was hesitant. So many questions bounced around in my head. I wasn't sure if he felt the same. I needed to know.

I couldn't move. I tried to close that final distance between us, but I was stuck. Was this even real? Was he finally standing there in front of me? After all of this time? After so many months of being apart, this day had finally come. I wanted to pinch myself to see if it was a dream. I told my daughter earlier that morning that I was bringing her daddy home. Her eyes had lit up. Even though she wasn't even a year old yet, she knew. God, did she know.

Jaron's dark eyes searched my face. His big body was stiff, rigid, like he was holding back from doing God only knew what.

With a shaky hand, I placed it against his chest.

His heartbeat thumped beneath my palm and I knew, God did I know, that his heart beat only for me.

I looked up at him, the vision of him blurring in front of me. Gripping his hoodie in my hand, I pulled him closer.

That was the only invitation he needed before he wrapped his arms around me.

A sob escaped me as I latched on to him and tried pulling him even closer. But no matter how close we were, I still felt like he was far away. But it didn't matter. I would help him. We would get through this and we would move on.

Together.

Tears fell down my cheeks, rolling off my chin and onto his black hoodie. I pushed my face into the crook of his thick neck and silently begged for him to take me away. We had so much to work through but first, we needed to work through us.

"I fucking missed you," he whispered into my hair, his voice thick. "I missed you so damn much, Piper."

Sobs continued wracking through me. I still couldn't believe he was back in my arms. After all of this time.

Jaron leaned back, cupping my face and swiping his thumbs under my eyes. He placed a soft peck on my forehead that only made the tears fall harder.

"Are my boys here?" he asked, his voice cracking.

"They parked their bikes over there," I murmured, nodding toward the end of the parking lot. "They wouldn't let me come by myself but wanted to give us a moment."

Jaron gave me a small smirk. "We need lots of moments, baby."

My breath hitched. "Yeah. We do." I paused. "They've been taking care of us."

"Good. I'm glad." Jaron leaned his forehead against mine. "You look good."

I smiled, wiping away the tears. "I still taste good too," I told him, using the line I had used so many months ago when I had gone five weeks without seeing him.

A deep chuckle left him, but it wasn't like before. No. Something inside of him changed. The laugh appeared as if it were forced in a way.

"I bet you do."

Cupping his nape, I ran my fingers through his dark hair. It had grown in some, especially his beard. And he filled out. A lot. He was big before but now he was outright huge.

I leaned back, cupping his jaw. "I like the beard," I whispered.

His face was impassive, something flashing behind his eyes. Normally, he would have said something dirty but now the words failed on his tongue.

My stomach twisted, unsure if I was happy about that or not. I didn't want him to change but I knew that being in jail could affect a person. For better. For worse. Both. I wasn't sure anymore.

"Did you get everything?" I asked him, taking a step back.

"I did."

Before I could walk away, he grabbed my hand, pulling me back into his arms. I gasped, slapping my hands against his chest. "Jaron."

"I need…" He blew out a slow breath. "I just need to touch you. I need you in my arms. I can't explain it. I'm not even going to try."

"Okay." I wrapped my arms around his neck. "Take all the time you need."

"How have you been?" he asked, brushing his thumb down the length of my jaw.

I shivered at the soft contact. Especially coming from someone like him. He had never been a gentle guy. Not that I ever wanted that side of him anyway. I preferred when he was rough and took from me exactly what he wanted, knowing that I wanted it just the same. "I've been alright. I've missed you." I ran my fingers through his beard, a tingle racing down my spine. "I really like this."

His eyes darkened. "Trust me, Piper. You'll like it more when it's between your legs."

And there it was. The dirty talk I always craved from him. I only smiled and pushed out of his hold before grabbing his hand. "Let's go see the guys."

He nodded, pulling his hand from mine and wrapping his arm around my shoulders. "Where is she?"

"Oh." I stopped, turning toward him. "I was going to bring her, but she was fussy. I think she was stressed. Or she knew I was stressed. I'm not sure. But she didn't sleep well last night." And neither did I. It was all due to excitement, nerves, and fear.

Excitement to see Jaron again.

Nerves over how he would be. How we would be together.

And fear of the unknown. Of what life would throw at us next.

"Her mama was stressed." Jaron kissed my cheek. "I get it."

I turned my head before he could pull away and brushed my mouth along his.

His stiff body relaxed, melting into my touch. He cupped the side of my neck, pushing his hand into the back of my hair and crushing his mouth to mine.

I breathed him in, taking the air that gave him life, down deep into my lungs.

Before the kiss could turn into something more, he pulled back. Brushing his thumb along my bottom lip, he let out a soft sigh. "I can't believe I'm here. Touching you again. Holding you. Kissing you."

"It's felt like years since I've seen you." I wrapped my arms around him, leaning my head against his chest. Others had spent longer without their loved one in their arms, but it was still too long without him at my side. I needed him more than I could ever tell him, and I knew that he needed me just the same.

"I know, baby." Jaron kissed me softly on the mouth. "I know."

Taking a deep breath, I released him and held out my hand. "Let's go find the guys. Sammy has been on edge all weekend, waiting for this moment. He's been worse than me."

"Nah, baby. It's probably the pussy he's been sniffing around." Jaron placed his hand in mine and brought it up to his mouth before kissing my knuckles.

"You know about her?" I asked, watching him.

He nodded, his slate gray eyes flicking back and forth over my face. "I hear things and I've known Sammy my whole life. I remember the first girl he had a crush on. She was his teacher. Obviously, she didn't want anything to do with him, but it still pissed him off. And it stemmed from there."

"Oh," I breathed out the word.

Jaron winked, dropping our hands to his side.

Clearing my throat, I led him to the twins, his cousins, our family. He walked along beside me as we headed to where Cyrus and Sammy parked their bikes.

"Brynn's at your parents' place," I told Jaron, breaking the unnerving silence that had fallen between us. "We spent the night there since they live closer." I took a chance and looked up at him. "She's such a good baby."

"I can't wait to meet her," he said, his voice low.

My eyes burned. God, I wasn't normally a crier but this, this was a set of emotions I could never have prepared myself for.

"Don't cry for me, Piper." Jaron stopped, pulling me in front of him and cupping my face. "I'm not worth it."

"But you are," I insisted. "I wouldn't be here if you weren't."

His jaw ticked. Placing a soft peck on my forehead, he let his lips linger.

A single tear rolled down my cheek at the pain and confusion seeping from him. I didn't know what happened while he was locked up, but I knew that he needed me. Even if he couldn't admit it to himself. He would. Over time. I would make sure of it.

Before I could tell him more, Cyrus and Sammy caught sight of us and came rushing toward Jaron. Sammy reached him first and threw himself around him, almost tackling both Jaron and I over.

"I missed you too, fucker." Jaron hugged him back but kept his hand wrapped tightly around mine.

"Asshole." Sammy released him, so Cyrus could get a hug in. "It's been way too fucking long."

"At least you got to see him," I mumbled.

Sammy's chocolate brown eyes met mine. "I know, kiddo. Trust me, I tried for you."

"It's not a place for a lady," Cyrus interjected, clapping Jaron on the shoulder.

"Not my lady, that's for damn sure." Jaron brought my hand up to his mouth. "Take me to her." His beard brushed my knuckles, sending a shiver racing down my spine.

I nodded, clearing my throat. "Did you want to drive?"

"Are you sure you want him to? It's been a while. He probably forgot how to." Sammy pulled a set of keys out of his pocket. "Unless you want your baby." He dangled the keys, waggling his eyebrows.

Cyrus rolled his eyes, shaking his head.

Jaron took the keys from him. "Did you bring both helmets?"

"Of course." Sammy held out his hand. "I'll drive your car."

"Oh." I looked ahead at my car. "The keys are in my bag. The doors are unlocked."

All three guys looked my way.

"What? I was a little distracted. Sue me." I tugged Jaron's hand. "Let's go."

"You watch horror movies with us, and you still leave your car unlocked." Sammy shook his head, running his hand through the mess of light brown hair that was longer on top and shorter on the sides. "Women, they never learn."

"Ignore him." Cyrus nodded toward us. "Take your time," he told us, following his brother to my little beater of a car.

"I need my girls." Jaron turned me toward him. "I need *you*."

My heart stuttered. "We can pick Brynn up; let you see your parents and everyone and then take a drive somewhere. Unless you want to stay at your parents' place tonight. I understand if you do."

"No." Jaron walked by me, pulling me toward his bike. "I appreciate everything they've done for you, but I need…" He stepped up to his bike, running his hand along the sleek black machine. He pulled both helmets off of the seat and handed me one before slipping the other onto his head.

"What, Jaron?" I asked, pulling on the helmet. "What do you need?"

"You." He pinched my chin, placing a soft peck on my mouth. He helped me do up the straps beneath my chin. "I need to get reacquainted with you." He gave me a final kiss before he straddled his bike. "Everything else can wait."

A breath I didn't realize I had been holding escaped me. A part of me feared that he would get released from jail and move on. I knew he would be a good father to Brynn. His parents raised him right that way but when it came to us, I had spent many lonely nights wondering how it would be when he got out. I still didn't know but all we could do was take it one moment at a time.

"We'll meet you at your parents' place," Cyrus called out, straddling his own bike.

Jaron nodded, starting up his bike that Sammy had driven for him and revving the engine. He glanced at me over his shoulder. "Ready?"

I cupped his shoulder, sliding onto the seat behind him.

He reached behind him, giving my knee a squeeze. It was as if he was saying, *We got this, babe.*' But a part of me wasn't sure if we did.

Or if we ever would.

TWO

JARON

FEELING PIPER HOLDING ONTO me like I was the only thing stopping her from going anywhere, hit somewhere deep inside of me. It had felt like a lifetime since I touched her, kissed her, heard her laughs, and seen her smiles. I wanted more from her, but I didn't know how to tell her that. Hell, I wasn't even sure if I could show her.

What we had, wasn't serious at first. Not by our doing. Friends of ours had a little thing for her and kept her from me. I shouldn't have let it stop me, but I also didn't want to cause a scene whenever I was around, so I played nice and kept to myself most times. But I watched her. I wasn't even sure if she knew that.

"Jaron."

My body stirred at the feminine voice coming up from behind me.

"How are you?" Piper sat on the patio couch beside me.

I looked around us, wondering where the twins were. Ashton and Aiden never let her out of their sight.

When I didn't see them anywhere, I took that single moment as my chance and inched closer to her.

Piper's breath caught, the sound shooting through every cell in my body. She stared up at me with wide eyes.

The private moment between us was short lived as the twins joined us but I savored that moment with her. Even if it had only been just a second.

Even though we had been kids, I always had a crush on her. I just wished I could have saved myself for her and her the same for me. But that didn't matter anymore. I would make her forget every single guy she had been with.

As if she could hear my thoughts, Piper ran her hands around to my front. They inched beneath my hoodie, the tips of her fingers brushing over my abs.

My dick jumped but not because it turned me on. There was that too, but this was more of us getting to know each other again. Getting reacquainted in ways neither of us were prepared for.

Piper leaned her head against my back. I could feel the shudder rippling through her. She wasn't a crier and the sobs that tore through her when we were finally reunited, made what I felt for her grow into something I had never experienced before.

Love.

It was definitely love I felt for the woman behind me. She held onto me like I was her lifeline when really, she was mine. She kept me sane. Her and our daughter were the only reasons I survived the months in jail. It could have been longer but the time we were apart, fucked me up. I did things to survive. Evil, vile things. Things I wouldn't wish on my worst enemies. I had been known to be a hothead, more so than my own father, and it was used against me.

Piper squeezed me, pulling me from my thoughts. It was like she knew.

I cupped her hand, giving it a squeeze, silently thanking her.

She looked good. So damn good. Her body was fuller. She was also curvier than I last remembered. Although I would have known this, if I would had let her come see me in prison. But I refused. It wasn't a place for her. As much as I needed it, I had to protect her from those monsters. And at the same time, I had to protect her from me.

Once we pulled up in front of my parents' place, I killed the engine, kicked out the kickstand and waited. For what, I wasn't sure. I looked out at the vast house. For some reason, it felt bigger since I had last seen it. My father wanted to expand on it, but my mother had always told him no. She said it was big enough.

I pulled off my helmet, resting it on the gas tank in front of me.

"Jaron?" Piper wrapped her arms tighter around me. "Whatever you need, I'm here."

I grabbed her hand and kissed her knuckles. I wasn't sure what I needed. A drink. Sex. To leave. I didn't know. Maybe I would never know but whatever it was that I needed, I knew that I needed it with Piper and only her.

She slid off the back of the bike, pulled off the helmet, and rested it on the seat behind me.

"What did you tell me months ago?" She cupped my nape, running her fingers through my hair. "You said we had this. That we always had this." Her chocolate brown eyes locked with mine. "I can't do this without you but whatever you need, I'm here. If it's space, time, to talk...something else...I am always here."

I swallowed hard, nodding slightly.

Her light brown hair was a mess of waves, the ends sitting just below her chest. I noticed then how freckles graced her skin even more now since I had seen her last, almost like the sun had kissed her beautiful body.

"I promise, Jaron." She cupped my face. "I'm not going anywhere."

I covered her hands with mine, staring intently at her. "I need you," I told her softly.

Piper leaned her forehead against mine. "You have me. You've always had me. Even when we were apart..."

"I know." I cupped the back of her neck, sliding my fingers into her hair. "I should have gotten my head out of my ass and searched you out long ago."

17

She laughed lightly, standing upright. "We're together now." She gave me a small smile. Reaching out, she brushed her thumb along my bottom lip.

That soft touch eased some of the anxiety rushing through me. Being without her was the hardest thing I ever had to do. But I would do it again and again, if it meant keeping her safe.

I pushed her back gently and slid off the bike before I pulled her back into my arms.

She sighed, melting into me.

Every inch of me pressed up against her and if we were alone, I would have taken advantage of the situation. But we weren't, and we wouldn't be for a while, so instead, I just held her.

"God, I missed you. I missed this. I just…I missed us," she whispered, pushing her face into my chest.

I pulled her tighter against me. "Me too, baby. Me too."

"I missed the way you touch me. The way I feel when your hands are on me." She wrapped her arms around my neck, holding me tight against her. "I missed how safe I feel in your arms."

"You are safe, Piper," I told her, rubbing my nose against hers. "Always safe."

I needed this. I needed her. Being without her tested my limits and I knew if I had gone any longer without seeing her, it would have made me fall into myself. I wasn't stupid, and I was man enough to admit it, jail scared the shit out of me, and I was afraid for my mental well-being.

Clearing my throat, I pushed away from Piper and grabbed her hand instead. "I should go see my parents before my mom kicks my ass."

Piper laughed lightly. "I know she's been waiting for this day."

I smiled. "Me too, beautiful." I brushed my thumb along her bottom lip. "I also need to meet *her*."

Piper's breath hitched, her eyes shining. "I'll go get her."

I nodded, my throat working over a hard lump. I wasn't an emotional man. It was one of the things I loved about Piper. She wasn't an emotional person either. But being reunited, this whole ordeal, it brought out feelings I never knew I was even capable of having.

"Where is he? Where's my baby?"

I looked up and found my mom running out of the large house with my dad following behind her.

Piper gave my hand a squeeze and walked away from me to head into the house. I knew where she was going. I knew she was going to get *her*. Our daughter. But it still didn't stop me from rushing after her. When I caught up to her, I grabbed her arm and spun her around.

She jumped, slapping her hands against my chest. "Jaron?"

"Just...just stay." I grabbed her hand, her touch calming every racing nerve in my body. "You can grab Brynn in a moment. I just need...I need you here."

"I'll be right here," she said gently. "Go to your parents."

"Okay." I blew out a slow breath and turned to my mom.

She stopped suddenly.

My dad stood beside her. He leaned down to her ear, whispering something to her.

She nodded, kissed his cheek, and ran toward me.

I held out my arms and waited.

When my mom closed the distance between us and threw herself against me, a sob left her.

"My baby," she cried against my chest. "I missed you so much."

I cupped the back of her head, holding her tight. I wanted to tell her I was sorry. Sorry for worrying her. Sorry for darkening that light that had been in her eyes ever since I was a small boy. Sorry for scaring her and for no longer being the son she raised but now a monster instead.

A dark shadow loomed over us and I didn't have to look up to know that it was my dad. He had agreed back in the beginning of my sentencing that we didn't want either Piper or my mom showing up. As much as it killed me not to see them, it wasn't a place for them. So, my dad came to visit me as much as he could, in their place.

I could never thank him enough. Either of them. For what they did for Piper. For our daughter, their granddaughter.

19

Mom leaned back, cupping my face. "You've gotten so big."

I only smiled because if I said a word, any word, I would have fallen apart at her feet.

"How are you doing?" she asked, searching my face.

"Eve." Dad cupped her nape.

She looked between us. "I can't imagine." Her breath hitched. "What you did for her."

My chest tightened, memories of that night slithering their way into my mind.

Him.

Piper.

Blood.

"Eve," Dad repeated, his voice firm.

"I know." Mom cupped my cheek. "She's perfect for you. She'll help you heal." She paused, her eyes searching my face. "You good?"

"I will be," I finally said, my voice thick. "I…" My voice trailed off when a loud rumble of engines made their way up the large driveway.

"I love you, Jaron." Mom gave me another hug.

"I love you too, Mama," I murmured, returning the embrace.

"I'll go check on your daughter." She turned, gave my dad and me one final look, and headed back into the large house.

When I caught Piper still standing nearby, I let out a slow breath.

"How are you doing, Son?" Dad asked, clapping me on the shoulder.

"I don't know." But before I could say any more, we were interrupted by other members of Hell's Harlem.

As much as I wanted to see everyone, I needed Piper and to meet our daughter. I needed…hell, I didn't even know what I needed anymore. I glanced around me while the club members got off their bikes and came toward me.

Piper was suddenly nowhere to be found. She said she would stay with me. She wouldn't leave without telling me. Mom said she was going to check on Brynn. She must have gone inside with her. But it still didn't make me feel any better.

"Jaron."

I turned back around and found my uncles Tray and Catch coming toward me. While we weren't blood related, they were the closest thing I had to family besides my parents. And now Piper.

Piper.

I needed to see her. I needed her in my arms. I needed to know that she was safe. That this was all worth it. That nothing would come between us again and we would be together forever. I needed her more than the air that was giving me life. I needed her in ways I couldn't put into words.

"Hey," I said, my voice not as firm as I would have liked it to be.

Uncle Tray raised an eyebrow. He lifted a tattooed hand and cupped the back of my neck. "You good, kid?"

No. I'm losing my fucking mind. I need my girls.

"Yup," I muttered.

Uncle Catch came up beside him. "Have you met her yet?"

I shook my head, unable to voice my thoughts.

"Shit."

I didn't know who spoke. I didn't care. I needed Piper. I couldn't explain it. It was like this unknown force was taking control of me and I couldn't think or do anything until I had her in my arms and knew that she was okay.

My vision clouded, my hands clenching into fists at my sides.

"Jaron."

"Get Piper."

Voices. One deep. One higher. Both male. I couldn't place who was talking. Hell, I didn't even care.

"What's wrong?"

I spun around, finding Piper coming toward me with…her…our daughter…in her arms. My heart raced.

"Jaron?" Her eyes were wide. "Hey, talk to me."

Once Piper stood right in front of me, I wrapped my arms around her and pulled her against me, careful not to hurt either of them.

"What's wrong?" Piper asked, her voice muffled by my shirt.

"I couldn't see you." I pushed my face into the crook of her neck. "I was looking for you, but I couldn't find you."

"I'm here, baby," she whispered, cupping my cheek.

I shivered, resting my head against her shoulder and finally looking at our daughter who was just over ten months old. Ten months where she didn't have me, her father. My chest felt like it was closing in on itself, but I forced the next words out anyway, "She's perfect."

Piper's breath caught. "She is."

"Hi, Brynlee," I murmured, my chest tightening.

Brynn sucked on her soother, her eyes locking with mine.

"This is your daughter, Jaron," Piper's voice cracked. "Our daughter."

I lifted my head, cupped the back of Piper's and kissed her fully on the mouth. "She looks like you," I finally said.

Piper laughed lightly. "Maybe, but she has your eyes."

Brynn stared at me, leaning her head against Piper. She held a small stuffed pink pig in her hands while sucking on a matching pink soother.

"Pigs?" I asked Piper, taking hold of Brynn's hand.

"Yeah." Piper laughed lightly.

"I thought you got over that obsession," I said, staring into our daughter's eyes. She did have my eye color, but the rest of her features were definitely Piper's.

"You remembered?"

"Oh yeah." Piper had been obsessed with pigs as a kid. I thought she outgrew it but clearly, I was wrong.

"Everyone else forgot."

I met Piper's stare then. "I would never forget anything when it comes to you."

Her breath caught. "We should go inside. Your parents missed you but when you're ready, we can leave and do whatever you want."

I nodded.

"Did you want to hold her?" she asked softly.

I nodded again.

Piper handed Brynn to me and much to my surprise, she came into my arms willingly. It was like she knew. When she snuggled her chubby face into my neck, my throat closed, working hard over a lump.

Brynn sighed, holding her pig tightly in her arms and let her eyes close.

Piper ran her hand down her back. "She knows, Jaron. I've been telling her about you since I first found out I was pregnant with her."

"Really?" I was taken aback by her words. "You did?"

"Of course." Piper started walking toward my parents' house which doubled as the clubhouse. "Come. We'll talk more later."

Holding our daughter, I followed Piper. How I lucked out and had a woman like her was beyond me. I had to tell her what I did to make it back to her. I just hoped she still wanted to be with me after she found out everything.

THREE

Piper

WATCHING JARON WITH BRYNN was surreal. He talked to her and she responded in her baby babble like they were having an actual conversation. It made others around us laugh and I couldn't help but sigh every time he smiled down at her.

I knew this time would come. I had been praying for it every day while he was gone. But seeing it right in front of me forced to the forefront all of these newfound emotions that I never imagined.

Although something was still very wrong with him, he held Brynn like she was his lifeline. Like he survived solely for her.

Jaron met my gaze, giving me a wink.

My stomach tumbled.

No. Correction.

He survived. For *us*.

"Piper."

My head snapped around, finding Tray coming toward me. "Hey, Uncle Tray." I remembered back to when I first met him, when he demanded that I call him Uncle.

"You're Jaron's girl. You call me Uncle Tray."

It seemed everyone knew about me before I knew about them. Word got around rather quickly over what Jaron had done for me. Not the exact details, but most knew that he had saved me.

"How are you doing?"

"Me?" I frowned. "I'm fine. Why?"

He nodded toward Jaron, his dark eyes zeroing in on his nephew. He crossed his thick tattooed arms under his broad chest and rubbed the graying scruff on his strong jaw. "He's off."

"Well, he did spend some time in jail," I muttered.

"True." Tray wasn't a man of many words and I found I liked that about him. His wife, Zillah, did all the talking for them. Along with their daughter, Bee, who I didn't see as often since she lived with her husband and son a few hours away in the middle of nowhere.

We stood in silence, watching Jaron mingle with people he hadn't seen in quite some time while holding our daughter. But while he talked to them, his family, he kept glancing my way. Probably making sure I was still there. I wasn't sure why he needed me close by, but I appreciated it just the same. He also didn't have to worry. I wasn't going anywhere. I was in this for life. I just had to prove that to him.

"You should go."

I glanced up at Tray. "What do you mean?"

Tray nodded toward Jaron. "He needs time with you and Brynn. His family. I know his parents will understand."

I looked back at Jaron. "But that's not fair."

"Yes it is, Piper." Tray gave my shoulder a squeeze. "Jail can do funny things to a person. Doesn't matter how long you're in there for. Trust me when I say this, he needs you and you need him. Both of you also need to be patient with each other. You can't expect to fall into a routine right away." Tray gave my shoulder one final squeeze before heading back to join his wife at the bar.

Zillah glanced my way, gave me a small wave and greeted her husband with a kiss.

I gave myself a shake, surprised that Tray had said all of that to me. I knew he cared for Brynn and I, but the man never said more than a few words at a time.

But maybe he was right. Jaron was on edge. I wasn't sure what he needed but I knew that I was willing to do whatever it took to make him feel better.

Heading toward him, I couldn't help the way my heart picked up speed the closer I got.

I had spent years having a crush on him, only to find him at the same café in Paris of all places. I never asked him how he found me. Maybe I should have but I didn't really care knowing that I was the one who would spend the night with him, and I had. It started our obsession with each other and only grew from there.

When I stood a few feet away, my palms became sweaty at the mere sight of him. He was big, intense, and powerful. God, I missed him. I missed his dirty and vulgar words telling me what to do and how to do it. I missed his sweet, vulnerable side that he never shared with anyone else but me. I missed how he controlled me in ways I never thought I would ever be interested in. I wasn't new to sex but for the most part, all of the partners I had were vanilla at best. But Jaron? He was anything but vanilla.

"Suck my cock, baby. Just like that. Your mouth is so damn hot."

A shiver raced down my spine at the memory rushing through me. A memory that had taken place so long ago. But no matter how hard I tried to forget that night, I couldn't. Not that I really wanted to. What I wanted to forget; was how I left the next morning.

Before I closed the distance between us, Jaron glanced over his shoulder, his gaze locking with mine.

I stopped suddenly.

A silent conversation fell between us. So many unanswered questions. So many emotions that neither of us could admit to.

Clearing my throat, I stood up taller and walked the last few steps toward him.

He was standing with Sammy, Cyrus, and a few other guys I had only seen a couple of times.

"Give us a moment," he said, not taking his eyes off me.

The guys grunted their responses but all I could focus on was the slate orbs peering into my soul.

"What's wrong?" he asked, shifting Brynn to his other arm.

"Nothing." I ran my hand down her back. "I was just wondering if you wanted to leave. We don't have to. Or you can stay here. Whatever you want. Brynn has a room here if you wanted some time alone with her."

"No."

My gaze snapped to his. "Okay but—"

Jaron pinched my chin, tilting my head back and staring into my eyes. "I said no. I'm going home with you. I *need* to go home with you. I need…" The air crackled around us, his eyes darkening. "I—"

"Are you guys leaving?"

Both of us turned as Jaron's mom approached us.

"We should," Jaron said. "I need some time with my girls."

Eve grinned, glancing between us. "Okay."

My heart skipped a beat like it always did whenever he referred to me as his.

Eve pulled me into her arms, squeezing me tight. "I'm happy he's home. But most of all, I'm happy your family is now complete."

I swallowed hard. I was happy too. Scared yes, but definitely happy.

"I know you have a lot to work through," she said, her voice low enough for only me to hear. "But he loves you." She leaned back, cupping my face. "Believe me when I tell you that."

I nodded, the vision of her blurring in front of me.

She smiled, glancing at her son. "I've never seen him look at a woman like he looks at you."

My cheeks burned.

Jaron gave me a small smirk, running his hand down my arm and linking our fingers.

I looked at Brynn.

She was fast asleep with her head against his shoulder.

My heart warmed. "She's never fallen asleep in someone else's arms before."

"What?" Jaron looked down at her. "Oh. She hasn't? I wonder why."

"I think she was waiting for you," I whispered.

He kissed my temple, letting his lips linger. "Just like her mama."

A slow smile spread on my face, my eyes welling. God, all of these new emotions were not the norm for me. If I let myself, I would be a blubbering mess, but I refused. I had to be strong. For me and for Brynlee.

"I'll let you say bye." I moved off to the side, still making sure I was in his line of sight.

He glanced my way every so often, his big body relaxing every time he saw me still standing there. Was that even possible? Could the mere presence of someone be calming?

When he was done, he walked toward me.

I turned and left the large house, taking in a deep breath of fresh air.

"Piper?"

I jumped, spinning around.

Jaron raised an eyebrow, hiking the strap of Brynn's diaper bag higher up on his shoulder. "You good?"

I nodded. "Thank you for grabbing her bag." I was in my head and completely forgot.

"You're welcome." He walked by me and headed to my beater of a car.

"I have stuff for you at my...our...home," I stuttered, following behind him.

"Really?" He unlocked the back door and placed Brynn in her car seat. She stirred, letting out a cry of protest. She held her arms out for Jaron. "I'll hold you when we get home, baby girl." He kissed her head, which seemed to settle her down. "What stuff do you have?"

I opened the passenger door and slid into the vehicle. "Clothes and anything else your mom thought you might want. It was her idea. I didn't want to force you into anything, but she insisted. She said that you..."

"What?" He buckled Brynn into her seat. It was so natural; it was like he had been doing it since the day she was born. He met my gaze. "Piper, what did she say?"

I cleared my throat. "I...uh...she thought you might want to live with...us."

He only stared at me. A few seconds went by and I thought for sure his mom had been wrong. Why would he want to live with us? It wasn't like we ever made it official. There was something there. Neither of us could deny it but to be tied down and so quickly...

Jaron made sure Brynn was buckled in safely before shutting the door. He took a minute. I almost thought he was going to bolt but when he opened the driver's side door and sat beside me, I let out a breath of relief I didn't realize I had been holding.

"I don't want to force you into anything," I said, wringing my hands in my lap.

"You know how I feel about you, Piper," he finally said, covering my hands with his.

"I don't want you to feel tied down." I took a chance and looked at him then.

"I don't feel tied down." He brought my hand up to his mouth, the scruff of his beard tickling my knuckles. "I want this. I want you. I want her. If I didn't, I wouldn't be here. I wouldn't be in your car about to drive us to our house. Unless the house is yours and you just want me as a random hookup. Or some stranger who sleeps on your couch. I am pretty handy, so I can help with fixing up the place if needed too."

"How about a babysitter?" I laughed lightly.

"That works." He chuckled, lowering our joined hands to my lap. As quickly as the humor fell between us, it soon disappeared.

We had a lot to work through.

I just hoped both of us were patient enough for it.

FOUR

Piper

ONCE WE PULLED UP in front of my house, my heart started racing. I had only ever lived with my best friends. Never a guy. Before Jaron, I never even spent the night with a guy. It's not that anyone I had been with never tried; it just wasn't my thing. It didn't feel right. I didn't want the guys to feel like I was hinting for more when I wasn't. But then Jaron came along and even though it only happened once, sleeping beside him felt natural. When I woke up the next morning, I realized that, and it scared me.

Now that Jaron was going to be living with me, even though I knew from the very beginning that it was a possibility, I never thought he would actually stay.

"You're not mad?" I asked, waiting for my dad to blow a fuse.

He raised an eyebrow. "Why would I be mad?"

"Well, I've had a baby before marriage and…and Jaron and I could possibly move in together once he's out."

My dad sighed, placing his mug of coffee on the table in front of him. "Listen, I like Jaron. He was raised well and has a good head on his shoulders. He's a better man than I ever could be and I'm glad that he's yours. And what he did for you..." He shook his head. "That's love, kiddo."

"This is your place?" Jaron asked, slowing the car down.

"It is. But I guess it's ours now. I moved in about six months into my pregnancy. My parents had been saving money for me to go back to school but that never happened. They gave me the money anyway and I used it as a down payment. It's small but it's perfect."

"How small?" Jaron asked, pulling the car into the driveway.

"There's a master bedroom, Brynn's room, a smaller room that I'm just using for storage right now but would like to turn it into a library one day. It also has two bathrooms. It does have a finished basement though and...I actually have a surprise for you," I said, leaving the car.

Jaron left the vehicle shortly after. "You have a surprise for me?"

"I do. The guys helped me set it up. It's nothing big but I thought it would make you feel more at home." The back of my neck heated. It wasn't much but I wanted to do everything I could to make Jaron feel better, knowing the time he spent in jail messed with him.

I opened the back door and leaned in to get Brynn out of her car seat. Once she was in my arms, I grabbed the diaper bag and kicked the door closed. Heading up the sidewalk to the house, I stopped at the base of the front steps. Glancing over my shoulder, I found Jaron standing with his hands in his pockets, staring up at the house.

"Take your time, Jaron," I told him. "There's no rush. For anything."

AFTER US

(Jaron)

I watched Piper take Brynn into the house. As much as I wanted to follow her, as much as I wanted her back in my arms, something was off. I couldn't figure out what it was. But maybe she was right. There was no rush. Although I wasn't a patient person, not everything needed to feel normal right away.

The house looked small from the outside, but I couldn't wait to make it a home with Piper and our daughter.

Taking a deep breath, I headed toward the house and followed Piper inside. I shut the door behind me, taking in every inch that lay before me. She was right. The house *was* small. But I liked it. It was perfect.

As soon as you entered, you were brought to an open concept which held the living room and dining room. The kitchen was off to the right with an island separating it from the rest of the large room. You also had to walk up two steps to reach it.

"I like it," I finally said.

Piper placed Brynn in her playpen and turned to me. "Yeah? It was fixed up a bit, but the backyard is huge. When Brynn gets older, she'll love it." She walked to the large patio door leading out to the back of the house.

I joined her, standing behind her and following her gaze. There was a sandbox, a swing set, and a shed. "It needs a pool."

Piper looked up at me. "I agree but I can't maintain it myself. That's why I haven't gotten one yet."

"I can do it."

She stared at me. "Really?"

"Why not?" But I knew the reason she was questioning me. We never did put a label on what we were doing. Hell, I never even wanted kids but when I found out she was pregnant with my baby, I wanted to fuck more babies into her. She had been the only one who could ever reach a part of me I never wanted to give to anyone else and I could never thank her enough for that.

"Why are you looking at me like that?" she asked, her voice lowering.

I pinched her chin, placing a soft peck on her forehead, nose, and then I hesitated before placing one on her mouth.

Her breath caught. Snaking her arms around my neck, she pulled me closer.

Wrapping my hand in her hair, I pulled her head back and deepened the kiss. This, this right here was the reason I survived. With her mouth fused to mine, it was the only thing I had been itching to come home to. Beside our daughter, Piper was my very existence.

She was the reason I made it out of jail alive.

She was the reason I didn't give up.

She was the reason I *lived*.

I swallowed her moan, taking in every inch of her mouth. Her breaths were mine. I consumed and breathed her in, reveling in the way she felt in my arms after all of our time apart.

Piper broke the kiss, leaning her head to the side, her chest rising and falling.

I took that as a hint and brushed my mouth up the length of her neck.

"Jaron," she whispered.

"Yeah," I murmured against her throat.

"We can't."

"I know." But it didn't mean I couldn't tease us a little. Running my hand down her back, I cupped her ass and pulled her flush against me. Making sure to push every inch of me into her, I wanted her to feel how my body reacted to hers. I didn't want her to doubt for one single second that I didn't want her as much as she wanted me.

"God," she panted. "It's been way too long."

"It has." I scraped my teeth along the length of her jaw. "I'm going to have so much fun getting reacquainted with your body."

"When Brynn goes to bed, we can…we can continue," Piper suggested softly.

I responded by placing a peck on her nose but we both knew that we needed to wait. Didn't we? Wouldn't it be too soon to jump right back into bed when that started our problem in the first place?

Piper pushed out of my hold, but she didn't get very far. I grabbed her arm and pulled her back against me.

"We can't do this here." But she didn't push away from me again.

"If you're worried about me fucking you in front of our daughter, I won't. I don't mind the kinky shit but that's too far. Even for me."

A breathless laugh escaped her. "What kind of kinky shit are you into, Jaron?" she asked, turning in my arms and placing her hands against my chest.

I covered them and brought them up to my mouth, kissing her knuckles. "Shit we'll eventually explore but right now..." I brushed my thumb along her bottom lip. "Whatever you're thinking, I'm here. I'm not going anywhere."

Her deep blue eyes met mine. "Promise?"

"Baby, I've been yours since Paris. Probably even before that." It had been a few months since before we met up in Europe, that I'd last had sex. Women hinted but I shot them down. Fast. The guys always gave me a hard time about it, but I finally decided to get my head out of my ass and search Piper out. "Didn't you know that I went to Paris, looking for you?"

"What?" Her eyes widened. "No, I didn't know that. I thought you were there on vacation and it was just a coincidence that we were there at the same time."

"I was only there because you were. I had been going through a rut," I explained. "Nothing was doing it for me. I saw you that summer before you went to Europe. Do you remember that?"

"I do. My parents held a going-away party for me. You hardly talked to me that night." She frowned. "Why was that?"

"Because the things I wanted to say to you..." My body stirred. "I wanted to fuck you, Piper. I wanted you to go to Europe remembering how my cock felt deep inside you. I wanted to own every inch of your body. I had every intention of pulling you to the corner of the house and swallowing you fucking whole in the shadows. But I never got a chance because when I went to approach you, you were with the twins. I could never get you alone."

"Oh." Her cheeks reddened.

How the hell she got me to say exactly what was on my mind, was beyond me. I always listened first before speaking. I watched and waited but Piper forced the thoughts out of me like she had control of my words.

I reached out, running my thumb along her cheek. "So instead, I brought Sammy and Cyrus with me and we went to Europe ourselves. But I gave you a little bit. And eventually found you at that café."

"How did you find me?"

"I followed your trip on Instagram." I shrugged like I didn't just confess to stalking her.

"You were stalking me?"

My body stirred. She had been the only woman to ever call me out on my shit. It was what made me fall for her in the first place.

"And then I went back to your hotel with you," Piper added.

"You did."

She licked her lips. "That was the best night of my life but now that you're home, this is the best night."

"I agree, baby," I murmured, kissing the side of her head.

She sighed. "Want to help me get Brynn ready for bed? She won't be going down for at least an hour, but I like to get her changed and ready anyway just in case she falls asleep. Then I don't have to disturb her."

I headed to the playpen, reached inside and pulled our daughter out of it. She had woken up on the car ride home but now, with her snuggled against me, I found I just wanted to hold her and never let her go. "Can she stay up a little later tonight? I just…" I swallowed hard, running my hand over her head of dark curls. "I need this."

"Of course." Piper gave me a small smile. "We can get her ready for bed and then we can come out here and watch a movie."

That sounded damn near perfect.

FIVE

Piper

WATCHING JARON WITH BRYNN was something I thought I'd never actually see. He had promised to come home to me whenever he was released, but a part of me felt that they were just words and he didn't actually mean them. I knew I shouldn't have doubted him, but it wasn't like we ever made our relationship official. We had a fling and then I got pregnant with his baby. I didn't want him to feel pressured into staying with me just because of Brynn. We didn't have to be together for him to be a good father. I just wanted him, us, happy.

Even before he went to jail, a part of me feared that he wouldn't want anything to do with me after a while. In the beginning when I told him I was pregnant, the silence that had fallen between us was deafening. He spoke without telling me. He liked the fact that I was pregnant with his baby.

"Have you ever changed a diaper before?" I asked Jaron, grabbing a onesie out of Brynn's dresser. We ended up watching a movie first. Brynn had been wide awake through the whole thing, so we made sure to watch something she liked. Now we were getting her ready for bed since she started yawning during the credits.

Jaron was standing by the far wall that had pictures of him hanging on it. I wanted Brynn to see his face as often as she could. Even if he wasn't around.

"Jaron?"

He looked at me over his shoulder. "Sorry, what?"

"Have you ever changed a diaper?"

"I have." He went up to Brynn who was lying on the change table and tickled her belly.

She giggled, slapping her hands against his cheeks. "Dada."

"That's right, baby girl. I'm your daddy." He grinned, grabbing her hands and kissing her fingers.

My heart swelled at the exchange taking place before me. "That's her second word."

"Yeah?" He tickled her belly. "What was her first?"

"Mama. She's said some other stuff, but it was mostly babble. Tell me about the time you changed a diaper."

"A club brother's son brought his baby to the clubhouse," Jaron told me. "They bet me a hundred bucks that I couldn't change the diaper."

"And did you?"

"Fucking right I did." He chuckled. "It was the easiest hundred I've ever made."

I laughed. "When I first changed hers, it fell off." I shrugged. "But we got it figured out."

"You did."

I handed him the onesie.

He took it and changed Brynn with no fuss from her. It had amazed me how she didn't cry with him like she did with everyone else. I was the only one who could hold her without her freaking out. It was like she knew. It had only been her and I for months and now that Jaron was home, things changed. It was different but she accepted it with open arms.

"There." Jaron picked her up off the change table. "How does she look, Mama?" he asked, bringing her over to me.

"Perfect." I kissed her cheek. "You sleep well, baby girl."

Jaron placed her in her crib and put her stuffed pig in her arms. "Dream of puppies and kittens, little princess."

I turned off the light before we left the bedroom and closed the door nearly all the way, but left it open partially.

I almost asked, now what?

But Jaron led the way into the living room. Just when I thought he was going to sit on the couch, he headed into the kitchen instead.

I moved to the couch, sat down, and breathed. Everything that happened in the past few hours, hit me. Jaron being back. The father of my daughter being here. With me. With us. Finally.

"I'm pregnant."

"Fuck me. You are?" Jaron's voice lowered.

The tiny hairs on my skin tingled. "I am."

He had been happy about it. And when I had Sammy bring him the picture of the ultrasound, he had called me as soon as he could.

"You're pregnant. With my baby. My baby is growing inside of you. That tiny, tight as fuck, little body."

I smiled to myself, remembering that it had turned him on.

Jaron took that point to join me on the couch. He handed me a beer before taking a swig of his own. "Fuck. I missed this."

"I guess you don't really have beer in jail, do you?" I asked, taking a sip of my own.

"No. Although I'm sure if you're a good boy, you could probably swindle your way into getting some but who the fuck knows what you have to do for that."

I lifted my knee onto the couch and turned toward him. "Are you happy to be home?"

His eyes flicked to mine. "Why wouldn't I be?"

"I mean…" I shrugged. "I don't know what I mean. I just want you happy."

Jaron turned his full body in my direction and grabbed my hand. "A lot of shit happened while I was…" He cleared his throat, placing his beer on the table in front of us. "I can't go back to the way things were. I don't think I'll ever get back there."

"What do you mean?" I asked, taking in the light scars on his knuckles. What did he have to do to survive? He was big, but I knew that if he had been jumped by several guys all at once, even *he* couldn't take them on.

"Piper." Jaron pinched my chin, tilting my head back to meet his dark gaze. "I'm not the man I was before."

I swallowed hard, taking in the slate orbs staring back at me. The air crackled around us. An electric energy zapped its way between us. I licked my lips, needing just a taste.

His eyes dropped to my mouth, his nostrils flaring. "I'm not him, Piper." His thumb brushed along my jaw line. "I'm not a good guy. I want to be. For both of you. But I had to do shit to survive. Can you handle that?" he asked, his voice lowering. His hand slipped into my hair, to the back of my head. "Can you handle knowing the father of your baby would do anything to make it through each day? To make it back to his family. To his girls."

I reached out, cupping his face.

He covered my hand, pushing his cheek into my palm. "You are the only reason I'm here. That I made it through that hell. The *only* reason."

"What about your parents?" I murmured, my heart jumping to my throat at his confession.

"I love my parents and the club. I love them with every inch of me but what I feel for you goes beyond that."

"Tell me," I demanded, my voice turning husky.

He gave me a small smirk. "Not yet, baby."

"Jaron, please. I need to know how you feel." We had been going back and forth for months. I needed to hear the words. I needed to hear him say that he was in love with me.

"I can't."

I pulled out of his grip and shot up from the couch. "Fine." Stomping to the kitchen, I downed the rest of my beer before throwing the empty bottle into the recycling bin.

"Babe." Jaron came up behind me.

"No." I spun around. "Don't *babe* me. I haven't seen you in over a year. I haven't touched you. Kissed you. Made love to you.

I need something. At least your words. Tell me. Please. Tell me how you feel."

Jaron's brows narrowed. "Then you tell me."

"What?" I frowned, taken aback by what he was suggesting.

"Tell me how *you* feel." He closed the distance between us. "You're demanding it from me, but I don't hear you saying it."

"That's because you told me you didn't want us to say it until I was wrapped around you."

Jaron chuckled. "Come on, baby. Since when do you ever listen to other people? Especially me? Your parents raised you better than that. Or did having my baby turn you into a pushover?"

My jaw clenched. I crossed my arms under my chest, jutting my chin defiantly. "Fuck you."

"Hmm…" His gaze raked over me. "I will. But not tonight."

"Whatever." I spun on my heel and headed down the hall. "Your surprise is in the basement," I called out. Once I reached my bedroom, I rushed inside and shut the door behind me. Blowing out a slow breath, I leaned against it and dropped to the floor.

(Jaron)

I wasn't sure where any of that came from. I shouldn't have been an asshole. It wasn't Piper's fault that I did what I had to, to survive. I went to hell for her. Literally.

It took everything in me not to go to her. To apologize. To tell her how sorry I was for being a dick. To tell her I loved her. But those words wouldn't leave my mouth, no matter how much I wanted them to. I wasn't sure why. I wasn't scared of commitment. I had been committed to her long before Paris ever happened. It was one reason I had stopped sleeping around. But I was definitely scared of something. Maybe I feared how she would respond once she found out all that I had done. The men I had taken out. The fights I started. The name I had made for myself so I wouldn't have to walk around in fear.

My phone took that moment to ring, interrupting my thoughts. "Mercer."

A soft laugh slid into my ear. "I don't think you've ever actually said hello whenever I've called you."

"Candace." I rubbed the back of my neck and moved to the couch. "Why are you calling?" Not that I didn't mind hearing from people now that I was out of jail, but she wasn't one of them. The bar she owned with her husband, Ronny, was a place for us to get away and unwind.

"Well, I wasn't expecting that," she mumbled.

"Yeah, listen, you can't be calling me anymore."

"I heard you got out and wanted to see how you were doing, that's all."

"I'm fine," I muttered, not liking how fast the news traveled that I was no longer in jail.

"Life's biggest lie." She sighed. "Did you meet your daughter yet?"

The hackles on the back of my neck rose, not liking that anyone outside of my family and friends, knew about Piper and Brynn.

"Lose my number, Candace."

A cough sounded.

My head snapped up, finding Piper standing at the entrance to the hallway.

"Jaron, you can't mean that."

"I do." I disconnected the call and made sure to block her number. Piper and I had enough shit to work through. I didn't need an ex causing any issues.

"Who the hell is Candace?" Piper demanded, her cheeks reddening.

"No one important." I rose from the couch and took a step toward her. "I just blocked her number. I didn't know she still had mine."

"Who is she to you?"

"No one, baby. I promise."

Piper spun on her heel and ran back down the hall. The sound of a door slamming shut jarred through me.

Fuck me.

42

AFTER US

What the hell just happened?

SIX

Piper

MAYBE I WAS OVERREACTING. I knew Jaron had other women before me, but I never expected one of them to be calling him. What did she want?

Did they date?

Was he ever in love with her?

Was she in love with him?

Did he think he wasn't good enough for her?

Why? Why the hell after all of this time, had he never told me about her?

I left my room to try and make peace. I also didn't want to be alone and was going to offer to show him his surprise, but when I heard him on the phone and the name Candace was mentioned, I couldn't help but listen in.

A soft knock sounded on the door. "Piper, let me in." The doorknob jiggled. "Please, baby. We need to talk. It's not what you think."

"You don't know what I'm thinking," I muttered, sliding down the wall until I landed on the floor.

"I promise it's nothing."

"Nothing? It's nothing?" I jumped to my feet and unlocked the door before opening it. "How could you say it's nothing?" I demanded, giving him a shove and glaring up at him. "If I only just got home and another man called me, you would search him out and light his house on fire."

"Fuck." Jaron raked a hand through his hair. "That's not..." He came into the room, shutting the door behind him. "I didn't know she was going to call me. Her and I..."

"Her and you...what?"

Jaron looked away.

"You had a thing?" My stomach clenched when he didn't respond. Of course he had other women before me. I knew he did. It wasn't like I had been a virgin either when we first slept together but knowing that a woman he had *a thing* with, called him, didn't make me feel any better.

"I just blocked her number. You and I need to work through us. I don't want any more issues. You have to believe me."

I looked at Jaron then. I wasn't sure what I was looking for. Maybe a sign that he was lying. Or some indication that he was going to throw his hands up in the air, say screw it, and leave us.

I slumped onto the edge of the bed. "Did she go see you in jail?"

"No." He shook his head for added effect. "Not at all. Only my dad came, Cyrus, Sammy, and a couple of the other guys. If she tried to visit, I don't know about it, but I made it very clear to the guys that no one was to show up unless it was them. I didn't even see my mom that whole time."

"That must have been hard," I said softly.

"It was." He showed me the screen to his phone. "See? I blocked Candace's number."

"You didn't have to show me. I believed you but thank you."

"I missed you." Jaron dropped to his knees in front of me. He covered my hands, placed soft pecks on my knuckles, and rested his head on my lap. "I missed you so damn much. I don't want anything else to come between us."

"I missed you too." My stomach flipped at his confession.

He lifted his head, giving me a small smile. "I know."

"Thank you." I cupped his face. "Thank you for saving me." My mind went back to that night. It felt like just yesterday that I was attacked by someone who was supposed to be a friend. Jaron walked in and stopped it from going further than what it did. But it still fucked both of us up.

"No." Jaron kissed the tips of my fingers. "That was nothing. I would do that over and over again, go back to jail, stay there for the rest of my life, if it meant keeping you safe."

"God, Jaron. I can't…you've only been back not even a day yet and I feel…" My eyes welled. Damn him for making me cry. Again.

"Hey." He pulled me off the bed and onto his lap, wrapping his arms around me. "I'm here. I'm not going anywhere and I'm sorry for not letting you come visit me in jail."

"It hurt too much." I sighed, my chin quivering. "I get it. But I needed you. I had everyone here, but I still felt so alone." I picked at a fuzz on his hoodie.

Jaron leaned his forehead against mine. "I know that feeling. I have to say that this is unnerving. It's so damn quiet. I'm not used to this."

I leaned back, searching his face. I never once thought how he would feel since getting released. I just assumed that he would be fine and could go on with his day-to-day life. "I had no idea."

He shrugged. "I had no idea either. No one tells you how it's going to be once you're out. It's why a lot of people who have been in jail for years, end up committing suicide. The world has changed for them. Technology is more advanced. The world is faster. Their loved ones are no longer there for them. It's hard."

"That's sad."

"It is." He ran his hands up and down my arms. "I met a guy who was getting released a month after I had been there. He was in jail for over thirty years and didn't want to be released, so he ended up killing a guard to get more time put on his sentence."

"Wow. I can't imagine what that must have been like."

Jaron looked me square in the eye. "I would have done the same thing. If I knew that you weren't going to wait for me, there would have been no point in getting released."

I shook my head. "Never. I'm here. I've always been here."

He kissed my nose. "I know."

"Who is she?" I heard myself ask.

He stiffened. "No one important."

"Jaron." I latched on to him when he went to pull out from beneath me. "Listen, I'm not going to freak out. I just want to know who she is."

Jaron met my gaze. "An ex."

My heart dropped to the floor beneath me. "Oh...was she before..."

"She was long before Paris if that's what you're asking me." Jaron wrapped his arms around me and stood, keeping me in his embrace. "She works at Rouge."

My eyes widened. "The club Gigi teaches at?"

Jaron nodded. "Candace is the owner, along with her husband."

Gigi talked about the club often, but I never heard her mention Candace's name. But I also hadn't been around much since she started teaching there. Our friend was a dance instructor after blowing her knee out several years ago. Clearly, I needed to get out more.

"We would stop by there whenever we were in her part of the city. Before you, I was bored. I had an itch that needed scratching and I used her." Jaron wrapped his arms tighter around me.

"Did she scratch the itch?"

He grunted, carrying me out to the living room. "Not even close, baby." He sat us on the couch, keeping me in his arms.

I pulled the blanket off the back of the couch and wrapped it around us. "Did you love her?"

"No. She was convenient. She was also married. Still is. Her and her husband have a fucked up relationship. He found out about me and didn't do anything."

"Really?" How could her husband be fine with that? "I know that if it were you, you definitely wouldn't be fine if I..."

"If you what?" Jaron asked, his body stiffening.

"Fucked someone else."

"Get that thought out of your head, Piper, because you are mine. And mine only. Understand me?"

I shivered at the deep vibrato rumbling from his chest. "I understand." I thought a moment. "Was she in love with you?"

"She said she was. But I think she was just looking for some form of happiness that her husband couldn't give her at the time. They're now in counseling and seem to be doing better." Jaron ran his hand beneath my shirt, brushing his fingers over my lower back. "I don't want her, Piper. Whatever you're thinking, you have nothing to fear. I'm yours. I'm Brynn's. Both of you are my girls."

I nodded, laying down and snuggling my face into the crook of his neck.

His breathing evened out, his stiff body finally relaxing beneath me for the first time since he was released earlier that afternoon.

"I love you, Jaron," I whispered, kissing his cheek.

Warm lips brushed down the length of my neck. A heavy cock rested between my thighs. Hinting. Begging. Swelling for more.

I bit my bottom lip to keep from moaning out his name. But it didn't stop me from thinking it.

Jaron. Jaron. Jaron.

My hips moved back and forth. Up and down. Side to side. The thick length between my thighs, pressed against my slick center.

I had gone to bed in shorts and a tank top, but I could still feel him everywhere. Was I dreaming? Was this just some delicious fantasy that my brain had conjured up because I had been lonely for so long?

"Please," I whispered, knowing he liked it when I begged.

Hands gripped my hips. Fingers dug into my flesh. As much as I knew he wanted me, he held me still and rolled his hips.

Pleasure shot through me. My core clenched. Aching. Throbbing. Needing to be filled by him.

With my eyes still closed, I let the ecstasy consume me and take control much like the man lying beneath me.

With a firm grip on my ass, he undulated his hips, forcing a groan to fall between us.

A spark shot through me when my clit came into contact with the hard ridges of his thick length. "Jaron," I finally cried out.

"Piper."

My eyes snapped open, the delicious dream vanishing and sizzling into a memory. But even though it had been just a dream, he was hard beneath me and his hands were on my hips.

"I'm...I was..."

He pushed me back and forward, sliding me along the thick length beneath his sweatpants.

"Oh God." I panted, shaking above him.

"I was dreaming," he said, his voice husky. "I was dreaming that you were riding me."

"I was dreaming that this was happening." I sat up, placing my hands on his chest.

"That what was happening?" he asked, his slate eyes meeting mine.

"Your hands were on me like this. Your cock was hard beneath me." I undulated my hips over him. "Like this."

"Fuck." His eyes rolled into the back of his head, his fingers tightening their hold on me. "We shouldn't."

He had said that he didn't want to take advantage of me. But he never said anything about no foreplay.

"We're not having sex," I panted, thrusting my hips forward and back.

"We might as well be."

"I need you. I need this. It's been too long."

He sat up, swinging his legs over the edge of the couch. "Then kiss me, baby."

A breath of relief left me that he wasn't going to fight me on this.

Licking along his bottom lip, I crushed my mouth to his at the same time he picked up speed with his hips.

A delicious burn spread through me. Although we were both fully clothed, it felt almost as good as if he were inside me.

"Faster," I pleaded against his lips.

"What do you want?" He kissed the corner of my mouth. "You want to come? You want to soak my pants with your sweet cream?"

I moaned, a fast release crashing into me like that of a tidal wave.

He chuckled. "That's my girl. So damn responsive."

I grinned. "Only for you."

Jaron cupped my nape. "Fucking right." He slammed his mouth down hard on mine and ran my center up and down the length of him. "Fuck, baby. So good."

Slipping my tongue between his lips, I reveled in the way he swelled beneath me.

"Piper." His body shook, a soft growl escaping him when I felt something warm rush between my legs. He released my mouth, breathing heavy. "I wasn't expecting that."

I smirked. "Neither was I."

"I know you want me to fuck you."

"Of course I do." I ran my fingers over his collarbone. "Why wouldn't I?"

"I don't want to take advantage of you. I know it's been a while for both of us. I'm just trying to be a gentleman."

"I don't want a gentleman."

He leaned his forehead against mine. "I know. And I'm having a hard time here."

"You've never been a gentleman before." And I had loved it. He could read me like an open book. He knew what I liked, took from me what he wanted and returned it tenfold.

"You complaining?" he asked, running his hands up and down my thighs.

"No. Never." I gave him a small smile.

"I should take a shower and clean myself up."

"Okay." I slid off his lap. I tried not letting the disappointment rush through me, but I missed him. That single orgasm wasn't enough.

Heading into the kitchen, I got the coffee brewing before I made my way to the bathroom. The sound of the shower running stirred something inside of me. It sparked an ache, a need, but I knew that I couldn't press Jaron for more until he was good and ready to take full advantage of the situation. I wasn't sure why all of a sudden, he was being a gentleman. It messed with my head and I didn't like it.

Quickly checking on Brynn, I saw that she was still sleeping, so I headed to the bathroom and stripped along the way. Throwing my clothes in the laundry hamper, I quietly opened the door and shut myself into the room with Jaron.

The black shower curtain shielded him from me, but I could still imagine every drop of water sliding down his hard body.

"You're making it difficult to say no, Piper," he said, his deep voice rumbling through me.

"Then why are you?" I was standing there, naked, offering my body and soul to him.

"I'm trying to be nice."

I scoffed, pushing away from the door and making my way to the shower. Pulling back the curtain, I stepped into the shower with him. Water rained down over his hard body, the large tattoo of the Hell's Harlem Club logo on his back, moving with every breath. The black skull grinned, its eyeless sockets peering into me. "You don't have to be nice."

He turned around, his gaze roaming down the length of me. "It's been a long time for me."

"It's been a long time for me too," I reminded him. "I've dreamt of you. Fantasized about what would happen when you were finally home. I thought you'd end up…"

"What?" He reached out, pinching my chin and tilted my head back. "You thought I'd fuck you last night? After being away from you, you thought I would take advantage of the situation because you were offering up your sweet pussy to me?"

"I just want you again. I want you to touch me. Hold me. Kiss me. Make love to me."

Jaron released me, turning around and pushing his head beneath the water. The stream rained down over him, covering every inch of the hard lines of his body.

"Jaron." I touched his back, sliding my hands up the length of him.

He shivered. "I can't make love to you. Not yet."

"Why not?" I sounded desperate but, in all reality, I was. I was so damn desperate for him, it hurt. Every inch of me hurt the longer time wore on where he wasn't inside of me.

"Because you deserve more than me just fucking you. You deserve to be pampered, savored, fucking devoured."

"Then do that." I grabbed his arm, spinning him around. "But I don't need hearts and flowers. You know that." I cupped his cheek, his beard tickling my palm. "I just want you. That's all I've ever wanted."

He covered my hand, giving my palm a gentle nip. Questions danced in his eyes. A war battled through him. It was a moment of should I, or shouldn't I? I didn't care that he had just gotten out the day before. We needed lots of moments and this was one of them. We had to take this one day at a time, I knew that, but it didn't mean that sex was off the table.

When I reached out to touch him, he grabbed my hand, linked our fingers, and pushed me up against the wall.

He leaned down, brushing his mouth along the shell of my ear. "The things I want to do to you should be illegal."

"Tell me what they are."

He lifted his head, something flashing behind his eyes.

Just when I thought he was actually going to listen to me, a phone rang, snapping through our intense moment.

"Fucking hell," he grumbled, placing a soft peck on my forehead. "I should get that."

"Why? They can leave a message if it's that important."

Instead of pushing me away, he placed a hard peck on my mouth.

The ringing stopped, only to start back up again seconds later.

Jaron grumbled a curse. "I'll take care of it but whatever you're thinking, whatever you're hoping for, forget it. Because when it does finally happen, it'll be so much better than what you're imagining." He kissed my cheek and left the shower.

I sighed, a shiver trembling through me.

I had no idea what the hell just happened, but I could only hope that Jaron would eventually make good on his promise.

Sex wasn't everything but it had been how we started.

Maybe it was all we could ever have.

SEVEN

JARON

WHEN I LEFT PIPER in the shower, alone and naked, very naked I might add, it took everything in me not to ignore my phone and give her what she wanted. But the fact that it kept ringing over and over again, made me wonder if it was one of my club brothers calling. I had missed so many club meetings, I had to do what I could to get caught up. Even though my dad, as well as Cyrus and Sammy, filled me in whenever they came to visit, it wasn't the same.

Quickly drying myself off, I slid into a pair of jeans and answered my cell. "Mercer."

"I heard you were out but almost didn't believe it myself. I was kind of hoping that because you killed my son, you'd stay there forever. But even I can't control that. And I am technically still the mayor of this fucking city too."

My back stiffened at the deep voice in my ear. "What do you want, Price?"

"You will refer to me as Mr. Mayor, Jaron," he bit out.

"Sorry, you lost my respect the moment you hired underage girls to work at your club." I leaned against the dresser, pinching the bridge of my nose.

"I have no idea what you're talking about." The mayor chuckled. "Listen, as much as I'm loving this, I just had to call and hear it for myself. I'm sure we'll chat soon." The call disconnected.

I swallowed a curse and threw the phone on the dresser.

"Everything okay?"

I glanced up.

Piper stood in the doorway to the bathroom with a towel wrapped around her body and another wrapped around her hair on top of her head.

My dick twitched, swelling with need for her.

"Jaron?" Piper chewed her lip, taking a step toward me. "What do you need?"

You. Beneath me. On top of me. I don't give a shit where. I just need you.

I wasn't doing either of us any favors by not giving us what we wanted. She could make me feel better. She could give me the strength I needed to go and live my life. Our life. For her. For our daughter. For us.

I glanced at the door. My body trembled, my hands shaking. The hairs on my skin tingled. With need. Want. *Fear.*

Fear of the unknown and what would come of this. Could she handle me at my worst? Jail fucked me up. I wanted to give her every horrible detail. I wanted to tell her what I did to survive. To make it so I could come back to her and our daughter.

When Piper stood a foot away from me, I could smell the sweet scent of her floral shampoo. I gripped the edge of the dresser, my nails digging into the wood.

"Jaron?" Piper closed the distance between us, placing a hand on my chest. Her eyes snapped to mine. "Your heart's racing."

I inhaled a sharp breath. The control was wearing thin as her scent wafted into my nose. It billowed around me, enveloping me in a blanket of ultimate desire and seduction.

She licked her lips, wetting her mouth.

That one movement, that tiny little action, made me step forward. In a quick move, I curled my arm around her waist and pulled her closer.

She gasped, slapping her hands against my chest.

Ripping the towel from her head, I fisted her hair and pulled her head back. Leaning down to her throat, I scraped my teeth up the length of it.

Her chest rose and fell, her breath coming out in small bursts of air.

Sliding a hand down the length of her back, I cupped her ass, making sure to keep my mouth against her throat. I could feel her pulse beating beneath my tongue. The faster it was, the harder I became.

Snaking her arms around my neck, she pulled me closer. The hold was so damn tight, it was like she was trying to burrow herself under my skin.

Yeah, beautiful. I feel it too. Fuck, do I ever feel it.

"Jaron." She shook against me.

Brushing my lips up the length of her throat and down the line of her jaw, I covered her mouth with mine.

I swallowed her sighs, held her against me, and just felt. The soft curves of her body. Her full breasts against my chest. Her pelvis rubbing against mine.

Fisting her hair with both hands, I spun us around and pushed her up against the dresser. She whimpered, reaching around me and sliding her hands into the seat of my jeans. She cupped my ass, pulling me between her legs.

My cock pushed against the fly of my jeans. Although the zipper wasn't done up, it still begged to be released and dive deep into her warmth.

Rubbing back and forth, I pushed and pushed until she was trembling beneath me. Her moans slid into my ears. Her nails scratched into my skin. But it still wasn't enough. It would never be enough where she was concerned.

I lived and breathed for this woman in my arms. I loved her. I loved her so damn much.

Every inch of me belonged to her. My heart. My body. My damn soul. But it wasn't enough. I wanted to give her more. I *had* to give her more.

Inching my hands up her bare legs, I pushed them beneath the towel, all the while keeping my mouth locked with hers.

Piper slid her hands to the front of my waist.

Anticipation sparked a feral need inside of me. A growl escaped me, the tiny hairs on my body tingling and getting ready for that familiar touch.

Releasing her mouth, I opened the towel wrapped around her. Her chest rose and fell with ragged breaths. I leaned down, closing my lips around a nipple, sinking my teeth into the hardening peak.

Piper whimpered.

Remembering a while back how she enjoyed being spanked, I decided to test my little theory. Sliding my fingers up her inner thigh, I brushed the tips along the soft, wet slit at her core. When I gave her nipple another bite, a gush of liquid left her body. My cock swelled.

"God, Jaron."

Licking up her chest, I kissed her chin before covering her mouth at the same time as I shoved two fingers inside her.

She jumped, spreading her legs wide for me.

Pushing my finger against the ribbed wall of her pussy, I grinned against her mouth as she shook in my arms. "Feel that, baby?" I asked, staring down at her. "That's your G-spot. I think it wants to come out and play."

"Holy shit." She arched against me, her thighs trembling.

I smirked, lowered my mouth to the spot between her breasts, and kissed my way down to her navel. "I suggest holding on."

Piper gripped the edge of the dresser, watching, waiting for permission to fall.

Suddenly, a cry sounded from the baby monitor, pulling a laugh from Piper's lips.

I smirked, placing a soft peck on her forehead. "Until later."

"Wait. If she doesn't cry again, she fell back asleep."

"Is that so?" I sunk my teeth into her hip bone.

"Yes," she breathed.

I was so close to the sweet spot between her legs but when a second cry came from the monitor, I knew that this moment was over. "We'll continue this later."

She nodded, gently pushing me back. She shivered when I pulled my fingers from her body.

Our chests rose and fell while we tried to gain control of our racing hearts.

I helped her off the dresser. "I think I need to get you alone," I told her, brushing my fingers that had just been inside her body, over her swollen mouth.

Her nostrils flared, her tongue peeking out to lick the juices off my fingers.

"You'll need to put your phone on silent." She gave me a small smile.

Kissing her softly on the mouth, I wrapped my arms around her. "I'll get Brynn up," I murmured against her lips, tasting her on her tongue.

"Really?" Piper leaned back, her brows raising.

"You've been doing it for months." I kissed her nose. "It's my turn now."

"Okay." She pushed me back. "Coffee should be ready by now and I'll get breakfast started."

I nodded, did up my pants, and headed to the bathroom to quickly wash my hands. Once I was done, I made my way to leave the bedroom when I stopped at the door.

Piper opened the drawer to her dresser, meeting my gaze in the mirror. "What?"

"You're beautiful," I told her and left the room but not before I caught the small smile on her face.

(Piper)

Once Jaron left the bedroom, I let out a breath I didn't realize I had been holding. What we almost did...what almost happened...I shook myself. Was it too soon? Was there a rule for this? I had no idea but what I did know was that it felt good to be back in his arms again and to feel him, even though it had been just his fingers, deep inside me. Although, when I thought of the last time, the passion then was nothing compared to how it was now. We had been interrupted twice. It was like it wasn't meant to be. Or it would happen when neither of us could take waiting anymore.

I quickly cleaned myself up, got dressed, and headed to the kitchen in need of coffee, and a lot of it. Last night had been the best sleep I'd had in months. Something was still off with Jaron and I couldn't figure out what it was. Or even how to help him through it. He went to jail one way and came out a completely changed man.

I made myself a cup of coffee and poured one for Jaron when I realized that I didn't know what he took in it. Or if he even drank coffee for that matter. Hell, I didn't know much about him.

"Fuck, baby, you have the tightest throat."

I remembered he liked it rough and that was it.

What was his favorite color?

Did he like watching movies?

Did he enjoy being a part of his dad's club?

What was it like being a biker?

Was he looking forward to being president of Hell's Harlem one day?

So many questions bounced around in my head that I didn't have the answers to. Would I ever get the answers I was looking for?

My cell phone rang, startling me. I had completely forgotten I plugged it into the wall socket the night before.

I smiled when I saw that it was one of my best friends, video calling. "Hey, Gigi."

"Hi." She gave me a wide smile. "I texted you yesterday and then I called but you were obviously getting reacquainted." She paused. "How's it going?"

I looked over my shoulder before turning back to her and placing my phone on the counter, leaning it against the microwave. "It's going."

"Yeah?" She chewed her bottom lip. "That rough?"

I shrugged, taking a sip of my coffee. "It's been a while. We're trying to get into a routine, but it hasn't even been twenty-four hours. So…"

"I get that." Gigi pulled her long curly hair up into a messy bun. "Listen, I'm getting ready to head out to the studio but wanted to check in first. I know everyone wants to see him. Even the twins have been asking about him."

My heart warmed. "Really?"

"Yeah, so you guys can come over whenever you're ready. No rush. Even if it's just the girls and us."

I thought a moment. "I think that would be nice."

"Babe, who you talking to this early?" Vince Jr. came up behind Gigi and kissed her cheek. "Hey, Piper."

"Hi. How's Hannah?" Their daughter was a few months younger than Brynlee and was simply adorable.

"Sleeping just like her mama should be doing." He took the phone from Gigi.

"What are you doing? Vince, give me back my phone," I heard her say in the background.

"We'll meet up soon," he told me. "But right now, I'm going to take my girl back to bed."

I laughed. "Have fun."

He winked. We said our goodbyes and I hung up the phone.

"You complaining to our friends about me?"

I jumped, spun around, and found Jaron standing at the entrance to the kitchen, holding Brynn. She was sucking on her soother, holding her stuffed pig toy. I went up to them and kissed her cheek.

"Sleep well, baby girl?" I asked, running a hand down her back.

She leaned her head against Jaron's shoulder.

"I asked you a question," Jaron said, his voice rough.

"I wasn't complaining about you." I went to walk away when he grabbed my arm.

"If you have an issue with me, talk to me. Not Gigi. Not anyone else. It's the least you can do."

My head whipped around. "What the hell is that supposed to mean?"

Jaron released me and walked over to Brynn's highchair before placing her in the seat and doing up the belt. She slapped the tray in front of her, throwing her pig on the floor.

He chuckled, picked it up, and handed it back to her.

"Jaron." I wasn't sure what he was accusing me of, but this shit needed to end and fast.

He straightened to his full height and peered at me over his shoulder.

"What are you accusing me of?" I demanded, finally voicing my thoughts.

"I'm not accusing you of anything," he mumbled, shoving his hands in the pockets of his jeans.

"No? Because it sure as hell feels like it." I headed back into the kitchen to make Brynn a bottle. While I was waiting for it to heat up in the bottle warmer, I felt Jaron come up behind me.

"I'm not accusing you of anything." He wrapped his arms around my waist, resting his chin on my shoulder. "I just don't like that you talk to Gigi and not me."

"Gigi called, asked me questions and I gave her an answer. What was I supposed to say?" When the bottle warmer dinged, I pulled the bottle from it and tested the temperature on my inner wrist. Satisfied that it wouldn't burn Brynn, I handed it to Jaron. "She gets one of these for breakfast, lunch, and dinner. I've started her on baby food as well, so once she's done her bottle, she can get something from the cupboard."

Jaron took the bottle from me and spun me around. "I like this. Being here with you. Being a family. But what I don't like is that I have to learn all of this when we should have learned it together."

My heart jumped to my throat at the coldness in his eyes. "It's not my fault. And it's definitely not yours."

His jaw clenched. "I know it's not your fault but..."

I frowned, staring up at him. "Jaron, do you think it's your fault?"

He looked away.

"No." I fisted his t-shirt and forced him to look at me. "You told me to talk, so you have to do the same."

"I'm just having a hard time here, Piper. I should have been there. I should have been with you throughout your pregnancy. Through the birth. Through her diaper falling off the first time you tried putting it on her. I should have been there."

Instead of waiting for me to respond, he pushed past me and left the kitchen to go feed our daughter.

My heart hammered in my ears. I had no idea that it bothered him as much as it did. I didn't know at all. I had no warning. Not one bit. And now I was left with a broken man who hated himself for what he did and for leaving me. Even though he saved my life, I knew Jaron wished things would have turned out differently. I just wondered how much of that he blamed on me.

EIGHT

JARON

I NEVER MEANT TO come off as an asshole but the fact that Piper had no issues talking to Gigi about our problems, instead of me, pissed me off. I knew she never really said anything, just that we were trying to get into a routine but that side of me came out before I could stop myself. Words spewed from my lips quicker than I would have liked and of course, Piper was on the receiving end of it.

While she rummaged around in the kitchen, I pulled up a chair beside Brynlee and gave her the bottle.

She clasped it with both hands and stuck the nipple into her mouth.

I sighed, leaning back in the chair and ran a hand through my hair. "Did you breastfeed her?"

Instead of answering me, Piper left the kitchen and went to a bookshelf sitting beside the TV. She pulled a box off the bottom shelf and brought it over to me.

"Everything is in here. The ultrasound pictures, doctor's notes, more photos and so on. I even kept journals," Piper told me, but she wouldn't meet my gaze. "And yes, I did breastfeed her."

I stood from the chair. "Piper."

"Read the journals, Jaron. Everything you want to know is in them." Her shoulders slumped, almost like she was admitting defeat.

"Hey." I pulled her into my arms when she went to walk away. "Stop this."

"Stop what?" She struggled against me, but I wouldn't release her. I refused, knowing we needed to work through this. "I can't do this with you. I don't know what I expected when you got out, but it definitely wasn't this."

"Don't push me away." I cupped her face, forcing her to look up at me. "I can't do this without you either. I know I've changed. I get that. But you don't know what I went through. And I know I should tell you and that you deserve to know but I also don't want you hearing that shit."

"I want to know everything." She turned in my arms, placing her hand on the spot above my heart. "I want to know what made you change. I want to know *you*, Jaron. That's all I've ever wanted. I went to make you a coffee and I don't even know if you drink coffee. I just..." She huffed. "I've known you since we were kids, but I still feel like we're strangers."

I opened my mouth to argue but no words came out. She was right. She was absolutely fucking right. "Then let's take this one day at a time. We can even start dating."

She leaned back, frowning. "Really?"

"Why not? We have a kid together, Piper, and sure, we may have done things out of order but that doesn't matter." I ran my hands up and down her arms. "I want to date you. We don't have to even go out for dinner. We can stay here, order in pizza, watch movies."

"I like that idea," she whispered, her eyes shining.

"Good." I kissed her forehead, breathing her in. "And we may not know every single thing about each other or what we like and don't like. Our hobbies and things like that but I *do* know you. I know every single inch of your body. And yes, I know it's been a while, but I can still read you, baby." I released her and sat down. "To answer your question, I do drink coffee. Black. And I know that you drink yours with half a spoon of sugar. Brown sugar if you can get access to it and a little bit of milk."

Her eyes widened. "How do you know that?"

"Because I paid attention in Paris." While Brynn drank from her bottle, I pulled the box closer to me. "I'm still waiting for that coffee."

I could feel Piper's gaze burning into me but after a couple seconds of silence between us, she headed into the kitchen.

When she left, I blew out a slow breath. "Your mama drives me crazy, baby girl."

Brynn babbled, probably defending her mama, and shoved the nipple back into her mouth.

I only shook my head and started looking through the box of items. When Piper said she saved everything, she meant just that. She saved every single thing she could from her pregnancy. I pulled out a bundle of notebooks. Five to be exact. Pulling the elastic off of them, I flipped through the pages. My eyes widened when I saw that every single page was written on.

"Geeze, Piper," I murmured. She really did keep everything. My eyes landed on a journal entry.

Not feeling well today. I really miss Jaron and wish he was here to massage my lower back. It hurts so much and I'm only five months pregnant.

My chest tightened. I flipped through a few more pages.

Meadow made me the best donut today. It was filled with peanut butter, icing sugar cream type stuff and chocolate. I probably gained ten pounds, but it was worth it, and baby is happy.

I picked up another journal and flipped to the middle.

I'm in my fourth month of pregnancy and I want Jaron. God, I want him so bad. Everything hurts. It aches. And knowing he'll probably read this one day is making it that much worse.

What would I say to him if he was here?

What would he do?

What would I do?

Would I get on my knees and beg?

Would he force—

I slapped the journal closed. "Fucking hell."

"You started reading about the fourth month into my pregnancy, didn't you?" Piper placed a mug on the table in front of me.

"Oh yeah." I took a sip of the coffee and let out a heavy sigh.

She sat across from me, drinking her own cup. A rosy tinge had hit her cheeks. I was going to have to read the rest of that passage later with her.

"There's other stuff in there. My mom bought me a Polaroid camera, so I took a bunch of pictures too. And I have digital copies as well. But I…"

I met her gaze, placing the mug on the table. "What?"

"I want some pictures with you. Family pictures and so on." She hesitated. "I mean…if you want that of course."

"I would like that," I told her and continued looking through the box. "Do you have videos too?"

"I do." She reached into the box and pulled out a smaller box. "I had these put onto CDs and also a flash drive. So you can watch them whenever you want. Gigi was in the delivery room with my mom and me, so she videotaped. I just made sure she stayed at my head." She laughed lightly.

I gave her a small smile. "I can watch you give birth to our baby." My body stirred, the tiny hairs on my body tingling at the thought.

Piper coughed, clearing her throat. "Yeah. You can. Oh, Luna gave birth to a boy. His name is Benjamin and named after your uncle who died. We were pregnant around the same time. Just a few weeks off from each other."

Luna Stone was one of Piper's best friends and was also engaged to my cousin, Zach. I was happy that they finally worked through whatever it was they were having issues with. I hadn't seen them since they came to the hotel my crew and I were staying at. Fuck, that was so damn long ago.

"They're also getting married in a few months," Piper continued. "Zach proposed a while ago but they were waiting for you to come home. Vince and Gigi are getting married too."

"Meadow and Shade already did," I added.

Piper nodded. "They couldn't wait. With everything they went through, I don't blame them."

My chest tightened, remembering back to when my dad told me that Sunny Harrison had been shot and killed. He was a good guy and had been a longtime member of Hell's Harlem, along with Roy Allen, known as Shade.

"They have a son together. Andrew." Piper reached across the table and cupped my hand. "I'm sorry about Sunny."

"Thank you. He was a good man." I sighed. "I look forward to seeing everyone and meeting the kids." My dad tried keeping me in the loop as best he could, but I completely forgot everything. With what had gone on, it fell to the back of my mind.

"We're invited to all the weddings of course."

"I'm sure you're in them."

"I believe both of us are in Zach and Luna's." Piper smiled. "Gigi and Vince had a baby as well. Her name is Hannah."

"I didn't know that." I rubbed the back of my neck, not liking the sudden sense of urgency I felt. Anxiety twisted at my stomach over the fact that I had missed so much.

"Jaron." Piper cupped my knee. "Everything will feel back to normal in time."

I covered her hand and gave it a squeeze, hoping she was right. I pulled out a stack of Polaroids and ripped off the elastic holding them together. "Babe, these are…" I looked through each picture. It was a progression of Piper's pregnancy.

"Which ones?" Piper pulled her chair closer to me. "Oh. Yeah, I had fun doing those. Luna helped me and then I did the same for her."

"Fuck, Piper, you're beautiful in these." And she looked good enough to eat. Especially knowing she was carrying my child in her swollen belly.

"I was huge, Jaron." She laughed. "And I didn't feel beautiful at all but thank you. I was definitely all belly with her."

"Tell me more." I needed to know every detail. "I know you wrote journals, but I need something. I need you to tell me. Anything."

"Oh, um…well I had a hard time breastfeeding at first, but we figured it out." She looked at Brynlee then. "It was stressful but the nurses at the hospital were wonderful. They came up with the idea for me to video tape it and act like you were there. So my mom recorded it and I talked to you through the whole thing. It's lame but it worked."

"You have a video of you breastfeeding our daughter for the first time?"

She nodded. "Why are you looking at me like that?"

I didn't know how I was looking at her, but I knew the way I was feeling. I had heard of this. My uncle Tray had reacted the same way when my cousin Bee was born. My aunt got drunk one day and spilled the dirty details not knowing that I was nearby and could hear it all.

I shot up from the chair. "Show me."

"Jaron." Piper stood, grabbed her mug, and headed into the kitchen.

"Show me."

"Really? Now?" She came back with her mug in hand. "I have to feed her."

"Fine. We can feed her together. Show me where everything is, and I can watch the video at the same time." I wasn't sure why I was being so demanding. Maybe it was because I missed it all and I wanted to make up for it. We had over a year that we lost between us and I knew it would take a while to get to that point where we could move on from it, but this would be a start. And it was a start I wanted to take with her.

"Okay." Piper placed her mug on the table. "Come with me and I'll show you where her baby food is. She's not a fan of carrots. I fed them to her once. I even tried them myself. And nope. I'll wait until she can have salt and stuff. I even tried mixing them with green beans. But blech." She grimaced. "So gross."

I chuckled, following her into the kitchen.

She opened the cupboard by the fridge. "This is all the stuff that doesn't need to be refrigerated of course and then everything else is in the fridge. I like to give her a mixture of stuff. Veggies, fruit, and so on. Luna's blending everything herself, but I didn't have the time for that. But now that you're home…" She met my gaze then.

"Whatever you want." But I really needed to see that video.

Piper nodded and pulled a couple of jars from the fridge and a tray from the cupboard. Once she was done, she handed me the tray and a small spoon. "She likes to get messy."

I smirked. "So do I."

Piper laughed, smacking my stomach gently. "Go feed our daughter and I'll get the video."

I saluted her and rejoined Brynn at her highchair. Her eyes rounded when she saw that I had a tray of food.

"Yeah, baby girl." I chuckled. "This is all for you. You need to get big and strong so you can fight off those boys who'll fall in love with those beautiful eyes of yours."

"Oh God. I don't even want to think about that." Piper stuck a DVD into the DVD player and grabbed the remote control before sitting at the table across from me. "I can continue if you wanted to watch it."

I nodded, handing her the tray and standing from the chair. I headed into the living room and sat on the couch, watching what was going on before me.

"I can't do this," Piper sobbed from the TV. She was holding Brynlee in her arms, covering her face with her other hand.

"Yes, you can," I heard her mom say from behind the camera. "Come on, Piper. Talk to Jaron like he's here with you and helping you through this."

Piper sniffed and took a deep breath. "But what should I say? This is so weird." She looked down at Brynn. "I just want to feed you. That's all."

I moved from the couch to the coffee table, sitting on the edge. It was like I couldn't get close enough. I wished with everything in me that I had been there. That I could have helped her through it. Through all of it.

I'm here, Piper. I'm always here. Even when I wasn't, I was always around.

Piper took a deep breath. "How do I start?"

"Take another breath and say something like…" Her mom paused. "What would Jaron say if he was here?"

She laughed. "He would probably tell me how beautiful I was. Even in my current messy state."

She was right. She was beautiful and that would be exactly what I would say to her.

Come on, Piper. Feed her. You can do it, baby.

I cheered her on even though it was so many months ago.

Piper took another breath and looked down at our daughter. "If your daddy was here, he would be coaching me on and telling me what a wonderful job I was doing." She smiled. "Yes, he would." She laughed, wiping under her eye. "He would also say, 'Babe, we got this.'"

I passed a glance at Piper.

She smiled, her eyes shining.

"He would also say that he loves us." She sighed, glancing back toward the camera. "I'm not sure what else to…" She gasped, looking down at Brynn. "She's feeding."

Her mom cheered.

The video ended shortly after that, but I found that I wanted to watch it again and again. She was right. I would tell her that I loved them because I did.

I shut off the TV and rose from the coffee table.

Piper headed into the kitchen and I followed.

"She needs a bath but for once, she actually ate really well." Piper placed the dishes in the sink. "I think it's because you're—"

Before she could finish her sentence, I grabbed her shoulders and spun her around. Pushing her back against the counter, I covered her mouth with mine.

She gasped, giving me the only invitation I needed to take the kiss a little further.

"Jaron," she whispered.

I released her, placing a soft peck on her swollen lips. "I'm sorry I wasn't here but I'm so fucking proud of you and what you've done. You're the strongest person I know."

Her breath caught, her eyes welling.

"I'm also sorry for putting you through hell all of this time. I should have been there with you during your pregnancy. I shouldn't have done what I did but my temper..."

"Hey." Piper cupped the back of my neck. "You saved my life."

My jaw clenched. "But I—"

"I had nightmares after that. For months, I had nightmares. And I heard that being pregnant can make you have some crazy dreams too, so that didn't help at all. But can you imagine what those nightmares would have been like if you hadn't stopped him, Jaron? Sure, I had to move out of that room. And yes, I jumped at every little thing for weeks. But that's not the point. It could have been so much worse."

"I still shouldn't have reacted the way I did." And I definitely shouldn't have killed the mayor's son.

"I was almost raped, Jaron. You stopped that from happening."

I looked away.

"Hey." She grabbed onto my t-shirt. "I'm being serious. Yes, it was hard without you but you're home now and I know you had it hard as well and you went through hell in there. But I hope that one day you'll let me help you through that."

"I will." I nodded, placing a soft peck on her forehead. "Thank you."

I pulled away and left the kitchen but not before I caught that look from Piper. It was pity, concern, but worst of all...*fear*.

(Piper)

"I just got off the phone with Gigi and told her that we would stop by soon. They asked us to come over this weekend, but I told her we might need a little longer. Whatever is good for you. She and Vince live outside of town. Did you hear that the house us girls lived in, was burnt down?" I joined Jaron on the couch, curling my feet under me.

"My dad mentioned something about that." He shook his head. "So fucking crazy what Gigi and Vince went through to be together."

Just like us but I kept that thought to myself.

Vince's friend's ex-girlfriend and another friend pulled some crazy stunts and both Vince and Gigi almost lost their lives because of her. I just prayed that she was able to get the help she needed before she hurt herself or anyone else.

"I look forward to seeing everyone," Jaron said, pulling me from my thoughts. He kissed my temple and went back to my journals. He had spent the afternoon looking through the box, watching the videos and reading the journals I wrote for him. It was now later in the evening. We had put Brynn to bed together and now we were spending some time, trying to find that connection again.

"Oh I just realized, I never actually showed you your surprise." I turned toward him. "It's just a home gym and it's in the basement for whenever you get bored."

"Thank you." He kissed the side of my head again. "But I just want to read these."

"Okay." I took a sip of my water and leaned my head against his shoulder. "I like that one," I told him, pointing at the current entry he was reading when I was craving mustard and peanut butter.

"Mustard and peanut butter?" Jaron made a face.

I laughed. "Yeah, but Meadow turned it into a cupcake. Ashton even liked it and had her make more."

"Huh…" Jaron shut the journal and placed it in the box on the floor.

"What is it?"

"How have the twins been with you?" he asked, not meeting my gaze.

"What are you really asking me, Jaron?" I sat forward, turning my body toward him. "If you're wondering if they've hinted for more, they haven't. They've been good to me and Brynlee while you haven't been here." I stood. "So stop with this jealousy bullshit."

He grabbed my hand when I went to storm away.

The touch was so soft and gentle, it brought tears to my eyes.

I couldn't look at him for fear that I would start blubbering like a baby. One day. One day he had been home, and I was a mess. *We* were a mess. And I didn't know how to fix us.

His thumb ran back and forth over the back of my hand. He tugged it gently, pulling me down onto the couch beside him.

A shuddered breath left me.

Jaron wrapped his arms around my shoulders, pushing his face into the crook of my neck.

An unspoken apology fell between us. This would be a give and take situation and right now, I was taking everything I could.

Turning in his arms, I brushed my fingers through his dark beard, over his cheekbone and across his lips. I wanted to memorize this moment. Where both of us were at a place where we didn't know what to do but knew that we wanted to do it together.

Fisting his shirt, I pulled him against me and wrapped myself around him. I held him as I tightly as I could.

His big body relaxed. With rough hands, they roamed beneath my shirt and up my back. The touch of his calloused palms against my naked skin, sent a flutter of peace through every inch of me.

I leaned back, cupped his face, and covered his mouth with mine before he could say or do anything. Before he could push me away again. Before he could stop me and tell me that it wasn't right. That this was the wrong time.

We needed to talk. I knew that. But right now, I just needed to feel. Even if it was just holding and touching, I would take it. I would take all of it and keep it safe in my arms.

Jaron ran his hands up my back, trailing one of them down my side and around to my front. His fingers brushed over the stretch marks covering my lower abdomen, a rough growl escaping him. He would have seen them before when I joined him in the shower, but he never said anything then. I wondered why they all of a sudden affected him.

Releasing my mouth, he leaned his forehead against mine.

"Jaron," I whispered, running my fingers through the hair at the back of his neck.

When his lips found the side of my neck, I let out a soft sigh.

He gripped the hem of my shirt and lifted it above my head, leaving me only in my leggings. His dark eyes fell to my breasts, his tongue licking along his lips.

My chest rose and fell, the tiny hairs on my body tingling under his scrutiny.

Reaching out, he brushed his thumb along my jawline before covering my mouth with his. Splitting my lips with his tongue, he pushed and shoved, licked and sucked. He devoured every inch, taking and giving and making it his own.

I grabbed onto his shirt, fisting it in my hands. I needed to feel his hot skin and his muscles jump under my touch. I craved the way he lost control and needed every inch of him against every inch of me.

Fisting his shirt in my hands, I broke the kiss long enough to get the fabric up and over his head.

Once he tossed it to the floor, he was back on me.

I gasped, taking his tongue deep into my mouth and wrapping my arms around him. My nipples peaked, my breasts pushing against his naked chest.

Jaron laid me back, lowering me to the couch. Kneeling between my legs, he pushed into me, igniting a burn I had never felt before.

Reaching between us, I ran my fingers down his stomach, his abs twitching beneath my touch. Once I reached the waist of his jeans, I undid the button and lowered the zipper.

He deepened the kiss, stealing the very breath from my lungs.

Jaron hooked his fingers into the waist of my leggings and broke the kiss. His eyes were dark, filled with so much damn lust, my heart hammered in my ears. He continued tugging the leggings lower until they were off one leg.

Spreading my legs even more, I opened myself to him. Although I was still in panties, I was sure he could see exactly how much I wanted him. How much I needed every inch of him inside of me.

He pushed his waist back between my knees and crushed his mouth to mine.

(Jaron)

The rational part of me said that this was too soon and that we should wait. But I didn't listen. When Piper accused me of being jealous of the twins, I almost yelled that I had every right to be jealous of them. Knowing she spent weeks with them fucking her, how the hell could I not be jealous? But then I saw the pain hidden behind her eyes and the wobble of her chin, and I closed up completely.

Now she was beneath me.

Wet. Ready. And all fucking mine.

I reached into my jeans and pulled out my cock. It had been so long since I had an orgasm, I knew I wouldn't last but right now, I didn't give a shit. This was all for her. Every inch. Every throbbing vein. It belonged to Piper and only Piper.

With my tongue deep in her mouth, I swallowed her moans and inched a hand up her inner thigh before hooking a finger into the crotch of her panties. Her breath caught, the kiss becoming frantic.

Yeah, baby. It's fucking time.

With a rough tug, I ripped the thin fabric from her body.

Before either of us could say no and that this wasn't the right time, I pulled her farther beneath me and lined the tip of my cock up with her soaked center.

Piper lifted her leg, wrapping it around my waist, giving me the only invitation I needed.

In one smooth thrust, I was deep inside her.

She cried out, arching beneath me.

As much as I knew I should have gone slow, it had been way too long that I couldn't. My hips quickened, my length pulsing and swelling inside of her. Her pussy was so damn hot, it took everything in me not to come right away.

She ran her hands down my back and into my jeans. Cupping my ass, she pulled me forward, taking exactly what she wanted from me.

Releasing her mouth, I wrapped a hand around her jaw and tilted her head back. Her dark eyes locked on mine. Her hips met me thrust for every powerful thrust.

Needing her orgasm, I picked up speed and gripped the arm of the couch. Pulling out until just the tip of my cock was in her, I thrust forward, slamming every inch into her swollen body.

She screamed, her thighs shaking.

Good girl. Give me more, baby. I want them all. Every orgasm.

Licking along her mouth, I slipped my tongue inside and devoured the hell out of it.

She broke the kiss, arching beneath me. "Faster."

Slipping from her body, I grabbed her waist and flipped her onto her stomach. I pulled her to all fours before thrusting back inside her.

Piper cried out, slamming her ass back against me. It was hard, rough, and bordered on violent, but it was everything that made up us.

I knew then that this was only the beginning and my feelings for her would only get stronger as time wore on.

NINE

Piper

"I WASN'T EXPECTING THAT," I murmured, running my finger in circles along Jaron's nipple.

He kissed my temple, wrapped his arm around my middle, and snuggled his face into the crook of my neck. It had been something he did often. It made me wonder if it calmed him in a way.

It was an hour later, and we were still on the couch. My leggings were still on one leg only, my torn panties were on the floor, and I could feel his cum dripping out of me. But it was perfect and needed.

Jaron's jeans were still undone but he had stuffed his cock away after he came inside me. The dark treasure trail ran from his belly button to what laid beneath his jeans.

His hold on me tightened.

I expected him to say something dirty, but he hadn't said anything. Not even during sex. I wasn't sure why, but it bothered me.

"Talk to me," he murmured, the deep vibrato of his voice rumbling through me.

"I don't know what to say," I whispered, turning away from him.

"Tell me how you feel."

"I like this. Being with you. Being in your arms again." I cupped his cheek. "I like getting to know you."

"I like this too." He turned his head, kissing my open palm. "Jail didn't start out that bad. Besides being away from you, it was manageable. But over the weeks that followed, word got out who I was." He kissed my shoulder. "As much as it sucked, like I said before, Piper, I would have done anything to get home to you."

Placing a hard peck on his mouth, I tried with everything in me to let him know how I appreciated what he had done for me.

"I'm going to go get cleaned up, check on Brynn, and then head to bed." I kissed him one last time before sitting up. "Thank you for this though." I pulled my leggings back on and slipped the tank top up and over my head. "Join me?"

"Of course." He grabbed my hand when I went to walk away and turned me toward him. He lifted my shirt, placing a soft peck on my stomach. "Did you have any depression or anything?"

My heart jumped. "Postpartum depression?"

He nodded.

"No. I was lucky that way. That had been one of my fears because you weren't here, and I couldn't see you. But I was fine." I pushed my fingers through his hair.

He leaned his forehead against me and took a deep breath. "I'm glad."

"Me too," I whispered.

Jaron stood, grabbed a hold of my hand, and brought it up to his mouth. His dark eyes never strayed from mine. They looked into the deepest parts of me. The parts that had only ever been his.

Stepping away from him, I led him to our bedroom. While we both got ready for bed, I could still feel him inside of me. All throughout me.

"Tonight was amazing," I told him, slipping into bed after getting pajamas on.

"It was." He joined me, pulling the covers up and over us before pulling me down and into his arms.

"I just want you to know that I understand if things can't go back to the way they were. I mean, you changed. Not that it's a bad thing, I just want you to know that I get it." I scrubbed a hand down my face. "I'm not making sense."

"I get it, baby. I'm still him but I'm not. Yes, I changed but I think I became stronger because of it, just like you have as well."

"I don't feel strong half the time," I confessed.

"I get that too." He cupped my cheek, turning my head to meet his stare. "As much as I may have changed, my feelings for you have not. It's like being away for all of this time, only made them become more intense."

"I agree."

"We do have to take this one day at a time though, baby. That's all we can do. That's all we have." He kissed me softly on the lips. "I wish I could tell you that you'll get that man back. The one who went to jail for you. The one you fell in love with. But you won't. Not completely anyway. The only thing I can promise is that I will be the best man for you. Do you understand me?"

I swallowed hard at the mere intensity rolling off of him. "I understand."

"Good." He hugged me closer.

"One day at a time," I repeated, a yawn trembling through me.

"One day at a time," he murmured in my hair, pulling me against him.

I agreed with him but at the same time, I felt like that one day would turn into a lifetime.

(Jaron)

Holding the shank in my hand behind my back, I zeroed in on my victim. This felt good. Too good. The blood that was already on my hands shouldn't have felt so damn perfect. These men. These vile human beings. They deserved everything that was given to them.

"Kill him and we'll protect you."

I didn't believe those words but listened to them just the same. It wasn't like I had a choice in the matter. It was kill or be killed and I had a woman who was pregnant with my baby to get home to. I would do anything to get back to her and unfortunately these men knew that. How they did was beyond me. But I wouldn't put it past the mayor to let that little tidbit slip into unwanted ears.

My dad told me to keep to myself, to stay safe and not get into trouble. Keep my nose clean so to speak. But when I was jumped last week by three larger fuckers and put in the infirmary, I'd had enough.

These men needed to know that I was not one to be messed with. That I would kill them first and ask questions later.

Cross me and die.

My eyes popped open, memories of my nightmare slithering over my skin.

I placed my hand on my chest, trying to ease the racing of my heart.

Turning onto my side, I stared at Piper's sleeping form. She was on her stomach, her head facing the other way. The covers had ridden below her ass, showing the curves of her rear that the pajama bottoms couldn't cover.

My palm twitched, itching to reach out to her. To hold her. To tell her everything. How I felt. What I had to do to make it back to her. To tell her that I loved her.

I leaned over, placed a soft peck on her shoulder, and slid from the bed. Pulling a pair of gray sweatpants out of the bag my mom had given Piper, I slipped into them and left the bedroom.

A part of me expected Piper to want things back to the way they were. But were they even good then? I fucked her three times. Once in another country after stalking her beautiful ass, once in a bar, and the last time was in a car. Although, I probably shouldn't have done that, she never complained.

Heading to the living room, my eyes landed on the box on the floor by the couch. Maybe I should read more of those journals, then I can get to know her better. I could figure out what she needed. What both of them needed and maybe I could figure out what I needed just the same.

Taking the box with me, I headed to Brynn's room. I opened the door quietly and slipped inside. I never had a chance to tell Piper, but I loved the design of the room. It was warm and inviting. With a soft yellow for the walls, white furniture, and pigs of all shapes and sizes everywhere.

I smiled, my heart thumping hard at the love you could feel just by standing within the four walls.

Brynn was sleeping soundly in her crib and as much as I didn't want to disturb her, I needed to feel her in my arms. I had heard that a baby could bond with their parent from having skin on skin contact. It was worth a shot and I was willing to try anything to help Brynn know exactly who I was.

Gently taking off her onesie without disturbing her, I lifted her in my arms. She cooed, stirring awake.

"Hey, baby girl," I murmured, holding her against my chest.

She sighed, sucking on her soother. Her deep gray eyes fluttered closed, another sigh leaving her.

I chuckled, bringing her to the rocking chair in the corner of the room and kicking the box closer, so I could read while holding her.

Getting comfortable, I rested an ankle on the opposite knee, grabbed a journal, and began reading.

I felt the baby kick for the first time today. It was an odd feeling. Kind of like butterflies fluttering around in my belly. I was alone when it happened, so I couldn't really celebrate with anyone. But I called up Luna and gushed and she did the same about her baby. I can't believe we're pregnant at the same time. I wish I could see her.

I frowned, wondering why she couldn't see one of her best friends.

I turned the pages until I came across one that was dated after Brynn was born.

I had no idea what to name our daughter. I went on Pinterest and spent hours trying to find something unique. I came across Brynlee and fell in love. It's perfect.

I agreed, running my hand in circles over Brynn's back.

I hope Jaron likes it. I also hope he doesn't mind that I gave her his last name.

My eyes widened. She didn't.

I lowered my leg, placing Brynn on my lap on her back and searching through the box until I came across what I was looking for. Her birth certificate.

Name: Brynlee Emma Mercer

"Fucking hell," I whispered. She did. She actually gave her my last name. I never expected it, knowing we weren't married. It wasn't even hyphenated with both of our names. It was my name. Only.

Picking Brynn up, I put the onesie back on her and placed her back in her crib. My feet carried me to Piper before I knew what I was doing. It was like I was looking down at myself and watching.

She was still sound asleep, but I didn't give a shit.

Turning on the lamp, I knelt on the bed and rolled her onto her back.

Her eyes popped open. "Jaron? What's wrong? Is it Brynlee?"

I shook my head, not sure what I wanted to do or say. *Thank you* was on the tip of my tongue, but I didn't know how to voice it. It was stuck, the words a dead weight between us.

"Jaron?" She frowned, sitting up. "What is it?"

Instead of answering, I pulled her against me and wrapped my arms around her.

Thank you for not giving up on us. Thank you for giving me a daughter. Thank you for this gift that I can never repay you for.

As much as I wanted to voice my thoughts, I couldn't, so I held her instead.

A shuddered breath left her.

Running my hands through her hair, I gently tugged her head back and stared intently into her eyes.

Something passed between us. We knew how the other felt even though we hadn't said it yet. But those feelings suddenly turned into something more. They became dark, feral. I needed her in ways I had never felt before. It went far past just love. It became possessive, bordering on insanity. The thought of her being taken away from me left me on the verge of snapping.

"You're scaring me," she whispered but I knew she could feel it too. Her nipples hardened, her breathing picked up. We had always been attracted to each other, but this took on a whole other meaning.

Piper licked her lips, wetting the full pout of her mouth.

My body vibrated, my skin tightening over my muscles.

"Hey." She ran her hands down my stomach, dropping them to my sides. "Talk to me."

"I had a nightmare," I finally said. "And then I went to see Brynn. I needed to hold her. I also continued reading your journals. I found the one where you gave her my last name."

"Oh. Well, I thought it was only right. You weren't there to help me name her and you weren't there for anything else. I thought it was only fair. And I know…we are…we'll be…"

"What?" I needed her words. Her feelings. I needed her to tell me that she loved me. I tightened my hold on her head. "What?" I repeated, my voice lowering.

"What's going on? Are you mad?" She cupped my face. "Please don't be mad."

"Fuck, baby. I'm not mad. I'm far from being mad. I'm turned the fuck on, and I have no idea whether I should rip you open, make love to you, or go take a cold shower. It's driving me fucking crazy because I can see your nipples through your tank top, and I can…" I closed my eyes, taking a deep inhale, the sweet scent of her desire wafting into my nose. "I can smell your pussy," I growled.

"Oh." Her breath caught. "I'm…sorry?"

I chuckled, leaning my forehead against hers. "I just…I need a moment."

"Jaron." She ran her hand over my crotch, her fingers grazing the line of my thick cock.

Another growl escaped me. "Piper."

"I don't know what's going on with you but I'm here. For whenever you're ready. You can make love to me, fuck me, rip me open…" She tilted her head back. "Whatever you want. I just want to make you happy."

"I…" A tremor of something unknown rushed through me. Instead of taking her up on her offer, I released her and jumped off the bed. Pacing back and forth, I shoved a hand through my hair, avoiding her eyes but needing her to look at me just the same.

"What's wrong? What did I do?"

"Fuck, Piper." I spun on her, making her jump. I blew out a slow breath, trying to take control of the sudden rage rushing through me. What the hell was going on with me? "First off…" I took another deep breath. "You don't need to make me happy. Do you understand?"

"What?" She shook her head, her hair brushing her shoulders with the movement. "I don't know what you mean."

"I'm saying that I'm happy. I am happy. Yes, I'm fucked up. But I'm happy and no, you didn't do anything wrong. You could never do anything wrong. I'm so fucking confused right now…I just…I need…" I didn't know what I needed but this wasn't right. She didn't need to worry about making me happy because it didn't matter. It shouldn't matter. Her happiness came first and foremost. That was all I cared about. Nothing more. Nothing less. Her happiness was it.

"I don't know what's going on with you but you're the one who suggested sex, Jaron." Piper pulled the blankets up to her chest, shielding her nipples from me. A growl was on my tongue. A demand for her to not hide herself from me threatened to fall from my lips. But like the stupid ass that I was, I didn't say shit.

"I need a moment," I mumbled, leaving the room. Shutting the door behind me, I leaned against it and blew out a slow breath. It had been less than two days since I had been home. I thought that we would have a happy reunion and that would be it. But I was wrong. I was so very wrong.

TEN

Piper

I DIDN'T SLEEP WELL after Jaron left my room last night. I knew I had to have patience with him. I got it but it didn't mean that it didn't hurt any less.

"I'm fucked up."

He had always been grumpy, saying exactly what was on his mind, but this time was worse. He changed and I understood why. Not that I needed him to be exactly the way he was before, but I did need him to see that we were meant to be together. He told me he felt he didn't deserve me. It made me wonder if he still felt that way.

Letting out a hard sigh, I saw that it was pushing five in the morning. Brynn would be up in a couple of hours, if she wasn't up already.

Not being able to sleep, I quietly made my way out into the living room.

Jaron was on the couch with his arm over his eyes.

I walked up to him and pulled the blanket off the back of the couch.

He dropped his arm, staring up at me.

No words fell between us. Instead, we had a silent conversation. One that neither of us could ever say no matter how much we tried.

He rolled over onto his side.

I sat on the couch and laid down, snuggling up to him and wrapping the blanket around us.

Jaron curled his arm around my middle, pulling me tight against him. He shifted, his body becoming tense.

"What is it?" I murmured.

"Take this off," he demanded gently, giving the hem of my tank top a tug.

I stood from the couch and stripped completely.

He pulled his sweatpants off and tossed them to the floor.

Laying back down, the tiny hairs on my body tingled when his cock pressed up against my ass. But even though we were completely naked, he never took it further.

Jaron kissed the side of my throat, letting out a soft sigh, his body finally relaxed. Brushing the back of his knuckles down my side, he ran his hand back up to just beneath my breast. He repeated the movement, as if he was committing me to memory much like I had done when I touched his face earlier. His hand moved to my stomach, his fingers leaving light feathery touches.

My body tensed that he was touching a part of me that I had become self-conscious about ever since I gave birth to Brynlee.

"This is my favorite part of you," he murmured, his deep voice so soft, I wasn't sure I had heard him correctly. "Do you know why?"

"No," I croaked.

"Because you grew something that belongs to both of us. That's a part of us. Our best parts. You did something that a lot of women can't do but wish they could. You grew another person. A baby. Our baby." He kissed my shoulder. "I'm in awe of you, Piper."

A hard lump formed in my throat, my eyes welling at his unexpected words. "I couldn't have done it without everyone."

He pulled me tighter against him, his length twitching against my ass. He grunted, reached between us, and adjusted himself. "You're squishing my dick, babe."

"Oh." I laughed. "Sorry."

He chuckled, pulling me even tighter against him.

"I thought I was squishing you."

"It's fine." He hooked his arm that was under my head, around my chest. "He's not used to having a beautiful woman pressed up against him. He'll get over it."

A hard laugh escaped me. "Well, tell him I'll kiss him better if it ends up hurting too much."

Jaron growled in my ear, his cock pushing up between the cheeks of my rear. "I think he likes that idea."

A breathless giggle left me. "We can go to bed. Might be comfier."

"No." Jaron brushed his fingers down my side before gripping the back of my thigh and pushing my knee up to my chest. "You're too far away in bed. This is better." He pushed the tip of him up against me.

I sighed, a shiver rippling down my spine.

He was hard where I was soft.

"Jaron." As soon as his name left my mouth, he thrust into me. I bit my bottom lip to keep from crying out. "God."

"Shhh…" He kissed my cheek and pulled my leg over his waist, but he didn't move. "I know you feel insecure about the added weight from the pregnancy. But you are beautiful, Piper, and I still want you. I will always want you."

I loved and hated when he spoke to me while he was fucking me. It was like as soon as he slipped into my body, all of the truths were revealed because he was right. He said it before, and I was sure he would say it again. Sex was the most vulnerable position. For us anyway. Because as much as we had trouble talking, we spoke with our bodies.

"Tell me you don't feel how hard I am right now, Piper." His mouth brushed along the length of my neck. "Tell me you can't feel every vein, every ridge, every fucking pulse. My heart beats for you, baby, and I know you can feel that beat in my cock."

An unexpected release hit me. I gasped, arching against him, my thighs shaking as the orgasm rippled through me.

Under normal circumstances, I was sure that I would be embarrassed over the fast release, but the growl that left from somewhere deep inside Jaron shoved the embarrassment away.

Jaron slipped out from beside me and turned me onto my stomach, all the while keeping his body connected with mine. He fisted my hair, sinking his teeth into my shoulder.

Our fingers joined, linking together as we spoke a silent confession.

"Your body knows that it was made for me, Piper." He kissed my temple. "Now I just have to remind the rest of you."

After we finally fell asleep with Jaron still inside me, I woke a few hours later alone on the couch. Grabbing my clothes, I trudged to my bedroom but not before I heard Jaron in Brynlee's room. I peeked through the door that was slightly ajar, finding him sitting in the corner in the rocking chair with her on his lap. He was reading her a story. My heart warmed at the sight before me. Not wanting to interrupt their little moment, I went to the bathroom.

Once I was done taking a quick shower, I got dressed. Deciding on something comfortable, I ended up choosing gray leggings and a dark green long tank top that hid some of the baby weight I still carried around the middle.

My body still burned over the words Jaron had said a few hours ago. He still wanted me. He would always want me. A part of me knew that I had nothing to worry about when it came to his attraction to me, but it didn't mean that I wasn't concerned any less. I had been skinny before having Brynlee. Maybe too skinny at times. It wasn't like I never ate. My metabolism hadn't caught up with me yet clearly.

Throwing my hair up into a messy bun, I gave myself a once-over in the full-length mirror sitting in the corner of the room. I had started doing home workouts while Brynn napped, and I did some short runs while pushing her in the stroller. But it still didn't stop me from feeling insecure about my curves.

Although Jaron looked at me like he wanted to devour me whole, I was still nervous to be naked around him.

Leaving my room and heading to the kitchen, I was swiping lip gloss along my lips when I was stopped short by Jaron feeding Brynn.

His head popped up, his gaze flicking my way. They roamed down the length of me, the deep gray orbs, darkening even more.

My heart fluttered. I looked down at myself. Was I not presentable? When I met his stare again, I lifted my chin defiantly.

He smirked, gave me a wink, and went back to feeding our daughter.

I huffed, heading into the kitchen to make some coffee.

"Coffee's made," he called out, his voice rough.

"Oh." The heavenly aroma wafted into my nose. "Thank you." I made myself a coffee and joined him at the table. He was feeding Brynn breakfast, dishing a spoonful of the grape jelly baby food that even I loved tasting from time to time, into her mouth.

She smiled at me, her face a mess while she played with what was in her mouth and slapped her hands against the tray of the highchair.

I kissed her head before sitting at the chair across from her.

"I made her a bottle," Jaron said, still not looking at me. "Did you know that shit is fucking disgusting?"

"You tasted it?" I asked, my eyes widening.

He looked my way then. "I did. I wanted to know what I was putting in my baby girl's belly. We need better food for her."

"I...I really have no idea what to say."

"Have you tried it?"

"I have. Breast milk tastes better," I told him, still finding it hard to believe that he actually tasted her formula.

He placed the dish on the table in front of him. "How long did you breast feed her for?"

"For the first three months but I dried up pretty quickly. I did what I could, but she wasn't getting the nutrients she needed, so I put her on formula. There is better tasting stuff out there, but I haven't been able to find it. There's so many different kinds, it's unreal." Shame weighed heavily on my shoulders that I couldn't give her the best of the best.

"Really?" His eyes burned into me, setting my heart a flutter.

"I had it the once when someone gave it to me as part of a present for my baby shower but ever since, I haven't been able to restock because the stores around here don't carry it," I explained. "People have offered to go to another city to try and find it, but the company changed the name, and I can't seem to locate it anywhere."

"We'll find it. If I have to go to another damn country, I'll get it for Brynlee. I'll order it online if I have to and try every single type of formula until we find the right one. Alright?"

I nodded quickly, a flush of heat washing over my skin at how he had claimed her as his and so quickly.

"Good girl."

Those two words made my body burn even more.

Clearing my throat, I picked my mug up off the table and headed back into the kitchen where I could drink my coffee in peace. Although Jaron never followed me, my thoughts sure did.

Passion. Lust. *Fear.*

I was scared of the feelings I had for him because I knew that I would rather he fuck me than talk about our problems. It wasn't normal. None of this was.

A warm body came up behind me. Jaron reached around me, placing his mug on the counter beside mine. He didn't touch me, but he was standing so close, he might as well have. My skin tingled, my body vibrating with want. With need.

"Cyrus and Sammy are coming over for supper on Friday," Jaron said, his voice taking on that delicious rasp whenever he was on the verge of losing control.

My throat went dry. All I could do was nod.

With a shaky hand, I poured some more coffee into my mug. "What was your nightmare about last night?" That was a safe topic at least and it would get my mind off of all the things I wanted him to do to me.

"Shit I had to do to survive, baby." His voice took on a low dangerous timbre. He trailed his finger down my arm, a path of goosebumps following it.

"But you did it."

"I did what?"

I took a chance and turned in his arms, staring up at him. "You survived."

His jaw ticked. It did that whenever he was pissed or thinking about something serious.

I reached up, running my fingers along the muscle, the beating of it in tune with my heart.

Thump. Thump. Thump.

"I have to get Brynn cleaned up," he murmured, closing the final space between us. "But I want you to remember."

I let out a soft sigh at feeling him pressed up against me. "I remember."

"Do you?" He stared down at me.

I looked away, fidgeting under his scrutiny.

"No." He gripped my jaw in a rough move, forcing me to meet his dark eyes. "Tell me that you remember that we belong together. That I'm not going anywhere. That you need me and that I need you. Tell me, Piper."

"I remember," I gritted out. "I also remember your dirty and filthy words. Your delicious way that you like to use me to make you feel better. Your need to dominate—"

Brynn took that moment to start crying. She usually fussed right after eating. I was surprised she waited this long to interrupt us.

I shoved out of Jaron's grip and stepped around him. No matter what happened or how much we fought, he was my safe place. He pissed me off, turned me on, and treated me like I was the only thing that mattered.

"Cyrus and Sammy used to come over for supper once a month," I told him, grabbing a cloth to clean up Brynn. "We would talk about you and they would fill me in on everything they could. Sammy also told me that he tried convincing you to let me come and see you. But you never agreed."

"I didn't want those bastards seeing you. It's bad enough I have to deal with friends who fucked you and probably wish they were still fucking you."

I stared up at him, scanning his face. "You can't seriously be jealous. I gave birth to your kid, Jaron." I could feel the rage burning through me and I waited for it to blow, but luckily for us both, his next words stopped that from happening.

"No, I'm not jealous." Jaron leaned down until he was eye level with me. "You want to know why? Because you gave birth to *my* baby. I'm the only man you've let fuck you without a condom and I went to Paris for you."

"I never asked you to do that." He couldn't possibly be blaming me for something I never suggested.

"I know that," he said, his voice rough. "Fuck, Piper." He pulled away from me and leaned against the wall opposite me. "Listen, I went to Paris because I needed to know that what I felt for you wasn't just one-sided."

"Really?"

"I did. When I told Cyrus and Sammy why we were going to Paris, they jumped on the idea. I only told them that I was going after you and they never asked any more questions. Even Sammy, and he hates the idea of a relationship. Or he did at the time anyway." Jaron ran a hand through his hair, blowing out a huff. "What I'm saying is that," he took a step toward me, "it's you and me against the world, baby. I knew this would be hard, but I didn't realize just how hard." And that was the most honest thing he had said since he had been home.

"Do you think we'd still be here if you never went to Paris?"

He tilted his head, thinking a moment. "I'm not sure," he finally said. "I'd like to say that if it was meant to be, which I know it was, then we would be here whether I went to Paris or not but maybe we'd have a harder time of it. Or you would be with someone else and so would I. But I'd like to take you back to Paris one day."

"Since it started it all," I finished for him.

"Exactly." He closed the distance between us and placed a soft peck on my mouth. "It started everything."

I cupped the back of his neck when he went to pull away and tugged him down harder, needing to feel him against me.

"Listen, I'll go to the grocery store and grab some new formula," Jaron murmured against my lips. "Anything else you need? What did you want for supper?"

It was on the tip of my tongue to ask if we could go out for dinner, but I hadn't been out in so long, just the idea of being around people, sent a nervous flutter racing through me. Maybe over time that could happen.

"What is it?" he asked, tilting his head.

"I just...I want to go on that date." My face burned at my confession.

He gave me a small smile.

Much to my surprise, he wrapped his arms around me, pushing his face into the crook of my neck like he always did.

"I want to go on that date too, baby," he whispered.

My heart stuttered. Returning the embrace, I pulled him tighter. "You do?"

"Yes." His mouth found the side of my throat, placing a soft peck there.

I sighed, wishing we could stay like this forever. Just him, Brynn, and I but I knew we would have to face reality sooner than later.

Jaron leaned back, cupping my face and placing a soft kiss on my forehead.

My eyes fluttered closed.

"We'll get through this." His voice was soft. "I promise we will."

I believed him. I had to. We had to take this one day at a time. While we needed to talk some more, for the moment, I just wanted to give Brynn a bath and snuggle with her while watching some mindless show on TV for the day.

While I got Brynn ready for her bath, I made it a mission to find out everything I could about Jaron. What his hobbies were. Did he have a job? His mom had told me that he worked for his Aunt Zillah at her auto repair shop but that was all I knew. His hands weren't stained with grease from a car. Not like Shade's hands.

"Hey, baby girl. Are you ready for a bath?" I lifted Brynn out of her highchair, getting a babble of baby chatter. I laughed at whatever it was she was trying to tell me.

Before I could bring Brynn to the bathroom, Jaron kissed my cheek and placed a peck on her head.

He kissed me one last time before leaving the house.

My stomach fluttered.

Placing Brynn back in her highchair, my feet carried me to the door before I could stop myself. Groceries could wait. I needed him. This was more important.

"Jaron," I called out before he could get in the car.

"What's wrong?" he asked, closing the driver's side door.

I ran up to him and threw myself around his middle, hoping for the moment that it was enough.

"Piper." He wrapped his arms around my shoulders, hugging me against him.

"I never told you to drive safe." I grabbed the collar of his hoodie and pulled him down to meet my mouth. "And I also wanted to tell you that you don't have to go now. We can go together in a few days."

Jaron hugged me tighter, every hard line of his body pushing up against me.

I leaned back, cupping his cheek.

"I should go. I won't be too long."

I nodded but we stood there like that for a few minutes, just staring at each other.

"The sooner I go, the sooner I can get back to you, baby," he whispered.

My heart stuttered. I kissed him one last time before pulling away and running back to the house.

When I reached the front door, I looked back at him.

Jaron stood there, staring at me. He lifted his hand, giving me a small wave.

I blew him a kiss and headed back into the house. With my back to the door, I let out a slow breath, a small smile creeping on my face.

AFTER US

(Jaron)

When Piper left the house and ran toward me and into my arms, that single moment would forever be burned in my memory. It had only been a couple of days since I gotten out of jail. Things weren't all hunky-fucking-dory right away, but this was a start.

When I originally stepped out onto the porch, I stared out at her car and my bike sitting in the driveway. Sammy or Cyrus must have dropped off my bike. I didn't even notice. Being too wrapped up in Piper and reconnecting with her, I had no idea they had even shown up.

My eyes scanned the street. The house was in a quieter part of town. Neighbors were few and far between. Even though Piper's home was small, both the front and backyard were huge. My eyes flicked to a light on the wall beside the door. I remembered seeing a security panel on the wall as soon as you stepped into the house. Knowing that Piper had protection when I wasn't around, set some of the anxiety rushing through me at ease. Her father wouldn't have it any other way and made sure to keep his girls safe. *My girls* safe. I made a mental note to thank her parents for taking care of them when I couldn't.

With my hand still on the screen door, I hesitated.

Before I could stop myself, I went back into the house in search of Piper.

She was in the living room, placing Brynn in her playpen. When she rose to her full height, she let out a soft sigh.

I rushed to her, letting my feet guide me to the person I needed most.

Her head whipped around. "Jaron, I thought you left."

Instead of answering her, I crashed into her and enveloped myself around her.

Her breath hitched as she latched on to me.

I didn't know what to say but I hoped, no, I prayed she could hear my words through my touch alone. I realized then I needed to spend as much time with her as I could. I couldn't just walk away. Even if it was just to get groceries. I'd figure that out later.

"Jaron." Her voice was muffled by my shirt.

I squeezed her, wrapping my hand in her hair. "I'm sorry," was all I said, fisting her hair with both hands and crushing my mouth to hers.

Let me in, baby.

She opened to me, flicking her tongue along mine.

A rough growl left me as I deepened the kiss.

Piper sighed, tilting her head back.

Breaking the kiss, I leaned my forehead against hers.

"What was that for?" she asked, her voice husky.

"It was an apology." I released her and grabbed her hand, pulling her to the couch. While Brynn played, I wanted to hold Piper.

"I thought you were going to the grocery store," she said softly, letting me tug her onto my lap.

"I changed my mind." I pulled the blanket off the back of the couch and wrapped it around her. "I can text Cyrus and Sammy and get them to pick stuff up if needed."

"Okay." Piper rested her head against my shoulder. "I think I know why we're having issues."

"Oh?"

She lifted her head. "We haven't had much time alone. This is new for both of us. I've never been in a serious relationship and neither have you. So we're bound to have some bumps along the way."

I kissed her jaw. "We got this, and I got you, Piper," I murmured, placing a soft peck on the top of her head. "I always got you."

"I know and I have you as well, Jaron." She snuggled against me. "But it's only been not even three full days yet. We don't have to fall into a routine right away."

"True but I'm not a patient person."

She sat up, a gasp leaving her. "No. I never would have guessed that."

"Careful." I jabbed a finger into her side, earning me a giggle. "You're not patient either."

Her laugh deepened. "Let's just wait a little bit and we can get groceries later."

I pinched her chin and covered her mouth with mine.

She moaned, wrapping herself around me.

I grinned against her lips, giving the bottom one a gentle bite.

While Brynlee played in her playpen, talking and babbling to herself, Piper and I cuddled on the couch. It was perfect if you asked me, even if we didn't talk about a whole lot. Just being together was enough.

ELEVEN

JARON

IT WAS THE FOLLOWING Friday. I had been home for a week and while things weren't perfect, we were slowly falling into a routine.

I would get Brynn up in the mornings so Piper could sleep in a little longer, since I was the one who made her go to bed late each night.

Whenever I went into Brynn's room in the morning, she would be standing in her crib and her chubby little body would jump whenever she saw me approach her.

It was the start to my day that I never knew I needed and looked forward to each morning. I would get her changed, place her in her playpen out in the living room, and wake up Piper with a kiss to any part of her body that was exposed.

It was now Friday and Sammy and Cyrus were coming over for supper later that evening.

"Did you want me to grab something for supper tonight?" I asked Piper as she fed Brynlee an afternoon snack of soft crackers.

"We can order pizza so you don't have to go to the store."

I kissed her head. "I don't mind."

"Okay, well whatever you want, I can cook it." She smiled up at me.

"Okay." I placed a peck on Brynlee's cheek before giving her mama another kiss. "Thank you for this morning," I whispered.

She laughed, her cheeks turning a light shade of pink. "Thank you for this week."

"One day at a time, baby." I gave her one final kiss and left the house.

We spent the week slowly reconnecting. We talked some more and even though it was only a couple of words shared between us, it was a start in the right direction.

When I reached the driveway, I hesitated between taking my bike or Piper's car. I knew she wasn't going anywhere, so she wouldn't care if I drove it.

Our fighting had been limited this week, thankfully, but we still had our moments. Of pushing. And then at the same time, a constant taking. I wanted to give, take, fight, and more. A part of me, that sick part, enjoyed fighting with her because I loved her angry eyes on me as they heated my skin until I felt like I was going to combust from the fiery stare. I bet my life that angry sex with her was dirty and hot as fuck.

Piper walked on eggshells around me. Not always. It had mostly been in the mornings after I woke up from a nightmare. She probably wondered when I would blow. I wouldn't. Because none of this was her fault. But I was itching for something. Not sex. She took care of that. Blood maybe? A fight? She had mentioned a gym in the basement. Maybe working out would help me. I could spar with Sammy. He was a dirty fighter, but it always helped my moods after getting into it with him. Maybe I could convince both him and Cyrus to fight me. I needed to fight. To hurt. To get fucking bloody.

Forcing myself out of my head, I took Piper's car and drove to the grocery store to grab some food and hopefully, better tasting formula for Brynn. I could still remember the taste perfectly. It was like rotten milk. Or worse. It was disgusting and there was no way I would feed that shit to her again. I found another brand in the kitchen cupboard that tasted a bit better at least, so we made sure to feed that to Brynn instead.

Piper wasn't aware but I had arranged for my dad to set up automatic deposits to her bank account. Every time I got paid from the club, it went to her and our daughter. It started as soon as I found out she was pregnant. My dad told me that she had thanked both him and my mom for the money. He never told her that it was me who was sending the money because he felt I should have been the one to tell her.

She spent some of it on groceries, but it made me wonder what else she spent it on. If it were me, I would pay the bills and set aside the rest as a college fund for Brynlee. That was probably what Piper did. I wouldn't have minded if she spent some of it on herself either. That had been why I sent the money to her in the first place. Since I couldn't be there for her, making sure she was financially taken care of was the least I could do.

When I reached the store, I leaned forward, peering at the large building. I remembered coming here as a child when my parents would need to grab some things on the way home from Uncle Coby and Aunt Brogan's place. It was bigger than before but not by much.

Putting the car in park, I took a breath and left the vehicle. It had been a long time since I was around people I didn't know. Even being in jail, you got to know everyone. Especially when you made a name for yourself. Word about who I was got around rather quickly. Whether I liked it or not.

Grabbing a cart from the rack, I wheeled it into the store when someone stepped out of the large building. They stopped in front of me, followed by two men dressed in black suits.

My chest tightened; my hands white-knuckling the bar of the cart. "Price."

Price Davies grinned, running two fingers along his mouth. He looked different than the last time I saw him, which would have been before I went to jail. He had lost quite a bit of weight and appeared as if he had taken up working out. His dark hair held some silver in it. Even the scruff on his jaw had some gray in it. While he may have changed his appearance, his eyes hadn't changed. They held so much damn hate for me, a tremor of unease rippled down my spine.

"You look well, Jaron." He cocked his head to the side. "It's been a while. How's that pretty little thing of yours? She still pining after you or did she smarten the fuck up and finally get herself a real man?"

I twisted my head to the side, looking around me. Two black SUVs sat at the outer edge of the parking lot, meaning the mayor had more security detail with him than the two men standing on either side of him.

"What do you want?" I asked instead, knowing full well he was trying to get a reaction from me. But I refused. It would come. In time. But not now and especially not when I was alone.

"I want to chat." Price jutted his chin. The two men behind him, stepped forward.

"We're in public," I bit out. "Don't be stupid."

Price grinned. He smoothed his hands down the front of his gray suit jacket. The weight he was sporting around the middle the last time I saw him, no longer there. I had never been attracted to men but even I noticed how better looking he had become. I wondered why. Price Davies had a reason for everything he did. He might have even been a half-decent human being in another life, but not in this one. No. He liked little girls and that didn't sit well with me, but it was something I had never been able to prove.

"What are you doing here anyway? Don't you have people that do this for you?" I leaned my arms on the bar of the cart, scratching my jaw.

"If you're referring to grocery shopping, yes." Price nodded. "I do. But I much prefer to do this part on my own. You see." He took a step toward me. "You took something important from me."

The hackles rose on the back of my neck. "What are you getting at?" His son had deserved what he got. Sure, I reacted first before thinking of the consequences, but he had attacked my girl. He was lucky I didn't do worse to him.

"My son was going to be the next mayor," Price said, his jaw ticking.

AFTER US

I rolled my eyes then. "Right." Brody Davies never wanted anything to do with politics. Of all the research I had done on him, he often looked bored in the pictures of him and his dad during his many public appearances and campaigns.

Price's brows dropped in the middle. "You questioning me, boy?"

I chuckled then. "You don't scare me, Price. Never have. Never will."

"That's Mr. Mayor to you, fuck—Jaron." His cheeks reddened.

I grinned. "Nice catch, Price," I said, drawing out his name. Calling him Mr. Mayor meant that I respected him. And that was something I had never done.

Price took a step toward me while his men stayed back. When he stood a couple of inches away, I could see the evil swimming in his deep sapphire eyes. "You want to know something?" he asked, low enough for only me to hear. "I don't actually give a fuck that you killed my son." He stepped closer. "He wasn't even my blood anyway."

That revelation didn't sit well with me. It meant that he threw me in jail, made a huge fucking scene about it, just to get under my skin. Because of him, my daughter didn't know her father the first ten months of her life. Because of him, my mother's heart shattered. And because of him, I could have lost Piper forever.

Price smirked, curling his fingers around the handlebar between my hands. "I suggest watching your back, Jaron. We wouldn't want anything to happen to those pretty little girls in your family. I could get a lot of money for your daughter. She would grow up in my world. She would be trained. She would be the perfect pet because she wouldn't have the influence of the world hanging over her." He leaned toward my ear. "I'd also have so much fun breaking Piper."

"You even think of going after my girls..."

"You'll what?" Price chuckled. "Remember what happened last time. You ended up in jail. Too bad it wasn't longer." He turned around, walking away from me but stopped suddenly. "I'd be careful if I were you. Your girls won't always be protected.

And your daughter will grow up." He continued walking away, his wicked grin the last thing I saw before he stepped into the black SUV.

As soon as both vehicles sped away, I let out a sigh of relief but before I did what I came there to do, I called Cyrus.

"Yeah," came his deep reply after the first ring.

"I need you to go to Piper's sooner," I told him, heading into the grocery store.

"On it. Where are you?"

"At the grocery store getting Brynlee some better formula and I was going to pick up food for Piper to cook but she needs a break." I suddenly felt all eyes on me. I looked down at myself. I wasn't wearing my cut. What could these people be looking at?

"Is it weird??" Cyrus asked.

I cleared my throat, not wanting to get into this with him. "Listen, just go to Piper's and I'll be there soon."

I disconnected the call before he could ask any more questions. He wouldn't. That was Sammy. He was the talker while Cyrus was the quiet, brooding type. That was how it used to be anyway. But maybe things had changed while I was away. I had found out during the times the twins came to visit me that there was a woman Sammy was sniffing around. But he refused to talk any more about it. So I never asked.

Quickly grabbing some food and more formula for Brynn, I made it to the checkout when the hairs on the back of my neck tingled. I looked around me, finding nothing out of the ordinary. People shopped, like they were supposed to be doing at a grocery store.

Biting back a sigh, I turned around and was greeted with a friendly smile from the young man working the cash.

"Newborn?" he asked, picking up the formula and scanning it.

"She's almost ten months actually," I told him.

"Ah. My sister uses this stuff for my nephew. She said it's the best she's found," he added, continuing to scan the items and placing them in bags.

My gaze landed on a stack of flowers. All different types and colors. I didn't know much about them. I probably should have paid more attention when my mom made me help her with the gardens in their backyard.

I picked up a bouquet of blue flowers, making a mental note to ask my mom what they were but I thought they looked nice, so it was worth a shot.

"Those are pretty."

My gaze flicked to the woman standing behind me with a cart full of food and other items.

"I think whoever they're for, will like them." She smiled.

"I hope so." I handed them to the cashier. "These too, please."

He nodded, scanning them and giving me my final total.

Handing him the exact cash, I pulled my phone out of my pocket and saw a text from Sammy that they were heading to Piper's.

"You're Jaron Mercer, aren't you?"

I frowned, glancing at the same woman behind me. "I'm sorry, do I know you?"

"Nope, you don't." Her gaze roamed down the length of me. "But I've seen your girl around."

I grabbed my items, bouquet of flowers, and rushed out of the store. As soon as I reached the car, my phone rang. Fucking hell.

These people needed to leave us the hell alone. Piper and I had shit to work through. While we were slowly getting into a routine, we still needed to learn to raise Brynlee together. We needed to not fight and actually talk about our problems instead of fucking our way through them. But I knew it would be a long time before that happened.

If ever at all.

(Piper)

After I had put Brynlee down for a nap, I decided to get some cleaning done. Turning the music on low, I inhaled a deep breath, letting the deep melody wash over me and guide my feet. An hour later and the floors were swept and mopped, the bathrooms cleaned, and toys picked up. I was just getting ready to grab a glass of wine when I heard the front door open and the alarm disengage.

My heart jumped, waiting for Jaron to greet me with a kiss, but it wasn't him at the door.

"Hey, kiddo." Cyrus came toward me, holding a case of beer. He brought it to the kitchen, placed it on the floor, and started putting some of the bottles in the fridge.

"What are you guys doing here already?"

"Jaron called us and asked us to come over early." Sammy raised an eyebrow. "He didn't tell you?"

"Not that you were coming over early, no." I blew a loose strand out of my face.

"We'll order pizza later, so you can have a break," Cyrus said from the kitchen. "Where is he anyway?" He grabbed a beer and popped the cap off. "He should be here already."

I glanced at the doorway, expecting Jaron to show up.

Sammy handed me a beer and sat at the table. "Something wrong?"

"Jaron left over an hour ago." Maybe he got caught in traffic. Not that there would be a lot between the grocery store and here. "Or maybe..." A tremor of fear rushed through me when suddenly, the front door opened.

I passed the guys a glance.

Jaron entered the house, a scowl on his face. He held a bouquet of beautiful blue flowers in one hand and a bag in the other. He walked past me, bringing them to the kitchen.

I followed him, the air suddenly becoming thick around us.

"These are for you," he mumbled.

"Thank you. They're beautiful." I put the flowers in a vase and was filling it up with water when I noticed that he hadn't budged from his spot beside me.

He gripped the edge of the counter, the muscles in his back, jumping beneath his shirt. He looked over his shoulder. When his slate eyes landed on me, his face softened.

My heart skipped a beat, the smoldering look making me pause.

"Thank you for the flowers, Jaron," I murmured, turning off the water and setting the vase on the counter.

He nodded, his jaw clenching.

Before I could ask what was wrong, he came toward me and cupped my face. "Have you ever had any problems?" he asked, running his thumb along the edge of my jaw.

I frowned. "What do you mean?"

He grabbed my hand, bringing it up to his mouth. "Have you ever had issues with anyone? Women. Men. Anyone at all."

"What's going on?" Cyrus asked, coming up behind him.

Jaron searched my face, something flashing behind his eyes. "Have you ever run into the mayor?"

"No. I haven't seen him since your trial." I shivered, remembering the way he looked at my pregnant body. I was huge and he looked at me like I was a piece of steak and he was the dog who wanted to rip me apart.

Jaron released me and started pacing back and forth. "I had an unexpected meeting with the good mayor at the grocery store."

"The fuck? Why? Doesn't he have people who do that shit for him?" As soon as the question left Sammy's mouth, a cry sounded from the baby monitor I kept on the kitchen counter. "I got her." He left, heading to Brynn's room.

Jaron stared after him, his jaw ticking.

My chest tightened. I knew that tick. I knew what it meant. He was pissed and he was going to blow. On his cousins. On me. On someone. I wasn't sure who, but I had a feeling that before the night ended, I would find out.

"This little one wanted to come and see what all the fuss was about," Sammy said, holding Brynn in his arms. She had her arms wrapped around her stuffed pig, sucking on her favorite soother.

I passed a glance at Jaron. He didn't budge. No emotion splayed on his face. "Um…can you guys give us a moment?"

"Of course." Cyrus clapped Jaron's shoulder, leaning down to his ear and whispering something I couldn't hear.

Jaron's gaze flicked to mine.

My heart jumped, the blood pounding in my ears.

Cyrus released him, gave me a small smile, and headed out to the backyard with Sammy following behind him.

When the patio door closed, leaving Jaron and I alone, I was expecting him to blow up. But when he only remained silent, it made the nerves fluttering through me that much more pronounced.

"What's wrong?" I asked, needing to break the silence. I stepped in front of him, placing my hand on his chest. Expecting his heart to be thumping hard like mine, I was surprised when it was calm. My eyes popped to his, finding him staring down at me. "Jaron."

"How long has he been helping you with Brynn?"

My throat went dry. I went to pull my hand away but in a quick move, Jaron grabbed a hold of my wrist and pushed me into the kitchen out of view.

"I..." He took a deep inhale and blew it out slowly. "I know I asked them to help you, but I don't like that they know Brynn better than I do. I don't like that she knows them better than she knows me. Her father. And I especially don't like that they know *you* better than I do."

"No." I cupped his face. "They don't. No one knows me like you know me. I haven't slept with anyone since you, I wouldn't do that. I'm not in...I don't like them like that. I don't..." My throat worked hard over a lump that suddenly lodged its way inside. "Jaron, please trust me. Nothing's happened. I promise."

"Fuck." He cupped my nape, leaning his forehead against mine. "I know you haven't slept with them. I trust you, baby. And I trust them. I wouldn't be with you...I wouldn't be here if I didn't. And I wouldn't have asked them to help you and watch out for you, if I thought something could happen."

"You'll get to know Brynn and she'll get to know you, but I talked about you constantly. You have to know that I did. Please believe me. And this past week with you has been amazing. It's a start, Jaron."

"I know." He cupped my face, kissing my forehead. "I have to tell you something. I don't know what it means. People are trying to cause shit and I don't like it. It's pissing me off."

"What's going on?"

"I ran into this woman at the grocery store. It was harmless but she's seen you around."

"Oh…" I thought back to my times at the grocery store. I never noticed anything out of the ordinary, but it didn't mean anything when I was stuck in my own head for the most part. "What do you think she wanted?"

"I'm not sure." Jaron ran a hand through his hair. "But I don't give a shit about her or the mayor or any of them. Working through us, is the most important thing right now."

My heart jumped to my throat. "I agree."

He titled his head, his eyes, eyes that I had fallen in love with so long ago, searched my face. "You better."

I laughed lightly. "I did think this would be easier though. No one warned me that it could be hard."

Tanned, rough, calloused hands covered mine. Warm lips kissed my forehead. "I will make this right. Us. Our family. Everything you need, I will provide for you. I'm here. I am always here. Forever."

"You better," I whispered, repeating his words.

Jaron smirked, ran his hand to the back of my head and crushed his mouth to mine.

Snaking my arms around his shoulders, I pulled him closer and held on. So many things still needed to be said. So many truths needed to be revealed. But for the moment, instead, I just held on and breathed him in.

The minty taste mixed on his tongue.

The scent of his cologne that mixed with the scent of him. Everything that made up him.

"Stop thinking," he murmured, his voice low. He held my hand between us, leaning his forehead against mine.

"I was just thinking how good you taste and smell." I tilted my head back, grazing my fingers through his beard. "That's all."

"Good. Enough with this heavy shit." His brows dropped, a deep vee settling in his forehead. "We'll work through this because I refuse to have it any other way." He paused. "I'm scheduling our date."

I leaned back. "You are?"

"Yes." He paused. "You said that we hardly know anything about each other. I want to get to know you more. I want to know your hobbies, what you want to do for a living, whether you like horror movies or romance movies. What music you like. I want to know all of your quirks, Piper."

"I want to know that about you too."

"Good, I'll make us a reservation."

"Thank you." I pulled him closer.

He gave my bottom lip a gentle nip. "No thanks needed because I wasn't taking no for an answer anyway." He released me and gave me a wink before joining the guys and our daughter out in the backyard. As soon as he shut the door behind him, he stood there, staring at me.

Something changed between us and I couldn't wait to explore more of whatever it was with him.

TWELVE

JARON

MY PARENTS WERE DRAGGING me to Uncle Coby and Aunt Brogan's place. It had been something we did quite often when I was younger, but we had skipped the past couple of summers for whatever reason. Adults were too damn busy all the time if you ask me.

"We're almost there." Mom turned to me with a wide smile on her face. "Are you excited? You get to see your friends again."

"I am." And that was the truth. We talked on the phone, texted, chatted on Facebook, and so on, but I hadn't seen them face-to-face in over a year. We lived a couple of hours away in a large house that held more than its fair share of people. I loved my cousins who lived with us, but they weren't blood. Not that it ever mattered of course but it still wasn't the same. They were also older and living their lives while I was stuck in school and trying to graduate without pummeling my fists through the other kids' faces just for being annoying half the time.

"I know Zach is looking forward to seeing you," Dad said, meeting my gaze in the rearview mirror.

I nodded, leaning my head against the back seat and watching the world fly past us. Half an hour later and we were pulling into Angel and Jay's driveway. I had come to understand that their house was the biggest, so that was why they always had everyone over. Their backyard was my favorite too. I would have the same one day. With a giant pool as well.

"Alright, let's go before your sister rips my face off for keeping her boys away from her." Mom laughed, leaving the car. Just as she shut the door behind her, Aunt Brogan came running from the backyard. She threw her arms around my mom, which was funny in a way seeing as she was so short.

Mom's body shook with laughter as she returned the hug.

Dad chuckled. "Let's go, Jaron."

I left the car as everyone else came from the backyard to greet us.

As we gave hugs, said hi, carried on like we had only seen each other the day before, I couldn't help but notice...her.

Piper stood off to the side. She was chatting with Gigi and Luna, other girls we had grown up with.

She laughed. Her long dark hair was pulled back into a messy ponytail. She wore a red tank top that was tucked into cut-off shorts and no shoes. Her skin glowed like she had just spent hours in the sun. Her head turned, her dark eyes meeting mine.

She gave me a small wave.

I did the same.

My heart thumped hard, my mouth going dry.

From that day on, I knew one thing. And it was the most important thing of all.

Piper Michaels, no matter how long it took, would be mine.

I had only ever gone on one date. Once. And that was when I was a teenager and had no idea that it would be Piper my dick would be lusting after. Not until that little reunion took place at Angel and Jay's place that summer so many years ago. I wish I would have waited for her. If we lost our virginity to each other, the wait would have been worth it, but neither of us did that. Life had different plans for us. It forced us a part only to bring us back together again in another country.

I knew then that Piper would be mine and now it was what I strived for. But there were still pieces to our puzzle that were missing. Maybe a date would help. It would surely set us on the right path. It had to because like I told her, I refused to have it any other way.

I would burn the mother fucking world down just to put a smile on her face.

"This pizza is so good. I could eat ten of them to myself." Sammy patted his stomach and leaned back in the patio chair he was sitting on.

Piper laughed.

Cyrus only shook his head.

"It is good." Piper wiped her hands on the paper towel and placed it on the coffee table in front of her. "Meadow is the one who got us into it. Although, she swears she can make it better. But she's never tried."

We ordered pizza after putting Brynn to bed. Piper was sitting on the ground with her legs crossed beneath her. After our moment in the kitchen, we had come outside. Piper had snuggled with Brynlee and ended up putting her to bed an hour later.

While Sammy and Cyrus talked amongst themselves, I couldn't help but watch Piper. She pulled the elastic out of her hair, smoothing her fingers through the long dark strands. She massaged her head, a wince furrowing between her eyebrows.

"Come here," I blurted.

Sammy and Cyrus looked my way.

Piper's gaze snapped to mine.

I pointed to the floor in front of my feet.

She looked from the spot I was pointing at, to my face.

"Sit in front of me," I told her, something sparking inside of me that I would soon have my hands on her again.

She chewed her bottom lip, a light flush gracing her cheeks, but she did as she was told. When she moved to the spot at my feet, I pulled her back between my knees and pushed my fingers through her hair and into her head. Massaging out the kinks, her worries, and everything else, I rubbed and kneaded.

Give me your fears, baby. All of them. I'll take care of you. Both you and our daughter.

Piper sighed.

"Hey, if you're offering free massages, I'm down for that." Sammy waggled his eyebrows.

Cyrus smacked him across the back of the head.

"Ow." Sammy punched his brother's shoulder. "That hurt, fucker. You have like fifty pounds on me."

Cyrus only smirked.

I leaned down to Piper's ear. "Better?"

"Yeah," she breathed, that single word husky and low, shooting right to the tip of my dick. "Thank you."

I wasn't there when her back hurt while she was pregnant with Brynlee, but I was here now. Any pain she had, was mine. I would make it go away. No matter what I had to do. I would take it on my shoulders and bear the brunt of her agony, whether she offered it to me or not.

Sitting back, I started braiding her hair. "Elastic," I said when I was done, holding out my hand.

"Did you just braid my hair?" she asked, trying to turn her head.

"Yes, but you're going to mess it up. So I need the elastic. Please."

She gave it to me, but I could see the shock on her face.

Tying the elastic around the end of the braid, I tugged the end, forcing her head back. "Surprised, Piper?"

She laughed. "Little bit."

Cyrus and Sammy only grinned.

"We were taught to braid hair a long time ago, kiddo." Cyrus pulled his pack of smokes out of the inner pocket of his jacket. He lit a cigarette and handed it to Sammy before lighting one for himself.

"All of you know how to do braids?" she asked, running her hand down the length of her hair.

"Yup." I released her and sat back, satisfied with my handiwork.

"You can actually thank Jaron for that," Sammy said, puffing on his smoke.

"Why's that?" Piper hooked an arm across my knee.

My breath caught in my throat, thankful that she didn't pull away.

"I got in trouble and Uncle Tray made us braid Bee's hair. She was five, had hair so fucking long, it kept getting in her way. I was being a little shit, so he made us braid it." I shrugged. "All of us had to learn."

"At first, I thought it was lame, but it usually ends up impressing the ladies. And…" Sammy sat forward. "It gives us something to pull."

"Truth." Cyrus winked.

"Interesting. I can see you guys now, sitting around and braiding her hair, but I can't picture you as boys. So all I'm seeing are grown men, braiding hair." She giggled. "Which is super adorable by the way."

"And hot right?" Sammy wiggled his eyebrows. "It's definitely hot." He elbowed Cyrus. "It's hot. Admit it."

"It's impressive." Piper laughed, shaking her head. Her gaze flicked to mine. "And yeah, it's definitely hot."

I grinned, cupped her nape, and pushed my thumb into her shoulder.

She sighed, leaning her cheek against my knee, but kept her eyes locked on mine.

"We should go." Cyrus butted his smoke out on the bottom of his Shitkicker. "We're driving up tomorrow to see Bee, so we should have an early night."

Sammy scoffed. "Right. Not like I'm going to sleep anyway." The air around him suddenly shifted.

Our cousin, Bee, named after their parents, lived off in the middle of the woods with her husband and their son. I didn't see them as much as I would have liked, especially since being home, but I knew she would understand. I could almost hear her now, telling me to get my shit together and sort things out with my own family first.

"Did you want to come with us?" Cyrus asked, sticking the smoke between his lips. "I know you have your own shit to work through right now but…"

Piper and I passed a knowing look between us.

"Tell her we'll come up and see them soon," Piper suggested.

Cyrus nodded.

"Strip club?" Sammy stood, stretching his arms out above his head.

"No. Let's go to a regular bar." Cyrus rose to his full height. "I don't want to be washing the club off of me for days."

"Whatever. That's because you choose the sluttiest—"

"I do not. That's you, asshole." Cyrus shoved him.

Sammy scowled. "Nah. Not anymore my man."

My ears perked up at that. "Are you telling us that you're finally a one-woman man, Sammy?"

Sammy looked between all of us, puffing on his smoke. "I'm not saying shit," he finally said. "But there's...someone."

"Red." Cyrus cupped Sammy's shoulder. "She's keeping our Sammy boy on his toes."

"This Red must have made quite an impression on you," Piper said. "You haven't told me much about her though."

"She's someone I call when I need an itch scratched," Sammy muttered. "It's no big fucking deal. She's just convenient. She's there."

"When you need her." I pointed out. "Sounds serious to me."

Sammy rolled his eyes. "Whatever. You sort your shit out first and then we can talk."

Cyrus chuckled, pushing his brother toward the side of the house. "Let's go. We'll call you guys tomorrow night."

Kissing the top of Piper's head, I slid out from behind her and followed the twins around the side of the house.

"You two will get through this," Cyrus told me, heading to his SUV.

"I know. But listen, I need you to do something for me. I need you to tell my dad about Price being at the grocery store. I'd call him but we all know how much he hates talking on the phone and would rather it be done in person." I rubbed the back of my neck. "I just need my girls safe. I don't know if he showed up because I was there or because he actually needed to get groceries."

"I'm betting on the former," Sammy mumbled.

"We'll tell Greyson," Cyrus said, clapping my shoulder. "Keep to yourself and if you need groceries or anything, you let us know and we'll get them for you. Until we can figure out what the hell Price wants, it's better if you probably just stay home."

"I'm taking Piper on a date." Both of us were nervous to be out in public but I knew a date was what we both needed. "I'll take her out for dinner and then come back home. But I know she wants to see her friends too."

"Text us when you're going and where you're going, and we'll be around." Sammy pulled a pack of smokes from inside his leather jacket. "We got you, J."

I nodded, blowing out a slow breath of relief. "Thank you." I turned and started making my way back to the house. "Have fun," I called out.

Once I was in the backyard, I closed the gate and clicked the lock into place.

Piper was still sitting on the ground, by the patio couch. Her gaze caught mine as I approached. "Everything okay?"

"Yeah." I sat behind her, needing the feel of her beneath my hands.

"Did Brynlee go down okay?" I asked, figuring that was a safe question to ask, and massaged my fingers into the base of her neck.

Piper nodded. "She usually does. She likes sleep just like her mama."

"Sleep is overrated."

"It can be." She sat up, turning her body toward me. "So, are we really going to go on a date? Like a normal couple?"

"Come here." I patted my lap, instead of answering her question.

She stood and straddled my lap.

"What is it?" I asked, brushing a thumb over her collarbone.

"Can we be a normal couple?" she asked, voicing thoughts that were putting that frown on her beautiful face.

"Why can't we?" But her question made sense. Our relationship wasn't normal. I had never asked her out on a date like a decent guy would. No, instead, I followed her to another country and fucked her at my hotel, only for her to leave the next day. Couldn't say I blamed her. I wasn't an easy guy to get along with then and I sure as hell wasn't easy to get along with now.

"We're not doing things the right way. But I want to date you," she quickly added before I could argue. "I want to be with you. I want what you said. I want to learn every little thing there is to know about you. I want us to work. I want us to be happy for Brynlee and also for us. I know a lot of couples stay together for their kids, but I can't do that, Jaron. I need to be happy first because I know she'll sense if I'm not. I also want to help you through your nightmares."

"I'm fine," I told her, the hackles raising on the back of my neck. I suddenly felt cornered and I didn't like it. Not one fucking bit.

"That's all you got from that?" She grabbed the collar of my jacket when I went to push her off my lap. "This is what I'm talking about. We open up, you demand for me to tell you what I want and then you push me away."

"You push too, baby." I shoved her off my lap that time, probably a little too hard when she bounced on the couch beside me. "Piper, I'm sorry."

"No. It's fine." She stood, smoothing down her shirt. "I'm going to get ready for bed. But I want you to know something, Jaron." Her gaze locked with mine. Hers was hard, determined and I could feel her soul reaching only for mine to cower away like the damn pussy I was. "You say you're in this for the long run. You say you're not going to leave me or your daughter, but I feel you keeping me at arm's length." She took a step toward me. "So I just want you to know that I am making a promise of my own. If you hurt me, if you break my heart like you keep telling me you're not going to do," she cupped me over my pants, "this dick won't please anyone. Ever again." She squeezed me hard, making me jump. She released me and with that she walked away. "You can join me," she said from the patio door. "Sleep on the couch or leave. I don't fucking care anymore." She headed into the house; the patio door slamming shut behind her.

I stared after her. I shouldn't want her more, but I did. Hearing her words, listening to her speak, and putting me in my place turned me on, but it also made me fall in love with her even more than I already had.

Slumping back onto the couch, I dropped my head in my hands. What the hell was wrong with me? I had a good thing. A very good thing. Piper had been the only woman to put up with my shit but also called me out when I fucked up.

My phone took that moment to vibrate in my pocket. Pulling it out, I didn't bother checking the display and answered. "Yeah."

When no answer came, I sat up straighter.

"Hello?" I stood and headed into the house.

No one answered. Instead, all I got was static. I heard what sounded like a car off in the distance.

When I went to demand who was there, the line went dead. Checking the phone, I saw that it was an unknown number.

"Jaron?"

My head snapped up.

Piper stood at the entrance to the kitchen. "Everything okay?"

"Yeah. Wrong number," I told her, shoving the phone in my pocket. "I'll lock up, but I think I'm going to check out that surprise."

She nodded. "Okay. It's all in the basement for you."

When she went to walk by me, I grabbed her hand, stopping her from going any farther. "Thank you, Piper," I murmured in her ear. "Thank you for everything."

Much to my surprise, she turned in my arms and stood on tiptoes. She placed a hard peck on my mouth. "You don't have to thank me for anything, Jaron." She kissed me one last time before pulling away from me.

I headed to the basement door but not before I caught a movement out of the corner of my eye. Piper was standing at the door to our bedroom, looking my way. "Enjoy your workout, Jaron," she said, slipping into the room, the door quietly shutting behind her.

The silence surrounding me suddenly became loud, the demons of what I had done while in jail, screaming for that release. But like normal, I ignored them, and I knew that if I didn't talk about it, they would eventually take over.

THIRTEEN

Piper

AFTER I LEFT JARON standing in the living room, I quickly headed to our bedroom. I went to get changed into pajamas when my gaze landed on his white t-shirt sitting on the edge of my bed. I couldn't even remember when he had put it there.

Stripping out of my clothes, I threw them in the laundry hamper. My gaze flicked back to his shirt. Lifting it to my nose, I inhaled. It smelled of spice and him. Everything that made up Jaron.

I slipped the worn fabric over my head and down my naked body. The Hell's Harlem logo sat above my left breast. I fisted the fabric and brought it back up to my nose. The scent of him washed over me, my nipples hardening. That familiar ache settled between my thighs.

My gaze flicked to the door. When I didn't hear anything, my stomach fell that he wasn't coming to join me. He said he was going to check out his surprise but a part of me hoped that he would join me instead. Not that I expected anything more than for him to just sleep beside me. But I wanted him to hold me. To tell me that everything would be okay. That *we* would be okay.

We went into this backwards. Before we actually became an *us* and I wanted to do everything I could to make it work. But I couldn't do it without him.

Taking a deep breath and then another, I let my feet guide me to the door. Leaving my bedroom, I headed out into the living room and saw that Jaron was nowhere to be found.

Deciding to check to see if he did go into the basement, I went down the stairs leading to the surprise Cyrus, Sammy, and I had done up for Jaron. It was my idea. I wanted to give him something as a form of therapy. Something that could help him out of his head, and I knew from speaking with Gigi, that working out could help.

Once I stood on the other side of the door that led to the home gym, I chewed my bottom lip. What would I even say to him? I could work out with him, but it wasn't like I was exactly dressed for lifting weights.

I lifted my hand to knock but hesitated. I could hear the weights moving. I hoped that it would become a routine for Jaron. To give him something that felt…normal. He had said that he wasn't used to it being so quiet. As much as I was sure there were things about jail that he didn't want to remember, working out was probably not one of them.

Cyrus and Sammy helped me design the home gym for him. When they went to see him, he told them that working out was what he did to keep out of trouble. So it made sense to have one at home for him.

I was still shocked at myself for my little outburst out in the backyard, but I'd had enough. He needed to hear my thoughts. I imagined what it would be like to have angry sex with him. It was probably dirty, hard, rough, and downright filthy.

Jaron needed more than just physical contact. He needed to talk. To me. To a professional. To someone.

I had heard of people having PTSD after getting released from jail. Stupid me thought that he wasn't in it long enough for that to happen, but I was clearly wrong. I didn't know what he had done to survive. He wouldn't tell me. God, I wish he would tell me. Just something. Anything. I needed to hear his voice. But he closed up. Completely.

My thoughts traveled back to how he used to be. He had been dominant when I first slept with him but now, he was worse. My core clenched, remembering the way he had control of my body. The tension had been building ever since he got home. I almost expected something to happen tonight, but it didn't. It threw me off. Jaron had never been a gentleman when it came to sex. It was one of the many things I loved about him because I was the same way. I enjoyed when he threw me up against the wall and took what he wanted, giving me everything in return just the same. But nothing happened. I needed it. I needed him. That rough side of him. He knew I could take it. It would happen. In time. Because I knew he wouldn't be able to stop himself. Eventually he would snap and give me everything that I wanted.

Placing my hand on the doorknob, I took a breath and then another. He needed to get out of his head. Working out and sex, they were the only ways I knew would help him. I would be his therapy. Whatever he needed. And whenever he was ready to talk, I would be there as well.

Before I changed my mind and ran, I opened the door and stepped into the gym.

Jaron sat on a bench, wiping the sweat off his face.

Every inch of me came alive. The tiny hairs on my body tingled. My stomach tumbled. My heart raced.

His head popped up, his dark slate eyes meeting mine before roaming down the length of me. He sat up straighter, tossing the towel to the floor. He pulled the earbuds from his ears before setting his phone on the bench behind him.

No words passed between us.

My heart picked up speed, pounding in my ears like tiny little drums.

Closing the door behind me, I leaned against it.

He watched me and waited. I could almost hear him saying, *'You want something, come and get it.'*

The few times we had been together, he was in full control. Well tonight, it was my turn. It wouldn't last for long, but I could have some control for a little bit at least.

I pushed away from the door and took a step toward him.

We were alone. Just he and I

This was our time. Our moment. Just Jaron and me. One of many moments that we needed. That everyone knew we needed.

He leaned back the closer I got to him.

Once I stood directly in front of him, he spread his knees. Accepting that as my invitation, I stepped between them.

No matter how many times I had seen him in them, the gray sweatpants always did it for me. Especially when he wore them with a white t-shirt.

Jaron reached up, cupping the back of my thighs and leaning his forehead against my chest. Inhaling deep, a rough growl escaped him. His hold on my thighs tightened.

My breath caught. Inching my hands into his dark hair, it took everything in me not to just throw myself at him.

Touch me. Kiss me. Destroy me.

I didn't need his dirty words. Hell, I didn't even need foreplay. I could feel my desire for him dripping down my inner thighs. I wondered if he could smell it. We had been so damned in tune with each other; it was almost unnatural.

Sliding his hands up the back of my thighs, he grazed his fingers over the curve of my ass, pushing the t-shirt up higher along with the movement. He licked his lips, his eyes darkening even more at seeing what laid beneath the material.

He slid off the bench, sitting on the floor and pulling me closer.

My breath caught, unable to take my gaze away from the man who was my undoing.

Jaron leaned against the bench, hooking his hand under my thigh and pulling my left leg over his shoulder. A low growl left him, his eyes locking on the spot between my legs.

I shivered at the mere intensity rolling off of him. He looked at me like he hadn't eaten in days and I was his last meal. His only meal.

He stretched his legs out in front of him, running his fingers lightly up my inner thighs. His touch was gentle but there was something hidden in his eyes that told me it wasn't what he wanted.

I took the hint and stepped closer toward him, pushing my fingers through his hair. Closing the distance between us, his hot breath fanned over my bare pussy.

Jaron reached around me and cupped my ass, pulling me closer toward his mouth.

My muscles shook, my bones vibrating beneath my skin. It was on the tip of my tongue to tell him to hurry up but at the same time, I was having fun watching him.

Leaning forward, he pushed his nose against my clit, taking a deep breath.

Chewing my bottom lip, I watched as he scented me.

Another rough growl left him as he pushed his nose lower and over my center. "Fuck," he whispered.

I whimpered, never knowing that it was like this. Not with him. Not with anyone. He was all I wanted. All I needed. Before I begged for him to do what both of us wanted, his tongue peeked out. He slid it from my center to the spot above my clit and back down. He repeated the movement, the desire I felt for him, heightening the longer he teased us both.

His lips moved to my inner thigh, his teeth biting down. Hard.

A gasp escaped me, a flood of heat spreading throughout every inch of me.

Jaron grunted, cupping my ass and pulling me closer.

He sat back on the bench, laid down, and tapped his mouth.

I took the hint and straddled his chest.

He gave me a wink and shuffled under me until he was face first with my center. Another wink and I was lowered onto his mouth.

He snarled against me, his beard scratching at my inner thighs.

Another gasp lodged its way in my throat, my eyes rolling into the back of my head as the unexpected pleasure slammed through every inch of me.

Jaron hummed, shaking his head between my legs.

I whimpered, grabbing onto the edge of the bench for support as I rode his face. His tongue was inside me, licking at the walls of my very soul. I could feel him everywhere but at the same time, it wasn't where I wanted him most.

Jaron released me with a wet smack and kissed both of my inner thighs before dropping me even harder on his tongue.

I moaned, undulating against him, trying to get the orgasm I was desperate for. That release I craved before I could do anything else. I couldn't focus on anything except getting him back inside me but right now, I wanted his mouth to make me come.

Please make me come.

He grunted, sucked my clit between his teeth, and bit down.

A gasp escaped me, my eyes widening at the delicious pain rushing through the tiny little bundle of nerves.

He did it again.

Bite. Suck. Repeat.

"God," I whined, rubbing myself over his mouth.

Faster and faster, I moved. The orgasm was so damn close, I could taste it.

My skin tingled. My muscles tensed. My bones vibrated.

So close but so far.

Jaron sunk his teeth into my clit one last time, a surge of wetness leaving my body at the delicious agony throbbing through me.

I cried out, his name leaving my lips on a hard scream as the release suddenly slammed into me.

He wrapped his arms around my thighs, holding me tight against his mouth as he swallowed my orgasm.

"God, I can't..." I shook against him. "Please."

Before I could come down from the high, Jaron pushed me off of him. I was drunk with the need for more. For him to fill me with every inch of him.

He straddled the bench behind me, grabbing hold of my waist and pulling my legs out from under me.

I landed on the seat of the bench with an oomph.

Jaron pulled his cock out of his pants. He towered over me, fisting my hair and thrusting into me in a rough move.

I screamed, another release slamming into me at the unexpected invasion.

He grunted his approval, pounding into me with a fervor I would always crave from him. Lowering his mouth to my cheek, he licked the corner of my mouth.

Taking a deep breath, I could smell the scent of my desire on his lips.

My body clenched down and around him, taking him even deeper. "Jaron, please."

"What do you want?" he murmured in my ear. "Want rougher, baby?"

I squeezed my eyes shut. I shouldn't want it this way.

"No." He grabbed hold of my braid, pulling me to all fours. "Look in the mirror, Piper."

I did as I was told, glancing at our reflection in the mirror staring back at us. I had forgotten that Cyrus had put up the mirrored wall like a real gym.

"I like that you're wearing my shirt." Jaron ran his hand up my back, pushing the fabric to my shoulders. "I really fucking like it."

Gripping the edges of the bench, I started moving back against him.

His eyes snapped to mine in the mirror. "Tell me what you want."

"Fuck me," I demanded. "Now."

A wicked grin spread on his face. He gripped the cheeks of my ass, digging his fingers into the flesh and picking up speed with his hips. His pelvis slammed into the seat of my rear.

"Harder," I heard myself say. "Jaron, please."

"Fuck." He reached up, grabbing my braid and pulling me back against him. "You want it? Fucking take it, Piper."

With his one arm wrapped around my middle and his hand in my hair, I slammed my ass back against him and took it. I took it all.

With his cock deep inside me and his name on my lips, I gave him all of me. Jaron had moved us so I could straddle him. But what I wanted most was to kiss him. To take his very breath deep into my lungs until all either of us could focus on was just our lust for the other. He was the beginning to my end. Everywhere I turned, he was there. Maybe not physically but while he had been gone, I could sense him in everything I did. Everywhere I went. It was like he had eyes everywhere. Watching me. Keeping me safe. Maybe he did and I just didn't know about it.

He had been the only one to ever know me. My desires. My fantasies. Everything that made up me. Us. I wanted to explore everything with him and make it ours.

Keeping his gaze on me, he reached between us and brushed the back of his knuckles up my inner thigh.

The higher he got, the harder my heart raced.

When his fingers reached my clit, a soft sigh escaped me.

His eyes twinkled but again, no words. I wondered why but enjoyed the silence just the same.

Keeping my arms around his shoulders, I held on, moving my hips back and forth against him and gave him all of me.

Jaron brushed his other hand down my back. When it reached the curve of my ass, it slid beneath the shirt and lifted the fabric up the length of my body and over my head.

"Say it," he demanded, his voice rough.

I smiled softly. "Please."

He smirked, gripped my hips, and started thrusting up and down in rough moves.

I had learned rather quickly that he loved when that word dripped off my tongue.

Jaron cupped my nape and pulled me against him, crushing his mouth to mine.

I sighed, taking his tongue deep between my lips.

Running my hands up his back, I dug my fingers into his hair and deepened he kiss, slamming my hips against him at the same time.

He growled, trying to gain control but both of us knew that neither of us had the control we liked to think we had. It just wasn't possible.

"Fuck, baby." He broke the kiss, sinking his teeth into my jaw. "You like my fat cock deep inside your sweet little cunt?"

My core clenched.

He chuckled. "I take that as a yes."

I smiled, a hard moan leaving me. This was the Jaron I was used to. The one I wanted. The one I fell in love with. "Jaron," I whined, my center throbbing.

"What?" He pulled me against him, kissing the side of my throat.

With the tight hold he currently had on me, I couldn't move against him. The longer time went on, the more it hurt. And the more it hurt, the more I throbbed for him.

"What do you want, Piper?" he asked, his mouth still against my throat.

"For you to move," I breathed. "Please. I need more."

"Hmmm…more? Are you sure?" he asked, pushing into me as deeply as my body would allow.

"God, yes." I leaned back, cupping his cheek. "Please fuck me. Harder. Rougher. I don't even care anymore."

"Yeah?" His mouth brushed along the shell of my ear. He lifted me and dropped me onto him.

I cried out. "Holy." I whimpered. "Hell."

"Is this what you wanted?" he asked, thrusting hard and fast. "You wanted faster, Piper?"

"I…I can't…" I shivered, my skin tingling as the pleasure consumed me.

"You started this. You came in here wearing my shirt and looking all sexy as fuck. So, you can, and you will. Take it all, baby."

I couldn't breathe. Spots danced in my vision.

Jaron held me tight against him, his mouth finding my throat. While his hips powered into me, his deep groans sent me over the edge.

My thighs shook, my body trying to bow against him, but he only thrust harder and faster.

"That's it. Come again for me, Piper. Come hard."

"God." A sob escaped me, my nails digging into his shoulders.

Jaron cupped the back of my head, forcing my mouth down on his. He stole the last bit of breath from my lungs and made it his.

He took. He controlled. He *owned*.

And I loved every second of it.

FOURTEEN

Piper

AFTER OUR MOMENT IN the basement, Jaron had gently pushed me off him and mumbled something about needing a shower.

I went to grab the shirt off the floor when his hand covered mine. I looked up at him then.

"Join me," he said softly, slipping his fingers between mine.

I swallowed hard, nodding.

We headed up the stairs to the main floor, hand in hand and silent. When we reached the bathroom, Jaron stripped out of his sweatpants and shirt.

Taking the clothes from him, I tossed them, along with the shirt I had worn earlier, into the laundry hamper.

Turning to head to the bathroom, I was stopped short by Jaron standing naked at the door. His hand was against the doorframe, his dark eyes locking with mine. Of the few times I had seen him naked, none of those moments compared to this.

He was bigger than when I had seen him in Paris. Wider to the point I felt even safer in his arms.

I took a step toward him. It took everything in me not to shield myself from him. I was curvy and stretch marks graced my lower abdomen. He had been right though when he said that I had done something a lot of women couldn't. Having a baby was a blessing and definitely something I never took for granted. My body showed the evidence of creating a life and I knew there were a lot of women out there who would do anything to be able to do the same.

As if he could hear my thoughts, his eyes dropped to my stomach. His nostrils flared, his eyes turning a shade of gray I had never noticed before.

Before anything was said, he turned and headed into the bathroom. The sound of the shower running started a moment later.

I took a breath and joined him, closing the door behind me.

Jaron slipped into the shower, holding the curtain open for me.

I went up to it, glancing up at him.

He held his hand out, waiting.

Taking a chance, I grabbed hold of it, letting him pull me into the shower with him. Before I had a chance to wrap my head around the fact that I was showering with him, he captured my mouth in a hard, bruising kiss.

Jaron pushed me up against the wall, sliding his hands down the sides of my body. Goosebumps followed in their path, making my skin tingle.

As much as I wanted to take this further because I always did when it came to him, I waited for his permission. I needed his control at this very moment. I couldn't explain why. Maybe I never would be able to but for now, I was his. To do with as he pleased.

Taking the hint, Jaron released me, gave my mouth a final peck, and started undoing the braid. Once my hair was loose, he pulled me under the hot water. He ran his hands through my hair, wetting it before reaching for the shampoo. He poured some into his palm and massaged his fingers through the soaked strands.

I sighed, the scent of lavender wafting through my senses.

He gave me a small smile, kneading his fingers into my head. His cock twitched between us, but he never took it further. He never even hinted. Not that he had to. But this was different. It was a silent apology of sorts. For letting his temper get the best of him, making him leave me and his daughter. For coming back to me but for it not being easy. For being hard to get along with. Maybe even for loving me as hard as he did. Even though we hadn't said those three little words yet, I knew how he felt about me. He wouldn't have killed Brody if he hadn't.

"I'm sorry."

My eyes opened, not realizing I had closed them.

Jaron searched my face, like he was looking for a sign. Any sign. When he couldn't find one, he continued, "I'm sorry for what I've put you through." His hands stopped, his grip on my head tightening as he held it in place.

With his rough hold, I couldn't get away and I was forced to listen. "Jaron."

"No, just…" He closed his eyes, took a deep breath, and opened them.

My chest tightened at the desperation coming from him.

"I need you to know that I'm not going anywhere. I know I've told you that already and I also know that words can only do so much, but I promise that I'll show you. I'll show you and Brynlee that I'm here. I'm yours. Forever, Piper."

"And I'm yours," I whispered.

We finished the shower in silence, washing each other and connecting in a way we hadn't yet. I could feel his soul entwining with mine.

Once we were done, we dried each other off.

He would smirk, his hands lingering a little too long in spots that were now claimed by him.

I shivered.

His smirk grew.

"You're a tease." I laughed lightly.

Jaron only winked, leading me to the bed and pulling back the covers.

I was thankful that it was late but still early enough that we could hopefully get some sleep before Brynlee woke up. I just wanted to feel Jaron beside me. I wanted our words and even our silence to speak for itself.

Crawling onto the bed, I slid beneath the covers as Jaron joined me. I went to curl away from him when he wrapped himself around me. "Don't think so," he murmured, pulling me against him.

"You know every time we sleep together, something happens," I reminded him, pushing my ass into his waist.

"If that's what you want, I'll give it to you, Piper. Never be ashamed for wanting to fuck your man." He pushed me onto my side, throwing his leg over mine.

I sighed, curling the blankets up and around us. "Later," I whispered.

A light chuckle left him. "Definitely later, baby."

I rolled back over and turned my head toward him.

Jaron reached over and flicked on the lamp sitting on the nightstand before laying back down beside me. "I want you to see my face when I tell you."

My heart jumped. "Tell me what? I thought we were going to sleep."

"We are but I need to tell you this first. I should have told you as soon as I got out of jail. Saying this should have been the first thing I did and for that, I'm sorry." He paused. "I'm in love with you, Piper."

I gasped. "Jaron, you said..."

"I know what I said." He cupped my face, brushing his thumb along my bottom lip. "I need you to know how I feel before I push you away for good. Before you leave and move on with someone else."

"No, never. That'll never happen." I wrapped my arm around his shoulders, leaning my forehead against his.

His body shook, a shuddered breath leaving him. "It'll hurt but I understand, Piper. If you need time. If you need me to go and give you space."

"Stop." I shook my head. "I don't want that. You're mine. I'm yours. And, Jaron..."

His gaze burned into me.

"I'm in love with you too," I whispered, my eyes were met by his stormy grays.

Jaron sat up, pulling me along with him. His shoulders slumped like my words relieved all of the tension in his body. "Jail fucked me up. I wasn't in there for as long as some people are, but it still messed with my head." His eyes flicked to mine. "But being without you was even harder."

I ran my fingers through the hair at his nape, my chest tightening and my heart hurting over the fact that this man, this strong but broken man, was a shattered mess. He did something to save me only to lose a piece of himself in the process.

"I don't know what I would do if I lost you, Piper." He leaned his forehead against mine, his hot breath fanning over my face.

I lifted my hand at the same time as he lifted his. Our fingers joined, sliding between each other. The touch was small but said so much. It said more than our words ever could.

"I love you, Piper," Jaron murmured, kissing my temple. "I've been to hell for you and would go back there if it meant keeping you safe. The rest doesn't matter."

"But it does." Our eyes locked. "I don't want to lose you in the process. I love you too much to let that happen."

"I can never thank you enough for that." He brought our joined hands to his mouth, placing a soft peck on my knuckles. "We're breaking our walls, baby."

I smiled up at him. "We are. Slowly."

"I'm a stubborn fucker, Piper. I chased you all the way to Paris. Don't ever forget that."

"How can I?" I ran my thumb down the length of his jaw. "It started...everything."

"No, baby." He kissed my forehead. "It started the moment both of us stopped sleeping with other people."

"I wish I would have waited for you." I sighed, my shoulders slumping. "I wish I would have lost my virginity to you and giving you all of me."

"I wish the same for myself." Jaron turned me in his arms, so my back was to his front.

I curled the blanket around us. "Gigi told me that she was Vince's first and he was hers. I'm jealous." I laughed lightly.

"Same, babe, but we can't go back in time," Jaron said, resting his arm across my lap. "So we can only control our future. I don't want anyone else."

My eyes snapped to his. "I don't want anyone else either."

"Good." He pinched my chin, holding my head firmly in his grip. "You're mine."

"And you're mine," I said breathlessly.

He gave me a small smile. "We should get some sleep."

I went to respond when a cry came from the baby monitor.

"I got her." Jaron kissed my head before leaving the bed.

My breath caught at the sight of him. The large black tattooed skull sat on his back, moving over his muscles. He was hard in all the right places.

He slipped into his sweatpants and headed to the door before turning back to me. He didn't say anything. Just looked at me. It was like he was reaching into my soul and trying to find out all of my feelings, my dirty and dark secrets. My fantasies. He didn't need to look very far because when it came to him, my fantasies were all laid out on the table.

Jaron gave me one final look before leaving the room.

All breath left me when he walked out the door.

Lying down, I stared up at the ceiling. Time was what we both needed. Now that we had finally confessed our feelings for each other, it was like another piece fit into our puzzle. It was a start and maybe one day our love would truly conquer all.

While Jaron checked on Brynn, I tried falling asleep but all I could do was lay there. I rolled onto my side, facing away from the door when it opened.

The bed dipped behind me.

"She good?" I asked softly.

"She is," he murmured. "Her pig had moved, and she couldn't reach it. I put it in her arms, and she fell back asleep."

"You know I don't care what you did in jail, right?" I blurted. I brought his hands up to my mouth and repeated his actions. Kissing the tips of his fingers, I pushed my face into his palms. "I don't care what you did to survive. You came back to me. You came back to your daughter. That's what I care about."

"I'm not that man you fell in love with."

My gaze snapped to his. "I don't care about that. I don't care about any of it. What you did or who you did it to. You don't have to deal with this alone."

"I know." He turned on his side, facing me. "Thank you but I need you to promise me something."

I raised an eyebrow. "What's that?"

"Even if we fight, never stop telling me that you love me."

I stared at him. "Well let's hope we don't ever fight then."

He scowled. "Piper, I mean it. Promise me. Promise that no matter how angry you are with me, don't ever stop saying that you love me."

My stomach flipped. "I promise."

"Good." He rolled over onto his back.

"But you have to promise too."

"It's not even a promise I have to make because I'll always tell you I love you. No matter what."

His words coaxed my eyes closed and for the first time since he came home, I actually believed him.

FIFTEEN

Piper

I WAS NERVOUS. BEYOND nervous actually. I hadn't been on a date since I was a kid. Not that it ever really counted either. I was sixteen at the time and it didn't turn out well. Not when I had my father's navy brothers to scare my date.

"Is this him?" Angel crossed his arms under his broad chest, nodding toward Steven, my date.

"Uncle Angel." I scowled, placing my hands on my hips, knowing he was trying to scare the poor guy who was currently trembling beside me.

"It is." Dad mirrored his pose, letting his eyes wander down the length of Steven before clapping Angel's shoulder. *"This is the fucker who wants to take my baby on a date."*

"Um…Sir, I…" Steven stammered, his face paling even more.

I sighed, throwing my head back. God, where was Mom when I needed her? Oh yeah. She had gone out shopping with Aunt Jay. It was convenient timing if you asked me. It was like my dad knew, so that was why he agreed for me to go out on the date in the first place. Because Mom wouldn't be home to keep him in line.

I grabbed Steven's arm, trying to drag him to the door but it was like his feet were glued to the ground beneath him.

"Steven, come on. My dad already said yes, and he wouldn't dare change his mind and break his baby girl's heart," I told him, locking eyes with my father.

He raised an eyebrow.

I glared, challenging him.

"She's good." Angel clapped his shoulder again before taking a step toward us. He peered down at Steven. "You hurt her, and it won't be her father that you'll have to worry about."

Steven took me out to get ice cream only and not dinner like he had told me. He dropped me off half an hour later because he was suddenly feeling ill. Yeah. Right.

I laughed to myself, shaking my head at the memories.

All of us girls had issues dating at one time or another. The guys had it way too easy if you asked me.

Rummaging through my closet, I was searching for something to wear when my phone rang. Quickly answering it, I placed it on speaker and sat it on my nightstand. "Hey."

"Hey, girl. How are you?"

I smiled as Gigi's voice greeted me. "Nervous."

"Nervous? Why?"

"Because Jaron's taking me on a date tonight." I frowned, still unsure as to what I should wear.

"Really? That's amazing! Did you need anyone to watch Brynlee?"

"My parents are watching her but thank you." After falling asleep in his arms the night before, I had woken to a note on his pillow. He had taken Brynlee out for the day and would drop her off at my parents' place before picking me up for our date. He told me to spend the day doing whatever I wanted. For as grumpy as he was, he was also sweet and so damn caring at times, I thought my heart would burst.

"Do you know where you're going?" Gigi asked, pulling me from my thoughts.

"No. He took Brynn out for the day and gave me some time to myself. I'll see him in about a half hour when he picks me up."

"He gave you a day off?"

I turned toward my phone. "Yeah…why?"

"Piper, that man loves you so fucking hard."

"Oh…well…yeah." I smiled. "He does."

"Queenie, who are you talking to?" I heard Vince ask in the background.

"Piper," she told him. "Her and Jaron are going on a date tonight."

"We should go on a double date some time," Vince suggested.

"I like that idea," I added.

"She likes that idea. Now go away, so I can talk to my girl." She yelped. "Jerk."

I laughed, shaking my head. "You two are well?" I asked, getting the subject off of Jaron and me.

"We are. Wedding plans are coming along nicely. Now that Jaron is home, Luna and Zach can get married, so then can Vince and I."

"I don't know why we have to wait," Vince mumbled in the background.

"Hear him? He's so damn grumpy because I refuse to get married before them. I wanted Jaron home anyway for you."

My heart swelled. "Thank you. I appreciate that." I loved that our friends were settling down, having kids, getting married, and finding the happiness they deserved. "Well let me know when you need help. We have to set up your bachelorette party."

"I was talking to Luna and she suggested we do a double one," Gigi explained.

"Oh that would be fun!" I exclaimed, pulling a red skirt off a hanger. It was formfitting and fell just below the knees. With a black tank top tucked into it and cute flats, it would be comfy and perfect.

"So tell me," Gigi paused. "Can I ask why you're nervous to go out with Jaron?"

I shrugged even though she couldn't see me. "It's…complicated." I pulled off the towel, slipped into my black lace bra and thong before putting on the tank top and skirt. I was tucking the top into the skirt when the door to my room opened.

"Well, listen. Jaron loves you," Gigi went on. "Whether either of you care to admit it or not. You're perfect for each other even though I'm sure you drive each other nuts at times."

Jaron leaned against the door frame; his arms crossed under his chest. He raised an eyebrow, his dark eyes sliding over every inch of me.

"I know he does." I took Gigi off speaker and placed the phone to my ear. "I have to go."

"Okay, have fun!" she sang.

I laughed, hung up, and stepped in front of the full-length mirror. "I can put on something fancier," I said, meeting Jaron's gaze in the reflection of the mirror.

He came up behind me and cupped my shoulders. Running his hands down my arms until he reached my hands, he let out a low purr. "This skirt does wonderful things for your ass."

I grinned. "Yeah?"

"Oh yeah." He leaned back, checking out my rear. "It's a good thing you'll be sitting most of the night because I wouldn't be able to control myself otherwise."

"Have you ever been able to control yourself, Jaron?" I turned back and forth, the end of the skirt swaying with my movements.

"Fucking hell." He groaned, dropping his hands in front of his waist. "You look so fucking good."

"Really? Well…you look pretty good yourself." And he did. He was wearing black jeans with a black long-sleeved shirt rolled up to his elbows. The veins in his forearms, popped every time he moved.

He gave me a cocky grin. "Let's go before I bend you over the nearest hard surface and show you exactly how good I think you look. I need to feed my girl."

"Well…" I stepped up to him, placing my hand on his chest and letting it graze down to his waist. "I'm not overly hungry yet."

He smirked, leaning down to my ear. "Tell me what you want."

I shivered. "Everything."

In a quick move, he gripped my hips and pushed me up against the mirror before he did what he did best and used me to make both of us feel good.

Jaron kissed the side of my neck, holding me tight as I fell apart in his arms. His name left my lips on a sob. He felt so damn good that I couldn't get enough. Never enough. The orgasm had been so hard, spots danced in my vision. My muscles rippled over my bones.

"I love you, Piper," he whispered in my ear. "Let yourself go for me."

And I did. At that point in time, I felt our souls connect in a way I never knew was possible.

"That's my girl." His words slid over me and right into my heart.

His girl.

It had been something I longed to hear for years. Ever since I was a teenager. Maybe even before. I wished, God, did I ever wish, that we would have been together right from the start, but life had a different plan for us. But now, we were one. We were together and I wouldn't have it any other way.

"We can stay in," Jaron said, helping me smooth down my skirt. "We can order food."

I looked at him then. "Is that what you want?"

He shrugged, searching my face.

"Jaron, I'll do whatever you want to do." I went up to him when he didn't respond. "Talk to me."

"It's weird going out in public and being around people I don't know," he confessed, his cheeks turning a rosy shade of pink.

"I'm sorry." I stood on tiptoes and kissed his cheek. "I had no idea. I seem to forget these things." Before I could pull away, he captured my mouth in a hard, bruising kiss. "Jaron," I said, breathily.

"Shhh…" He pushed me back until I hit the edge of the bed.

"Once wasn't enough for you?" I asked, tilting my head.

He chuckled, sinking his teeth into my collarbone. "Once is never enough with you."

(Jaron)

"Was Brynn good for you?"

"She was." We were out in the living room after I fucked Piper for what felt like the hundredth time that day. Once I had her thighs shaking around me, that was when I started fucking her the way she wanted. My dick still hurt from the rough hold her pussy had on it earlier.

Piper sat beside me, handing me a beer.

I took it, kissed her head, and sat back.

She gave me a small smile.

My eyes flicked to my leather cut hanging over the arm of the love seat. I hadn't put it on since being home.

"I'd still like to take you out for dinner." I would have to get over my fear of being around people. Piper deserved to be wined and dined. She deserved it all. Food, presents, love, and more. Even if it was something small, I needed to show her how I felt about her. Words meant shit if I wasn't showing her that I loved her.

"You sure?" she asked, smoothing her hands down her skirt.

I finished off the beer and placed the empty bottle on the table in front of us before sliding off the couch. I moved in front of Piper, kneeling at her feet. Taking her hands in mine, I brought them up to my mouth and placed soft pecks on her knuckles. "I remember the first time I wanted to make you mine. I shouldn't have been a pussy and let Ashton and Aiden stop me from making a move, but I didn't want to cause a scene either in front of everyone." I nipped her fingertips.

Her breath caught, her chest rising high with a deep inhale.

"You were wearing these teeny tiny little jean shorts. Fuck, Piper, your legs were so damn long and tanned. I wanted to lick from your feet all the way up to that special little spot between your thighs." I looked at her then. "I wish I would have saved myself for you."

"Jaron," Piper said gently.

"No." I bit the base of her palm. "Just listen. You want to know how I survived being in jail?"

She chewed her bottom lip, nodding slightly.

"It was because of you, Piper. Even before I found out you were pregnant. It was all you. You may have had nightmares. Hell, so did I. But you are strong. You survived and I only survived because of you."

Her eyes welled, her chin wobbling. She cupped my cheek, leaned forward and placed a soft peck on my lips. "I love you," she whispered.

"I love *you*, Piper," my voice cracked. Running my thumb along the edge of her jaw, I slid my hand into her hair and deepened the kiss. "I love you more than I could ever say but promise to show you just how much, for the rest of our lives."

She nodded, a tear falling free down her cheek.

"Don't cry." My stomach twisted, hating her tears.

"I'm…" She sighed, her shoulders slumping. She wiped her cheeks, giving me a small smile. "I'm happy. I feel like we're finally moving forward. That's all."

I pushed to my feet and towered over her. "Forward is the only way we can go because I refuse to go back to before I loved you." I cupped her jaw, tilting her head back. "Falling in love with you was the best thing I've ever done."

"God." Piper stood and wrapped her arms around my shoulders. She pushed her face into the crook of my neck, her body shaking with soft cries.

"Shit." I lifted her into my arms, hugging myself around her. "I did it again. I hate making you cry."

"I'm fine." She laughed. "I promise. Just emotional. Everything has me crying lately."

I leaned my forehead against hers. "I meant everything I've said."

"I know, Jaron." A shuddered breath left her. "I know."

Kissing her softly, I stepped out of her embrace and held my hand out. "Go out for dinner with me?"

She nodded, slipping her fingers in mine. "You don't even have to ask me."

"Good." I tugged her closer, slapping my other hand against her ass.

She gasped.

I grinned.

And did it again.

"God." She shivered.

I chuckled. "The mood was getting too heavy."

Piper snorted. "No kidding."

Fisting her hair, I stared down at her. "You good?"

She nodded.

"Are *we* good?" It was a question that I wasn't sure I was ready for the answer to or not, but I still needed to know. Add to the fact that the question just fell from my lips anyway before I had a chance to stop it.

"I think we are," she said softly.

Kissing her one last time, I released her and went to my cut that was hanging over the arm of the love seat. I wasn't sure why, but something was stopping me from putting it on. It was like a part of me felt that I didn't deserve to wear it.

"Did you want to wear that?" Piper asked.

I caught her gaze.

"I mean…" Her cheeks reddened. "I'm not sure of the rules or anything but shouldn't you be wearing it all the time?"

"Tonight, I'm not a biker. I'm just a man taking his girl out on a date to try and save their relationship."

"Okay." She gave me a small smile.

My body stirred. Fuck me, she was beautiful.

Her long dark hair fell down around her shoulders in waves. Her lips were red from the many times I had nibbled at them over the past hour or so. Her eyes were dark with lust. From that point on, I vowed to myself that I would do everything I could to keep a smile on her face. She deserved it. She deserved all of it.

Holding out my hand, I waited. I often wondered if she would run. When I had gone to jail, a part of me feared that I would come home, and she would be shacked up with another guy. Maybe even with one of the twins or both. I hadn't seen them yet. Hell, I hadn't seen anyone yet. I didn't want to, but I knew at the same time that if I was going to be with Piper, I had to make an appearance and not be so damn grumpy and broody.

When Piper finally closed the distance between us and took my hand, all the struggles we bore, left me. Even if it was just for a moment.

SIXTEEN

JARON

WITH MY HAND IN Piper's, I drove us to a small Italian restaurant that my cousin, Zach, had recommended. He said it was a little on the expensive side but the atmosphere and food were well worth the cost. It also always put a smile on his fiancée's face, so that would definitely be worth every penny dropped.

Piper had been silent on the drive over. She kept looking out the window, chewing her bottom lip. She was thinking. And I knew it had to do with us, Brynn, her future. *Our* future.

Was she thinking about the mayor and what he wanted? She shouldn't. That was my job. It was because of me that he came around. It was because of me that he threatened the lives of my girls. For that, he would die.

Piper squeezed my hand then.

I blew out a slow breath, her touch calming my anxiety.

No matter how much we fought, I wouldn't rather be anywhere else. She was the only one I wanted to fight with. That I wanted to fight for.

Something deep inside of me thought that maybe once I told her that I loved her, that everything would be fine. All of the pieces would fall into place and we would no longer fight. But I was wrong. There was still a wall between us. It was smaller than before, but it still lingered.

I told her that we needed time, but time was also a dangerous thing. Especially if I didn't man up and tell her the shit I did in jail. I didn't want to bother her with it, but I knew that I needed to talk to someone. There was no way in hell that I would see a shrink over it, so Piper would have to be the person I spoke to.

She felt like we didn't know each other enough but we did, and we would continue to learn. I already knew that I liked what I *did* know. She was passionate and kind. Caring and so damn sweet. It made me want to take a bite out of her just to get a little bit of that flavor.

"I can feel you watching me." Her head turned around, a small smile creeping on her face. "You should be watching the road."

"I can do two things at once," I told her, my gaze flicking back out ahead of us. But she was right. She was a distraction and I never wanted it to stop.

"My parents didn't mind taking Brynn unexpectedly?"

"No. They were good about it." In fact, her father knew that Piper and I needed to be alone. He said so in not so many words. It was also good to see them.

Dale and Maxine had been through a lot in the beginning. I didn't know the exact details, but I had heard through others that Piper's dad had been a dick.

"Don't do what I did, Jaron," Dale said, bouncing Brynlee on his knee. *"Don't push Piper away just because you're scared of those feelings."*

Dale and I hadn't talked much over the years but every time we did, I took his words to heart.

"Have you ever been on a date before?" Piper asked, pulling me from my thoughts. Her thumb brushed over the back of my hand.

"Once. I was in high school. It was after we came up here and I saw you." I had been pissed because I couldn't get Piper alone even to just tell her hi. Ashton and Aiden took up all of her attention.

"I went on a date too. He was a nice guy I went to high school with. Steven. My dad and Angel scared him. The date didn't last long." She laughed lightly. "God, that was so long ago."

"And look where we are now," I murmured. The lights to the restaurant came into view. "Did your dad give you a hard time about us in the beginning?"

"Surprisingly, no, he didn't. I'm not sure why. Maybe it's because you weren't around for him to do anything about it. Who knows?"

I pulled into the parking lot, killed the engine, and turned toward her. "Has he said anything about what I did?"

"No. No one has. It's like everyone just brushed it under a rug and left it as a dirty little secret." She scowled. "I don't know if it's because Brody was the mayor's son but..." Her head whipped around. "He almost raped me."

"That's my girl." I grabbed her hand. "Get fucking mad, baby, because no one deserves that shit."

"I saw a therapist a couple of times. It was one the hospital had provided, and I felt like it did nothing." She huffed. "I wanted to talk to you and not a stranger. I tried talking to my parents. Your parents. Even our friends. But everyone just kept asking me how I was doing. They still ask me. Well you know what? I'm not okay. I'm not. Even though it's been almost two years, I can still feel him. I can still hear the vile words he said. I can still smell him." She shivered, pulling her hand from mine and hugging her arms around herself. "I'm *not* okay."

Before either of us knew what I was doing, I left the car and went around to her side. Opening her door, I reached in and unbuckled her seat belt.

"Jaron?" When her fingers touched my cheek, I lost it.

In a rough move, I pulled her from the vehicle and shoved her up against the side of it. The door slammed shut behind her, the sound reverberating between us.

I stared her down, expecting her to push me away but when she grabbed my waist and pulled me closer, I crushed my mouth to hers.

Her lips opened, inviting me in and speaking every silent word she could never say. That *neither* of us could say.

Pushing her harder against the door, I ground into her. Not to hint for more but to let her know that I was hers. Every inch.

"What is it?" she whispered, breaking the kiss.

"You are in control. With me. With your life. With everything. What you and I have, it wouldn't be happening without your complete consent." I pushed into her harder. "This, all of me, it's all yours but only when you give the go-ahead." As dominating as I could be, I wanted her to know that she was in control of the situation. It was all her.

"I know." She looked up at me through her lashes. "I would never think that you would do something without my consent. Is that what this is about?"

I released her and began pacing, blowing out a slow breath. "I don't want you to think that just because I'm a biker, I take whatever I want from a woman even if they tell me no. I've never been like that. Most of the guys in my dad's club aren't like that. Yes, it happens. I'm not going to lie and say it doesn't, but I want you to know that *I* am not like that."

"I know that." She held out her arms. "Now come here."

"Piper." I stopped pacing.

"Baby, I know you would never hurt me. I know that you would never do anything without my permission. Trust me, everything we've done already has been because we both wanted it. You're not manipulative. You are *not* Brody." Her gaze hardened. "You hear me?"

A breath of relief left me. I knew I wasn't him. I wasn't like him at all.

"Now come here. Please."

I charged for her, crashing into her and messing up her hair.

"You never have to worry about me thinking that of you," she said, her voice muffled by my shirt. "I promise."

I gripped her hair, tugging her head back. "I love you," I said, my voice firm.

"I love *you*." She frowned. "But why did that sound angry?"

"It wasn't...I'm not..." I huffed again. "Fuck. If we weren't in a public parking lot, I'd have my cock inside you right about now." But it was still too early in the evening for that to happen. Especially when the parking lot was filled with cars.

Piper gave me a small smile, her cheeks turning pink.

"I didn't know how you felt," I blurted.

"I love my parents." She sighed, hugging an arm around my middle. "I love yours and I love our friends. But I didn't want them to ask me how I was doing. I wanted them to just be there. I wasn't ready to talk about it. I haven't been ready at all. Not until you came home. I just wanted to sit there in silence knowing those I loved understood my need for that. But that never happened. It just...I don't know. I'm not making sense."

"We can sit in silence for as long as you need." I cupped her cheek. "If you want to talk, we can. If you want to light shit on fire, we can. If you want to fuck so damn hard, the walls shake, we can do that too."

A husky laugh left her.

My thumb grazed under her jaw, pushing her head back. "I mean it, Piper. Whatever you want to do, we can do it. I can even talk to some of the guys and see if they have an old vehicle that you can destroy if you want."

"You think that would help?" she asked softly.

I gave her a small smile. "Maybe. Maybe not. If it doesn't work, we can find something else that does. We can keep trying until you feel better. That's all I want. I'm not going to ask you how you're feeling. The answer is obvious. Brody was a dick and he almost took something from you that was never his to take in the first place."

"Thank you," she whispered.

"You don't have to thank me." I kissed her forehead. "Ever."

I looked down at her, expecting her to say something but when she didn't and was suddenly closed off, my stomach clenched. "What is it?"

"It's nothing." She went to pull away from me, but I caught her arm.

"Talk to me."

"Are you okay?" she finally asked me.

"Why wouldn't I be?" But I knew why she was asking. We hadn't talked about what I had done or even gone through while being locked up. Whenever I closed my eyes at night, I kept thinking that I would wake up in the morning, back in that hell. That being with her had only been a dream. I couldn't imagine being put away for years. The time I had been gone, was long enough.

"I love you." Piper placed her hands on my chest. "You know that right?"

I only nodded, my throat suddenly working over a hard lump.

"Good." She grabbed my hand again and led me to the door of the restaurant.

I knew it wasn't fair; me expecting her to talk when I wouldn't. But I couldn't tell her everything. Not yet. Maybe never. I wanted to. God, I wanted to. I wanted her to help me heal. I wanted her to save me much like I did for her.

"Wait." I tugged on her hand, spinning her around and crashing her into me. I wrapped my body around hers, needing to let her know without saying so many words how I felt. I told her that I loved her but even I knew that sometimes words weren't enough.

I wasn't proud of what I had done. My temper got the best of me and I took a life. Even though Brody deserved it, it still wasn't right. But what scared me most of all was that I didn't regret it. Not one bit. What I *did* regret was having to go to jail and leaving Piper to fend for herself and our daughter.

"Does your dad know?" Piper asked softly. "What you went through in jail?"

"He knows some." I pushed my nose against hers. "I didn't give him a lot of information because I know he tells my mom everything. I didn't want her worrying." But I knew she did anyway.

"I get that." Piper's hand dropped to my hip. "We should go before we miss our reservation."

I nodded, staring at her.

The air suddenly became thick between us, the tension almost suffocating.

"Let's go." I released her, took a step back and held out my hand.

She chewed her bottom lip, tentatively placing her hand in mine. "Jaron," she said, before I could lead us to the restaurant.

"Yeah?"

"I love you."

I cupped her face and crushed my mouth to hers.

"I love you too," I whispered against her lips. Clearing my throat, I pulled away again but kept her hand tight in mine.

"How did you find out about this place?" Piper asked, following along beside me.

"Zach's taken Luna here a few times." I didn't talk to my cousin as often as I would have liked but we did text back and forth a bit. I reached out to him earlier today over where I should take Piper, and this was his first choice. "He said it's a little expensive, but the food and atmosphere are worth it."

When we entered the building, Piper gasped. "Wow, this place is beautiful."

We walked through a second set of doors and was greeted by a female hostess. She looked up from the podium she was standing behind and gave us a wide smile.

"Hi there. Welcome. Do you have a reservation?"

"We do. It's under Mercer," I told her.

She looked down at her tablet. "Perfect."

Another woman approached us. "Welcome. I'll take you to your table."

Piper and I followed behind her, entering farther into the large restaurant. The looks on the outside were deceiving because you would never know just how far back the restaurant went until you were inside it.

"Here's your table." The hostess placed two menus on top of it and stepped out of the way so we could slide into the booth that was shaped like a half-circle. I was thankful for that because then I could be close to Piper.

"Your server will be with you in just a moment." The hostess looked between us, her eyes lingering on me a little too long if you asked me, before she turned on her heel and headed back toward the front of the restaurant.

When we were finally alone, I turned to Piper and grabbed her hand. Brushing my thumb back and forth over the scar on her palm, I thought back to the day she got it. She said she had been trying to impress us boys. But she didn't need to impress me. Ever.

"How did you find out you were pregnant?" I was sure it was in one of the journals, but I hadn't gone through all of them yet and I needed her voice. I needed to hear her as she told me how she found out she was pregnant with *my* baby.

"I...I took a sip of beer and threw up after," Piper said softly.

I looked up; being met by the most beautiful eyes I had ever looked into. Eyes that hid so much love for me.

"Really?" I curled my fingers in hers and brought our joined hands down to my lap. My cock twitched beneath them.

Her breath caught.

Yeah, baby girl. This is all yours. Every inch. Every vein. Every fiber of my damn being is yours.

She cleared her throat. "Luna had already found out she was pregnant at the time. She jokingly suggested that maybe I was as well. We all laughed but then I started doing the math."

"Were you upset?" I inched closer to her. "Did it bother you having my baby in your belly, Piper?"

She swallowed hard. "No. Not at all. I was excited to tell you. I wanted to tell you in person, but I knew that I couldn't. That's actually what sparked the whole journal idea. I wanted you to know everything. Even before I told you that I was pregnant. At first I thought it was Paris that..."

"You thought I got you pregnant in Paris?"

She gave me a small smile. "Yeah. But then I remembered I got my period. I have a confession though."

"What?"

"I was scared at first that it would have been Ashton or Aiden's."

The hackles on the back of my neck rose. "Why?"

"I liked them. I cared for them. I still do but not the way I care for you. Even when you're an asshole." She winked. "And I'm not in love with them."

"But you're in love with me."

"Oh yeah," she breathed.

My dick jumped.

She gave me a small smile, looking away. Her pinky reached out, brushing ever so subtly along my cock.

"I'm glad Brynlee's mine too," I told her, my voice rough.

"I used condoms with them, but I know they're not one-hundred-percent, so she could have been either of theirs. The math didn't add up though. And when I had the bloodwork done and my first ultrasound, it proved that she was in fact yours. Also, she has your eyes. No one I know has eyes as gray as yours. That's one reason why I don't talk to the twins much anymore though."

"Really? How come?" My eyebrow raised.

Piper played with the napkin sitting on top of the small white plate. "They're jealous. Ashton more so than his brother. Aiden doesn't come around much and spends most of his time at a bar. That's what I've been told anyway. I think that's one reason why Ashton has become the way he has. He's worried for his brother. All I can do is wish the best for them, but I also want our friendship back." She shrugged.

"I heard that Aiden has a drinking problem." But I never knew how bad it was. I held Piper's hand tighter, unsure of what else to say.

Our waitress took that moment to approach the table.

"Good evening." The young woman smiled, looking between us both. "My name is Lisa and I'll be taking care of you tonight." Her gaze met mine, something flashing behind her bright blue eyes. She cleared her throat, her smile widening. "Can I start you off with some drinks?"

Piper ordered a glass of white wine and I ordered a beer.

Lisa poured us both a glass of water and left after that, but not before I caught her staring. What the hell was with these women tonight?

Piper laughed, shaking her head.

"What?" I brushed my thumb back and forth over her palm.

"You have an effect on women, Jaron." She leaned her head against the back of the booth.

"I don't do anything." I wasn't Sammy or even Cyrus. Hell, I wasn't half the men in our club. I liked sex, sure, but I didn't go out of my way for it. And I never enjoyed it as much until I started sleeping with Piper.

"You don't have to do anything." Piper sat up and turned her body toward me. Her gaze fell to my lap. "I feel like you're reminding me of something."

"I am." I turned toward her, shielding us from anyone that came up to the table. Releasing her hand, I spread her fingers and made her cup me. "This is yours. All of it. Every inch. All of me belongs to you, baby."

Her jaw clenched.

With my free hand, I pinched her chin, forcing her to look at me. "I mean it, Piper. I belong to you."

Her breath caught.

I covered her hand that was in my lap and held it against my crotch. "Every inch."

The waitress came back at that moment and placed our drinks on the table.

Both of us muttered a thank you but wouldn't look anywhere else but at each other.

"Are you ready to order?" Lisa demanded, her voice curt and to the point when she realized that I had no interest in anyone but Piper.

Only when we placed our orders, did Piper look away from me.

"And for you, sir?" Lisa asked.

I gave her my order, keeping my eyes on Piper the whole time.

She looked my way, a flush spreading up the back of her neck before it hit her cheeks. She gave me a small smile.

Lisa muttered something that I couldn't quite make out and left to put our orders in.

"Piper," I demanded, my voice rough.

Her nostrils flared, the tension between us crackling into something that neither of us had control of. If ever at all.

"Yes?" she whispered.

"Say it."

"Say what?" She licked her lips, her gaze falling to my lap.

"Tell me that I'm yours. That I belong to you. That you would do anything right now to get me back inside your tight little body."

She looked away, pulling her hand from my lap.

"No." I snatched it, pulling it back against me. "I don't give a shit where we are. You want something from me, you take it."

She snorted which was fucking sexy as hell. "I can't when we're in public, Jaron."

"I fucked you at that bar. Remember?"

"Of course, I remember. We conceived Brynlee that night at the bar." Piper pulled her hand from my lap and cupped my jaw. "This is a nice restaurant. I don't want to taint it with our dirty desires."

"And why not? It would give us something to remember this place by." I covered her hand that was resting against my cheek and kissed her palm.

"This place already has something to remember it by," she whispered.

"And what's that?"

She linked her fingers in mine. "Us."

SEVENTEEN

JARON

AFTER GOING OUT FOR dinner the night before, we came back home and spent the rest of the evening watching movies and snuggling.

I received several texts throughout the evening, from both Sammy and Cyrus, letting me know that Price was laying low and hadn't been spotted anywhere near us. I appreciated the information, but it pissed me off that the good mayor was fucking with me.

It was now later in the afternoon the following day and we were going to Gigi's place for a couple of hours before picking up Brynlee.

My nerves were on edge, knowing I had to see people I hadn't seen in almost two years. I had always considered them friends but knowing that the twins were probably going to be there as well, set me off.

"Hey." Piper wrapped her arms around my middle, snuggling her face into my chest. "You good?" she asked, looking up at me.

I am now.

Giving her a gentle kiss, I pushed out of her hold and finished getting dressed.

"We don't have to go," she offered. "We can just pick up Brynn and come back here."

I met her gaze in the full-length mirror.

"I know that the girls are wanting to see you. And I…" She looked down at her feet. "I haven't seen them in a while."

I turned to her. "Why is that?"

Piper sat on the edge of the bed. "I don't know really but when you went to jail, I fell into myself. Everyone was as supportive as they could be, but it wasn't enough. I needed you and I couldn't have you." She lifted her hand when I went to speak. "But I don't want you feeling guilty. I'm just telling you the truth."

Moving to the spot between her legs, I knelt on the floor and rested my head on her lap. "I am sorry. I'm so fucking sorry for everything."

"I know, baby," she whispered. "But like I told you before, you don't need to be sorry, Jaron. You saved me."

"I'll make up for it." I lifted my head and rose to my feet, towering over her. "I promise."

"I know that too, but this isn't your fault. None of it is." She pushed me back and slid off the bed. "We'll go for an hour or two and then pick up Brynn. I miss her anyway."

I nodded, sitting on the edge of the bed. Dropping my head in my hands, I pushed my fingers through my hair and tried warding off the impending headache that threatened to take over. I heard her words and understood them, but it didn't make me feel any better. My temper got the best of me and someone died because of it. It wasn't right.

Wrapping my arms around her waist, I pulled her onto my lap and just held her.

"Jaron," she whispered.

"Just…let me have this." I leaned my forehead against her chest, taking a deep inhale. There was a faint scent of sex. It only lingered but it was still there. It reminded me of what we did. What we were.

For as long as I could, I would hold on because it was the only thing I knew how to do at the moment.

When we arrived at Gigi and Vince's place, I shut off the car and sat there.

"Vince surprised Gigi with this home," Piper said, pulling me from my thoughts.

"My dad told me." My Aunt Brogan had let him know what had gone on and he, in turn, told me. He thought it would help me feel like I was still a part of everything even though I was sitting behind bars. It didn't help but I appreciated the gesture just the same.

"I'm glad that Gigi and Vince are okay." Piper shuddered. "But a part of me is happy that the old house no longer exists. Is that bad?"

I took her hand, enclosing it in mine. "You had a trauma there, Piper. It's understandable that you feel that way."

She nodded, chewing her bottom lip. "Gigi doesn't throw parties anymore. Vince doesn't like them anyway, but they have people over every now and again. I'm looking forward to their wedding. And Luna and Zach's."

And ours. My heart clenched. It was way too damn soon to think about it, but I still liked to hope that one day it would happen.

"Did you live with your parents after everything happened?" I had learned that she never went back to the old house, but I still wanted her to tell me everything. I wanted Piper to reveal every feeling, every dark secret. Her pain, her agony, and her love. I wanted to know her fantasies, her kinks, and her desires. I wanted to know every single thing that made up Piper.

"Yeah." She sighed. "I felt bad. I think Gigi feels that it's her fault but it's not. God, it's no one's fault but Brody's," she said, her voice wavering.

I squeezed her hand. She said that it wasn't my fault either. And while I knew that, I still acted out before thinking. I caused so much damn pain for her and my parents, I didn't know how to make up for that. I just wanted to move on but the noise in my head was too loud at times.

"We should go." Piper left the car, staring up at the house.

I forced myself to do the same and joined her at her side. Linking our fingers, I brought our hands up to my mouth and kissed her knuckles. "We can stay an hour and then go."

She nodded. "It looks like everyone's in the back."

With her hand in mine, Piper led us to the backyard. The voices from our friends carried, getting louder and louder as we neared them.

She took a deep breath and then another. "Jaron." She stopped.

I stepped in front of her, cupping her cheek. Brushing my thumb along her bottom lip, I kissed her forehead. "Deep breath."

She inhaled, mirroring my own breathing. "I don't get out much anymore. It's kind of...it's scary." Her voice trembled, hitting somewhere deep inside me that had never been reached before.

"Again," I demanded, not liking the sound of fear in her voice.

Inhale. Exhale. Repeat.

"Better?"

She looked up at me through her dark lashes. "Yeah. You?"

"Yeah." Leaning my forehead against hers, I cupped her arms. "We got this, baby, and I'll help you through it all. I promise."

She nodded. "I'll help you too."

"Good because we do have this. I refuse to have it any other way." I grabbed her hand again. "Remember, I'm a stubborn fucker."

She laughed. "Yeah, I know."

"Hey."

Both of us turned at the sound of a deep voice.

Ashton Donovan stood behind the fence leading to the backyard.

My hackles rose, my stomach twisting at the sight of him. Knowing that both he and his brother used to have a thing with Piper, didn't sit well with me.

His eyes locked with mine, a slow smirk spreading on his face.

My jaw clenched, my teeth grinding together so damn hard, a pain shot up the side of my face.

"You joining us or just going to stand there the whole night?" he threw at us.

I could see out of my peripheral that Piper was looking up at me, but I could only focus on the cocky fucker staring at us.

Ashton lifted his chin as if he were egging me on.

"Jaron." Piper tugged my hand.

My gaze slowly slid from Ashton to her. "Why don't you meet me in the back? Grab us a drink and save me a seat."

She frowned. "What are you going to do?"

Something I should have done a long time ago. In a quick move, I had my hand wrapped around her throat before I could stop myself.

A gasp escaped her. Her eyes darkened, lust billowing between us.

I took one last look at Ashton before lowering my mouth to Piper's.

She sighed, opening to me and, being the type of woman she was, didn't care that I kissed her in public. She didn't care that I was staking my claim in front of a guy she used to fuck. I didn't give a shit that it had only been a handful of times. The fact that Ashton and his brother both knew what Piper looked like, tasted like, and sounded like, didn't sit well with me. Especially when he threw it in my face without so much of a word.

"Jaron," she whispered against my mouth.

I cupped her cheek, placing a soft peck on her forehead. "I love you."

A shaky breath left her. "I love you too. But please behave."

"Always." I kissed her cheek and released her.

Ashton stood a few feet away, watching us with his arms crossed under his chest.

"Please behave," Piper repeated, pointing at Ashton. "That means you too."

His gaze flicked to hers. "Sorry, babe. You don't belong to me, so that means you can't tell me what to do."

With her shoulders pulled back, she took a step toward him. "You know what, Ashton—"

"Piper." I grabbed her shoulder, stepping between them and looking down at her. "How about that drink?"

Her jaw clenched. "Fine." She huffed, spun on her heel, and joined her friends in the backyard.

When she was out of earshot and I was satisfied she wouldn't see me kick Ashton's ass, I turned to face him head on.

He raised a dark blond eyebrow. "It's been a long time, Jaron. If you're worried that I still want your girlfriend, you're wrong."

"What the hell is your problem, Ashton?" I bit out. I had to remind myself that I grew up with him. Even though I hadn't lived close by as a kid, I still saw him at every get-together, holiday, and during the summer. But now that we were adults, I realized something. I had never actually liked the guy. Even before he started fucking Piper.

"Problem?" Ashton held his hand out, checking out his nails. "I don't have a problem."

Cocky fucker.

I went to follow Piper when he stepped in front of me. Crossing my arms under my chest, I sized him up. I was impressed. He had gained a few pounds since I had last seen him. His chest was filled out, his arms thicker than I last remembered. Someone had been working out.

"You're in my way," I told him.

"You broke her heart," he said instead of moving.

The muscle in my jaw ticked. "I saved her life." And lost a piece of myself in the process but that was beside the point.

"Right," he said slowly. "I heard about that. We all did. And we were here to pick up the fucking pieces too."

I took a step toward him, getting in his face. "What's your deal, Ashton? You got beef with me? Say what you want. Tell me what's on that fucking mind of yours, buddy."

"I am not your buddy. I never have been and never will be." He reached out; swiping his hand along my shoulder to wipe away whatever it was he was trying to get rid of. "It seems though that she loves you. I don't know why. Do I want her for myself? No. Not anymore. I've moved on. Especially when she's ignored us this whole time. Her fucking friends."

That explained some of his bitterness. "What happened messed her up."

Ashton's face softened. "It did but it didn't mean she had to ignore us."

"So you're being a dick because Piper handled her trauma the way she needed to and poor little Ashton felt ignored? Get the fuck over yourself, that wasn't about you. You sure as hell don't get to tell a victim how to handle their shit and you aren't entitled to her time. A real friend would see that. You of all people should know that people deal with their issues differently, Ashton." His brother was a drinker. Even though I had been locked up, I still heard how Aiden shoved his demons aside by swimming at the bottom of a bottle. He had joined the navy like their father, was deployed and something happened. He was home and discharged within a year. But no one knew why.

"Leave my brother out of this." But as Ashton said those words, I could see that pain in his deep blue eyes. He was hurting for his brother. I had seen it in the bikers I had grown up with. If you weren't careful, alcohol was like a noose, eventually tightening its hold around your neck until you were no longer breathing. I just hoped Aiden could loosen the rope before it was too late.

"I know we're not close. We've never been close but…" I glanced out at the yard, finding Piper smiling and talking with the girls. As much as she pushed everyone away, you could see the happiness etched all over her face now that she was back. "If you need anything." I coughed, clearing my throat and met Ashton's gaze.

"Yeah, okay, buddy," he mocked. "You don't give a shit about me or my brother."

"I don't like you. I never have but I know you don't like me either. Your brother is a different story."

"He fucked Piper too," Ashton reminded me.

"Yup. He did. But I don't see him standing here trying to cause shit." I clapped Ashton's shoulder. "I do suggest leaving this alone though. Piper is here. Play nice and we won't have any problems."

He raised an eyebrow. "Are you threatening me?"

"Nah." I lightly slapped his cheek. Not hard enough that it would hurt but just enough that it would get my point across. "Be a friend to Piper and you and I won't have any issues." I looked back at her standing with Gigi and Vince. Piper laughed at something Gigi said while Vince stared down at his fiancée. "Where's Aiden?" I asked, suddenly realizing that Ashton's brother was nowhere to be found.

"He's…" Ashton stepped up beside me. "Around."

"Is that your way of saying that he's not here?"

"Leave it alone, Jaron. You got the girl, didn't you?" Ashton took a step forward.

"Maybe Aiden needs a good ass kicking. It's been a while. I could go for a bloody match." I crossed my arms under my chest, scratching my jaw.

"I'm sure we could both use that," Ashton mumbled, heading back to the group I had grown up with as a kid but no longer knew as an adult. "Lots has changed, Jaron," he called out, meaning he was implying that he could now kick my ass.

Sorry, buddy, I'm still bigger, faster, and dirtier. I'd scrub the ground with your face before thinking twice about it.

I only smirked.

Ashton walked up to Piper, scooping her up into a hug and swinging her around.

My jaw clenched so damn hard, I thought my teeth were going to shatter.

He met my gaze and winked.

Motherfucker.

AFTER US

(Piper)

"Ashton," I squealed. "Put me down."

He laughed, placing me back on my feet.

I smacked his hands away. The hairs on the back of my neck tingled and I knew before looking that Jaron was watching the whole exchange.

"What do you think you're doing?" I demanded, placing my hands on my hips.

"Just having a bit of fun." Ashton winked. "You look good though, Piper. It's nice to see you." All amusement left his face as he stared down at me.

I sighed, that familiar flutter I had felt years ago whenever he looked at me, no longer there. I was glad for that because Ashton wasn't the type to settle down. I wasn't even sure he ever would be.

"Is she here? Is she here?"

I smiled, turning to find Luna Stone running toward me. I laughed, rushing toward her. We hugged and laughed some more and hugged again. "It's been so long."

"I know. God, I could cry," she said into my hair.

"Please don't." I had done enough crying for the both of us put together.

"Is Jaron here too?" She looked around the yard.

Jaron was leaning against the far fence, talking to his cousin, Zach Porter, who was also Luna's fiancé.

"He looks good," Luna said softly.

"He does." And he felt good too. Really damn good.

Jaron caught my gaze. He lifted his chin, giving me a wink.

My stomach tumbled, the desire I felt for him unfurling deep in my belly.

Luna giggled. "I know that look."

"I have no idea what you're talking about," I said, looking away from Jaron's gaze before our friends caught us eye fucking each other from across the yard.

"You good?" Gigi asked, coming up to us, followed by her sister, Meadow.

"Yeah." I wished everyone would stop asking me that.

"How's he doing?" Meadow asked, nodding toward Jaron.

"We have our moments." I followed her gaze, my heart jumping when I saw that he was coming toward us.

Jaron glanced at the girls. "Ladies."

Luna gave him a hug. "It's good to see you, Jaron."

"You too, Luna." He returned the embrace. "You treating my cousin well?"

She laughed. "Always."

"How's your son?" Jaron stepped up beside me, slipping his fingers between mine.

My stomach somersaulted. Leaning the side of my head against his shoulder, I wrapped my other hand around his bicep.

"You good, babe?" he whispered, kissing the top of my head.

"He's growing so fast but he's good," Luna said before I could answer Jaron's question. "I don't know if anyone told you, but we named him Benjamin after your uncle who passed away."

"Piper told me. Uncle Benny would have been proud," Jaron said. "I only wish I could have met him too."

"I know." Luna sighed.

While he continued talking to Luna about her son, I glanced around the yard. Ashton was standing on the other side of the bonfire with Zach. I wondered where Aiden was.

Zach gave me a small wave.

I waved back.

Ashton's head snapped up. He scowled.

I frowned. *Asshole.*

I quietly excused myself from the group and made my way inside the house. I had only been in it a couple of times. I was thankful that the old house no longer existed. As much as I was sorry that it happened at the expense of almost losing Gigi and Vince, it was as if the house had been cursed.

Even though their home, looked nothing like the one I had shared with the girls, memories of that night came rushing back.

It had been the last time I hung out with my friends. The last time I had seen Jaron before he was taken from me.

My feet carried me down a hall that led to the bathroom but before I reached it, I stopped in front of a closed door. Placing my hand on the doorknob, I took a deep breath and opened the door. Glancing into the room, I saw that it was Hannah's bedroom.

My thoughts took a dark turn. It didn't make sense as there was nothing there to trigger me. Memories shouldn't have hit me like they did, but I had learned from the little research I had done, that anything could be a trigger. From a touch, to a scent, to something that happened so damn quickly, you couldn't control it, it could all bring you back to that certain trauma.

When I closed the door, I was brought back to that night.

"I like you, Piper."

I ran around him and jumped onto my bed when my feet were pulled out from beneath me. I cried out, struggling against him. I kicked and fought with all of the strength I could muster. My foot landed against Brody's crotch, making him grunt, but it didn't stop him from ripping at my clothes. His fingers dug into my sides, his knee pushing into the small of my back.

No matter how much I fought him, I couldn't get him off me. It took Jaron breaking into my room for that to happen and even then, it wasn't enough. It would never be enough.

Brody still touched me. He still put his hands on me when I never wanted him to.

"Brody, please stop this."

But he never listened to me.

"I will make it so you never forget me."

He was right. He was right this whole time. I never forgot him. I tried to. Lord knew I tried. But it never worked.

Even though the house no longer existed, I was still brought back to that night. Leaning against the wall for support, I tried to forget. A night that had changed everything. I had been pregnant with Brynlee at the time. Brody's punches could have killed her, but they didn't. She was strong and I knew once it was confirmed that I was in fact pregnant, that she was a fighter and would do amazing things for this world.

My mind was playing tricks on me as I continued making my way to the bathroom. Even though I knew this wasn't the house I used to live in with Gigi and the other girls, that sense of fear still slithered over my skin like I was back there. Back in my old room. Back in my old bed with Brody on top of me.

The room that had held so many happy memories was tainted by one fucked up night. And then Jaron was taken from me and that night became even worse.

A sound at the end of the hallway made me spin around. Jaron stood there with his arms crossed under his chest and a deep scowl on his face. He was pissed. Not at me. I knew it wasn't at me. But he was mad at the situation. He was mad that I went into the house without him. He was mad that I was losing myself and he couldn't do anything about it. He was mad that the simplest things triggered a memory of that horrible night. He was mad. Period.

My heart raced, my blood pounding in my ears. "I just...I had to...I..."

I shook my head, Brody's words from that awful night still ringing in my ears. My head suddenly started pounding, remembering the many times he had punched me in the face.

"Piper." Jaron closed that final distance between us, wrapping his arms around my shoulders.

"I had to pee," I told him, a sob wracking through my body.

"Shhh..." With his arm around my shoulders, he guided me down the hall to the bathroom. We walked into the small room and instead of leaving like I thought he would, he shut the door and leaned against it. "Take all the time you need, Piper."

I looked at the toilet, my bladder screaming for release.

"I'm not leaving," Jaron said, tugging the thought right out of my head. "Tell me what happened."

"I had to go to the bathroom. I didn't think I would get a trigger, but something made me think of that night. It doesn't make sense. Maybe it's because I'm here. Maybe it's because I'm with the same people as that night." A sigh shuddered through me. "I thought maybe I was over it," I told him, deciding to get used to the fact that he was there and went about my business.

AFTER US

When I finished, I was washing my hands when his next words made me pause.

"How the hell do you expect to get over something like that, Piper? It could take years. And even then, you might not ever get over it." Jaron came up behind me, wrapping his arms around my middle. "I'm sorry I wasn't here."

I shook my head, pulling away from him so I could dry my hands. When I was done, I turned toward him. "Do you get triggers? Anything that reminds you of whatever happened while you were in jail?"

His jaw clenched, a sharp exhale leaving him. "Yeah. I do."

"How do you deal with them?" I asked, leaning against the wall opposite him.

"I have you, Piper." He took a step toward me. "You help me deal. I know I haven't told you every nitty gritty detail of what I did but…" He closed the final distance between us, reaching out and locking my chin in his grip. "I love you and without you, I would have done far worse shit than I did."

I swallowed hard. "Really?"

His gray eyes darkened, something flashing in his intense stare. A stare that I could get lost in if I ever let myself.

"Really," he murmured, placing a soft peck on my forehead.

My eyes fluttered closed at the gentleness coming from him. "I'm here for whenever you want to talk about what happened."

"I know." He pulled away, putting some space between us, but it wasn't space that I needed. No. I needed him. Every inch. Every dark stormy stare. Every smirk. Every word. I needed him to tell me that this was going to be okay. That *we* were going to be okay.

When I went to walk past him, he grabbed my upper arm. I looked up at him.

"Did someone tell you that you should be over it by now?"

"What?" I pulled from his rough grip. "No. God no. I was thinking it myself. But no, everyone has been wonderful and supportive. Even though I haven't seen people as often as I'm sure I should have…it's my own fault that I haven't been around. And I don't know what Ashton's problem is. He was a dick before. He caused problems for your cousin and Luna but he's

175

dealing with Aiden." My stomach clenched. "Not that it matters anyway. It's no excuse."

"Piper, listen to me." Jaron cupped my face, forcing me to look up at him. "What you went through was traumatic. And you haven't been able to hang out with your friends since. Luckily, as sad as it is, you never have to go back to your old place. A trigger can be caused from anything. You don't have to be in the location of where the trauma actually happened for you to get one. But I wish you would have come got me."

"You followed me," I reminded him. "And I only had to go to the bathroom. I didn't think something would happen."

"Of course I would follow you. I followed you to Paris remember." He kissed my forehead.

A shaky laugh left me. "I still can't believe you did that, creeper."

Jaron chuckled. "I followed you to the bathroom to make sure that you were okay. Seeing as saving your life means shit to some."

"What?" I leaned back. "What does that mean? You did more than just save my life, Jaron. I don't know who you were talking... you were talking to Ashton. Did he say that?"

Jaron's jaw ticked. "It doesn't matter."

"Of course it matters." I pulled away from him. "God, he's such an asshole. I just want..."

"What do you want, Piper?"

"I want you. I want to move on with you. I want to spend my life with you. But I also want this shit to end and I'm going to kick Ashton's ass." I huffed. "I really am."

Jaron smirked. "There she is. The little firecracker I fell in love with."

I stared at him. Really looked at him. His beard had grown in some more. His light brown hair was longer on top, giving it a shaggy look. He was ruggedly handsome in a way I had never been attracted to before.

My core clenched, aching to be filled by him. Even though we weren't at home, it was like my body didn't care. I wanted him to fuck me. Didn't matter where we were.

He tilted his head, probably wondering why the hell I was staring at him for so long.

When I took a step toward him, a knock sounded on the door. I jumped, our little moment ruined.

Jaron came up to me and leaned down to my ear. "Until later, Piper. I want to know where your thoughts went just now."

"You, Jaron," I whispered. "My thoughts were about you."

He kissed the side of my head before heading to the door.

"Some of us have to take a piss," Ashton grumbled from the other side of the door, banging it again.

"You say the word and I can make him disappear." Jaron opened the door, pushing Ashton back. "Problem?"

Ashton shoved Jaron into me.

"Hey." I stumbled back a step.

Jaron caught my hand, steadying me. "You can hit me, fight me, whatever the hell you want, but you sure as fuck better be careful when it comes to *my* girl."

Ashton shoved past us. "Sorry, Piper," he mumbled.

"It's fine." I closed the door, giving him some privacy. "Maybe we should go," I told Jaron.

"You go outside." Jaron smacked a hard peck on my lips. "I'm ending this."

"But…" I looked between the door and him. "Now? Really?"

"I didn't end this last time." Jaron pinched my chin. "I'm ending this now. You and I have enough shit to deal with on our own. We don't need Ashton's jealousy or whatever it is that he's dealing with, added to it." He released me and leaned against the wall, waiting for Ashton to come out of the bathroom.

"Fine…just…"

Jaron's hard gaze met mine. "What?"

I waited for Ashton to come back out into the hall, standing my ground. This shit needed to end.

"Piper."

"I got this," I told Jaron.

The door opened, revealing Ashton. "Problem?"

"I never came to see you all because I was upset. I missed Jaron and had to raise his baby on my own. Not that I need to explain anything to you. But you could have called, Ashton. You could have even shown up and checked up on me. But you never did. So this isn't just my fault." I stabbed a finger into his chest. "So stop being a dick." Not waiting for him to respond, I spun on my heel and headed down the hall. "Don't kill him. Whatever you do," I called out and left Jaron to deal with the guy I had once considered a friend, but now, I wasn't so sure.

(Jaron)

Ashton watched Piper head down the hall.

I cleared my throat.

He slowly looked my way. "We doing this now, fucker?"

Stepping toe-to-toe with him, I grabbed hold of his shirt and shoved him back into the bathroom. Kicking the door closed, I spun him, and pushed him up against it. "What the fuck is your deal?"

His brows narrowed, a tinge of red hitting his cheeks. "You broke her heart. You left and she ignored all of us. People who love her. Her family. I hardly know your fucking kid because of this shit."

"I didn't leave because I wanted to, Ashton." I got in his face, our noses mere inches apart. I was so damn close, I could see the gray specks in his blue eyes. "You know I didn't."

"That's the thing, Jaron," he spat. "I don't know shit. Sure, we've had our issues but…"

"What?"

"I thought we were friends," he muttered.

I laughed, pushing away from him and moving to the other side of the bathroom. "Have we ever been friends? I wanted Piper. I wanted her this whole time and yet, you and your brother were always in the way. It was like you knew."

Ashton crossed his arms under his broad chest. "I saw the way you watched her. I used to tell Aiden that we had to make our move before you did. And even though we did make our move, you were still able to do something better."

"Oh?" I paused. "And what was that?"

"You made her fall in love with you."

My blood stirred at that. Even though Piper and I had only just started confessing our feelings for one another, every time she told me she loved me, it brought out this force in me that I had never felt before. It was possessive and controlling. It was a darkness I craved.

"I don't give a shit what you do or even say to me, but you need to show Piper that you are a friend. It's not her fault that she's been distant this whole time. It's mine. And I know she's a big girl and could have kept in touch but what happened…" My fists clenched at my sides. "It fucked her up."

"I've always been a friend. And so has my brother." Ashton took a step toward me. "It's you who keeps getting in the way of that. And it's her who stayed away this whole damn time." He went to turn to open the door when I grabbed his arm.

"She's been through hell, Ashton. None of this is her fault."

"How can I believe that when I have no idea what the fuck is going on?" He shrugged me off of him, left the bathroom, and started walking down the hall.

"Have you ever thought that maybe it's none of your damn business? Or that if you asked her nicely, she would tell you? No. Probably not because you're too damn jealous that it's not you and your brother who she's fucking anymore."

Ashton spun on me. "I have no idea what the hell you're talking about."

"No?" I closed the distance between us and got in his face. I was vaguely aware that we were no longer alone. "What's in this for you?"

"I want her happy," he muttered.

"She *is* happy." And I would make damn sure that she would be happy for the rest of her life too.

"Is she?" Ashton raised an eyebrow. "Can you honestly stand there and tell me that Piper is actually happy? With you?"

"Ashton," said a soft voice but neither of us looked to see who it was that was speaking.

"What are you getting at, fucker?" I growled. "Is there something that I don't know?"

179

"Do you love him?" he snapped at Piper.

I realized that she was now standing beside us.

Her eyes widened, a flush hitting her cheeks. "Yes, I do."

"Interesting." He scratched his jaw. Instead of answering, he shouldered past me and headed out to the backyard.

I glanced at Piper.

She chewed her bottom lip, looking between me and the door that led outside.

"Jaron, you got a moment?"

I turned as Vince Jr. came up toward me.

"Something's wrong with Gigi's car again." He gave my shoulder a squeeze and headed to the front door.

Going up to Piper, I cupped the back of her head and kissed her forehead. "I love you."

"I love you too," she whispered.

Releasing her, I followed Vince out of the house and into the front yard. "Trying to stop me from kicking his ass?"

Vince chuckled, leaning against the railing of the front porch. "I'm keeping my girl happy. She asked me to stop you two."

I grunted, slumped onto the patio couch, and let out a hard sigh. "I thought it would be normal, coming back here."

"Has it felt normal yet? Since you've been out?"

Stretching my legs out in front of me, I crossed my arms under my chest. "Nope. Not at all."

"Didn't think so."

"I heard about what you and Gigi went through." I wasn't sure where that had come from. It wasn't like guys usually talked about this shit, but I said it, so there was no taking back the words now.

Vince's gaze slowly slid to mine. "Gigi still has nightmares."

I nodded. "So does Piper. I've heard her mumbling in her sleep. She won't admit it though and says that everything's fine."

"Sounds like Gigi." Vince pushed away from the fence and joined me on the couch. "Our girls need each other. You and I can only do so much."

"I know." I rubbed the back of my neck. "I'll get Piper to stop by more often. I think now that I'm home, it'll help."

He nodded. "I agree. Gigi didn't want to pressure her, but I know she's been missing her."

"Piper misses her too."

As if they knew we were talking about them, both Piper and Gigi walked out from the side of the house, arm in arm. They spoke amongst themselves.

My body stirred at the smile currently on Piper's face. She laughed lightly at something Gigi had said and gave her a hug.

Her eyes caught mine.

I ran my fingers along my mouth.

Her eyes twinkled.

"You leaving?" Ashton asked, coming out of the house.

"Yeah." Piper pulled away from Gigi. "We have to go pick up Brynn and then head home."

I stood, preparing myself for whatever shit it was that Ashton had to say.

His eyes narrowed at me. "After all this time, you finally got her to admit that she loves you." He glanced at her. "Do you think of us when he's inside you?"

I'd had enough. I had no idea what the hell he was going on about, but I was sick of this shit. Grabbing his shirt by the collar, I shoved him against the wall.

Gasps sounded around us, but I ignored them.

"Stop being pathetic and man up, Ashton," I bit out.

"Fuck you."

Leaning down to his ear, I lifted him onto his tiptoes. "If you're giving me shit because you want Piper for yourself, I suggest thinking again. Remember, I know where you live. I know where you sleep. If you're not careful, my ugly face will be the last thing you fucking see." I tightened my hold on his shirt. "I also heard that you gave my cousin a hard time as well. Is this your thing, Ashton? You can't be happy without making your friends' lives fucking miserable?"

"You're not my friend," he ground out through clenched teeth.

"No, I guess I'm not." I leaned back, giving his cheek a light slap then releasing him completely. Without giving him or anyone else another look, I left the porch. When I was heading down the driveway, I texted Gigi and thanked her for having us.

My bones vibrated beneath my skin. My muscles ached. I needed to hit something, run, or fuck. Preferably the latter.

"Jaron."

I spun on Piper.

She stopped suddenly.

Before she got a chance to ask me what the hell was going on, I closed the distance between us. "Why are you with me?"

"What?" Her eyes widened. "Why are you asking me that?"

I turned away and continued walking to her car.

"Jaron." She rushed to my side, grabbing my hand. "Hey." She stopped me. "What's going on?"

"Would you be with him if I wasn't here?" I didn't want to know the answer but at the same time, I did.

Instead of answering me, Piper opened the passenger side door and slipped into the car.

I took a breath and joined her. When I was seated behind the wheel, Piper started laughing.

I frowned, slowly turning toward her. "What's so damn funny?"

"This. Everything. Ashton is an asshole, Jaron. I don't know what his problem is. I really don't. I've tried coming around. Maybe it's my fault. Maybe..."

"No." I took her hands in mine, giving the tips soft pecks. "Everyone deals with trauma differently. People need to understand that."

"Drive us to pick up Brynlee and then take us all home."

I nodded, giving her fingers one last kiss before I pulled away.

"Ashton's a dick," Piper said softly, breaking the silence between us. She gripped my hand that was resting on her inner thigh. "I don't know what his issue is."

She had been friends with Ashton and Aiden since we were kids, and I could never control that part of her life or whether she was still friends with them. In bed, she was completely submissive but outside of that, she was the strongest woman I knew.

"I think Aiden's drinking is messing Ashton up and he's taking it out on everyone else. I've seen Ashton yell at his dad for no reason, but his brother is worse." Piper sighed. "I'm sorry for how Ashton was."

"I'd probably be the same way." I had to admit it. Ashton liked her and I could only assume that Aiden still did as well.

"They slept with other women while sleeping with me. So them being jealous doesn't make sense. We were never exclusive." Her thumb brushed over the back of my hand. "I've only ever been exclusive with you, Jaron. I just wish that we would have started this thing a long time ago."

"You mean before I got you pregnant," I corrected her.

Piper turned her body toward me, her eyes burning a hole through the side of my head. "I don't give a shit that you got me pregnant. What I do give a shit about is you constantly blaming yourself. For you shutting me out. I know we've come a long way since you've been home and...I love you."

"I love you too." Looking back out at the road ahead of us, I wished I could have taken her away. To go back to Paris and start over.

"Why do I feel like it isn't enough?" she murmured.

My head whipped around. She was staring out the window, her hand tight in mine that was currently gripping her inner thigh.

"It has to be enough," I finally said.

"What if it isn't? What if it means that we're not meant to be together? What if—" Her eyes shone.

I brought her hand up to my mouth because, truth was, I had no idea what to say. She was right. She was always fucking right. What if this wasn't enough? What if our love couldn't sustain the shit that life threw at us? What if it only got worse and we couldn't handle it and it broke us apart?

"Piper." I gave her hand a tug.

She turned toward me. A shaky sigh left her. She moved closer, leaning her head against my shoulder.

"I'm not going anywhere, baby."

"Neither am I, Jaron." Piper sighed. "Neither am I."

EIGHTEEN

Piper

JARON HAD BEEN ON edge the whole time after we picked up Brynlee. He hardly said anything, even when we went to my parents' place. I wondered if they noticed he had been acting differently. I wasn't sure what all was said between him and Ashton or even Vince. I tried asking but he just brushed it off and that familiar tick in his jaw became more pronounced. The tiny hairs on my body tingled under his intense scrutiny. It only seemed to get worse as the minutes trickled by.

When we got home, he muttered something about putting Brynlee to bed. I gave her a kiss on the head and watched as he walked away with her in his arms.

There was a war going on inside of him. Although he felt like he had to deal with it on his own, he didn't. I would help him battle whatever demons he was trying to fight. We hadn't talked about what happened to him in jail. I wanted to ask but at the same time, I didn't want to fight with him anymore. But I wanted to help him. God, did I ever want to help him.

Jaron was a private man. Especially when it came to the things going on inside his head.

I wished I could get him to open up about everything. Maybe in time. But for now, all I could do was give him whatever it was that he needed.

While Jaron was putting Brynn to bed, I decided to get ready for bed myself. When I was pulling on my tank top, I felt warm arms wrap around me, followed by a kiss to the neck.

I sighed, dropping the hem of the shirt and leaning back against Jaron.

He held me against him, hugging me from behind. "I'm sorry. For everything. I'm sorry for not being able to talk. I'm just..."

I turned around and snaked my arms around his shoulders. "Enough is enough. We have time and I'm here for the long haul. Whenever you are ready, I'm here but for now we can just be us and that *is* enough."

"What do you want to do instead?" he asked, his voice low.

I placed my hand over his heart. "I want you to make love—"

Before I could get the rest of the sentence out, Jaron crushed his mouth to mine. He lifted me in his arms, carrying me over to the bed and dropping me gently on top of it.

Breaking the kiss, he ripped his shirt up and over his head.

I swallowed hard, staring up at him.

"I'm not going to make love to you, Piper." He crawled onto the bed, kneeling between my spread legs. Towering over me, he placed a soft peck on my forehead. "Ask me what I'm going to do."

"W-What are you going to do?" I asked, my heart hammering behind the walls of my rib cage.

"I'm going to fucking own you." Jaron flipped me onto my stomach and ripped my shorts off of my lower body, before sinking his teeth into the cheek of my ass.

I yelped, fisting the blankets beneath me.

"Are you ready for me, baby?"

I looked at him over my shoulder. "I want you. All of you."

"Good." He cracked a hand against my ass, and I knew, God, I knew, there was no way in hell that I would come out of this without some marks on my damn soul.

(Jaron)

I was brought back to that night in Paris. The night that truly sealed the deal for Piper and me. With her on all fours in front of me, I couldn't help but just sit there and stare. Her body vibrated. A slight flush caressed her cheeks. When she glanced at me over her shoulder, waiting and wondering when I would make my next move, my heart stuttered. I loved this woman. Fuck, did I ever love her.

I wanted to spend my life with her. I wanted to give her everything she deserved and more. She loved traveling. I wanted to take her around the world. See new places. Grow together. Learn about other cultures. I wanted to make her my wife and have a dozen more kids. With her. It had only ever been her.

"Jaron?" My name fell from her lips like a petal from a flower. It caressed my skin, kissing every inch of me. As much as I wanted to take this further, I was stuck. In my head. In my own body. My hand stopped moving on my cock, my grip loosening on her hip.

Piper turned around and knelt in front of me. Instead of asking me what was wrong like most people would, she covered my hand and pushed it down the base of me. A hot tingle shivered down my spine. She placed a soft peck on my mouth, our hands stroking and caressing the part of me that had only been hers for the past couple of years.

She trailed hot kisses down my neck, over my collarbone. Her tongue licked along my nipple before she delved lower. Rolling onto her back, her mouth soon found my balls. Sucking and licking until a hard groan finally fell from my lips.

Bending over, I rested my hands on either side of her hips and watched as she slipped my cock into her hot mouth.

My dick lengthened even more, bumping the back of her throat as she swallowed every inch of me. She hummed around me, caressing her hands up my abs and lower, constantly touching me.

Her knees fell apart, revealing the very part of her that I had become addicted to. The scent of her desire for me wafted into my nose. Her pretty little clit peeked out from the soaked folds of her pussy.

Much to my surprise, her hand fell to her center, stroking and dipping into her tight heat.

A growl left me, my hips bucking forward.

She gagged, opened her mouth wider, and took me even deeper.

When she lifted her hand that was currently between her legs it seemed to snap me out of my trance. I grabbed her hand and stuck her fingers between my lips, sucking the juices from her body off them.

Shoving my hips forward and back, I began fucking her throat. Giving and taking everything I wanted from her, I used her mouth to make me feel better. Tonight had been a shit show with Ashton, and Piper was the only one who could pull me out of my head. I knew that now.

Looking beneath me one last time, I saw the outline of my dick in her slender throat as I thrust hard and fast.

She took everything I had to give her. She let me use her to my liking and only when I was good and satisfied, did I return the favor.

Ripping my cock free from her mouth, I gave her a chance to breathe.

Piper panted, wiping the drool that had slipped out the sides of her mouth.

"Turn over," I demanded, my voice rougher than I imagined it would be.

She did as she was told, revealing her beautiful naked ass to my hungry eyes.

Wrapping my hand in her hair, I held her head in place. "Take a deep breath."

She inhaled, opening her mouth wide at same time I slammed my dick between her swollen lips. She jumped, gagging around my cock but moaning just the same.

"Fuck," I whispered, holding her head in place as I throat fucked the hell out of her. Gearing my hand back, I landed a hard swat on her ass.

She yelped, arching on the bed.

So I did it again. And again.

Swat. Swat. Swat.

She moaned, the sound vibrating down the length of my cock and hitting me right in the balls.

Swat. Swat. Swat.

With each hard blow of my hand, her ass lifted into the swings of my palm.

Swat. Swat. Swat.

Her ass reddened, covered by my handprints. That only made me fuck her face harder and slap her ass more.

Swat. Swat. Swat.

Piper cupped my ass, taking me even deeper.

That's my girl.

That single action made my balls draw up into my body. I took a deep breath and then another. I didn't want to come. Not yet. Not until I was deep inside of her.

Holding the back of her head, I pushed my hips forward.

She opened her mouth wider, taking me as deeply as her throat would allow.

A hot shiver raced down my spine. "Fuck, baby." Pulling free from her mouth, I gave her ass another swat. "Turn over and spin around."

She did as she was told, staring at me with that lust in her eyes I had come to crave.

Crawling between her knees, I kissed her forehead and swiped my thumb over her swollen mouth.

Piper wrapped her hands around my cock, gave it a couple of pumps, and lined it up to her center. "Please," she whispered.

I crushed my mouth to hers at the same time I slid into her body.

189

She sighed, wrapping her legs around my waist and lifting her hips to meet me thrust for every thrust.

"You looked beautiful with my cock between your lips," I murmured against her mouth.

A breathless laugh escaped her.

Releasing her mouth, I pushed into her as far as I could go. Cupping her jaw, I turned her head and kissed the spot beneath her ear. "I love you, Piper," I whispered. "I hope you know that."

"I do," she panted.

Pumping slow and deep, I pushed my face into the crook of her neck. "I'm so fucking in love with you."

"Jaron, I…" Her voice shook, her thighs trembling around me. My name left her lips again on a scream.

"Say it," I demanded, keeping my thrusts at an even pace.

"I-I love you," she cried out. "God, I love you too."

As soon as those words left her lips, my release poured into her.

(Piper)

After we came down from our passionate high, we were lying in bed, content and secure, just comfortable in each other's arms.

"I'm scared," Jaron blurted, breaking the silence.

"What?" My eyes were wide as I stared up at him. Never in my whole life would I think Jaron would admit to being scared of something.

"I'm here." I cupped his cheek.

His eyes fluttered closed.

"I'm always here," I murmured.

"I don't want you to stop loving me when you find out what I did." He looked at me then, peering down into me. With both of us naked, the vulnerability slid between us.

"That would never happen, Jaron." Placing my hand on his chest above his heart, I kissed his cheek. "Look, I know we don't have a lot to go on as far as our history together. I also know it takes time for us to trust how we feel about each other...but Jaron, my soul recognizes yours. You. Are. The. One."

He fisted my hair, crushing his mouth to mine and pushing me onto my back. His cock grew, hardening between us. It rested against my lower belly, reminding me of the reaction I caused in him. The need for more. The will to please.

Wrapping my arms around his shoulders, I pulled him even closer.

A low growl escaped him. In a rough move, his hand tightened in my hair as his tongue devoured every inch of my mouth.

Lifting my hips, I hinted for more, needing him back inside me. I wanted him slow and gentle and then rough and fast. I wanted everything that made up him. The man I was in love with. The man I was going to marry.

Jaron slid his other hand down my side before hooking my leg around his waist. He slowly slid back inside me, forcing a sigh from somewhere deep inside when we were connected once again.

NINETEEN

Piper

A KNOWING SMILE PASSED between us as I got dressed. Jaron watched me in the reflection of the mirror.

He would smirk.

My cheeks would become hot.

His smirk would grow.

And I would laugh.

When I pulled the gray sweatpants up over my hips, fingers wrapped around my wrist. I jumped, my eyes shooting to Jaron. I didn't even realize he had left the bed.

His jaw ticked, a dark shadow passing over his face but before I could question it, it was gone. Releasing me, he went to the dresser and grabbed my white tank top. He slipped it on over my head, smoothing it down my middle before pulling me into his arms. His body shook with a shuddered sigh.

"Jaron?" I wrapped my arms around his shoulders, unsure as to what was going on but wanting to help him with whatever it was. No matter the cost or what I had to do. I would help him.

Before Jaron came home, I probably would have cried over the fact that he still hadn't told me what was going on with him. But then, on the other hand, I had to be patient. He did tell me that he was in love with me. He told me often how he loved me, so I couldn't fault him for not revealing all. It was too soon. He needed time. We had so many lost moments together that we had to take what we could.

"Jaron? Hey." I brushed my mouth over his. "You good?"

"You smell like me." He nipped the side of my neck. "So yeah, I'm good."

A breathless laugh left me.

He winked, kissed my neck one last time, and released me. "I'm going to hop in the shower."

"Okay." I went to the door when a throat clearing stopped me. "What's wrong?"

Jaron was looking at my ass. "Nothing but your ass looks hot as fuck in those pants."

A laugh burst through me. "Now you guys know why us girls like when you wear them. We can see everything." I waggled my eyebrows.

His eyes popped to mine. "Good thing I have a pair to put on after my shower."

I giggled, shaking my head. "Enjoy your shower."

"You can join me," he called out, heading into the bathroom.

"I have to check on our daughter." Heading to Brynlee's bedroom with a smile on my face, I went to her crib. She was sound asleep, resting on her little belly with her thumb in her mouth. Her dark head of hair matched both Jaron's and mine. Her small nose along with her full lips, mirrored my own. Her skin was darker and that was all Jaron. His lineage was European, and those genes were definitely dominant in Brynlee.

I knew in the beginning people questioned whether I was in fact pregnant with Jaron's baby. I wasn't stupid. I heard the whispers. I heard my mom talking with her friends. She didn't mean any harm by it, I knew that as well, but everyone was aware of the fact that I'd had a fling with Aiden and Ashton. Aiden kept it to himself, while Ashton bragged. Even though the fling was short lived, and we always used protection, it didn't mean anything. Science was science. Condoms and birth control weren't foolproof. I was just thankful that Brynn was all Jaron. As soon as she looked up at me with those beautiful eyes of hers, I knew.

"You're doing so well, baby girl," my mom coached. *"Just one more push."*

I screamed, putting everything into that single push. Suddenly, the pressure released from somewhere deep inside of me. I fell back against the bed, my body coated in sweat.

Loud cries sounded around the room, forcing a sob from my lips.

"Want to meet your daughter?" Mom placed the small bundle in my *arms, tears flowing down her cheeks.*

When I glanced at my daughter through unshed tears, I knew before she opened her eyes that she was Jaron's. And when she looked up at me, everything felt…right.

The scent of spice wafted into my nose.

My body heated.

Jaron came up behind me, resting his chin on my shoulder.

"I still can't believe we made her," I told him, gripping the edge of her crib.

"She's the best part of us," he said, his voice low. He curled his fingers around the edge of the crib on either side of mine, caging me in. He moved his hands closer to mine, his thumbs reaching out to brush along the sides of mine.

"She is," I whispered. "She's the only parts that matter."

"I caved and was going to call you and get you to come visit me," he confessed, still brushing his thumbs along the sides of my hands.

"Really?" I looked up at him then.

"Yeah, but somehow it got out. Someone was listening because I told Sammy and that evening, I got jumped."

"Jaron." I gasped. I wanted to ask if he was okay, but he was standing in front of me, so of course he was okay. But I wondered if it still hadn't left a lingering effect.

"I don't know who they were." He pushed away from me and began pacing. "I thought maybe they were with a rival club or someone we had issues with, but no one would tell me anything. I had never seen them before. And I had a hard time seeing them anyway when they had me on the ground and..." He cleared his throat, a dark shadow passing over his face. "It doesn't matter."

"Were you hurt badly?" I slipped my fingers between his.

"I was put in the infirmary for three days." He ran his other hand through his hair. "My dad found out and almost lost his shit and ended up in jail right beside me. But of course, my mom doesn't know."

"I'm just glad that you're okay." I brought his hand up to my mouth.

"I know we've had our issues, but I promise that I'm here. I'm always here. She doesn't deserve my anger. Even though it has nothing to do with her." He nodded toward Brynlee. "I'm sure she can feel it. And you definitely don't deserve it either, Piper." He led me out of the room and turned off the light.

When we were standing in the hall, he pulled me into his arms. "I love you."

My heart stuttered. "I love *you*." I returned the embrace. "I...I have something for you." My stomach tumbled, knowing that what I was about to give him was not going to be easy for either of us.

Jaron cupped my face. "You've already given me so much. And you put up with my shit."

I laughed lightly, kissing him softly on the mouth. "Go sit." I released his hand and went to our bedroom. Once I reached the closet, I opened the door and grabbed a small box from the top shelf.

Joining Jaron back out in the living room, my palms became sweaty the closer I got to him. He was sitting on the couch with his long legs stretched out in front of him. Those damn gray sweatpants hung low on his hips, even while he was sitting. He was hot before, but those pants made him look even hotter. As much as I wanted him, this was not the time because I knew that both of us needed what I was about to show him.

"Another box of stuff?" he asked, nodding toward the small shoe box in my hands.

"This is different." I sat beside him. "This stuff has nothing to do with the pregnancy. It's little things that reminded me of you." I opened the lid, took out a small envelope and handed him the box.

"What's that?" When he reached for the envelope, I snatched it back.

"I'll show you in a moment." I reached into the box, pulling out a coaster. "This is from the bar."

"The night I fucked you in that bathroom?" he asked, cupping my knee.

"Yeah. I stole it when no one was looking. I forgot I had it until I looked through my purse a few weeks later." I snuggled into his side, watching him root through the little things I had saved over the last few years.

"Geeze, babe. This stuff...it's not just from when we started sleeping together." He pulled out the shard of glass I had cut myself with when we were kids. "Is it?"

"No. I even kept a napkin from the café in Paris." I rummaged through the items in the box until I found what I was looking for and picked it out of the box.

"Piper." Jaron took the napkin, wrapped his arm around my shoulders, and kissed the side of my head. "Thank you."

"It's no big deal. I'm sure most would think it lame, but I needed these items. It's like something told me that we wouldn't have it easy."

Jaron leaned his forehead against the side of my head, placing the napkin back in the box. "It's perfect."

Taking a deep breath, I gave him a small smile and handed him the envelope. "Before you read this..." I chewed my bottom lip.

"Hey." He pinched my chin, forcing me to look up at him. "Whatever it is, thank you."

"It wasn't easy to write. It was before I found out I was pregnant. I was upset. You know how they say to write out your feelings and then burn the letter or delete the email and so on? Well, I wrote it, but I didn't burn it. I'm not sure why."

Jaron pulled the letter from the envelope.

"It's only a couple pages but it's double-sided. Sorry." My cheeks burned. "Apparently, I was a writer in my previous life." I laughed lightly, trying to make a joke.

Jaron kissed the side of my head. "Read it to me."

"What?" I shook my head. "No. I can't. It's too…it's too weird."

He shoved the letter in my hands. "Don't care. Read it."

I looked down at the letter now in my hands and back up at him. What if I read it and he ended up hating me? What if I read it and we would never move forward and past this hurdle between us? What if…what if…what if…? So many damn what ifs. But one thing I knew was that if I read it and he didn't react the way I hoped he would, I would never forgive myself for not burning the damn letter in the first place.

(Jaron)

I wasn't sure what the letter consisted of but by the way that Piper was munching on her bottom lip, it couldn't have been good.

"Come here." I wrapped an arm around her shoulder and pulled her back against me. "Read it. Please." I needed to hear her words. I needed to know what she went through when I was taken from her. I needed to know what I missed out on. I wasn't sure if it was the guilt eating away at me or if I just wanted to suffer, but I wanted to know everything. Every single thing that made up the woman in my arms.

Piper unfolded the stack of papers and cleared her throat. "I'm sorry," she whispered before clearing her throat again. *"Jaron, you were taken away from me,"* she said, louder that time as she read her own words. *"I never thought that you and I would end up together. I actually thought at one point that you hated me."*

Never. That would never happen.

"It's been a couple of days since the police took you. Since I felt Brody's hands on me. Since I thought he was going to…" Her breath hitched.

I tightened my hold on her.

"Rape me.

I think what bothers me most is that I had no idea. Brody was nice. Kind. I saw him help an old lady cross the street and nurse a dying bird back to life. It didn't make sense and I feel stupid for falling for his games.

I'm not sure what's going to happen or even when your trial is. No one has told me anything. I keep getting an 'I don't know' or 'I'll let you know when we find out something' but no one has told me shit."

Piper took another deep breath.

"I shouldn't be writing this letter. My wounds are fresh. My emotions are raw. But I've always kept a journal, ever since I was a little girl. So a letter is no different I guess. They say that writing letters and then destroying them after can be therapeutic. Well, I'm not going to destroy this one and I hope you see it. I hope you read it and know the pain your absence has caused me. God, I sound like a bitch. I'm sorry.

I'm sorry for everything. I'm sorry for Paris and for leaving you the next morning. I'm sorry for not starting whatever this is between us, sooner. Jaron, I've been in love with you since we were kids, but I've also been terrified of those feelings. Because they go far beyond love. I'm obsessed.

With you.

When you showed up in Paris, I thought 'This is it.' Jaron and I are going to be together forever, and we'll be happy. Little did I know that being with you, isn't easy. Although, being with me isn't easy either, I'm sure.

I've heard rumors. Stories about the women you've been with. It's like now that we started sleeping together, I'm hearing more and more about how you truly are with the women you've fucked. But you know what? I don't care. I don't care at all because I know I have your heart. Or I hope I do."

I kissed her temple. "You do, baby," I whispered, petting my hand over her head.

"Loving you hurts but living without you is worse. It hasn't even been a week yet and I don't know if I can do this. I'm not strong," Piper continued, a lone tear rolling down her cheek. *"Because I know that if you hurt me, I'll never recover from it. That's why I've been so scared to reveal my feelings for you.*

Jaron, you could break me, and I know if that happened, it would be the end of me. I shouldn't depend on someone like I depend on you, but I can't help it. I need you. I need your stormy eyes and deep voice. Your cocky smirk and your crude words. I need your rough touch and your spicy scent. I need you."

Piper looked at me. "There's more but I can't. God, Jaron. I sounded so desperate."

"Never." I cupped her cheek and placed a soft peck on her mouth. "I thought this would be easier. They never tell you how hard love can be. My parents never taught me this shit."

Piper laughed lightly. "Neither did mine. My parents had it hard in the beginning. My mom told me. I'm sure most parents don't talk about that." She looked at me then. "They probably want their kids thinking they had the happiest of marriages and so on. But not mine. They wanted to be honest with me. They just never said how hard it could be."

"I want to finish reading the letter."

Her breath hitched. She handed it to me. "You can finish it on your own if you want. I just go on to tell you that I love you."

Holding the letter tight in my hands, I continued reading it. She was right. Her words proved how upset and hurt she was. Nothing I didn't already know was in it. She went on to say how she loved me and couldn't wait to see me. The letter ended with her saying that she would never send me the letter but would wait for me to read it when I got out of jail. She had also promised in it that she would show me that we were meant to be together and she also thanked me for saving her life.

I placed the letter on the coffee table and pulled her against me. Petting my hand over her head, I kissed her temple. No words passed between us. We just sat there in silence. But the words from her letter dug into my heart, threatening to rip it out and stomp all over my feelings for her. She thought I would be mad. No. I wasn't mad. Not in the least. In fact, I was almost relieved. Relieved that it wasn't just me second-guessing everything. Our love for each other was very real but everything else made me question whether we were strong enough to get through this.

My phone buzzed, vibrating on the coffee table in front of us but I never moved to answer it.

"You going to get that?" Piper asked softly.

"No. They can wait." I kissed her head. "This is more important."

My phone buzzed again, the person who was calling, clearly not getting the hint.

Piper sighed, reaching for it and handing it to me. "Looks like someone wants to speak to you." She stood, a cold draft suddenly billowing around me.

"Mercer," I said, answering the phone.

When no response came, I frowned. "Hello?"

The call disconnected before I could demand to find out who it was.

I stood, following Piper into the kitchen. "Have you noticed anything weird while I was gone?"

"No." She frowned. "You asked me this already."

"I know. But I need you to think really hard." I pulled out a chair from the dining room table and sat before patting my knees.

Piper came toward me and lowered herself onto my lap. "Did something happen?"

"People know who you are." Even though it made sense that her name was out there, it still didn't sit well with me.

"That's not a good thing, is it?"

She was smart. Fucking hell. "No, baby." I leaned my forehead against her chest. "It's not."

"What does it mean?" she asked, brushing her fingers through my hair at the back of my neck. "Should I be worried? I've stayed home and only went out if I had to. I know you were defending me but of course my name made the news. It's why I don't watch a lot of TV. I didn't want to see it and be constantly reminded of that night."

"I get that." My head snapped up. "But you let me do the worrying. You hear me?"

Piper slid off my lap and began pacing.

"What is it?" My heart picked up speed the longer she didn't answer me.

"I remember seeing something odd when I was at the grocery store before you came home. I didn't think anything of it but now, it makes sense." She stopped, facing me. "There were a couple of women standing by the produce section. They were whispering and looking at me when I walked by with Brynlee. I don't know what they were talking about, but they kept staring at me. So they were obviously talking about me. But I've never seen Price around. It was in the news a few times that he was taking a vacation or a break from politics. I didn't know you could do that while being mayor." She rolled her eyes. "He probably paid people off."

"Probably." I pulled my phone out of my pocket and sent a quick text.

Me: I need you both to watch over my girls.

Cyrus: Already on it.

The reply came almost instantly from Cyrus. The guy hardly ever slept anymore and for whatever reason, that forced the guilt I had been feeling for the past several years, down harder on my chest.

"Jaron."

I looked up, placed my phone on the table, and sat back in the chair.

"Can we get through this?" Piper asked, pulling at the hem of her tank top.

I wanted to tell her yes. I wanted to tell her that this was only a bump in our road and that we would get over it together. But none of that came out. Instead, I just sat there and stared at her. We had confessed our love for each other. I thought as soon as those three powerful words were said, that everything would be easier. But I was wrong. The air around us grew thick. The passion that was there became electric, bordering on insanity as I couldn't think about anything else but getting back inside her tight, hot, wet body.

"Jaron." Piper's voice took on that husky tone I had fallen in love with. It proved to me that no matter how much we fought, that lust would always be there.

Running two fingers along my mouth, I stared at her.

Her eyes followed the movement, her mouth parting slightly. She shivered, hugging herself. "God, I can feel you when you're not even touching me."

I chuckled, my body stirring at her confession. "Good."

AFTER US

She gave me a small smile and took a step toward me. Just when I thought she was going to hint for more, a yawn trembled through her.

My laugh deepened. "Let's go to bed, baby."

She nodded, making her way to the bedroom but not before she gave me a look over her shoulder.

My dick jumped.

Maybe she wasn't that tired after all.

TWENTY

Piper

IT HAD BEEN A few weeks since the night at Gigi and Vince's place. While I missed the girls, I knew that Jaron and I needed to work on us. There was no way we could get through this if we didn't. He would spend every evening reading through my journals. Even re-reading them, to the point he had them memorized. I was impressed that he was committed to finding out everything there was about me that he could.

I started writing another journal but didn't let him read it yet. It wasn't time. Maybe in a year or more but right now, it was for my eyes only. He never pressed. Just asked what I was doing when he saw me scribbling away in the notebook. I would tell him. He would nod, kiss my head, and leave me to my thoughts.

It was later into the evening on a Friday. We were invited back over to Gigi and Vince's place but decided to stay home instead. Brynlee was in bed and Jaron and I were snuggled on the couch. He was going through my journals again but there was one that he missed. I often wondered if it was intentional.

"My body hurts. It's not pregnancy pain either. No, I'm turned on and I can't do anything about it. Jaron isn't here to please this ache."

Jaron looked at me then. "Did you masturbate?"

I gave him a small smile. "Keep reading."

He cleared his throat and continued.

"I talked to Jaron today and without telling him, I told him. It was weird. It was like he knew that I was aching for him but couldn't do anything about it. I think he was hinting for phone sex but that never happened. It wasn't like he was alone anyway. Someone could overhear and I know he wouldn't want that. Maybe I should use my fingers."

"Fucking hell." Jaron blew out a slow breath.

"If he were here, I know he would help make me feel better. Maybe I should live with the pain. I know it'll go away eventually."

Jaron turned to the next page, a deep frown settling between his brows. "You didn't do anything about it, baby?"

"Nope." I rose from the couch and headed into the kitchen. Pulling two beers from the fridge, I went back to the living room and handed Jaron one before sitting back down beside him. "I think I was punishing myself. Or I didn't think it was fair that you were stuck in jail and here I was, playing with myself because the pregnancy was making me..."

"Making you what?" He placed the journal on the table and took my beer from me. He put both of the bottles on the table before turning to me. "Tell me."

"Horny," I whispered.

He chuckled. "You can let me fuck you in public, but you can't say that one word without blushing?"

"Shut up." I laughed, punching his arm. "It's embarrassing."

"Why?" He turned me around and pulled me back against him. "There's nothing to be embarrassed over." He grabbed my hand and stuck it between my legs. "I think you should show me what you would have done if you *had* touched yourself though."

"Oh? And why would I do that?"

"Because it's hot as hell." He kissed the side of my neck. "Do it." He released my hand.

Getting a better idea, I moved to other side of the couch. Bending my knees, I spread my legs and slid my hand up my inner thigh.

Jaron's eyes followed, watching what I was about to do for him. "Show me."

I licked my lips, pushing my shorts down my legs, leaving my bottom half completely naked for him.

His eyes darkened.

Just as I was about to touch myself like he wanted, his cell rang.

He muttered a curse, pulling it from his pocket. "It's Sammy."

"Take it." I slid off the couch and got dressed. "He only calls if it's something important."

He nodded, putting the phone to his ear. "Yeah."

As I was walking by him, his hand grazed my hip. I stopped, glancing down at him.

I love you, he mouthed.

"I love you too," I whispered.

Jaron sat back, pushing his fingers through his hair. "What's up, Sammy?"

Grabbing my beer, I headed to the kitchen to clean up from our dinner earlier. I heard Jaron's muffled voice coming from the living room. Unsure as to what Sammy could be calling for, I gave them a moment of privacy. Just in case it was club business that I shouldn't be privy to. Not that Jaron ever kept things from me but both Cyrus and Sammy had told me often how they filled him in whenever they went to see him.

Letting out a hard sigh, I leaned against the counter and finished off my beer. From where I stood, I couldn't see Jaron, but I could hear him. His mumbled words, the gruff deep vibrato of his voice. Something was wrong. I wasn't sure how I knew but I could feel it deep in my gut.

Jaron suddenly appeared in the entranceway to the kitchen. He was no longer on the phone but there was a deep scowl on his face. Whatever Sammy told him, couldn't have been good. The lines etched on Jaron's face told me that he was pissed. About something. But I had no idea what. It was on the tip of my tongue to ask, to beg for his words, to plead for him to give me all of him. Every word. Every syllable. Every damn breath as he spoke his truths.

His hands were shoved into the pockets of his jeans, but I could still see the outline of his thick length.

My eyes glanced up, locking with his.

He smirked.

My cheeks heated at being caught staring at his crotch.

"Don't."

I swallowed hard at that single word.

Jaron took a step toward me. "Don't ever be embarrassed for looking at me. You want something, you don't even have to ask. Just take it, Piper. Take whatever it is that you need. I'll always be willing to give it to you."

"Even if we're fighting?" I asked, my voice small and unsure. I loved him. I loved him with every inch of me, but I had never been in a relationship before. Were there rules that I didn't know about?

He took those final steps between us and cupped my face.

I shivered, pushing my cheek into his calloused palm.

"Especially when we're fighting," he said, his voice low.

"Is everything okay?" I didn't want to ruin the moment, but he didn't look happy after his conversation with Sammy.

"The mayor's still causing shit." Jaron cupped my jaw. "I don't want you going anywhere alone. I know it makes me sound controlling but it's the only way I know how to keep you safe. You want to go out, we go together."

I nodded. "Okay but what if I went somewhere with the twins?"

A dark shadow passed over Jaron's face. "I sure as fuck hope you mean Cyrus and Sammy."

I rolled my eyes. "Of course."

"Don't roll your eyes, Piper." His grip on my jaw tightened. "I remember how jealous you got when Candace called me."

"That's different." But was it?

"It's not but good try." He smirked.

I huffed. "I won't go anywhere with either set of twins, alright? Does that make you feel better?"

"No." Jaron cupped my shoulders, running his hands down my arms. "Normally, I wouldn't care if you went anywhere with Cyrus and Sammy but with the mayor sniffing around, I'd rather you be with me, so I know where you are at all times. I know that sounds even more controlling…"

"I get it." Maybe it *was* controlling but after what we had been through already, I didn't care so much. "Anything else going on?"

"No." But as he said that single word, something flashed in his eyes.

I leaned back, staring up at him. "You're lying."

"It's nothing, babe." He kissed my forehead. "Let me worry about it."

"No." I gently pushed him back, keeping him at a distance so I could get these words out. "We are a couple. That means we worry together. Tell me what's going on."

"It's shit that's added to the pile, Piper." Jaron pulled away from me and began pacing. "The mayor said some nasty shit when I saw him weeks ago, but I never told you because I didn't want to worry you. Now, he's saying more shit." He shook his head. "He was a monster before but now, he's worse."

"How can someone like him be worse? I've heard the rumors." I shivered at the thought of what that man was capable of.

Jaron stopped pacing, his eyes connecting with mine. "What have you heard?"

"That he had underage girls working at one of his strip clubs. But no one actually knows if it's his club or not but, come on, the guy is shady as fuck." I rolled my eyes. "I remember the way he looked at me when I was at your trial."

"So do I." Jaron's hands clenched into fists. "I should kill him just for that."

"No." I took a step toward him but the look on his face made me hesitate.

"What?" His tone was short and clipped. There was a battle in him. Stay and keep his family safe or go after those who wronged him and us.

"I don't want you to lose yourself more than you already have." I placed my hand on his chest, feeling the beating of his heart beneath my palm.

"I'm fine," he bit out, covering my hand with his.

"Are you, Jaron? Can you honestly stand there and tell me that you are, in fact, fine?" I searched his face, waiting for a sign that he was going to run. That he was going to fall to his knees and break before me but instead, I got something far more than what I expected.

He pulled me into his arms. Just when I thought he was going to hug me, he cupped my ass and lifted me into his arms. I wrapped my legs around his waist, holding on and waiting for him to tell me what was going on with him. Whatever he needed, I would be there to give it to him.

When he brought me to our bedroom, he gently placed me on the edge of the bed. "Jaron, what is it?"

"I had to kill people while in jail, Piper. I didn't relish being their Grim Reaper. And maybe they didn't all deserve a death sentence, but they were also all vile scumbags who would have hurt people again. Not that it makes it right. Nothing does. But that's it. That's me. That's what I did and can't undo. I couldn't risk never seeing you again or meeting our daughter, so I did everything I could to survive."

"You never got in trouble?" I asked, wondering how he wasn't still in jail, paying for his crimes.

"The guards were paid to look the other way. The system's corrupt."

No wonder he was haunted by his demons. "Jaron."

"No." He placed his thumb against my lips. "I need to get this out. I should have said all of this a long time ago but to be honest, I'm scared, Piper."

I ran my hands up his strong arms, reveling in the way he shivered beneath my touch. "Talk to me."

Before I knew what was happening, he fell to his knees in front of me.

"Jaron," I gasped, clapping a hand over my mouth.

"I'm here, on my knees, begging you to forgive me." His eyes held so much sorrow, so much pain. So much agony over something he never had to worry about.

"Baby." I knelt in front of him, cupped his hands, and brought them up to my mouth. "I love you. I'm not going anywhere."

"But what I did..."

"Stop." I straddled his lap. "You don't have to ask for my forgiveness, Jaron, and I'm not going anywhere. What you went through in jail was so you could get home to me and our daughter. I could never repay you enough for what you did. For us. For me. You saved me and over time, I'll save you too."

He blew out a slow breath, leaning his forehead against mine. "You already have, baby."

Pushing out from under my hold, he rose to his full height. Holding out his hand, he waited.

I slipped my fingers in his, letting him pull me to my feet.

Jaron stripped before helping me out of my clothes until we were both standing naked in front of each other.

"Clothes get in the way," he murmured.

"They can," I whispered, backing up until I hit the edge of the bed. "Come here." I crawled onto the bed, lifted the covers, and waited.

Jaron joined me, slipping beneath the blankets and pulling me down and into his arms.

"How many?" I asked, turning to face him.

"I..." He drew in a sharp breath. "Two by myself but I assisted in many fights and started one when I first arrived." Jaron rolled onto his back, staring up at the ceiling. "My dad had warned me that some of Tanner's crew was in jail with me."

I had heard about Tanner Horsch and his club, Devil's Rejects. Tanner was no longer the president of the club after a shady bastard took over and kicked him out. I liked to think that things happened for a reason. Tanner was now married to Jaron's cousin, Bee, and they had a son. He was happy. I'd only met him a few times, but I could see the love he had for Bee whenever he looked at her. He was curt and to the point most times with others but when he spoke to his wife, it was like his personality completely switched. His tone was softer toward her. Almost like how Jaron was with me.

"Did they leave you alone?" I asked, needing Jaron's voice to drown out the fears in my head.

"They did. I don't know who told them, but they never messed with me. But it didn't matter."

"What do you mean?"

Jaron looked at me then. "I had to do something. I'm a biker, baby, and I'll be president of Hell's Harlem eventually. Most of the guys I was locked up with knew that. They also knew that my dad has been trying to clean up Hell's Harlem's messes for years. Before I was even born." He turned onto his side, facing me. "I was fresh meat for them."

I swallowed hard. "Did you start a fight to make a point?"

"I did." He reached out and pushed a loose strand of hair behind my ear. "It's not something I'm proud of and my demons will follow me to my grave, but knowing that I made it out of there and back to your arms was worth it."

"Did they leave you alone after that?"

"They did until that time I told you about. When I was visiting with Sammy and told him I wanted to see you." He muttered a curse. "I should have been more cautious about that shit but I missed you."

My heart jumped. "I missed you too."

Jaron inched closer and wrapped himself around me. "Sleep, baby. I got you."

"No, Jaron." I yawned. "I got *you*."

TWENTY-ONE

JARON

TELLING PIPER WHAT I had done to survive while in jail lifted some of the weight resting on my shoulders. I wouldn't give her every bloody detail but I gave her enough so she would understand where I was coming from. Why I was quiet and withdrawn. Why I struggled in the beginning to tell her. I didn't want to fill her head with those gory details, but she needed to know.

It was a few hours later and Piper had fallen asleep in my arms like I wanted her to. My phone vibrated, hers chimed, but we completely ignored them. Did people not sleep? Maybe it was emails coming in. Who knew? I had learned that Piper worked at the center whenever she could, but it wasn't full time. Not that she would have to worry anymore since I was home. I would have to ask her what she did with the money I had sent her.

Piper stirred, rolled over onto her stomach, and lifted her head. "Hey, you're awake." Her voice was rough with sleep. She rubbed her eyes before reaching over me to turn on the lamp. "You okay?"

"I have a naked beautiful woman in bed with me. How could I not be okay?"

She smiled, a tinge of pink hitting her cheeks. "You haven't slept at all, have you?"

"No." I pushed her hair out of her eyes which earned me a soft sigh.

"How come?" she asked softly.

"Couldn't sleep but knowing that you did, is all I care about." I ran my hand over her upper back in small circles. "Can I ask you a question?"

"Of course." Piper tilted her head. "You don't have to ask permission. Ask me anything."

"How have you been able to afford the house? I know you work at the center whenever you can but it's not full time. And the money you got from your parents for college, wouldn't pay all the bills." I would eventually ask her what she did with the money I sent her but first, I wanted to know how she got the house in the first place. It wasn't overly big. It was perfect if you asked me but someone on a single income wouldn't be able to afford it. Not that she had to worry about that anymore of course.

Piper sighed, running her finger over a scar on my side. "As soon as my mom found out she was pregnant with me, they started saving money right away. My dad put most of the money in. I guess it was his little way to make it up to my mom. He put her through hell in the beginning. I really don't know how she forgave him."

"Love conquers all," I muttered.

"You believe that?" Piper asked, staring at me with wide eyes.

"I don't know but I've seen love come and go from the house I grew up in. The love my parents have for each other is something I've always wanted. I just never looked for it anywhere else when the twins wouldn't leave your beautiful ass alone."

"I'm so sorry about that." She leaned her head on my chest, running her finger in circles over a freckle. I liked that she wasn't scared to touch me. I liked that when she needed something, she took it from me, knowing I would never turn her down.

"Why are you sorry?" I asked, needing to hear her words.

"If I would have known that you had feelings for me, I would never have started sleeping with them. That was the reason I got drunk. I was upset because I thought you hated me," she explained, her voice shaking.

"Hey." I slipped out from under her and pushed her to a sitting position. "I love you. You hear me? I've never hated you."

She looked away, her chin wobbling.

"Baby." I cupped her jaw, forcing her to look at me. "I promise that I've never hated you. I shouldn't have let the twins come between us, but that's on me. I admit that I was scared of my feelings for you and that I tried to ignore them. I shouldn't have done that. But that's on *me*. Not you."

Piper looked at me, her eyes shining. "You forgive me?"

I gave her a small smile. "Of course. Now let's get some more sleep before Brynn wakes up."

"Actually." She pushed me back and ripped the blankets off of us.

"You want something?"

Her eyes dropped to my waist. "Yes," she breathed, licking her lips.

I laid back, crossing my arms under my head. "Then take it."

"I plan on it, Jaron." Her gaze snapped to mine, a sly grin spreading on her face before she jumped onto my lap.

Laughter broke free from us both, billowing around us like the love we shared. I made a promise to myself right then and there that no matter how much life became heavy, to talk it out and eventually fuck it out just the same. But talking came first. It had to. We wouldn't survive if it didn't.

(Piper)

After Jaron and I talked during the night, everything felt almost lighter. My mood had changed. Even his. Brynlee woke up in a good mood too.

Jaron's good moods were few and far between. Talking helped us both. It lifted our spirits and made us realize that communication was key to a healthy relationship. I had seen our friends go through it all and I didn't want that.

We spent the morning as a family. Jaron played with Brynlee while I cleaned. He offered to help me but I refused. I didn't mind cleaning so much, especially now that he was home.

"Babe." Jaron stood in the doorway. "You ready?"

"I am." I gave myself another glance in the mirror. When I was satisfied with my outfit, I went up to Jaron and stood on tiptoes. Giving him a soft peck on the cheek, I went to walk around him when he grabbed my arm.

"Don't think so." He spun me around and crushed his mouth to mine.

I gasped, breathing him in.

He gave my bottom lip a gentle bite which shot a shiver right down the length of my spine. "Hmm…"

"Jaron, we have to go." I was excited to go grocery shopping with him and Brynlee. It probably didn't make sense for most but it was our first outing as a family, and I was looking forward to it. Even if it was just to buy food.

"You kiss me? You kiss me like you mean it. None of this pecking and soft kisses shit anymore." He pinched my chin and tilted my head back. "You got me?"

"I can't kiss you like that in front of family," I whispered, my body tingling at the rough demand.

"I don't care who we're around. We went over a year without seeing each other, Piper. We will spend the rest of our lives making up for that shit." He lowered his mouth to mine again, pushing me up against the door frame. Before I knew what he was doing, he had me in his arms and my legs wrapped around his waist.

"We have to go." Although I said the words, I never stopped him. How could I? So many things were revealed while we talked last night. I knew this was his way of showing me that he meant every word of what he had said.

"I want you walking through the store thinking of me every time you take a step," Jaron murmured against the side of my throat.

Once Jaron took and gave me what both of us had wanted, he placed me gently on my feet. I pulled up my panties and leggings, making myself look somewhat presentable again.

He kissed the side of my neck before placing a hard smack on my mouth. "Go get cleaned up. I'll grab Brynn and get her ready."

"Okay." When I went to take a step away from him, he grabbed my hand. Glancing at him over my shoulder, I waited.

Jaron brought my hand up to his mouth, kissing the back of my knuckles. "I love you."

My heart swelled. "I love *you*."

"Good. Now go before I change my mind and call someone to come watch Brynn while I spend the day fucking my woman."

I laughed, pulling away from him before he could get any ideas. "We need food, baby."

"Yeah, I can call Sammy to grab it." Jaron stalked toward me, cupping himself over his jeans. "My dick misses you already."

I rolled my eyes. "You would think I deprive you or something with how needy you are."

"Needy?" Jaron raised an eyebrow. "I'm needy?" he asked, charging for me.

I squealed and got two steps away from him before I was tackled to the bed. A bubble of laughter left me.

He chuckled. "You're lucky, babe. But don't worry. I'll just get you back later." A wicked grin spread on his face.

"I look forward to it." I cupped his cheek, placing a hard peck on his lips.

"What did I say?" he growled, when I went to pull away. "Kiss me like you fucking mean it, Piper."

A breathless laugh escaped me. "But that always leaves us wanting more."

"Don't give a shit about that." Jaron slipped his tongue between my lips, pulling a moan from the center of my chest. "I have a lot of lost time to make up for."

I smiled against his mouth but as much as I wanted to continue this, we needed to grab Brynlee and get some groceries. We needed to move on and be a family. Even if it was just by doing the small tedious and boring things. I wanted it all.

I gently pushed him back. "We have to go or else we won't be going anywhere."

Jaron slid off the bed and helped me to my feet. "I like the sound of that. Spending a weekend in bed." He waggled his eyebrows.

I giggled. "We'll make it happen."

"I look forward to it." He walked by me but not before giving my ass a light swat. "Get ready and I'll grab our girl."

My heart swelled. Every damn time. No matter how many times he claimed Brynn as his, which she was in fact, it still did funny things to my belly. If my ovaries could explode, I was sure they would.

After I cleaned myself up, I met both Jaron and Brynn by the front door. He had dressed her in a red sweat outfit that said 'Daddy's Girl' in light blue on the front of the sweatshirt.

"Hi, baby girl." I kissed her cheek, pulling her from Jaron's arms so he could get his shoes on. "Did you sleep well?"

She leaned her head against my shoulder, letting out a hard sigh and sucking on her soother.

I laughed. "That hard?"

"I think she was dreaming when I woke her up," Jaron said, a frown settling between his brows.

"Really?" I ran my hand down her back. "I don't think babies can actually dream. I'm not sure though. Google says different things."

"Well…" Jaron came up to us and petted his hand over her head. "Whatever it was, she didn't look happy about it and I want to kick the ass of whatever it was that was bothering her."

"Maybe she just slept really hard." I kissed her forehead, inhaling the fresh scent of her soft skin. "She could be grumpy that you woke her up."

"Maybe." Jaron kissed my temple. "Either way, I still don't like it."

I laughed. "She's not a morning person, just like her mama."

He smirked. "You're a morning person when you wake up to my face between your legs."

My body burned. "That's different."

A deep laugh rumbled through him. "Is it now?"

"Yes." I walked past him and left the house.

"How?" He locked up before following us to my car.

"Because I can't think of how tired I am when you have your tongue shoved deep inside me," I threw at him, making my way to the vehicle.

He groaned. "You say the sweetest things."

I laughed, putting Brynn in her car seat.

Jaron sat in the driver's seat, glancing back at us.

The hairs on my neck tingled but when I looked at him, he didn't say anything. "What?"

"Just thinking how good you are with her."

"She's an easy baby. I lucked out I guess." Joining Jaron in the front, a contented sigh left me when he placed his hand on my inner thigh. I covered it with my own, brushing my thumb back and forth over a small scar in between his thumb and forefinger. "What happened here?" I asked, noticing the slightly raised jagged flesh that I hadn't seen before.

"A fucker bit me in jail."

My eyes widened, my head whipping around. "Really?"

Jaron nodded. "He was crazy as fuck and completely unstable. I had to get a whole bunch of tests done after to make sure I didn't catch anything from him. I've been hit, bones broken and all that shit, but being bitten almost hurt more."

"Wow." I ran my thumb over the light pink flesh. "What happened to him?"

Jaron glanced at me quickly before looking out at the road ahead of us. "I stabbed him in the eye with a pen I stole from a guard," he muttered.

"Oh." I knew going in that Jaron wouldn't be like the other guys I knew. Hell, he wasn't even close to being like Aiden and Ashton. While they could take care of their own when provoked, it was nothing compared to what Jaron could do or had done.

"I told you that I'm not the same man you fell in love with, Piper," Jaron said, pulling me from my thoughts. He brought my hand up to his mouth and kissed my knuckles. "But I love you and I will prove to you that I am a good guy."

"You don't need to prove anything to me, Jaron." I pulled my hand from his grip and brushed the back of my knuckles down his cheek. "I love you too and I know that what you did was only so you could survive and make it back to us."

"You are too fucking good to me, baby." He captured my hand in his and brought it down to his lap. "Way too fucking good."

"You make it sound like a bad thing." I turned toward him. "Do you think I'm being too understanding? Is that it? Should I yell and scream or cry that you had to beat up some assholes, stab them, hurt them, kill them, just so other assholes would leave you alone? You have no idea how much I thought of what you had to do or were doing while you were in jail. But I made a promise to myself right away that I wouldn't care. You were put in jail because the mayor is a monster who has it out for you, and his son was just as bad. Am I sorry for what you did to Brody? No, because if you wouldn't have stopped him, it could have been so much fucking worse, or he could have done it to someone else."

Jaron white-knuckled the steering wheel. "I keep having these thoughts that I should have made him suffer. That I shouldn't have ended it so quickly, but being at the party, I didn't want to cause a scene and make it worse for you. I can't tell you how many times both Cyrus and Sammy told me what they would have done if it was either of their girls." He shook his head. "But that doesn't matter." He squeezed my hand. "I can't do this without you, so thank you, Piper. Thank you for not giving up on me, on us, and for waiting it out."

Pulling my hand from his grasp, I cupped him over his pants. "This is mine. All of you. Remember? You told me those words yourself."

He nodded, placing his hand on top of mine. "Always yours."

"Finally mine," I whispered, his cock jumping under my touch.

Jaron leaned over, placing a soft peck on my forehead before lightly brushing his nose against mine. "I love you, baby."

My heart stuttered. "I love you."

He gave me a small smirk. "Let's get this done and over with, so we can spend the rest of the day doing nothing."

"I like that idea."

Once we reached the grocery store, Jaron parked and left the car first. He grabbed Brynlee from her car seat as I slipped out of the passenger side.

It was on the tip of my tongue to tell him that he could have brought her in her car seat but when he sighed as he held her against him, I thought better of it.

I grabbed the stroller from the trunk of the car. If Jaron wanted to put her in it, he could, but I was happy with him holding her.

We walked into the large building as a family. I looked at Jaron every now and again, almost expecting this to be a dream. I found myself pinching my arm every so often just to make sure this was actually a reality. Even though he had been home for a few weeks already, we had a hard start to our relationship. A part of me feared that he would move on after he got his fill.

"I can feel you looking at me," he said, glancing at me over his shoulder.

I stopped abruptly. "I…"

He tilted his head, hugging Brynn against his chest. "What's wrong?"

A sigh left me. "Nothing." I went up to him and kissed his cheek before placing a peck on Brynn's head. "Nothing at all." My fears were unwarranted because I knew, I felt, Jaron wasn't leaving. Ever.

"You sure?" He moved Brynn to his left arm, reaching out to cup my cheek with his free hand. "You can tell me."

"I know." I smiled up at him, liking the way my stomach tumbled whenever he touched me. "We can talk later."

Jaron leaned toward me, pressing his lips to my ear. "If you don't talk to me, baby, I'll force my cock so deep inside you, the only word that will leave your mouth, is *more*."

My body heated. "I don't believe you." I walked away but not before I caught the look of shock on his face. I bit back a laugh and sauntered down the aisle.

"Fuck." I heard Jaron breathe.

I laughed to myself, enjoying this newfound awareness between us. No matter the issues we were having, we were still able to flirt, touch, kiss, and just hold each other.

The tiny hairs on my body suddenly tingled.

I looked over my shoulder, finding Jaron staring back at me. He closed the distance between us and placed Brynn in the stroller. After he buckled her in it, he came up to me and cupped my jaw.

My breath caught. Even though we were in public, I couldn't help but get lost in him. His gray eyes. His life. It was like his damn soul was calling out for mine.

Just when I thought he was going to kiss me, he gave me a smirk and released my jaw before pushing the stroller down the aisle.

I huffed, shaking my head.

He chuckled. "Your mom's a tease, baby girl."

I scoffed. "I'm a tease." I stuck my tongue out at him. "Please."

A wicked grin spread on his face. "I'll remember that," he said, walking away from me.

Letting my eyes roam down the length of him, it took everything in me not to bite my knuckles at the way the dark blue jeans sat low on his hips. They did wonderful things for his ass. Mixed with the black hoodie, although it was casual, I found it hotter than if he were wearing a suit. Though, I bet he'd look good in one just the same.

"I can feel you staring at me, babe," he called out over his shoulder.

I laughed, shaking my head and following him and Brynlee down the aisle. We ended up picking up whatever we needed and even some things we wanted. Whenever I went grocery shopping, I usually only bought things we absolutely had to have. I got maternity pay from the center while I was currently off. Since my mom was one of the owners, I got more time off than usual. I would also get random envelopes in the mail each month with a check in them. I bought what we needed and put the rest in a bank account as an education fund for Brynn.

"Jaron, I need to tell you something," I said, before I forgot again.

"What is it?" He came up to me and threw a box of Cheerios into the cart.

"I forgot to mention when you first got home how your parents have been helping me each month. I've been getting deposits into my account from them and from my parents. I never asked for the money and have put most of it away into a bank account. I figured I'd start saving for Brynn's education now."

He cupped my cheek, placing a soft peck on my forehead. "That makes sense, but I want you to know, it wasn't my parents sending those transfers."

My eyes widened. "What? But the transfers said Mercer on them. I just assumed..."

"You shouldn't assume, Piper." Jaron winked.

A thought came to me. "They were from you. Weren't they?"

"Let's pay for this stuff and get out of here. Then we'll talk on the way home." He grabbed the cart from me and wheeled it to the nearest checkout.

This was something we should have talked about before. If I would have known that it was him sending me funds, I wouldn't have been so worried about actually spending the money. I loved his parents, and I loved my own, but they struggled just like the rest of us. I didn't want them thinking I was taking advantage. I knew it didn't make sense when they wanted nothing but the best for their granddaughter.

While Jaron paid for the groceries, the hairs on the back of my neck tingled. I looked around me, but found nothing out of the ordinary. It was early afternoon, so the store wasn't overly packed. But that familiar tingle didn't go away.

"Piper, what's wrong?" Jaron asked.

"I don't know." I continued putting the items on the conveyor belt but that feeling of being watched wouldn't go away.

"Babe."

I met his gaze then. "I feel like we're being watched."

Jaron stood up taller, his dark eyes moving around the vast room.

"Not to butt in or anything," the young cashier said softly. "But you probably are being watched."

Our heads whipped around.

"What the hell are you talking about?" Jaron demanded, his voice rough.

"She's been in here before." She nodded toward me. "I've seen other women whispering about her. They would point. But you never noticed," she told me.

"I was more worried about other shit," I mumbled.

"Our city is getting bigger, but it still has that small-town mentality," the cashier continued, still ringing through our items. "There was a woman who would ask us about you. Apparently, she saw you at Rouge, picking up two guys."

Jaron's dark eyes shot to mine, his jaw clenching.

"She's talking about Cyrus and Sammy." I rolled my eyes but appreciated the jealousy rolling off of him just the same.

"Still hate that shit," he mumbled. "We need to go."

"Thank you for the information," I told the cashier.

She nodded. "One last thing. The mayor has been asking about you two."

"Fuck." Jaron paid for the items and tossed the bags into the cart.

I thanked her and grabbed the stroller, following Jaron out of the store. The mayor. I hadn't seen him since Jaron's trial. Not in person anyway. I had seen him on TV and in the newspaper. He'd lost weight but it was like as soon as the pounds came off, he became meaner. There was something in his dark eyes that whenever I looked into them, I knew that he was the devil in disguise.

"Jaron." I rushed to keep up with him. "Have you seen the mayor since the last time?"

"No. I've been home with you."

When we reached my car, Jaron put the groceries into the trunk and slammed the hatch closed. The sound jarred through me. The tension rolled off him in waves. He was plotting and I didn't know how we were going to survive his wrath.

AFTER US

Once I put Brynlee in the back in her car seat, she babbled about something, probably warning me that her father was about to lose his mind. I kissed her cheek and closed the door.

I folded up the stroller and put it in the trunk as well while Jaron paced.

"Jaron," I said gently, fearing that he was once again closing up on me.

"I need a moment," he muttered, heading around to the driver's side. Once he was seated behind the wheel, he slammed his fists against it.

My heart jumped, knowing that this was either going to turn into a discussion, a fight, or worse.

TWENTY-TWO

JARON

I HADN'T SEEN OR heard from the mayor in weeks. Cyrus and Sammy tried keeping tabs on him as best they could, but it was like Price just disappeared off the face of the fucking earth.

I tried keeping my nose clean, not caring in the least about the shit he did but I wasn't kidding anyone. I *did* care about what he did because the fact he was mayor of our small city, was only a cover-up. He was a shithead and the worst kind of human. If you could even call him that.

When he had made those threats about Piper and Brynlee, I instantly put a watch on them. Not that Piper ever left the house much anyway and especially not without me, but I still wanted to her to be safe for when she got over her anxiety of leaving the house. She would become stronger and leave the house again on her own. Especially now that was I home to make sure that they were safe.

"Tell me about the money you received," Piper said, turning toward me.

We were still in the parking lot at the grocery store. I could have driven us home already, but I knew that we needed to talk. I texted Sammy and Cyrus, asking them to meet us at the house. Besides my parents, they were the only ones I truly trusted when it came to my girls.

"I had them transferred to you every month," I told her. "Not all of the money was earned the legal way, Piper, but it's yours."

"Who did you take it from?"

I leaned my elbow on the windowsill, scratching my jaw. "The mayor."

She barked a laugh. "No wonder he hates you."

"I also killed his son, so I'm sure that has something to do with it too," I said, my voice flat.

"How did you get the money?"

"That doesn't matter." I looked at her then. "The less you know, the better. It's already dangerous for you to be with me."

"Hold on." She pointed at me. "You better not be saying that you're going to leave me just because the mayor has it out for you."

"No, I'm not leaving you but I'm giving you a choice, Piper. It's not safe. Being with me is not safe. I should have realized this weeks ago, but I missed you so fucking much, I couldn't think about anything other than being with you and our daughter."

"And future baby," she whispered.

My heart jumped. "What the fuck did you just say?"

Piper sighed, leaning her head back against the seat. "I wanted to make it a surprise or do something fancy, but I think I might be pregnant."

Every cell in my body stirred. "You think?"

She nodded. "My period is almost two weeks late. I had some home pregnancy tests that I had from when I was pregnant with Brynn. I took a test this morning."

I turned toward her and grabbed her hands. "Tell me."

Her eyes slid to mine. "It was positive, Jaron."

All breath left me at what I was hearing. Cupping her cheek, I slid my hand to the back of her head and leaned my forehead against hers.

"I want to take another test and go to the doctor's to make sure everything is fine before we tell anyone," she murmured.

I nodded, brushing my nose against hers before placing a soft peck on her full mouth.

"I know Brynn's still young…"

When her voice trailed off, I lifted my head. "I don't care about that. People have twins and triplets and more, all the time. And with them being close in age, it could help them not fight as much and shit."

Piper smiled. "True. So, you're not mad?"

"Fuck." I kissed her harder. "No. Never, baby. But I do have to warn you of something."

"Oh?" She leaned back. "What's that?"

"If the test confirms that you are in fact pregnant, I'm not letting you out of my sight. Ever. I wasn't there for your pregnancy with Brynlee, but I'll be here for this one, every single step of the way. I'll be so damn annoying, I'm sure it'll drive you fucking crazy, but I can already tell you, I won't be able to help myself." Add to the fact that when her body becomes big and swollen, I could already guarantee that I would fuck her every chance I get. Pregnant women were beautiful, but seeing the woman I love swollen with my baby? I was going to be a fucking goner.

"I look forward to that."

"Seriously?" I was taken aback by her words. Most women wouldn't want their men being so damn protective.

A husky laugh left her. "Yeah. Even though I didn't see them often, I heard about how Zach and Vince were when both Luna and Gigi were pregnant. I often wondered if you would be the same way."

I gave her a smirk. "No, baby. I'm going to be worse."

Her laugh deepened. "Somehow, I'm not surprised."

Starting up the car, I reached across for her hand.

Piper linked our fingers, holding my hand on her lap. "I'll make an appointment with my doctor."

"I'll be there," I said before she could ask me. Not that she had to. Ever. I would be there. Now. Tomorrow. Forever.

"I love you, Jaron."

I brought her hand up to my mouth. "I love you, Piper. More than I could ever tell you."

I was on the verge of snapping. I wanted to know now if she was in fact pregnant or not. But deep down, I had a feeling that she was. It was the only thing that made sense. I had been home for nearly a month already and never once did I see her buy feminine products and she never asked me to pick them up for her. I never even saw her use them when I walked in on her going to the bathroom. She also never told me if she started or not. It had never gotten in the way, especially when it came to us having sex. And we had a lot of it. Especially recently.

"Jaron, that car's been following us for a while." Her words pulled me from my thoughts.

My eyes snapped to the rearview mirror. The car was dark. It was farther back but it was big, so I could only assume that it was an SUV of some sort. I didn't remember seeing it following us out of the parking lot at the grocery store but now I couldn't keep my eyes off it. "When did you first see it?"

"We left the grocery store and then I saw it pull out from a side street."

As much as I appreciated her being observant, it didn't sit well with me that we were being followed. For most people, it would be nothing and just a pure coincidence, but with the people I knew, especially the mayor, I feared for the worst.

Between the grocery store and Piper's house, there was a stretch of open road that didn't consist of any other houses or buildings. It was a farmer's field while the houses were a few miles from the main road.

My stomach twisted, my heart suddenly picking up speed that this damn SUV wasn't going anywhere.

"Jaron, something's wrong," Piper said, her voice shaking.

"Call Cyrus or Sammy," I told her. "They're supposed to be meeting us at home."

She pulled her phone from her purse and dialed a number before placing it on speaker. "I called Cyrus."

"Yeah," came a deep reply.

"Sammy, where's Cyrus?" I asked, clenching the steering wheel.

"He's in the shower and then we're heading over," was all he said.

"I think we're being followed," I told him, getting right to the point. I knew with the twins they hated small talk. Especially Sammy.

"Shit. Where did you go?"

"We needed to get groceries before you guys stopped by," Piper told him. "We have Brynlee with us."

"Fuck." There was some movement on the other line. "Cyrus," he yelled, banging on the door. "We got a problem." We could hear the running water shutting off as Cyrus stopped his shower.

"What's wrong?" he asked in the background.

"You're on speaker, J," Sammy said.

"We went to get groceries and Piper noticed someone following us. An SUV pulled out of a side street as soon as we left. We were heading home but they're still following us." I would drive for the rest of the day trying to get them off our tail if I had to, before I led them to our house.

"Make your way to the clubhouse but take every side street you can," Cyrus instructed. "We'll head there now."

"See you soon," Piper whispered.

We said our goodbyes but even after talking to the twins, it didn't make me feel any better.

"I'm scared," Piper finally said.

I wasn't a man who got scared often. Not until Piper and I started doing our thing and I ended up in jail as a result of my rage taking control of me. Only when that happened and I was taken from her, did I actually become scared.

Scared that I would never see her again.

Scared that I would never meet our daughter.

Scared that I would never be able to tell Piper how I truly felt.

Even after telling her that I loved her and confessing those feelings, it wasn't enough. There was so much more I wanted to tell her.

We continued driving in silence. I drove us past the road that would lead to home. I went down every side street I could and yet, the SUV was still following us. When we reached the outskirts of town, a shuddered breath left Piper.

As the headlights got closer, I could almost sense the depravity rolling off the person driving the vehicle. I would bet my life that the mayor had set it up. Price was out for blood and because of me, Piper and Brynlee were now brought into this mess.

When we got a couple of miles outside of town, the SUV sped up.

"Jaron," Piper gasped. "They're going to hit us." As soon as those words left her mouth, the SUV bumped the back of the car.

My eyes shot to Brynn. She had fallen asleep, thankfully, so she was none the wiser but if the vehicle kept hitting us, she could get hurt. I just prayed that she would never remember this shit.

"Hold on," I told Piper and pressed my foot on the gas. If I had been by myself, I would have driven off the road and into the field, but I wasn't. My main focus was keeping my girls safe.

The SUV continued speeding up, hitting the bumper and backing off. They were fucking with us and that pissed me off.

"Grab my phone and call the second last number that called me," I told Piper.

She did as she was told, thankfully not asking any questions. She placed it on speaker, her wide eyes burning into the side of my head.

When a click sounded on the phone, my eyes shot to the rearview mirror. I couldn't make out who was driving the SUV behind us. "Tell your boys to back the fuck off," I growled.

A deep chuckle sounded from the other end of the phone. "Do you kiss Piper with that filthy mouth?"

A soft gasp left her.

"Ah, it sounds like she's there with you," Price taunted. "Piper, how are you? Did you miss me?"

"What do you want?" I asked even though I already knew the answer.

"I want something of yours, Jaron. Something you don't deserve but have anyway. I want you to fucking pay."

Piper's hand trembled, the phone shaking in her grip.

"You can have me. You can do whatever the hell you want to me but leave my girls out of this shit." Even though I said those words, I knew it wouldn't be enough. I was also grateful that Piper didn't argue. She may not have been around the biker life until meeting me, but she also wasn't stupid. She knew when to keep her mouth shut when it came to hers and our daughter's safety. Especially when she could be pregnant again, her life was all that mattered to me.

"Yeah, you see." Price paused. "That doesn't work for me. You took my son."

"He almost raped me," Piper said, voicing her thoughts. "That bastard should have gotten more than what he did."

My head whipped around.

She raised an eyebrow, daring me to say she was wrong. She wasn't. But Price wasn't one to be messed with or egged on. He was going to use her words against us.

"Listen, you little bitch. Maybe you shouldn't have teased my son then we wouldn't be in this fucking hell," Price growled.

I grabbed the phone from Piper, took him off speaker, and held it up to my ear. "I will give you one last chance to call your boys off. If you don't, this will be war, Price."

"That's Mister Mayor to you, Jaron."

"Oh I'm sorry. I didn't realize you actually earned my respect. Forgive me for not noticing." The sarcasm dripped from my voice.

"Jaron." He chuckled. "I'm going to have so much fun ripping Piper apart. I was going to feed her to my dogs, but I've changed my mind. I'm going to keep her for myself. You know what else I'm going to do? I'm going to record every single detail and send it to you, so you can watch her die."

The sound of the click in my ear, forced a curse from my lips. Tossing the phone in Piper's lap, I gripped the steering wheel and pressed my foot against the gas as hard as I could.

"Jaron, what happened? What's going on? What did he say?"

I didn't answer because I couldn't. I needed to get these fuckers off our tail. I needed to end Price before he made good on his threat. I needed to keep Piper and Brynlee safe.

I was pissed that she let her mouth get away with her, but I was more pissed that I couldn't do anything about it. My temper had gotten the best of me before and I almost lost Piper as a result of it.

"Jaron." Piper's scream pulled me from my thoughts.

As soon as I reached for her hand, the SUV's headlights were the last thing I saw before everything went dark.

TWENTY-THREE

JARON

THE ONLY THING KEEPING *me from just up and quitting, was the fact that Piper had my baby at home. She gave birth a week ago and I hadn't been able to talk to her yet. Sammy and Cyrus had both gone over to check on her and Brynlee. They reported back that they were both healthy and safe. That was all I cared about. As much as it hurt that I wasn't there, I was thankful that Sammy and Cyrus could be there for her.*

They were the brothers I never had. We were family without being blood related. But even though we didn't share the same DNA, we shared a bond that most blood relatives didn't. Sure we fought, argued, and let our egos get in the way every now and again, but I couldn't ask for two better men to look after my girls when I couldn't.

While I stared down at the picture of Piper holding our newborn daughter, I ran my thumb along the colored image of them. She was beautiful and had a glow about her. Brynn was staring up at her mama and even though I wasn't there, I could feel the love they already had for each other.

I craved the day that I could meet our daughter and see Piper again. A question had crossed my mind on if we would have still been together if she hadn't gotten pregnant. I wondered if Piper felt the same way. The question had only crossed my mind once before I knew the answer was yes. She wasn't pregnant when I went to Paris for her. She wasn't pregnant when I found her at that bar and fucked her in the bathroom. She was mine before she had my baby growing inside of her.

From the moment I remembered being attracted to her when we were teenagers, I wanted her. And now that she was in fact mine, in almost every sense of the word, things were threatening to tear us apart.

But I refused to back down.

No matter the cost.

A loud ringing erupted in my ears. Pain slid between my eyes, forcing a breathless gasp to escape me. I tried thinking back over the last little bit. I didn't know what had happened but what I did know, was that I hurt. Everywhere.

Opening my eyes, I blinked once and then a second time before my vision cleared and I looked around me. The car was in a ditch with smoke coming up from under the hood.

Clicking the seat belt free, I did a quick scan of my body. When nothing seemed broken, I looked around me.

Piper was still beside me, but her eyes were closed. There was a gash on her head.

"Fuck," I bit out. I leaned over her, checking her pulse. When I felt the beating of her heart beneath my finger, I kissed her cheek. "I'm so sorry, baby. I'm so fucking sorry."

Satisfied that she was okay, I turned around to check on Brynlee. They say that when you're on the verge of death, you see a white light and your life plays out before you, but they never tell you what happens when your daughter disappears.

So many different emotions traveled through me, they were damn near suffocating.

How could I tell Piper that her daughter was missing?

Bile rose to my throat at the thought we would never see her again. Anger tore through my soul that Price had taken it this far.

The car seat was empty with the belt unbuckled, and the back door was open. The SUV who forced us off the road, was nowhere to be found and neither was our daughter.

Opening the driver's side door, I left the vehicle and searched around it for Brynn, but I couldn't find her. I kept thinking over the past few weeks. Did I make the right choice in being with Piper? If I would have stayed away, maybe Price would have left them alone. The things he wanted to do to Brynlee as she got older, forced the air from my very lungs. This was going to kill Piper. She would never forgive me.

"Jaron," I heard Piper call out from the car.

Fuck, what was I going to tell her?

"Jaron, where's Brynn?" she cried. "Where is she? God, my baby. Where is she, Jaron? Tell me!"

I rushed to her before she left the car. As I ran around to the passenger side door, she left the vehicle and fell to her knees.

A scent hit me. It smelled like…

"Gas." Shit. I grabbed Piper and all but dragged her to the road away from the car just as it went up in flames.

"Brynlee!" she screamed, trying to push away from me and run toward the car. Her cries of anguish ripped through my very soul.

"She wasn't in there, baby." I wrapped myself around her. "I promise she wasn't."

"Where is she?" Piper sobbed, gripping my hoodie tight.

"Whoever was in the SUV must have…they…" My throat closed, my tongue thick.

"No!" She shoved away from me and took a step back toward the car.

"Stop." I grabbed her hand, pulling her back against me. Just when I was about to ask her if she had her cell phone, a vehicle started coming down the road toward us. My heart jumped to my throat.

"Is that them?" Piper asked between sniffles and soft cries.

"I don't know who that is." I stepped in front of her, shielding her from whoever was driving down the road.

"Jaron, I need my baby back."

"I know. I'll get her." If it was the last thing I did, I would find Brynlee. I would find our daughter and make the bastards pay for taking her in the first place. If Price thought me killing his son was bad, just wait until I got ahold of him for taking my baby girl.

(Piper)

I was stuck in my head as the vehicle rolled up toward us. I didn't know who it was or if it was the same vehicle as before. The one who ran us off the road and took our daughter.

My baby.

The pain etching through me was nothing I had ever felt before. It was like these bastards had taken a piece of my soul. No. They took my whole entire being. If we didn't get her back, there was no point. I couldn't move on or get over it. Jaron and I were talking, we didn't fight as much anymore, we loved each other, and now this. This would destroy the progress we'd made.

"Who are they?" I heard myself ask.

"I don't know." Jaron kept his hand in mine.

The SUV came to a stop a few feet away. Three men filed out of the vehicle. Two were large and reminded me of the bikers I had spent some time hanging around while Jaron was gone. The third man was smaller. Much smaller in fact. He was still tall but had more of a swimmer's build. He reminded me of Spencer Reid from *Criminal Minds*. His hair was longer, the ends hitting just above his ears.

"Who are you?" Jaron asked when the Spencer Reid lookalike came toward us followed by one of the bigger guys.

The third man stood back. He moved his leather jacket, revealing two guns in a holster sitting on his hips.

"Who we are doesn't matter," one said. His friend who was still standing by the SUV, was big but this one was large. With tattoos lining both sides of his thick neck, his piercing blue eyes locked on us. Bits of silver sprouted from his black hair. He had dark scruff on his strong jaw that held a hint of gray. While he looked to be in his late forties, a gold nose ring made him almost appear young. It was a contradiction, the metallic ring sparkling in the sunlight. "We saw the vehicle pull out of the parking lot and start following you."

"You couldn't have done something before they ran us off the road?" Jaron bit out, tightening his hold on my hand.

"This isn't a movie, kid." The man looked at his friend before back at us. "You two need to go to the hospital."

"No. We need to find our daughter," Jaron told him.

"Your daughter's missing?" the man with the nose ring, asked.

"Yes," Jaron answered, his voice cracking. "She was taken before we woke up. We don't even know if she's..."

A dark shadow passed over the other man's face. He appeared to be younger and even though he was much smaller than his two friends, there was an air about him that I didn't like. His clothing didn't seem to mirror his personality either. He was definitely no Spencer Reid, even though he could have been his twin. With dark blue jeans, a button-up plaid shirt with all sorts of pastel colors, and a light gray vest, he seemed almost geeky. When he caught me staring, the corner of his mouth pulled up into a smirk.

My stomach twisted. Inching closer to Jaron, I grabbed his hand.

He looked down at me, probably wondering what the hell had made me suddenly so nervous but I couldn't explain it.

This guy...he terrified me.

"Someone took your daughter?" the larger man asked.

"Yes, they did," Jaron said, his voice rough.

The smaller man who had been silent this whole time, turned around and headed back to the SUV to join his other friend.

"Jaron." I grabbed onto his hoodie, leaning my head against his strong back. Everything inside of me hurt. From my bones to my muscles. My body ached but I needed Brynn. I needed her in my arms. I would never again take it for granted that I had her with us, always.

"We'll get her," he said, reaching around for me. He pulled me into his side, hugging me tightly and keeping me close.

"We'll drive you to the hospital," the man who had stayed behind said.

"No. We'll go somewhere else. The hospital isn't safe." Jaron grabbed my hand, slipping his fingers between mine. "We'll go see Shadow."

Shadow, or Nero Wolf, was Bee's grandfather and a retired biker. He had his own little hospital at his clubhouse which was safer than going to an actual hospital. No one asked questions there.

"We'll take you." The man spun on his heel, pulling a phone from his pocket.

"Wait." Jaron stepped forward. "Did you see who took our daughter?"

The man's face softened. "No. I'm sorry, we didn't. We were driving home, saw the other SUV start following you. They were sitting in the parking lot and pulled out as soon as you left the grocery store. So we started following them. We were cut off by another car and then got stuck behind a tractor. We finally made our way to you and saw the explosion but we thought it might have been too late." He put the phone to his ear. "Yeah, I'd like to report an accident." He gave the location and hung up before the dispatcher asked for anything else. "Call whoever you need," he said, handing Jaron the phone.

When we reached the SUV, Jaron paused in his steps. He looked down at the cell in his hand before meeting my gaze. "I don't know who to call."

"Everyone, Jaron. Call every single fucking person we know." My eyes welled. "I need my baby back."

He nodded, putting the phone up to his ear and walking away. "Dad, I need your help," he said, his voice trailing off as he stepped out of earshot.

"Here."

I looked over my shoulder.

The man who had stayed behind was now sitting in the passenger seat, holding a bottle of water out the window.

I hesitated but ended up taking it and downing half the bottle. "Thank you."

He nodded.

"I'm Piper and he's Jaron," I said, breaking the unnerving silence.

He nodded again, rolling up the window.

The back door opened then, revealing the guy who made me nervous for some unknown reason. The two men in the front of the SUV were tattooed up to the nines. With dark clothes and black leather jackets, they looked like bikers. But their jackets had no patches, so I wasn't sure who they were.

"Who are you?" I asked even though I knew they weren't going to tell me.

"We're here to bring you to wherever you need to go, sweetheart," the younger guy in the back of the SUV said. "That's all you need to concern yourself with."

"I need my baby," I said on a sob.

"Piper." Jaron came up behind me, pulling me into his arms as I cried against him. "We'll go to Shadow's and go from there. But most of the police are paid off in this area. We can't trust them. I have other people looking into this shit." He cupped my face, leaning down so he was at eye level with me. "We will get her back. I promise you. But you need to get checked out." Because I could be pregnant going unsaid.

I stifled another sob and nodded.

Jaron kissed my forehead before brushing his nose against mine. "I'll kill him for hurting you."

My throat burned, the tears rolling my down cheeks again.

He helped me into the back of the SUV, holding me against him as he shut the door behind. He gave the driver the address. Jaron tried making conversation with them and I knew then that he was scared. He wasn't a talker, but he was trying to distract us. There was a possibility that we would never see our daughter again and that thought alone was enough to drive us both mad.

"What do you guys do?" Jaron asked, tightening his hold on me.

The younger man shifted beside me. "We help people."

The driver's eyes flicked to the rearview mirror.

"Thank you," Jaron muttered.

The closer we got to Shadow's clubhouse, the less I knew what was going to happen.

I didn't know if Brynn was safe. I didn't even know if she was alive. I shouldn't have yelled at Price. It was my fault. All of my fault. Why couldn't they take me instead? Or Jaron? If it was the mayor who had a hand in this like we assumed, why did he take her? Maybe it was to get back at Jaron. I didn't know. But I could sense the fear in him that I would blame him. I didn't. I just wanted our baby back. I wanted to know if there was a new baby growing in me. I wanted to know that we were fine. That all of us were in fact fine.

While the strangers drove us to our destination, Jaron held me and whispered sweet words in my ears. They were words of encouragement. Words telling me how much he loved me. Words telling me to be strong and that although the mayor was an evil bastard, he wouldn't hurt her. Words telling me that we would get her back, but they were only words. I didn't believe him. I wanted to. I tried to. But until I had my daughter back in my arms, I couldn't believe a single thing Jaron told me.

TWENTY-FOUR

Piper

THE GUYS HAD DRIVEN US us to the Mayhem's Revenge clubhouse, but I couldn't even remember how we had gotten here. The drive could have been minutes or hours and I never noticed.

"How can I pay you back?" Jaron asked, helping me out of the SUV.

"You don't need to, kid," the guy in the passenger seat said.

Jaron grunted. "Everything comes with a price. I don't want to owe you if I don't have to."

The back window rolled down, revealing the smaller guy. "You don't owe us and there's no catch either. We help people. It's what we do."

"Tike," the driver barked.

"Now you know my name, so I guess we're even," he said, glaring at his friend.

Instead of waiting for us to answer, the window rolled back up.

Before we could find out anything about them, they drove off, the tires screeching out of the parking lot. I found I had more questions about the silent strangers but couldn't dwell on that too much when we were surrounded by several members of Hell's Harlem.

To say that I was surprised to see his parents, was an understatement.

"Dad, I..." A shuddered breath left Jaron, his hand tightening around mine as he kept me close.

"I can't believe this is happening." Jaron's mom, Eve, shook her head, wiping under her eyes.

"Do you know anything?" Greyson asked his son.

Jaron only shook his head, his jaw clenching.

"How the hell did you get here?" Sammy demanded, rushing toward us followed by Cyrus. "We followed the route you took and only saw the burnt-up car. You weren't there and then Cyrus gets a call from Greyson that there was an accident."

"Follow us," Jaron said. "And I'll explain all I know but Piper needs to see Ricky."

Ricky was the in-house doctor for Mayhem's Revenge, Shadow's old club. Now that he had retired, his own son, Kian, had taken over much like Jaron would eventually do for Hell's Harlem. Even though his dad was still the president, we all knew he was wanting to retire. It was only a matter of time before Jaron took over the club. I also knew that his father had been itching to spend the rest of his days with his wife. Now that his son was grown up, he could focus on her and their grandchildren.

As much as I just wanted my baby girl and to go home, I didn't argue with Jaron. There was no point trying to find our daughter if I wasn't taking care of myself. I knew that Jaron would go look for her. He didn't have to tell me. I needed to make sure he didn't worry about me at the same time, so I did as I was told like a good little girl.

"Jaron." Eve went up to her son. "Please tell me this is all some sick joke."

A sob left me. I pushed my face into Jaron's chest, crying against him over the fact that I may never see our daughter again.

"I wish it was," he told her, his voice thick.

"Oh God," she cried.

"We'll find out what's going on." That was his dad.

There were so many voices, all angry and curt, I couldn't place who was who, but I found that I no longer cared. I just wanted Jaron. I wanted Brynn. I wanted to move on as a family. When he first came home, I thought our biggest struggle would be how to reconnect, but this was so much worse.

"Let's get you looked at, baby," Jaron whispered in my ear. "I need to make sure you're good."

All I could do was nod while he led me to the back of the club. I was in a trance while Ricky, a smaller older man, looked at me. He was nice enough, but he could have also been a douche and I wouldn't have overly cared.

"She could be pregnant," Jaron muttered to Ricky.

He nodded. "I'll be careful. I have pregnancy tests here but if you want me to take blood..."

"Do it," Jaron said.

"You'll owe me, boy," Ricky said, trying to keep his voice firm but when he looked at me, the hard lines on his face, softened.

"I don't give a shit, Ricky. I already owe Shadow and Kian for letting us be here." Jaron nodded toward me. "We want to know."

Ricky did as he was told and took some blood. After, he checked out my head and neck. When he was satisfied that I didn't have a concussion, he checked Jaron out just the same. Much to his grumbling of course. He kept saying that he was fine but if he was going to go after Brynn like he said he would, he needed to be one-hundred-percent healthy. The crash had knocked us out, so Ricky mentioned something about taking it easy, but being the kind of guy that Jaron was, the instructions only went in one ear and out the other.

He kept looking my way, probably making sure I wouldn't snap. No. I wouldn't. That would be him. It was on the tip of my tongue to beg for him not to go after the guys who took Brynn. While I didn't know exactly who they were or even where to start, his dad had people looking into it. I wasn't stupid. They knew people. I was sure they owed some favors or were going to cash in on the favors that other people owed them. I didn't care how they found my daughter. I just needed her back in my arms.

When Ricky checked Jaron out, he went to leave the large makeshift medical room, but stopped at the door, checked his phone, and came back toward us. Showing us the screen, he gave me a small smile. "Congratulations again, little mama."

My breath hitched when I read the text saying that I was pregnant.

Jaron closed the distance between us and cupped my stomach. "Thank you. Let me know when you want to collect."

"I will." Ricky left the room, leaving Jaron and me alone.

Sammy and Cyrus, along with Greyson and a few other guys from the club, took that moment to join us in the room. Even though it was big, being stuck in there with them, made it seem almost smaller.

Jaron sat on the bed behind me, wrapping his arm around my middle.

"You can't."

"I can."

"You shouldn't."

"I will."

Jaron was arguing with someone, but I didn't care to look up to see who he was talking to. I didn't care. About anything. It felt like a piece of me had been ripped away. Like an appendage was torn free from my body, leaving my sorrow to bleed out on the ground beneath me.

I was pregnant. Again. With Jaron's baby. Our second baby.

Pain consumed me.

Agony threatened to tear me apart.

Rage coursed through my veins, making every nerve ending inside my body tingle beneath my skin.

As Jaron crushed me back against him, these dark thoughts took hold. They destroyed and yet gave me some sort of solace at the same time.

"We'll get her back," I heard him say.

Words. That was all they were. Nothing more. Nothing less. They were empty promises because how could he know? How did Jaron know that we would get her back? He was smarter than that. Than this. Than us. He lived and breathed destruction. He tore through my life like a hurricane, unleashing every feeling, every emotion he felt, on me and me alone.

He took. He gave.

He loved. He hated.

And right now, when he turned me around and stared into my eyes, without saying it, I knew, because I felt it too.

He was scared. He knew his words were fake and that I didn't believe them. Hell, neither did he, but he said them anyway. Why? Why would he make a promise when he wasn't sure if he could keep it?

He fisted my hair, keeping a tight hold on my head and making me look into his eyes. "I will get her back," he said, that deep raspy growl brushing over my skin like thousands of tiny kisses.

And there he was, the man I loved. The man I knew who would destroy everything in his path to get what he wanted most. That was the Jaron I wanted. Not the one promising me lies.

I wasn't sure anymore what was going on. What was real? What was a dream?

Voices sounded around us. Some high. Some deep. Some soft and gentle. Others rough and demanding.

Jaron placed a soft peck on my forehead before pulling from my clutches. He left the bed and began pacing.

A soft cry escaped me, and I reached out for him.

His dad, along with other club members, his brothers, with their dark eyes and jaws as hard as granite, mumbled amongst themselves.

I was vaguely aware of someone enveloping me in a hug. Who? I had no idea. It didn't matter. I couldn't take my eyes off of Jaron.

His mouth moved, talking to Cyrus and Sammy as well as the other guys standing with him. But his eyes never strayed away from mine.

Something switched between us in that moment. In the beginning, it was like we were treading water. We walked on eggshells around each other. The passion was thick, the love was intense, but the fear that something would come between us, was suffocating.

I didn't know why. I probably never would. I trusted him. I trusted him with every fiber of my very being. It was the other women I didn't trust. The quiet whispers whenever I had gone to the store. The looks and stares. The jealousy that seeped into the air every time I picked Sammy and Cyrus up from the club.

Jaron didn't trust the guys I had been with either. Even though I wanted nothing to do with them romantically. Ashton had caused problems for our other friends, so I got it. I understood Jaron's fear. Even though I had basically shoved them out of my life for no apparent reason but to wallow in my own self-pity.

Jaron said something, his words curt and to the point. He shoved the guys off of him and came back to me. He cupped my face, brushing his fingers over every crease, every line, every freckle. With each touch, he followed it with a kiss. A soft peck. A silent cry for me not to give up. Brynn wouldn't want that.

Someone cried in the distance.

I realized then that his mom had joined us.

Deep voices cursed.

Jaron stared at me. Begging. Pleading. It had only been a couple of hours since our daughter was taken, and I was already willing to stop fighting. But that part of me, the strongest part, fought with the side of me that was terrified I would never see her chubby little face again. Or kiss her fingers and toes. To watch her grow up into the amazing woman I knew she would be. To see her grow up and be an amazing big sister. She may never know her sibling.

I cupped my stomach, the tears rolling freely down my cheeks.

Hands covered my own. They were women's hands, so I knew they were Eve's, but I couldn't look up. I couldn't look into her eyes and see the pain that both Jaron and I had put there. If only we stayed home and had someone else grab us groceries. Especially when the mayor had already threatened us.

It was our fault.

AFTER US

Please God. Wherever she is, watch over her. And please give her back to us.

TWENTY-FIVE

JARON

PIECE BY PIECE, PIPER was breaking. Right in front of me and there wasn't a damn thing I could do about it. Not until I brought Brynlee home and safely tucked her back into her mother's arms.

I had pulled Ricky to the side and asked him if there was something he could give her that wouldn't harm the baby but would help her sleep. I didn't care how many favors I ended up owing him after all of this. I just needed my girls safe, healthy, and home.

He ended up giving her a light sedative that knocked her out rather quickly. I kissed her forehead, brushed my nose against hers, and whispered I loved her until I was satisfied that she would get some sort of sleep before everything continued to go down.

When I left the room, a new prospect who had just become part of Hell's Harlem and who came highly recommended by Shadow himself, came toward me. He was taller than most of the prospects and had an air about him that set me on edge.

"Cheesy," I greeted.

"Jaron." He nodded once. "I got you a phone."

"Do you have any news?" I asked, taking the phone from him.

"No but I was told to watch over your girl," he said, leaning against the wall by the door leading to the room she was currently sleeping in.

"I appreciate that, but I don't know you." Not that I wanted to be rude but after everything Piper and I had been through, Sammy and Cyrus were lucky that I even trusted them enough to watch over her when I wasn't around.

"I get it." Cheesy shoved his hands into his pockets. "I wouldn't trust me either, or anyone else for that matter, but Greyson and Shadow both told me to stand watch. So I'm just doing as I'm told."

"You can stand watch like you were told but I'm not leaving." I slid down the length of the wall until my ass hit the floor. Just then, the phone rang.

Cheesy and I glanced at each other before I looked at the small display and saw a number I didn't recognize flashing across the screen.

"Where the fuck is my daughter, Price?" I demanded, shoving to my feet.

"Now, that's not any way to talk to someone who could very well end your life."

"Where are you?" I repeated, my voice raising.

"She's safe."

"Give her back to me. You can have me instead."

He grunted, the sound grating on my nerves. "Unlikely, but I do have instructions for you. I want to see you." He listed off an address and before I could comment, he hung up. I tried calling him back, but the number had suddenly been disconnected.

"Fuck." I shoved the phone into my pocket.

"What's going on?" Cheesy asked, taking a tentative step towards me.

I looked at him then.

He brought his knees up to his chest, leaning his head against the wall behind him. A faraway look splayed on his face.

He was young but there was something deep within his eyes that showed more than he let on. I had only met him a handful of times. He had become a prospect for Hell's Harlem when I was in jail. Sammy and Cyrus briefly mentioned him and a few other new members. He was a good kid.

"Jaron."

My head whipped around, finding my dad coming down the hall toward us with Catch and Tray on either side of him.

"Price just called me and told me where he is but I don't know if Brynlee is with him." I shoved a hand through my hair. "I need to go. I need to get her back."

"Lucas was looking into things." Dad looked at Cheesy. "You taking a break?"

Cheesy cowered. "I—

"I told him I wasn't leaving Piper." I glanced back at the door. It took everything I was made of not to go back to her and pull her into my arms. But I needed to find out what was going on. I needed to go back and bring her information. I needed to meet up with Price and find our daughter.

"Fine." Dad jutted his chin. "You can leave."

Cheesy did as he was told and walked back down the hall, leaving us alone. My dad wasn't normally a dick, but this wasn't one of those times. Especially where his granddaughter was concerned.

"I need to give Piper an update," I heard myself say.

"I know." Dad's jaw clenched.

A breath left me that I didn't realize I had been holding. Placing my hands on my knees, I bent over, taking another breath and then another. "I need to give her information," I repeated.

"I know." Dad clapped my shoulder. "We'll find her."

But it was a promise he couldn't make. "You don't know that you will." I shoved away from him and opened the door leading to Piper. All breath left my lungs when I saw her sitting up. Her cheek was creased by the pillow. How much time had passed? It didn't feel like long, but it must have been. Time was lost on me as we stood around, waiting.

Waiting.

I hated fucking waiting.

Dad cupped my shoulder. "Go to her, Jaron, but don't you dare deal with this on your own."

I pushed away from him but never made any promises. Because I couldn't. There would be no point. We both knew that I was going to go after the bastards who took Brynlee, who hurt my girlfriend. The mother of my daughter and the baby currently growing inside of her.

"Jaron," she whispered.

I rushed to her, throwing myself against her small body.

She shook against me, trembling beneath my touch. "I thought it was a nightmare and then I realized it wasn't."

I fisted her hair, hugging her tight. Breathing in the faint scent of her sweet perfume, I let it soak beneath my skin, trying to give me all the strength I needed to do this. To hurt her again, because I knew that I would. I wasn't sure how she would forgive me for the things I had to do.

"Jaron," she murmured, pushing her face into my chest. "You're shaking."

"So are you," I mumbled, kissing the soft spot beneath her ear.

She shivered. "Have you heard anything?"

"No." I lifted her in my arms and sat on the bed.

Piper straddled me, holding onto me for dear life. As cliché as it sounded, I took it and welcomed her rough hold into my heart.

"What if we can't get her back?" she asked, her voice soft and unsure.

My jaw clenched, a tremor of rage coursing through my body. It rippled beneath my skin, promising pain and torture to those who wronged my girl.

"We will. We have to." I leaned back and brushed my hand through her hair, pushing it off her forehead. Her eyes shone, her cheeks red and tear-streaked. "I refuse to have it any other way, baby."

"I want to go home. I want to be by her stuff. I just..." Her chin wobbled. "I want her."

"Your parents are on their way to the clubhouse. We were waiting for you to wake up, but I'll bring you there." I realized then that it would only be the second time we would be at the clubhouse since I got home. "My dad told me that you put Brynn's stuff in my room."

Piper nodded. "I needed to be as close to you as I could. So I slept in your bed whenever I was there and there's a crib for Brynn there too." A shuddered breath left her. "I forgot to tell you."

"Don't worry about it." I gently pushed her off my lap and stood. "There's something I need you to promise me."

Piper stared up at me with those dark eyes of hers. "What's that?"

"I need you to promise that no matter what happens, you are in this for the long run. That you won't leave me."

She searched my face. "What are you talking about?"

"Promise me, Piper. Promise that you love me and are willing to stick this shit out." I wasn't making sense, I knew that, but there was no way that I could actually tell her that I was going to leave and go after the mayor myself. I knew that he had a hand in this shit. I just needed to prove it.

"Of course I'm willing to stick this out." She paused. "You're going to go after them, aren't you?"

I went to walk away when her hand caught my arm.

"You can't."

I spun on her, forcing her back a step. "I can and I fucking will."

"No." Her eyes welled. "I can't lose you too."

"You won't lose me, Piper."

"You can't make promises like that, Jaron," she screamed, shoving me. "You can't promise that nothing will happen because you don't know. You are not God."

"These bastards took our daughter," I yelled. "Our baby girl. So yeah, Piper. I am God when it comes to this shit because I hold their lives in my hands."

"Let the police do their job. Let your dad, the other guys, let them do this because I can't be without you. I need you, Jaron. I need your strength." She shook her head, tears streaming down her cheeks. "I can't. You can't. Please."

I spun on my heel, heading to the door but not before I caught the look of pure and utter agony written all over her face. I could see her heart breaking before me and I hadn't even left yet. But if hurting Piper meant I was able to get our daughter back, then I would do it and deal with her wrath later.

TWENTY-SIX

Piper

JARON WAS GOING TO leave. He was going to leave and take care of whatever and whoever took our daughter. Maybe I should have been grateful. I was sure some people would be, but not me. No. Because I knew that Jaron's temper got away from him sometimes. It was why he ended up in jail in the first place.

I didn't want him to go. I wanted others to do it for him. For us. But I knew that he wouldn't have any of that.

I just wanted to go home and curl up in his warmth and hold our daughter. I missed her. I ached for her the longer time went on where she wasn't in my arms. If I knew that she was safe and alive it wouldn't hurt so much, but I didn't. No one told me anything and it was driving me fucking crazy.

Jaron had insisted that I rest but he wasn't around to make sure that I did, so I left the lumpy bed and trudged out into the hall. I was thankful for Ricky who made sure that I was okay and also for whatever favor Jaron owed him, so we could get the blood test results back quickly.

I didn't know motorcycle clubs had setups like this. Although, I was sure that a lot didn't. Shadow, or Nero, as I liked to call him since that was his actual name and all, had been around a while. I became fast friends with his granddaughter after Sammy and Cyrus forced me to take a drive to get out of the house when I was still pregnant with Brynn.

"Piper."

I jumped, spinning around and found a young man coming down the hall toward me. I didn't know him well, but I had seen him around at Jaron's parents' place from time to time. "I'm sorry. I don't remember your name."

He gave me a small smile. "That's okay," he said, holding out his hand. "I go by Cheesy."

"Cheesy?" I asked, returning the handshake.

He chuckled, his cheeks turning a light shade of pink. "Yeah, it's dumb. When I was a kid, my parents couldn't afford a whole lot, so I brought cheese slice sandwiches for lunch quite often. I was teased about it, but truth was, they tasted good. My mom made sure to buy the best kind, even though it wasn't much. Some kids are worse off. So yeah. I got called Cheesy and it stuck."

"I like it." I pulled my hand from his and crossed my arms under my chest. "Have you seen Jaron?"

"No. Last I heard, he was with Greyson." He nodded to the room I had just come out of. "You should be resting. I was instructed to watch the door, but I'll get my ass kicked if you're not in there."

I opened my mouth to argue with him, but truth was, I had no idea if what he was saying was true or not. Jaron hadn't really been living the biker life since he came home. His dad was giving him time.

"I rested and then I got bored," I mumbled. "I need to find my daughter."

"Not happening, babe."

Cheesy's eyes snapped above my head as the deep voice boomed from behind me. "She left the room."

"Yeah." Jaron closed the distance between us. "I see that."

"*She* needs to find her daughter," I told Jaron, not caring in the least if Cheesy or any of the other guys heard our argument.

"*She* is not going anywhere." Jaron grabbed my hand, attempting to pull me toward the room, but I was having none of that shit and roughly pulled my grip from his.

"No." I went to storm past him when Jaron quickly grabbed me around the waist. He lifted me off my feet and carried me back into the room I had spent the last few hours in. "Stop. Put me down!"

Jaron ignored me and brought me to the bed.

"Jaron." I struggled out of his grip, landing hard on the bed. "You're an asshole."

"Yup. I am." He towered over me and grabbed my shoulders when I tried shoving him back. "But I'm an asshole who loves you and is looking out for you and your protection."

"I don't care about that. I need to find our daughter." I tried shoving him again, but he was too damn strong for me.

"*I* will find our daughter," he insisted, stepping closer and forcing me onto my back.

"Jaron, stop." When I went to move out from under him, he grabbed my shoulders again and pinned me down.

"You will listen to me." In a quick move, he gripped my jaw, forcing me to look up at him. "Are you going to listen?"

"Fine." I glared up at him. "I'm listening."

His jaw clenched but instead of arguing with me like I thought he would, he let out a hard sigh. "If you go after them, whoever they are, and look for Brynn, I won't be able to concentrate and do my damn job."

"What job is that?"

"To protect you, Piper." He pulled away from me. "You can't go after them because if something happened to you, it would kill me."

"And you don't think if something happened to you, that it wouldn't kill me?" I slid off the bed and went up to him. "Jaron, I can't lose you. Not when I finally found you. Not when I got you back. Not when your second baby is growing inside of me." I grabbed his hand and placed it on my stomach.

His shoulders slumped. "I need to find her," he murmured, pushing his nose against mine. It had been something he did quite often and each and every single time, it sent a wave of calm over me. "I have to, Piper. I know you don't understand."

"I *do* understand. I get it. But if it was the mayor like you think it was, he's dangerous. I can't have you going after him by yourself." I cupped Jaron's nape, pulling his mouth down to mine. "You're smarter than that."

He kissed me one last time before pulling away.

Just as I opened my mouth to yell, scream, demand for him to give me something and reassure me that he wasn't going to leave, Sammy and Cyrus came into the room.

"Sorry to interrupt," Cyrus said, sticking an unlit smoke behind his ear. "Your dad has news," he told Jaron.

Sammy looked at his brother. "That's it?"

Cyrus grunted. "What the fuck more do you want me to say?"

"How about the fact that Lucas got back to Greyson." Sammy looked at Jaron. "He did. Your dad is on a damn rampage."

My heart jumped to my throat. Was Brynn found?

Jaron looked back at me over his shoulder. He held out his hand, which I knew was a moment of truce. At least for a little bit.

I slipped my fingers in his and silently prayed that he would let the club take care of it but with the air that rolled off of him, I knew.

Jaron was on a warpath.

I almost felt sorry for the people who crossed him.

(Jaron)

Brynlee was found. Sort of anyway. We had her picture printed and passed out everywhere. Add to the fact that she wasn't even a year old yet, and the clubs would be dropping everything to make sure she was found. Shady or not, most of them had families of their own, so I prayed that they would do as they're told and bring her home to us. To Piper. I didn't overly care about me, but I *did* care about Piper. She was fighting it, but I could sense that she was losing herself and falling within.

"Where is she?" Piper demanded as we walked hand in hand down the hall toward where everyone was.

Dad was sitting in a booth with a few other guys. Catch and Tray were the only ones I knew. Cheesy walked up to them, placing a tray of beer on the table.

"Jaron." Dad stood when he saw us approach.

"Greyson, where's my baby?" Piper asked, her voice shaking.

"She was last seen at a gas station about two hours from here. She was spotted on the camera in the arms of a man." He looked at me. "We need to talk."

The hackles on the back of my neck rose. "Who the fuck was he?"

Dad's face softened. "Jaron."

"No." I could feel Piper's eyes burning into me, but I didn't care. "Tell us."

"We need to have this conversation in private." Dad went to sit back down when I charged for him.

"Tell me where the fuck she is!" I yelled, shoving him back.

In a quick move, he grabbed me by the collar and slammed me up against the nearest wall. "Careful, boy. I don't give a shit that you're my son. You put your hands on me again and I'll be bringing your mother to your funeral."

He was so damn close that I could see the specks of gold in his blue eyes. "I need my baby. For Piper," I murmured, knowing when to back down.

Dad leaned his forehead against mine. "I know, Jaron. Trust me, I know. I've been where you are. I know how you feel. I do."

I remembered when he and my mom told me about how I was taken when I was first born. I had been so focused on my own issues that I forgot that my dad could relate.

"Let's go talk." He leaned down to my ear. "I don't trust Shadow's crew." He released me, fixed my hoodie, and patted my cheek. "You are so much like me, it's unreal. But there's something you have that I don't."

"What's that?" I asked, feeling all eyes on us but the only one I cared about was Piper's.

"You have your mom's fire." Dad went up to Shadow who was sitting at the bar, watching the whole exchange. He said something to him, looking back at me over his shoulder.

Shadow nodded, standing and clapping dad on the shoulder.

"Jaron."

I looked down, finding Piper standing right in front of me. She had been so quiet this whole time, I didn't even hear her approach.

She slid her fingers in mine and started leading me out of Shadow's club.

Sammy and Cyrus followed behind us, muttering to themselves, but all I could focus on was how much I loved the woman holding my hand. How much I needed her. How I couldn't go on without her. How stupid I was for wanting to go after Brynn myself. But with the information that dad was withholding, I knew that she was with the mayor. How he played it off, I had no idea. The press would be all over him. Maybe he convinced them he adopted a baby. I wasn't sure but then a thought came to me.

"Have you seen anything in the news about the mayor or his whereabouts?" I asked the twins. "Or anything online?"

A knowing glance passed between them before Sammy pulled a pack of cigarettes from the inner pocket of his cut. He stuck a smoke between his lips and for whatever reason, that act alone sent a tremor of rage rushing through me.

Releasing Piper's hand, I stomped up to him and pulled the smoke from his lips.

He raised an eyebrow. "We gonna play, Jaron?"

"Sammy," Cyrus warned.

"What?" Sammy frowned. "He's clearly itching for a fight."

"Jaron." Piper came up beside us. "Stop. We don't want to do this here."

"You should probably listen to your girlfriend." Sammy stuck another smoke between his lips and that set me off.

I shoved him, pulled my arm back, and slammed it against his jaw.

He stumbled to the side, a slow grin spreading on his face.

"Jaron," Piper gasped.

Sammy caught his bearings and in two steps, he threw his own punch. When his fist connected with my jaw, my head rang. Pain shot up the side of my face, but it felt so damn good at the same time.

"Stop this, please!" Piper cried.

But as much as I knew this wasn't right, I couldn't stop.

"What the hell is going on?" That was said by my dad, but I still didn't stop.

Sammy and I landed blow after blow on each other. We fell to the ground, shoving and kicking. It was messy and not the least bit organized but the pain rushing through me forced these new feelings to the surface.

I was scared. No, I was damn near terrified that if something happened to Brynn, that it would be it for Piper and me. Our relationship was rocky at best. While we loved each other, we had already been through so much in such a short amount of time. I couldn't lose her.

My chest tightened, a sob of anguish lodging its way in my throat.

"Jaron." Sammy straddled my waist, clutching the collar of my hoodie.

"Fuck." I lifted a trembling hand, trying to cover my eyes. I didn't need him to see me cry. I didn't need any of them to see me break.

"Go back inside," Cyrus instructed. "There's nothing to see here."

"You heard him. Do as you're fucking told for once," Shadow barked.

Sammy slid off of me and knelt at my side. He helped me to a sitting position and wrapped his arms around me. "We'll find her."

I latched on to him, a sob finally breaking free. "I can't...I can't lose them."

"I know." Sammy squeezed me. "You won't. If it's the last thing I fucking do, I promise you, Jaron. You will not lose them."

"Jaron." Piper was suddenly beside me, her arms wrapping around my shoulders.

Sammy released me, giving me a crooked smile with his cracked lip and bloody nose.

A shuddered sigh left me. Roughly wiping the tears from under my eyes, I chanced a glance at Piper.

Her cheeks were wet.

"I'm sorry." I swiped a thumb under her eye. "I didn't mean to make you cry."

She shook her head. "Thank you."

"For what?" I asked, taken aback by her words.

"For finally breaking," she said softly.

Instead of answering, I crushed my mouth to hers. A sharp pain shot through my bottom lip, forcing me to pull back.

"I got you good, J." Sammy stood, holding out his hand.

I let him help me up, pulling Piper along with me. "Thank you for knowing what I needed."

"Anytime. I'm actually surprised it hadn't happened already." He cupped my shoulder. "We used to fight all the time."

Cyrus grunted. "That was until Aunt Eve almost kicked our asses worse than what we did to each other. Remember when Jaron had to pop his shoulder back into place?"

Sammy chuckled. "Oh yeah. I thought she was going to throw up."

"Hey." Piper turned me toward her. "You okay?"

"No." I bent at the waist and brushed my nose against hers. "But at least my nose isn't broken."

"What the fuck ever man." Sammy gently shoved me, pulling the hem of his shirt up to wipe his nose. "You're bigger than I am."

I scoffed. "Right."

"You two fuckers done fighting, so we can get this shit on the road?"

All of us turned at the sound of Shadow's deep voice as he stalked toward us. "The shit I have to clean up while my son is off doing fuck all. He's lucky I enjoy pretending that I'm still the president." He held two ice packs in his hands. My dad followed behind him with Tray and Catch on either side of him.

"We're good," was all I said. I wasn't but fighting it out, mixed with the pain from Sammy's punches, helped more than one would think.

Piper stepped closer to my side, wrapping her arm around my lower back.

I looked down at her and kissed the top of her head. "We'll find out what's going on and then go home."

"We can stay at the clubhouse," she murmured. "I just want to get out of here."

"Okay." I kissed her head again.

"You good, Son?" Dad asked me, clapping my shoulder.

"No but I will be. Both of us will be." I cleared my throat. "I'm sorry about—"

"Don't worry about it." Dad walked away. "We'll meet you at home."

Linking my fingers with Piper's, I led her to the twins' SUV. "Thank you for everything, Shadow."

"No thanks needed. You don't even owe me this time," he said, following us.

I helped Piper into the back seat before turning to him. "What's the catch?"

He grinned, scratching his jaw. "No catch." He nodded toward Piper and handed Sammy and me an ice pack each. "I like your girl."

I raised an eyebrow, the hairs on the back of my neck tingling. "Should I be concerned?"

A laugh boomed through him. "You're a jealous fucker. That's not what I meant. I like her as if she were my own granddaughter. She makes me not miss Bee so much." He shook his head. "I like them young but not that young." His laughter shook his shoulders.

"I've come over here with Sammy and Cyrus," Piper explained. "I would have a drink with him while the rest of the guys did their thing. Since he's not president anymore."

"She kept me entertained. Spent many nights talking about you, Jaron." Shadow leaned an arm on the hood of the SUV. "You don't need to worry about anything. You have Piper's heart."

I knew that but it still didn't mean that I liked the fact that he got her alone when she should have been with me. But my stupid temper got in the way and ruined everything.

"We should go," Cyrus said, his eyes flicking to mine.

"Right." Shadow closed the door, give us a two-finger salute, and headed back into the club.

"What did your dad find out?" Piper asked softly, snuggling into my side.

"I don't know." But I had a feeling that we were about to find out something that neither of us could prepare ourselves for.

No matter how much we tried.

TWENTY-SEVEN

Piper

ONCE WE REACHED THE Hell's Harlem clubhouse, I was met by both of my parents. Tears of relief streamed down my face that I had them with me, but anguish ripped through my soul just the same. I had given them their one and only granddaughter and I knew that the fact she was missing, hit close to home. My parents struggled in the beginning. Together and apart. My dad was a dick, his words, and he vowed to this day that I would end up with someone who wasn't like him.

"Daddy, I'm…" I looked down at my hands folded in my lap. *"I'm going to have a baby and the father is Jaron Mercer."*

When my father had covered my hands and gave me a small smile, I knew that it was Jaron I was meant to be with. I had dated a handful of guys, Ashton and Aiden not counting, and my dad never liked any of them. But he never questioned what I had with Jaron. Not once. I often wondered why but with everything that had gone on, I never had a chance to ask.

"Greyson told us everything," Mom said once we were inside and seated in the living room. It wasn't a spot I had been in before, since it was on the side of the house where Greyson and Eve spent most of their time. But he wanted to give us some privacy. I appreciated it. I appreciated all of it.

"I don't know what to do," I finally said. I expected the tears to continue but when they didn't, it concerned me. My pain was turning to rage and that didn't sit well with me. Jaron had gone through the same thing and was taken from me. This time, I could sense the fury in him, and I knew that he was going to go after whoever was doing this shit.

Whether I liked it or not.

"You're strong, baby." Mom wrapped her arms around my shoulders, pulling me in close.

I didn't know where Jaron was but even though he was close by, I missed him. No, correction, I ached for him. I missed his wrath, his rage, his passion as we argued.

"Where's Dad?" I asked softly.

"He's with Greyson, probably trying to figure out what the hell's going on and make it so Jaron doesn't burn the world down in the process." Mom sighed. "I never wanted this for you. I prayed for an easy life. You would meet someone, have babies, if that's what you wanted, and spend the rest of your days happy and content."

"No mother wishes this on their kid." I leaned my head against the back of the couch. "I just hate not knowing what's going on. I hate not knowing where my daughter is. I hate that this is making Jaron lose himself. I hate..." My throat closed, working hard over the lump suddenly lodged in it. "I hate what it's doing to us."

"You're strong," Mom insisted.

I jumped to my feet and began pacing. "Are we though? It's not like our relationship is conventional by any means. He went to jail before we could ever date. I had his kid by myself. And..." I cupped my stomach. "I'm going to have his second baby." A shuddered breath left me.

Warm hands covered mine. "We will help you through this."

"But I don't want help. I want my daughter back," I screamed, shoving away from her.

The door suddenly opened then, revealing Jaron. He didn't say anything. Just stared at me and probably wondered what the hell was going on and why the sudden outburst.

"I'll give you two some privacy," Mom said softly. She pulled me into a side hug.

"I'm sorry." I returned the embrace but kept my eyes locked on the man who had invaded every inch of my damn soul.

"Don't be." Mom released me, went up to him and whispered something in his ear.

He nodded.

When she left the room, finally leaving me alone with him, she shut the door behind her.

Jaron stalked toward me, closing the distance in two strides before he was on me.

"Jaron," I whimpered, my eyes welling.

"Shhh…" He held me tight, enveloping me in his strong arms.

I grabbed a fistful of his hoodie, trying to pull him even closer, but it wasn't enough. Not until we got our daughter back. Not until we could move on and finally be happy. I thought we were. Happy and all. But life was cruel and was like a kid using a magnifying glass on the ants trying to scurry away from him.

"I love you, Piper." Jaron fisted my hair, backing me up until I hit the wall.

"Stop." But even though that single word left my mouth, I couldn't push him away. It wasn't like I wanted to anyway.

"I'm not doing anything." His mouth found my cheek and then the corner of my lips before covering them completely.

I sighed, opening to him almost instantly.

The kiss picked up speed, bordering on desperation.

He pushed his pelvis into me, the hard lines of him proving how much he wanted me. How much he would always want me.

When he didn't take it further and only kissed me instead, a sob broke free.

"Let it out, baby." He licked up the saltiness of my tears, his mixing with my own.

"Jaron." I broke away from him, but I knew it was only because he let me. "I need her back."

"I know." He grabbed my hand before I could walk away for good. "We know who has her."

I stopped, spinning on him. "Why the hell didn't you lead with that?"

"Fuck, Piper." His jaw clenched. "I'm losing you. Forgive me for wanting to kiss you."

"So it could lead to more, Jaron?" I knew my accusation wasn't warranted but I was pissed, upset, hurting over the fact that someone had taken our baby girl.

"No." He pulled me back into his arms, much to my dismay of course. "Stop fighting me." He cupped my face, tilting my head back. "I kissed you because you are my strength. You are the reason that I keep fighting. You've been the damn reason all along. You are my rock, Piper."

The back of my eyes burned, my nose tingling as a new wave of anguish threatened to rip me apart. "Tell me," I whispered.

He sighed. "You know that pictures of her have been sent around. Thanks to the people my father knows, every police service in the damn country has an image of her. She was last seen at a gas station in the arms of…"

I leaned back, frowning. "Of who?"

"Price."

I gasped, pushing out of Jaron's hold. "What?"

"I'm sorry, Piper. I'm so fucking sorry. I knew he had it out for us, but I didn't think he would go through this much trouble. I should have followed my gut when I saw him the first time. I should have done more to protect you and Brynn. This is my fault." Jaron fell to his knees, wrapping his arms around my middle.

My eyes widened.

"Please forgive me."

Tears finally fell free, rolling down my cheeks and dripping off my chin.

"I'll find her. If it's the last thing I fucking do." He pushed his face into my stomach. "Please, Piper. I need you to forgive me. I need to hear you say it."

But I couldn't. Not that I knew if this could have been prevented or not but if the mayor had made threats back in the beginning and Jaron didn't take him seriously… "Did he say he was going to take her?"

"Piper, I—"

"Did he, Jaron?" I pushed out of his hold.

His shoulders slumped. "He threatened to take both of you."

Bile rose to my throat. "Did you think he was kidding?"

"What?" Jaron's eyes widened. "No." He shoved to his feet and closed the distance between us. "Not at fucking all."

"Then why the hell didn't you take us to your parents' place?" I pushed him back. "Why didn't you do something? Anything?" Sobs wracked through my body that I would never see my baby girl again. If I didn't, I wasn't sure if I could ever forgive Jaron. No matter how much he said he was sorry.

(Jaron)

She blamed me.

I got it. I did. I would probably blame me too. Maybe I wanted to call the mayor's bluff.

After Piper demanded to know why I never took the mayor seriously and brought both her and Brynn to safety, I left the room. I couldn't look at her for fear that I would do something both of us would regret.

As much as I wanted to dive deep inside her and never come out, I didn't and left her alone to her cries of anger.

Price didn't call again but as I neared the entrance to the house, I was stopped short by my dad approaching me. "I'm leaving," I told him.

"He's moving but the video footage that I've been sent, shows that Brynlee is unharmed."

That didn't make me feel better. I wouldn't be satisfied that she was in fact fine until she was back in Piper's arms. "Where is she now?" I asked, stepping around him.

"Jersey," was all Dad said. "If you go after him alone, you have to remember that it could very well end what you and Piper have." His eyes burned into the side of my head. "She needs you. I get your rage. I've been there. But if you were taken and your mom wasn't…"

"You still would have gone after me whether it tore you and Mom apart or not," I answered for him and walked away.

I knew what I had to do, and if things ended between Piper and me as a result of it, as long as our daughter was home and safe, that was all that I cared about.

TWENTY-EIGHT

JARON

I THOUGHT BACK TO before Brynn was taken and how I took everything for granted. How I assumed that Piper loved me before we even uttered those words to each other. Or how I assumed that she would always be there when she had waited for me to come home. Nothing that happened to me while I was in jail was like the pain I was currently feeling. Her love was there but it was mixed with something else just the same.

Pain. Hate. Agony.

I couldn't be sure but what I did know was that I needed to move fast. I walked around the house like a damn zombie, trying to soak up every single piece of information that I could. I needed to make my escape to go find our daughter and bring her home to her mama.

It was late in the morning and I had just checked on Piper. She was finally sleeping, although I was sure her mind was racked with nightmares that she would never see her daughter again.

The house was quiet except for the gentle murmurs of my father and a few of the other guys in the meeting room. They were still trying to figure out where the mayor was now. While I appreciated their help and what Lucas Crane, a friend of the family had done for my dad, I had a little contact of my own.

Thanks to Cyrus, Rowan Crane dug a little deeper than his father had and gave me the current whereabouts of the mayor. Not that Lucas wasn't good at what he did, but Rowan didn't fear getting caught by the law like his dad had. His words. I wasn't one to ask questions, so I took the help where I could get it.

Making my way to the back of the house, I texted Cyrus and Sammy and asked them to meet me. I knew this meeting wasn't going to end well. Sammy and I would probably get in a fight again. But it needed to happen. I couldn't sit around anymore. Not when Piper looked at me like it was my fault this happened. Maybe it was.

Stepping out into the large backyard, I let out a heavy sigh. There was a swing set that sat in the far back corner. A little house sat to the right. It was my parents' reading nook and a shed to get away when needed, so they wouldn't have to go far. That was what they said anyway but I knew that it was so they could have some privacy.

"Jaron."

My back stiffened at the sound of Cyrus and Sammy joining me in the backyard. I knew this conversation wasn't going to go over well, so I had to prepare myself for the fallout. But as much as I tried, I knew I wasn't ready.

"What's going on?" Sammy asked, walking up to an ashtray that sat in the middle of the patio table. It was a ceramic frog holding a turtle and the shell was hollowed out for the butts. It was an ugly thing, but Piper had seen two of them at a yard sale. She picked up both, gave one to my parents and kept one for herself. I only knew of this because Sammy had mentioned how ugly it was when they had come to see me in jail. It was a small thing, but I had appreciated at the time that little tidbit into my girl's life while I couldn't be with her.

"Jaron, what's up?" Cyrus came up to my side, while Sammy stood by the ashtray and lit up a smoke. He had been trying to quit, both of them had been, but we all knew it would never happen.

I had no idea what I wanted to say, let alone tell them that I was leaving. It wouldn't be for good. But it would be until I could get Brynlee and bring her home to Piper. The longer she was gone, the further Piper and I grew apart. Maybe it was selfish of me, but I needed my girl. I needed both of them. Along with the baby currently growing inside of Piper.

I caught Sammy's gaze.

He leaned against the fence, puffing on that damn cigarette.

"Jaron," Cyrus barked, pulling me back to him.

"I need you to watch Piper," I told Cyrus finally.

"The fuck?" He stiffened.

I could feel Sammy's gaze burning into me but instead of looking his way, I stared his twin down.

"Where are you going that you can't watch her yourself?" Cyrus's brows narrowed in the center. "What's going on?"

"I need to leave for a little bit." Fuck, I was thankful that Piper wasn't around. There would be no way that I could do this if she was.

"Leave. Why?" Sammy butted out his smoke and came toward us.

"I just have to." I went to walk back into the large house when a heavy hand cupped my shoulder.

"You're not leaving without explaining what the fuck's going on."

I glanced at Cyrus's hand on my shoulder, met his gaze, and waited. But he didn't budge. I knew he wouldn't. He wasn't one who backed down easily. I had learned that he got that trait from his father.

Cyrus's jaw clenched. "Explain."

"I need to find Brynlee and bring her home to her mama before I lose Piper for good." I shrugged him off. "Not that I have to explain shit to you."

"Not that you have to…" Cyrus's lips pressed into a firm line. "Listen here, Kid."

The hackles on the back of my neck rose, knowing he only referred to me as *kid* whenever he was pissed at me. It didn't happen often and when it did, it was usually warranted on my part.

"Kid." I shoved him back. "I'm your fucking VP."

"Then fucking act like it." Cyrus gripped the collar of my jacket, lifting me onto my tiptoes. "You have no idea what she went through. The screams we had to hear. The crying. The anguish. Those walls bled with her tears. Still do. And you're so damn selfish, you're going to leave because you're a fucking pussy."

"I am not a fucking pussy. I'm going to find my daughter." I waited for Sammy to step in. Cyrus was usually the levelheaded one. He kept his brother calm but when Sammy just stood back and watched, I knew that I had overstepped.

"You think going after Brynn yourself is going to make this shit better?" Cyrus shoved me back, roughly releasing me. "This will kill Piper."

"She already blames me," I confessed, not liking the bitter taste of pain on my tongue.

"She doesn't blame you." Cyrus shook his head. "For a smart guy, you're acting fucking dumb right now."

My stomach twisted.

"She's upset. Should you have brought them here when you had the first run-in with the mayor? Maybe. But you also had Sammy and I watch the house. Someone was always watching. Add to the fact that you were run off the damn road and your daughter was taken then. That is not your fault." Cyrus took a step toward me, the hard lines on his face softening. "You can't leave. Let the authorities do their job."

I scoffed. "Right. And both of us know how reliable the cops are."

"The mayor doesn't have everyone paid off," Sammy interjected. "Let your dad, Lucas, us, and everyone else help."

"They're taking too fucking long!" I yelled.

"How are you going to find Brynn?" Cyrus asked, his brows narrowing in the center.

"I've been in touch with Rowan," I said, like it was the most obvious thing in the world. My dad had been friends with Rowan's parents since before I was born. But living in different cities, we just never saw each other much over the years.

Sammy laughed, shaking his head and walking away.

Cyrus glared at his brother before meeting my gaze. "Rowan will take payment. He had a good life but is still shady as fuck."

I shrugged. "I don't give a shit about that." I would never classify Rowan as being shady. He just did whatever he could to make ends meet. Couldn't fault the guy for that.

"Fine, then we'll go with you," Cyrus said, crossing his arms under his chest.

"No." The people in this club had already lost their parents. It would kill the club if something happened to Cyrus and Sammy.

"No?" Cyrus scratched his jaw. "Yeah, you see, you don't get a say in—"

"I need you to watch over Piper and our unborn baby," I told him.

"Unborn…" Cyrus sighed. "Fucking hell."

"You can't go after these fuckers by yourself," Sammy added.

"I can. I handled it on my own in jail, I'll handle it on my own outside of it." I wasn't taking no for an answer. They could fight me all they wanted.

"We wouldn't know, Jaron. You haven't told us shit about your time in jail. Whenever we went to see you, you redirected the conversations to Piper." Cyrus raked a hand through his jet-black hair. "You haven't said shit since you've been back, and you've been back for weeks. Hell, Brynn is almost a year old. If I was Piper, I would have left your ass long ago."

"Fuck you." I charged for him, getting in his face. "You don't know what I had to do to survive. She's safer without me here anyway. The mayor—"

"You leaving is not going to keep her safe. It's what they want." Cyrus tapped my temple. "Use your damn head, Jaron."

I slapped his hand away, pushing him back. "Doesn't matter. You can say whatever you want but it's not stopping me." I went to walk by him when his next words stopped me.

"So this is it."

I paused, slowly turning back around. "She deserves better. You have to know that."

"No." Sammy stepped in front of his brother. "We don't because all we see is how she looks at you. We heard her cry herself to sleep. You don't know the pain she went through. And when she found out she was pregnant. Jaron, that pain was raw. She was alone even though she had all of us."

Guilt resonated on my shoulders over everything that I had done but it didn't matter. I needed to find Brynn and if something happened to me, Piper would be better off anyway. She would be safer.

"Piper needs you. This unborn baby needs you," Cyrus added. "We didn't grow up with parents. Look at how we turned out."

"Hey." Sammy smacked his brother's shoulder. "I turned out just fine."

"Brynlee needs me too." I wouldn't rest until I had her back in Piper's arms. Even if I died trying, knowing that my daughter was safe was all that mattered. . Piper would be pissed, angry, hurt, enraged. So many different feelings would course through her. I knew because I felt them too. But she would get over it. She had to. I wouldn't have it any other way.

(Piper)

I no longer had a sense of time. When I saw the look of agony on Jaron's face after I demanded to know why he never brought Brynlee and me to his parents to keep us safe, I knew that I had fucked up. My mouth had gotten the better of me and made it seem like I blamed him. Did I? No. Not really. I couldn't even be sure anymore. But what I did know was that I needed him. I needed our daughter. I just needed us to go home and move on. I knew the mayor had it out for Jaron, but I never expected him to go this far.

Jaron had tucked me safely in his bed. It was on the tip of my tongue to ask him to make love to me in it. To distract me and himself. Even if it was just for a moment. But those words never left my lips as he backed up and slowly left the room.

I cried myself to sleep then. I couldn't help it. I could already feel him pulling away. He was going to go after the mayor. I knew because it would be what I would do if I knew exactly where he was. And if I wasn't pregnant.

A light but firm knock sounded on the door. My heart jumped.

"Come in," I called out, sitting up.

The door slowly opened, revealing Cyrus and Sammy.

A hard sigh left me at the sight of them. "When did he leave?" I heard myself ask.

"How did you know?" Cyrus asked, leaning against the wall.

Sammy came into the room and went to the window. He opened it and lit up a smoke. "She knows him, that's how."

"He's going after him. The mayor." I couldn't even cry, I was so damn furious. It was like this newfound rage coursing through me, closed up my tear ducts.

"He is, kiddo," Cyrus said gently.

"And neither of you could have gone with him?" I asked, my voice a little more curt than I had intended.

Sammy muttered a curse.

Cyrus's jaw clenched. "We tried but he wouldn't let us. He asked us to take care of you."

"Well it seems to me that you should have been keeping me and my daughter safe and that hasn't happened. She's missing. Remember?" I regretted it as soon as I said it.

Cyrus flinched. "That's not fucking fair."

"I know." I shook my head. "I know. I'm sorry. He didn't even say goodbye. He just left. What if I don't see him again? What if something happens and he's taken from me? What if he just gives up on us? What if..." A sob broke free, tears finally filling my eyes. "What if he leaves me because he can't handle it?" I dropped my head in my hands, covering my face and letting the cries wrack through my body. All of the emotions weighed heavily on my shoulders, making them shake and tremble.

The bed dipped in front of me and I could only assume that it was Cyrus. He was the hugger between the two of them. Sammy not so much. He didn't like being touched. It made me wonder why when he'd had a damn good childhood. Both of them did. Even though they lost their parents and I could appreciate the pain and anguish they had felt and still felt, it made me wonder if something else had happened.

"You have no reason to apologize." That was Cyrus.

I looked up, being met by his dark eyes. Sammy still stood by the window, puffing on his smoke. His jaw clenched and unclenched but he wouldn't meet my gaze. He was probably as pissed as I was.

"Did he say when he would be back?" I asked softly.

"He'll be back when he has your daughter in his arms, Piper. He couldn't wait anymore. His contact told him where she was, and he went after her." Cyrus stood and began pacing. "I've always known something was shady about the mayor, but I never knew what. We tried proving that he was operating an underage strip club but couldn't pin anything on the bastard."

Sammy only grunted.

"What about Greyson? What about the other guys? Do they know that Jaron went off by himself?" None of this made sense. No bike club would let someone fight a battle by themselves. They were like a brotherhood. I had seen that over the years with my mom and her sisters from the King's Harlots. I had seen that with Shadow's club. They must know that Jaron left.

Cyrus stopped pacing, his dark eyes locking with mine. "We were asked to keep this to ourselves."

Sammy muttered another curse, slamming the window shut. "Why the fuck are we even listening to him? He's been selfish this whole time and we haven't seen…" He shook his head. "It doesn't matter."

"But it does matter." I slid out of bed and went to the door. "You two can come with me if you want but I will tell Greyson that his son left." I lifted my hand when Cyrus and Sammy both took steps toward me. "Try and stop me and I will tell him that it was your idea for Jaron to leave." I left the room, not waiting for them to respond. Knowing they would follow, I went to the one source who I knew could find Jaron and bring him and our daughter home.

Before it was too late.

TWENTY-NINE

JARON

WHEN I WAS A BOY, I spent most of my time going through the motions. I was searching for something, but I didn't know what. It could have been anything really. A new hobby. A new class at school. Maybe even a new friend. I had grown up around the same people. Saw them day in and day out. We spent so much time together, we would fight for no apparent reason. It drove my mom crazy and my dad and the rest of the guys would only laugh and shrug it off. *Boys will be boys*, they always said.

Sammy and Cyrus were the brothers I never had. They were older than me and I looked up to them with so much damn respect, I always felt guilty that I had both of my parents when they had neither of theirs.

They never said anything about it, but I could sense the longing. Although my dad took them under his wing, as did the other guys in the club, it wasn't the same. I knew that. They knew that, even though they would deny it if asked.

It wasn't fair. They didn't have their dad to teach them how to throw their first ball or give them tips for their first date. They didn't have a father who would tell them to man up and stop being a pussy when it came to the women they secretly loved. I wasn't sure if there was anyone in Cyrus's life, but I knew there was someone in Sammy's. He had become grumpier over the past few months. I found that I couldn't wait to meet her, knowing that no other woman had ever caused him to react this way.

While the twins had my dad, Tray, Catch, and a few of the other guys within the club, I knew it wasn't the same.

I had never been jealous of their closeness with my dad, knowing what they had been through as children. Luckily for me, I didn't remember any of it as I was just a newborn when Butcher and Trixie died. But I could feel the pain. The walls of the clubhouse wept with silent cries as vacant memories of their deaths still resonated in the air.

Sammy never went upstairs or down the hall with the pictures on the walls. Maybe in time he would. Cyrus did and then he fell into a bottle shortly after. It had been the same routine for the past few years.

See the pictures.

Drink a bottle.

Or fuck. A lot.

I tried not to let the guilt consume me, but it was hard not to. Especially when I had my parents, and they didn't. Although they never lacked in family, there had still been something missing.

Before I left the clubhouse, I made Cyrus and Sammy promise that they would look after Piper and that they wouldn't follow me. I knew as soon as Piper found out I had left, she would want to come after me. I just prayed that the twins prevented that shit from happening. She was carrying our second baby. I didn't need anything happening to either of them.

Now that I had a family of my own, I fucked up and took advantage of it. That had been what it felt like anyway.

Whenever Brynlee had looked at me, it was like I was the only one who mattered in her little world. If I had it my way, I would be the only man she would ever love, but I knew that it was unreasonable to think that way. When the time came, I would deal with it then but first, I had to find her. I had to bring her home to her mama.

I shouldn't have left like I did but I needed to avenge our daughter. I would get her back and if I lost Piper in the process, at least Brynlee would be safe in her arms. I would hold my head proud as long as my girls were together.

If I made it out of this alive, I would be lucky. I would then have to deal with Piper's wrath. My body buzzed at the mere idea of fucking each other because we were furious. It would happen. In time. And I couldn't wait.

It had been several hours since I left the clubhouse. Even longer since I left Piper in my bed. I was now sitting in the parking lot of a motel a couple of hours away. But it didn't make sense. Rowan had told me that Price was on the move, but he was heading back in the direction of the town Piper and our friends had grown up in. Did he want to get caught? Did he want to face my full wrath head on? I wasn't sure, but what I did know was that I needed to see that Brynn was, in fact, okay.

It was now later into the night, well past Brynlee's bedtime but if my contact was correct, Price was staying in one of these rooms. My phone dinged and buzzed every so often. When I started getting messages that my father and some of the crew were on their way, I put my cell away. There was no point in arguing with them. The only thing I had asked was if Cyrus and Sammy were joining them and when I got back a *no*, I ignored the rest of the messages. I owed them. I owed them everything. I was thankful that they cared enough about Piper to look out for her and our unborn baby. But I had to do this. Without them. Our family, even though we weren't all blood, had lost a lot over the years. It would kill them if they lost the twins too. So they had to stay home because I refused to be the reason they died.

A sudden movement in front of me, caught my eye. I was hidden in the shadows across the street of the motel. So I knew I wouldn't be seen. My bike was parked a block away. It was close enough that I could run for it if I needed to. Or that was what I liked to tell myself anyway. In all reality, I was strung out. I shouldn't have done this alone, but I didn't want any more blood on my hands. What I did in jail and the guys I had killed was enough.

A door to one of the rooms on the second floor opened. I thought I was prepared for whatever happened but when I saw a man come out of the room with a small child in his arms, all breath left my lungs.

My knees shook.

My daughter – Piper's daughter – was only a few yards away. It had felt like an eternity since I had seen Brynlee. Even though I couldn't see for sure that it was her from where I was standing, everything in my gut said that it was her along with the jackass that called himself the mayor of a fucked up town.

"Baby girl," I whispered, my feet carrying me forward.

I scanned the area around us. Nothing was out of the ordinary, but it didn't mean that Price didn't have his men standing close by. It made me wonder why he didn't have a few walking with him.

My feet carried me forward another step before I could stop myself when a sound suddenly came from behind me. I stopped, slowly turning my head to look over my shoulder. When I realized that no one was behind me, I took a deep breath and jogged across the street to confront Price himself.

As he was nearing a car, his head snapped up. A slow grin spread on his face, when it dawned on him who was coming toward him.

When Brynlee looked my way, she cried out, struggling in his arms.

He scowled, moving Brynlee to his other arm and holding her tight. That single movement pissed me off.

"Give me back my daughter," I bit out, not liking the sudden cries coming from her.

"You going to give me something in return?" Price placed a soft peck on her forehead, keeping his eyes locked with mine. "She smells so good. I could get a lot of money for her. She would be conditioned and trained. She wouldn't know the difference and would spend her life as a slave."

"You can have me." I took another step forward. The closer I got to my daughter, the harder my heart raced. I just needed to get her away from him. My car wasn't far. I could make it. I *had* to make it.

"Why, Jaron. Do you have a pussy?" Price paused. "Didn't think so. Men don't get me much money, so as much as I appreciate the offer, it's not happening."

"Why the fuck are you doing this? Is it because of Brody? Is it because you just hate bikers in general? What is it, Price?" I didn't give a shit how desperate I sounded. Now that I had my daughter in my line of sight, there was no way that I was letting him leave with her.

"Why am I doing this?" Price nodded once, his gaze moving past me.

The sound of a gun being cocked, sent a tremor of unease rushing through me.

Brynn started crying, trying to get out of his arms.

Price ignored her, hugging her even tighter against him.

As I stared down the man who had taken the other love of my life, I realized that seeing Piper earlier that morning could have been the last time I saw her. I should have told her I loved her. I should have made love to her one last time. I should have had a conversation with the baby currently growing inside of her. I should have done a lot of stuff, but I didn't. Instead, I let my anger get the best of me once again and left.

Knowing whoever was behind me was working with Price, I didn't bother to turn around. Instead, I crossed my arms under my chest and leaned against the side of his car. "You still doing the mayor thing? Kidnapping a baby doesn't look too good in the public eye you know."

Price's jaw clenched, a dark shadow passing over his face. Looked like I hit a nerve. "How did you find me?"

"Well, it wasn't like you tried very hard to hide. Did you want to get caught?" None of it made sense. Price knew people. He had his hands in everyone's pockets. The fact that he had remained out in the open and didn't even bother to put on a hat or sunglasses to disguise himself, was odd.

"I wanted you to find me," Price finally said.

I was taken aback by his words. "Why?"

"I was hoping you would have brought that sweet little thing with you but of course, you actually have to be a good guy and leave Piper at home. Where she's safe." Price sneered. "For now anyway. Think those twins don't want her though? I know she's been with other brothers. Seems like she has a type. Think you can satisfy her? There's only one of you, Jaron. Piper's a slut who needs more than one dick at a time to satisfy her needs."

My back stiffened at his words, rage coursing through me. "Fuck you."

Price chuckled. The smile suddenly fell from his face. He nodded once.

Something hard pressed against the back of my head, the sound of a gun cocking exploding through me.

"Knees," Price demanded.

My jaw clenched but I did as I was told and lowered to the ground.

"Good boy." Price chuckled. "Maybe I can get something for you after all." He opened the back door of the car and placed Brynlee in the back seat.

"No." My heart started racing. "Please. Kill me. Whatever you want to do. Just give Brynn back to Piper."

Price looked from the guys standing behind me, down to me, and back to them. "Fine."

"How do I know you'll do it?" I was grasping at straws, but Brynn needed to go back to her mom. I didn't care about me. I would do anything. I would die first before letting something happen to either of them.

"I guess you'll never know." Price shut the back door of the car. "Kill him."

The last thing I heard was a gunshot going off before everything went black.

THIRTY

GREYSON

WHEN I WAS TOLD by Piper that my son had done something stupid and went after the fucker who took his daughter, I couldn't say I blamed him. At all. But I still didn't like it. Especially when his mom found out and I had to watch her shatter in my arms again because of her son's temper. Or the fact that it brought us back to a dark time in the beginning of our relationship where I almost lost them both.

I channeled that anger, the rage that my son felt, and let it be the driving force behind my actions. Eve knew I was going after Jaron. But I did my best to reassure her that I would bring him home along with our granddaughter. I had to. For her and for Piper.

I respected the hell out of Piper Michaels. Knowing that she could have left Jaron long ago, and never did. Even though in the beginning, things had never been official, I felt their love for each other even before I found out that she was carrying my second grandbaby. The twins let it slip and it only made me need to find

Jaron more. This shit needed to end and the only way that could happen, was by putting a bullet between Price's eyes.

I wasn't sure why he had it out for my son. Even before Jaron killed Brody for attacking Piper, Price always hated him the most.

"Boss." Catch, my former vice president before my son took over that role, came up to me and pinched the bridge of his nose. "Jaron isn't here." He dropped his arm to his side and looked back at the motel. "We searched the room, and no one is in there. We even talked to the staff. The one maid recognized Price but didn't see him with a baby, so she never called it in."

"Fuck." We had gone to the last known address that Price and Brynlee had been seen at, but it meant shit when they were no longer there, and neither was Jaron. "We have to find them."

"I know." Catch went to put his phone to his ear when something inside of me snapped.

I slapped the phone out of his hand and grabbed him by the collar of his leather cut.

"Greyson." His eyes widened.

Bodies surrounded us, my men, guys I had known for years. Guys who were my family. They were my life besides my wife, son, and now grandbabies. Even Piper held a special spot in my heart because of the love she had for my boy. But for whatever reason, the fact that Catch thought he knew shit, pissed me off.

"You need to find my son and granddaughter," I bit out through clenched teeth. My voice was so low, even I didn't recognize it. "If you don't." I looked out at the men surrounding us. "If any of you don't bring them back to safety, I will kill you and your families. You hear me?"

They shifted but nodded and muttered their agreements.

"Do you hear me?" I asked Catch.

He swallowed hard but nodded.

Smart guy.

I released him roughly and pulled my phone out of my back pocket. I knew it wasn't my men's fault. They didn't take my granddaughter. They didn't make Jaron disappear. But if I couldn't bring them home, I was going to lose my wife and future daughter in-law.

When I dialed the number of the one person I knew I could trust and find out what I needed to know, I walked away from my men.

"Why, Greyson. I was just talking about you."

I stopped walking. "You are not who I called."

"Well, luckily for you, I have my dad's phone and decided to answer for him. 'Cause I am a nice guy and all."

I rolled my eyes. Rowan Crane was the epitome of his dad. No matter what happened, Lucas would always walk this earth as long as his son was around.

"Fine, you'll do I guess," I muttered.

Rowan chuckled. "Aren't you sweet? I really have no idea how you landed a nice lady like Eve."

"As much as I enjoy this banter, I need answers. I can't find my son."

"Shit. I thought it was just Brynlee who was missing?" The humor quickly left and was replaced with the serious side of Rowan. While his parents were experts when it came to computers, Rowan liked to venture a little deeper. He enjoyed teetering on the edge of the law and what was considered morally sound, just to see if he could get caught. One of these days it was going to backfire on him. I would love to be a fly on the wall when that happened and his mom kicked his ass.

"It was and then my son found her location thanks to you and now he's missing as well."

"He called me asking for help, so if you want it as well, you'll refrain from accusing me of shit. Got it?"

I let out a slow breath, trying to ease my racing heart. "Yeah. I got it."

"Good." I heard the sound of keys clicking in the background. "Um...Greyson?"

"What?" My back stiffened as my guys approached me with caution.

"I was able to hack into the security cameras at the motel. Surprisingly, for a shitty establishment, they have a good system, and the picture is crystal clear."

"What aren't you telling me?" I asked, needing to know what the hell was going on.

"Jaron approached Price, who was holding your granddaughter. A couple guys came up behind Jaron and it looks like something spooked them but..."

"What?" I demanded.

"I think Jaron was shot," Rowan said gently. "It was probably why they didn't shoot him in the head. Something startled them."

"Do you see them take him?" Red clouded my vision, my throat working over a hard lump. If Jaron was gone...

Catch came up to me, clapping my shoulder. That single touch alone calmed some of the nerves rushing through me.

"No. This shit is fucked up. Greyson," Rowan continued. "Price placed Brynn on the ground, and they left. Just like that."

"So they're here," I told him. "They have to be."

"That's what it looks like, but the video cuts out after that. They must have seen the cameras. I don't know. Greyson, it doesn't look good. Jaron dropped and was unmoving. He..."

"Thank you, Rowan." I disconnected the call and turned to my men. "Jaron and Brynlee are still here. Find them. Please for the love of God, I need you to find them. Not for me. But for Eve and Piper."

"We will." Catch gripped my shoulder, gave it a squeeze, and went to walk away when I caught his arm.

"Listen, I'm—"

"Don't." Catch shook his head. "I would have reacted the same way. We'll find them."

A sharp scream had our heads turning toward the noise. A maid was backing up out of a room on the second floor.

The closer we got to her, the harder my heart raced.

"Ma'am." Catch went up to her as Tray went into the room, followed by Cheesy and another prospect, Jamie Locke. A couple of other guys joined them. "Tell us what happened."

"Blood. So much blood." Her chin wobbled, not even mentioning anything about the fact that it was bikers going into the room unannounced.

Tray came out a moment later. "It's Jaron."

"What?" I rushed past him into the room. "Where is he?"

"Greyson, wait," Tray called out, but I ignored him.

The room wasn't overly big, so Jaron couldn't be very far. Where the hell was my son?

That was when I saw Locke and Cheesy in the bathroom. Cheesy was crouched down by an unmoving body.

All blood drained from me, leaving me ice cold as I closed in on them.

When I neared the door to the bathroom, the scene before was like it came right out of a horror movie. Cheesy and Locke stepped aside as I entered the small room. Jaron was lying on the ground in a pool of blood. Another guy was in the bathtub with the shower curtain and rod on his lap. His dead vacant eyes stared back at me, sending a shiver down my spine.

But what bothered me most by the whole situation in front of me, was Brynlee lying beside Jaron. She had a pig soother in her mouth and was covered in blood. But she stared up at me and was sucking on that thing like her life depended on it.

"I searched the body and didn't find anything," Cheesy told me.

I crouched by my son and picked Brynlee up. Using my shirt, I wiped the blood off of her face. Jaron was not moving but I could see the faint rise and fall of his chest.

"Boss, I called for an ambulance," Catch said from behind me.

"Cheesy, your dad still a cop?" I asked, reaching out to check my son's pulse.

"He is," Cheesy answered. "I'll make a call."

"Alright, Jaron. You need to stay with me. Help is on the way." I wasn't sure where he was bleeding from, but I didn't want to move him in case there were other injuries I didn't know about.

Brynlee pulled the soother from her mouth, drawing my attention back to her.

I hugged her against me and kissed her head.

"Dada."

My chest tightened, a lump forming in my throat. "Yes, baby girl. That's your daddy."

Brynlee looked up at me with her big gray eyes. "Dada." Her eyes welled.

I cupped the back of her head and cradled her into my chest. My stomach twisted, a sharp exhale leaving me as a wail left my granddaughter.

THIRTY-ONE

Piper

DEPRESSION HAD SETTLED IN rather quickly. I stayed in Jaron's room at the clubhouse while Cyrus and Sammy remained close by. It was probably to make sure that I didn't do something stupid. I didn't know because I didn't ask. I stayed in the bedroom. The scent of his cologne lingered in the room. The smell was faint, but it helped ease some of the anxiety rushing through me.

I didn't know where he was. No one told me anything. He had gone after Price. Some of the guys had followed him but I didn't know anything more than that. Had they found him yet? Had they found Brynn?

Time was lost on me the longer I didn't have my daughter and the man I loved in my arms. I was pissed at him, but I got it. I did. I was mad with the way we left things. He probably thought I blamed him. A part of me did at first. I couldn't help but admit it. But that didn't matter. I got over it and just wanted my little family home safe and sound.

I slept off and on, crying myself to sleep only to wake up from a nightmare that I would never see Brynn or Jaron again. I kept dreaming that I could see them but no matter how much I ran toward them, I could never catch them. It made me wake up in a cold sweat with tears streaking my cheeks.

This pain was nothing like when Jaron was in jail. At least then I knew he was alive because Cyrus and Sammy told me so. But now they couldn't tell me anything because they didn't know themselves. I had told them to go with the guys to find Jaron, but they refused. They made a promise and no matter what happened, they planned on keeping it.

I cupped my stomach, praying that my unborn baby could survive this stress resting on my muscles. I tried swallowing my emotions, so the baby wouldn't feel it, but I couldn't.

Be strong, little one. Please be strong.

One morning, I was restless. I wasn't sure how much time had passed since I last held my daughter or seen Jaron. Maybe a day. Maybe more. I wasn't sure. No matter how much I tried to sleep, I couldn't. So instead, I took a shower, got dressed, and went to see if Cyrus and Sammy had any news for me. But before I could ask any questions, I was stopped short by several members of Hell's Harlem filling the vast room on the main floor of the clubhouse.

Cyrus and Sammy were talking to the guy I had come to know as Cheesy. Sammy caught my gaze and came toward me.

"What's going on?" I asked, my heart racing hard.

"Jaron and Brynlee have been found," he said gently.

"What?" My eyes widened. "Where are they?"

"At the hospital. The guys only just showed up here or else we would have woken you up sooner," Sammy explained. "Brynlee is fine. There are no injuries. Price didn't hurt her."

"Oh." I latched on to his arm to keep from falling. "Thank God."

"But…" Sammy looked back at his crew.

"What is it?" I gripped his arm tight. "Tell me. Please. I can handle it."

Sammy looked down at me. "Jaron was shot. He was in surgery last we heard."

"I…" My chest tightened, tears streaming down my cheeks. "Take me to the hospital. Please."

"Stay here in case Greyson needs you," Cyrus instructed the guys. "We need to stick together until this shit dies down."

"Let's go, kiddo." Sammy hooked his arm around my shoulders and led me out of the house.

"Let's go see your daughter and Jaron." Cyrus stood back. "I'll join you in a moment."

"Sammy." I turned to him when we stopped at his SUV. "Tell me how bad it is."

He searched my face before letting out a hard sigh. "I don't know. Greyson said there was security footage showing Price holding Brynlee. Jaron approached them and guys came up behind them. Brynn is fine but she was found lying beside Jaron. She was covered in blood."

"God." I shivered, bile rising to my throat. "I'm glad she's young enough that she won't remember this."

"Same," Sammy said as Cyrus joined us.

We filed into the SUV with me in the back and the guys in the front. Cyrus drove like he usually did.

"Who shot Jaron?" I asked.

"One of Price's men but he was found dead in a tub in a motel room," Cyrus explained. "But we don't know how Jaron got into the motel room. The footage shows Price leaving in a car. Unfortunately, the car didn't have a license plate."

"Of course," I mumbled.

"We'll find Price and he will pay for what he's done, Piper," Sammy said, his voice taking on an edge that made my stomach twist. I could feel the rage coursing through him. Through both of them actually, but Sammy's anger set me on edge.

"Is Jaron going to make it?" I heard myself ask.

"I don't know, darling." Cyrus's eyes met mine in the rearview mirror. "But whatever happens, we'll protect you."

"Oh, we should tell you that your parents are staying at the clubhouse for a few days," Sammy pointed out.

My eyes widened. "What? Why?"

"It's safer there and more secluded. I'm sure they won't have to stay there for long but after your dad talked to Greyson, they both agreed it would be best. And we don't know what's going on with Price. He's no longer the mayor according to the media. They're saying he's on leave due to personal reasons." Sammy scoffed. "Right. We've always known he was a fucker, but we didn't know how far that went until now."

"Having a bar that underage girls work at, proves he's sick in the head." I shivered at the thought.

"Yeah, that's only part of it, kiddo." Cyrus pressed a foot on the gas. "But don't worry about that shit. We'll take you to your daughter and hopefully we can get an update on Jaron as well."

I nodded, sitting back in the seat. I was on edge, my nerves racing and jumping through me. I was vibrating with excitement that I would get to see my daughter again. To hold her, smell her baby scent, to have her back in my arms and never let go. It wasn't rational to think that, but I would keep her to myself at least for a few more years.

"We're here," Sammy said gently.

Hesitation coursed through me when I looked out at the large building. I wanted my baby girl back in my arms but then I also worried about how I would react when I saw Jaron. No one told me how he was actually doing. Just that he was shot, and he was fighting. No more details were said.

The door opened, revealing Sammy. "Come on, kiddo. They need you. Jaron..." His jaw clenched.

"Sammy?" I whispered.

Cyrus joined him, clapping his shoulder. "He'll make it through this."

Sammy shoved away from him. "You don't know that." Spinning on his heel, he stomped away.

My eyes welled, my chest constricting over the thought of losing Jaron. "Cyrus, I..."

"I know." He held out his hand. "Give Sammy time. Jaron's like our little brother, so it's...hard." When his voice cracked, a sob escaped me. "Shit."

I covered my face, letting the cries shake through me.

"Piper." Cyrus reached into the back seat and pulled me out of the vehicle and into his arms. "He's a strong, stubborn fucker. He's going to make it through this. He has to."

I latched on to him, the scent of his leather cut wafting into my nose. While the smell was familiar, it wasn't Jaron.

"Come. Everyone is here, including your parents. You need them and so does Jaron." Cyrus wrapped his arm around my shoulders, closing the door behind me and leading me to the front doors of the building.

I was like a zombie, walking with him. Both he and his brother had been good to Brynlee and me. I remembered back to when Sammy first held Brynn. He was gentle with her. It shocked me at first because there were rumors that he had a violent streak. Whenever I had picked them up from Rouge after they had too many drinks, I had seen the women fawning over Sammy. But he would either give them a look or mutter something in their ear that would make them slap him or run off crying.

"Do you think Sammy will ever find his person?" I asked, my voice weak and hoarse.

Cyrus looked down at me. "You don't worry about that shit, darling."

"I just want you both happy," I murmured.

"And we love you for that, but you know Sammy. He's struggling. He won't admit it, but he is. It'll take a strong woman to put him in his place and not back down when he gets in one of his moods." Cyrus shook his head. "But enough of that. You have more important things to worry about than our love lives."

"It's distracting." But before I could say anything more on the subject, we reached the floor where I could only assume Brynlee was.

"This way." Cyrus led me down the hall. "Your dad texted me that they were here with her."

"You texted my dad?" I asked, my head whipping around.

Cyrus gave me a small smile. "Ever since Jaron went to jail, kiddo. I got your parents' cell numbers and gave them mine in return. So did Sammy."

"How come?"

"Because Jaron asked us to take care of both you and Brynn. His girls." Cyrus nodded once. "They're this way."

As we continued down the hall, I kept thinking over Cyrus's words. I wasn't sure why I was surprised that the twins had my parents' numbers. Looked like they took Jaron's request and ran with it.

When we neared a room at the end of the hall, I could hear voices. My dad's deep one along with my mother's higher pitched voice. They were talking to someone.

Once I stood at the entrance to the room, I took a deep breath and let it out slowly. A part of me kept thinking that my daughter actually wasn't here, and that Price still had her but when everyone glanced my way and my eyes landed on her, a sob broke free from my lips and I ran toward her.

THIRTY-TWO

Piper

SHE WAS BACK IN my arms. My daughter. I didn't know I could love someone as much as I loved Jaron. Not until I held Brynlee in my arms for the very first time. What would have made it better was if Jaron had been there, but he was making up for it. He loved her. I could see it. With the way he looked at her, spoke to her, interacted with her. She was his world and this second baby, would be as well. We were his life.

Please, Jaron, fight to come back to us. We need you.

"How are you doing, sweetheart?" Mom asked, running her hand over Brynlee's head.

"Now that I have my daughter back, I'm better but…" I still couldn't stop thinking about Jaron and how he was fighting for his life.

"Jaron's strong." Mom kissed the side of my head. "I'm glad you both are safe. We'll keep praying for Jaron."

"Thank you," I whispered, my eyes welling.

Brynlee was sleeping against me, with her soother in her mouth and her stuffed pig in her arms. She was safe.

I had learned that after the guys found Jaron at the motel, Greyson brought Brynn to the hospital to get checked out. Thankfully, she was completely fine, and Price never hurt her. The hospital staff cleaned her up from the blood she was covered in. My mom had told me that she brought a change of clothes for her, so she wouldn't have to stay in the bloodied clothes. I still couldn't believe Price had left her that way. I knew he was beyond evil but it made me wonder why he didn't just take her with him instead.

We were now sitting in the waiting room that was supposed to be for family members only but held most of the Hell's Harlem members that were from this area. The hospital staff only said once that they had to leave. When the guys stood and stared at the young male nurse without even saying anything, the nurse left rather quickly. It had been amusing and something I never expected to see.

When my mom left my side to join my dad, Sammy and Cyrus sat on either side of me. I realized then that it had been something they did quite often. Even if we were standing, Cyrus was usually on my left and Sammy on my right. I never noticed the routine until now.

"Thank you," I blurted.

All heads turned my way. I looked out at the faces before me. Most I had seen before and met at least once.

Jaron's parents were off to the side.

My parents were beside them.

They had been talking amongst themselves before I spoke.

Clearing my throat, I shifted in the hard seat beneath me. "I just wanted to thank you all. For being here for Jaron."

"We're here for you too, darling," Tray said from the other side of the room. His hand was clasped in his wife's. Zillah smiled at me, her eyes sad.

A shuddered breath left me. "I need to see him," I said low enough for only Cyrus and Sammy to hear.

"I know." Cyrus stuck an unlit smoke behind his ear. "Sammy."

"Not leaving her," Sammy muttered, stretching his legs out in front of him.

"Fine. I'll talk to the doctor and see if I can get more information on...yeah." Cyrus cleared his throat, leaning over and kissing the top of Brynn's head. "I'm glad you're home safe, little one." He stood, signaled for Cheesy and Locke to follow him and they left the room.

"I'm going to kill Price," Sammy muttered, crossing his arms under his chest.

My head whipped around but he never met my gaze.

"Greyson has tried keeping our noses clean. Jaron did what he had to do in jail to survive but still remained out of trouble as best he could. Price has gone too far this time and if Grey and Jaron won't..." Sammy's jaw ticked. "I'm going to take care of him, so Jaron doesn't have to. He needs to behave for you. His family."

"Sammy, you—"

"He's done a lot of shit, Piper. A lot. Things that he needs to die for. I have no idea how he even became mayor in the first place. Clearly, he's paid off everyone to cover his tracks, but he doesn't know that I know people too." Sammy looked at me then. "I'm going to uncover all of his dirty little secrets and make him fucking pay for hurting you and Jaron. For hurting the other girls and women. I will avenge you. All of you." His head turned back to the front and I realized then that the conversation was over.

Before I even had a chance to respond, a man dressed in white, came into the room. He was looking at a clipboard in his hands. He was young with dark hair and features, but you could see the lines in his face from the stress his job had given him.

"Mrs. Mercer?" he finally asked, looking up then. His eyes widened a bit as he saw all of us sitting or standing around in the waiting room.

"Yes?" Eve stood up, keeping her hand locked in her husband's.

The doctor frowned, looked down at his clipboard and back at us. "Piper?"

Eve gasped.

301

My eyes widened. "W-What?"

"Are you Piper?" The doctor asked me.

"I am." I stood, holding Brynlee tight against me. I could feel all eyes burning into me over the doctor referring to me as Jaron's wife.

"I'm Dr. Rainn. Will you step out into the hall with me please?" Dr. Rainn asked, looking past me.

"No. You can tell me here," I insisted. "This is Jaron's family."

"Fine." He looked back down at me. "Jaron was shot twice. Once in the abdomen and once in the shoulder. His right kidney was severely damaged and had to be removed. His liver, stomach, and intestines were also hit. The wound in the shoulder didn't hit anything vital and both surgeries went well. But he has a long road ahead of him as we now have to worry about infection—"

"But he's alive?" Eve asked, coming up to my side.

"Yes, ma'am. He is alive. You can see Jaron now, but I will warn you, he isn't awake."

I nodded, looking back at Jaron's parents.

"Let me take Brynn," my mom said, coming up to me. "I know you just got her back a few hours ago but..."

"No, I...I know she's young, but I don't want her to see her daddy like that." Or for her to see me break down. "Thank you, Mom." I looked at my dad who was still sitting by the far wall. "And Daddy."

He nodded once.

"We love you, sweetheart." Mom took Brynlee from my arms and kissed my cheek. "Now go see Jaron. He's going to need you."

I nodded, petted a hand over my daughter's head, and went up to Jaron's parents. "We aren't married," I said, grabbing Eve's hands. "I promise you that. We would never get married and not invite you."

She threw her arms around me, knocking me back a step. "I know. Jaron did tell me he was going to marry you one day."

I leaned back, finding Eve's red rimmed eyes staring down at me. "He said that?"

She gave me a soft smile. "You were kids. We had gone to see his Aunt Brogan and Uncle Coby and the rest of you. It was the first time he had seen you in a couple years. He told me…" She laughed lightly, a lone tear rolling down her cheek.

Greyson placed a hand on her shoulder.

"His words were, 'I'm going to marry her, Mama. And I'll follow her around the world until I convince her to say yes.'"

"He…" I swallowed past the hard lump that had suddenly taken up residence in my throat. "Really?"

She nodded. "You must have been talking about traveling or something. But that's what he said. I never really believed him but now…" She shook her head. "He has you down as his wife and you're not even married yet. God, I never realized…I just…He's so much like his father, it's unreal. He's a stubborn one and can be a jerk at times, but he loves you. He loves you so damn much, Piper. Go see him. Our boy needs you. God, does he need you." She cupped my cheek. "Take care of him."

I nodded, swallowing hard.

Following the doctor, he led me to Jaron's room. I tried to expect the worst, but nothing could prepare me for what I saw before me. A large tube was down Jaron's throat. The doctor explained what it was for but the only thing I could focus on was how Jaron looked. Tubes were sticking out of his arms. The machines that he was hooked up to, beeped and controlled the life inside of him.

Jaron was usually strong and sure of himself. Now he just looked weak and like he was barely holding on.

My knees buckled beneath me when an arm wrapped around my middle.

I jumped, staring up at Cyrus.

"Eve said you were in here. I know I'm not supposed to be, but I also knew you wouldn't be able to handle it."

I nodded, words lost on my tongue.

I couldn't handle it. He was right. Jaron didn't deserve this. Neither did his parents. And neither did I.

I pulled out of Cyrus's grip and rushed to Jaron's side, falling to my knees. "Oh Jaron. I'm so sorry." I kissed his cheek, pushing my face into the crook of his neck. He was back. But at the same time, fighting for his life.

Tears streamed down my cheeks. "Cyrus, I can't do this."

"You can. He needs you to be strong for him."

But I wasn't sure if I could.

I had never seen Jaron lose it. Even after everything that had happened to us, he never reacted or allowed me to see that side of him. Not until Brynlee was taken from us, had I truly seen him break.

Cyrus pulled up the chair behind me, gave Jaron's arm a gentle squeeze, and left the room. As soon as Jaron and I were alone, a breath left me. I didn't know what to do or say. I had heard of people being in a coma and their loved ones talking to them, but Jaron wasn't in a coma. He just hadn't woken up from surgery yet. But I needed him to. I needed to see his gray eyes as he told me he loved me. I needed to feel him as he whispered dirty words and sinful truths into my ears.

Slipping my fingers between his, I brought our joined hands up to my mouth and kissed the back of his knuckles. "I love you, Jaron," I whispered.

Just then, Greyson and Eve entered the room.

It was a blur of emotions as Eve cried for her son and Greyson tried to console his wife while keeping his own feelings in check.

I wasn't sure how much time had passed but when I was once again alone with Jaron, he moved. I gasped, shooting to my feet.

His eyes remained closed, but his brow furrowed in the middle. He started struggling, the beeping of the machines becoming faster.

"Nurse!" I screamed, watching Jaron shift and move as he was probably trying to figure out what the hell was going on and why that damn tube was down his throat.

Several people filed into the room, yelling instructions to each other and trying to calm Jaron down.

I was pushed back. A young nurse came into my line of sight, her lips moving over words I couldn't hear.

Jaron was struggling, fighting the nurses and doctor.

Pushing past the nurse standing in front of me, I placed my hands on Jaron's shins. "I'm here, Jaron. Stop fighting them so they can help you, baby."

His body seemed to relax a bit after that.

When he finally calmed down, the nurses and doctor removed the tube from his throat and continued making him as comfortable as they could. His wounds were checked, the machines were silenced, and further instructions were given to each other. But no matter how much they spoke, I couldn't hear anything but the pounding of my heart.

(Jaron)

I was alive.

That much was clear anyway.

But my body hurt like a bitch. Time was lost on me, so I didn't know when it was or even what day it was. I tried thinking back to the moment at the motel with Price. He was shady as fuck, popping off one of his own guys before shooting me, just to make a point. Truth was, he didn't scare me. No. Instead, I had been terrified for my daughter. I didn't want to call out Price on his bluff over the shit he had said about training her. Add to the fact that he had wanted Piper, something inside of me snapped and the next thing I knew, I was waking up in the hospital.

My parents had visited briefly once they found out I was awake. My mom cried. My dad choked back his own emotions. It was hard but warranted.

"How did you and Brynn end up in that motel room?" my dad asked me.

"Price's men put us in that room. I must have passed out, but I woke up for just a second and saw them standing over me." I pinched the bridge of my nose, trying to ward off an incoming headache. "Price came into the room after them and shot one of the guys. I don't know why he did it. With him, it was probably for no reason at all."

My mom looked up at my dad. "Greyson, stop."

Dad wrapped his arm around her shoulders, pulling her into his side. But even though he had his wife close, I could still see the rage trembling through him. I saw it and felt it.

Nothing else was said about what happened. Instead, Brynlee was brought to me.

"Dada," she cried out.

I hugged her close, kissing her little nose. She was beautiful. Just like her mama.

"Where's Piper?" I asked my parents.

"She went to get some food with Cyrus and Sammy. She hasn't eaten much while you've been here," Mom said softly.

I must have passed out again because when I woke next, Piper was curled up in a nearby chair and too damn far away.

Everyone who visited was as quiet as they could be so Piper could sleep. The rest of the crew would come see me later, but my dad had said they were all there, waiting.

"Piper," I croaked, my voice hoarse. I had been through a lot. Beaten within an inch of my life. Bitten by that fucker in jail. Shot. But waking up to that tube down my throat, would be something I would never forget.

Reaching for the Styrofoam cup, I took a sip of water and cleared my throat. "Piper."

She stirred, her eyes fluttering open. They landed on me, sending every nerve ending in my body on high alert.

"Come here," I demanded, a little too rough.

When she didn't listen, my blood boiled through me. She sat there, staring at me.

"Piper," I barked. "Get your ass over here and into my arms."

She rose from the chair but still stood too far away. "I considered leaving you," she finally said.

"I would have left my ass long ago," I told her. "But you didn't because you are a good fucking woman. Now come here."

"I was going to take Brynlee and leave." She looked down at the floor, wringing her hands in front of her. "But I didn't because I love you too much."

"Piper, please." My voice cracked and I didn't fucking like it. Her words hurt. I got it. I understood. But it didn't make it any easier to hear her say it.

"This was before you came home." She met my gaze then. "I never told you because once I had you back, everything seemed right. It was perfect. We struggled and I'm sure we'll continue to struggle but I wouldn't want to struggle with anyone else."

"Piper," I whispered.

She closed the distance between us and threw herself around me. Finally.

I latched on to her, pulling at her clothes, trying to get her closer but no matter how close we were, it would never be enough. I hadn't been gone for long, but it was long enough.

Piper's body trembled against me, her shoulders shaking with her soft cries.

Fisting her hair, I captured her mouth with mine. Her tears coated my tongue, making my tastebuds tingle.

"Jaron," she whispered, sniffing.

I pulled back, cupping the sides of her head and covering her face with soft pecks. "I love you, Piper. You're the beginning to my end. The calm to my wild. The sanity to my crazy."

She smiled, covering my hands, a soft breath shuddering through her.

"You have given me the greatest gifts a man could ever ask for. I'm sorry. For everything. For all of the pain I've caused you. But I'm not sorry for getting rid of Brody and I'm not sorry for going after Price. I know my temper gets in the way, but I promise, it'll never be geared toward you, baby. Ever." My hand moved to the back of her head, my fingers tightening in her hair. "I know that we've struggled but there's no one else I'd rather do this with. Even if we need to go get counseling, take a trip, or just fuck it out, as long as it's with you, I'm down for anything."

A breathless laugh left her. "I didn't leave because I knew then that I didn't want to spend my life with anyone else."

A sly smirk tugged at my lips. "Oh, I know."

Her cheeks turned pink, her smile widening. "How are you feeling?"

"Now that our baby girl is home and you're back in my arms, I feel fucking perfect." I laid back down, pulling her into my arms until she was lying down beside me. The bed was small, but we made it work. "I'll feel even better when I have your pussy choking my cock though."

"Once you're released, baby," she whispered.

I looked down at her. Her eyes were closed, her breathing becoming deep and even. She hadn't slept well since this whole thing started. I let her rest, finally letting out a breath of relief.

While Piper slept, I inched my hand beneath her top and brushed my fingers over her stomach. We would have to make an appointment for her to get checked out and make sure that the baby she was carrying was strong and healthy. Especially after all of the stress.

A light knock on the door interrupted my thoughts. Even though the door hadn't been closed, whoever was at it, still indicated their arrival ahead of time.

"Come in," I called out.

Cyrus peeked his head into the room. "Are we interrupting?"

"No." I tightened my hold on Piper. "Not at all."

"Good." Cyrus came into the room followed by Sammy.

"I'm glad you're awake and well," Cyrus told me, pulling up a chair beside the bed.

"Me too. Have you heard anything about Price?" I asked, not wanting to dwell but needing to make sure my girls were safe.

"Not at the moment. I have Rowan looking into it in the meantime," Cyrus told me.

I nodded, noticing how Sammy stood back. "What's up with you?"

He shoved his hands in his pockets, his dark eyes locking with mine.

My stomach fluttered. I knew that look. He was plotting. "You leave that shit alone," I ordered.

Sammy grunted. "I have no idea what you're talking about."

Piper stirred, sitting up and rubbing her eyes. "You know you can't tell him what to do."

"Maybe not but I am your vice president," I reminded him.

"I'm glad you're well, Jaron." Sammy pulled a pack of smokes from the inner pocket of his cut. "You also have nothing to worry about. Take care of each other."

I frowned. "Sammy."

Instead of listening, he left the room.

"Don't worry about him." Cyrus stood, giving my arm a squeeze. "He's upset that you almost died, that Brynlee was taken in the first place, and that Piper was in the middle of this shit." He shook his head. "He needs time."

"He better not do anything stupid, Cyrus," I warned.

"Take care of yourselves," he said, ignoring my comment. "We'll stop by tomorrow." And with that, Cyrus left the room.

"Sammy said he's going to go after Price," Piper told me, placing her hand on my thigh.

"I figured." I pinched the bridge of my nose, closing my eyes.

"I'll let you get some rest."

My eyes popped open when she went to pull away from me. "Don't you even think about fucking leaving."

"But you need rest, Jaron. You need to heal and get better so I can bring you home and take care of you."

Before she could leave the bed, my hand was wrapped around her throat.

A little gasp left her, making my dick twitch.

Pulling her forward, I stared directly into her eyes. "The only thing I need right now, is for you to lay down beside me." I licked along her bottom lip. "I don't give a shit that I just got out of surgery either. If you don't listen to me, I will leave this bed and do what I do best."

"What's that?" she breathed.

"Fuck my girl." I kissed her hard.

A husky laugh escaped her. "You're not strong enough."

"Try me, Piper." Laying back down, I tugged her down beside me. "This is what I want right now. It'll help me feel better."

"Okay." She curled against me. "As you wish, Sir," she said, a teasing lilt to her voice.

"Careful," I growled.

Her laugh deepened. "I love you."

"I love you too, baby." I kissed the top of her head. "More than you will ever know."

THIRTY-THREE

Piper

JARON WAS GETTING OUT of the hospital today. He had been stuck in it for almost a week and was on the verge of losing it. I had stayed with him while my parents and his parents watched Brynlee. They would bring her to us every day. She stayed for a few hours until it was time to be picked up.

Price was still nowhere to be found. Cyrus said his contact lost track of him but was continuing to look into it. I couldn't understand how a person could just disappear like that. It didn't make sense to me and while I didn't like the fact that I felt like I had to constantly look over my shoulder, if Price disappeared for good and I never had to see him again, I was fine with it.

I went back to Jaron's room after getting us a cup of coffee each, only to find him standing by his bed in gray sweatpants and nothing else.

"Geezus," I heard a nurse say as she walked past me.

I laughed, shaking my head.

Jaron's head turned, his slate eyes finding mine. "Something wrong?"

"No." I went up to him and sat on the edge of the bed. "I think the nurses here are going to miss you."

He chuckled. "They were good to me, so I made sure to leave a little donation to the hospital."

"Oh, that's nice of you." My heart warmed at the thoughtful gesture.

Jaron slipped a white t-shirt over his head and smoothed down the material.

I handed him his coffee before taking a sip of my own.

"Thank you," he said, watching me over the rim of the cup as he leaned against the wall.

I shivered at the intense scrutiny. "Why are you looking at me like that?"

"Because I'm thinking of all the ways I'm going to fuck your body when we get home." His eyes darkened even more as the words left his mouth.

"You need your rest. The doctor said no strenuous activity," I reminded him. "You're still healing anyway."

"I don't give a shit. I'll just lay there if I have to but I'm fucking my girl."

My body burned at the idea but him calling me his, reminding me of something. "You told the doctor that I'm your wife."

"I put you down as my next of kin after Paris. Once I was released from jail, I then put you down as my wife to make things easier for you if anything ever happened to me."

I stared at him, letting his words sink in. "Really?"

He nodded. "I knew you were mine long before I found out you were pregnant with Brynlee. Maybe it was a little presumptuous, but I planned on dating you after Paris. When I saw you at that bar with the girls, I was struck stupid that you were there. My thoughts were messed up and I couldn't focus on anything but getting back inside you. I should have asked you out first instead of being such an asshole, but my feelings for you fucked me up."

"I had no idea. I wanted to tell you that I loved you when we were in Paris. I had been in love with you for a while…" I sighed. "I'm sorry."

"Don't be." Jaron placed his cup on the table and stepped between my knees. "What's in the past, stays in the past. We have each other now. It's just you and me." He cupped my jaw, tilting my head back. "I want to date you. Travel with you. I want to walk the journey of life with you. I want to raise Brynlee and this baby and all our future babies, with you." He bent at the waist, giving me a soft peck on the lips. "I want to marry you, Piper."

Throwing my arms around his neck, I deepened the kiss. "I want all of that too," I whispered.

He shivered. "I need to get you home. Please, baby."

I gently pushed him back and stood from the bed. "Take me home."

With a firm grip on my jaw, Jaron held my head in place and licked up the length of my throat.

"I fucking love you, Piper." His teeth sunk into my jaw. "But right now, I need…I need you so fucking hard. I want to hurt as we find us again."

It was the first time we had been alone since getting Brynlee back. While we had our moments where it was just us two at the hospital, staff always interrupted us to make sure that he was fine and healing okay. Now it was the first time we had been truly alone since he came back to me. The first time we had been alone since he almost died.

This wouldn't be making love. This wouldn't be us reconnecting. This would be a rage fuck. We would take out our pain, heartache, and wrath on each other.

"Piper." His rough use of my name slid over my skin. "Piper. Please."

A soft gasp left me at hearing the desperation in his voice.

I turned my head, meeting his hard gaze. We were at home, finally. I had brought his things to the bedroom while he followed behind me. I could feel him staring at me, his body hard and begging for that release only I could give it.

I had suggested to him that he have a nap first, at least, but he refused. So now, there we were, about to do what we did best. Speak through our bodies.

"Sit up." I wasn't the dominant type but when Jaron needed that control from me, I was willing to comply. He had always taken over, giving me everything I could ever want and more. But it had been so long since we were together, I knew he needed this from me. It was a silent apology for leaving me. For leaving us. I knew why he had left. I understood. But it still didn't mean that it hurt any less. And while we had our daughter back, we still didn't know where Price was or if he would ever be back. I wanted to tell Jaron that I didn't care, but I did. I wanted to tell him that we didn't need to know, and we could just move on. But I didn't. Because I knew that as long as Price was alive, the guys wouldn't rest until he was gone. For good.

Jaron moved to the edge of the bed, his eyes not leaving mine the whole time.

My heart jumped. The hairs on my skin tingled.

The longer he watched, the wetter I became.

Sliding off the bed, I stepped in front of him and began stripping.

When I was finally naked, I stepped between his knees.

Jaron ran the back of his knuckles over my stomach. "I love you."

I straddled his lap and ran my fingers through his beard. "I know."

"I'm sorry," he murmured, kissing my fingers as they passed over his mouth.

"I know that too." I kissed his forehead, breathing in the fresh scent of him. Pushing him back until he was laying on the bed, I reached into his sweatpants and pulled out his thick cock.

He groaned, his eyes rolling into the back of his head. "Piper."

I slowly lowered my body onto him.

His jaw clenched.

I moaned.

Once I was seated fully on his lap, I took a deep breath. His cock stretched me, making my body open to him completely. I wasn't fully wet, but I didn't care. I wanted to feel the burn of him being inside my unprepared body. I wanted to hurt. To ache. To be in agony as we made each other feel better.

"Piper," he growled through clenched teeth. His fingers gripped my hips, digging into me, but he never took over. No. Instead, this was all for me. He was letting me be in control to make up for the fact that he left. It wasn't enough but it was a start.

"Harder," he pleaded.

"I don't want to hurt you." It had only been a week since his surgery. Sex was probably not something he should be doing yet but he didn't listen.

"I don't give a shit, Piper. I need you to ride me. Hard."

Running my hands beneath his shirt, I lifted my hips up and down in rough moves.

"Fucking hell." His dark eyes locked with mine. "Bounce for me, baby."

"God, Jaron." I placed my hands on his chest for leverage and picked up speed. Riding him. Fucking him. Giving him what he needed. What we both needed.

"That's it," he grit out. "Faster."

His cock swelled inside of me.

His hands on my hips tightened, pulling me forward and back. His pelvis thrust up and down.

We worked up a rhythm. Fucking each other hard, rough, so damn deep, I could feel him through every inch of me.

"Piper," he shouted out, his back bowing off the bed as his release spilled into me.

Once he calmed down, I slowed but his fingers tightened.

"Don't stop. Don't you dare fucking stop."

Even though he was now soft inside of me, he continued to thrust into me.

"Get hard again, baby," I told him.

He sat up, wrapping his arms around me and crushing his mouth to mine.

Getting the hint, I slipped my tongue between his lips.

His hands roamed down my back before cupping my ass.

I sighed, breaking the kiss.

"Marry me."

I stopped moving, my eyes snapping to his. "What?"

"Marry me, Piper. Doesn't have to be now. Or next month. Or even this year. I want you to promise me that you will marry me." He pinched my chin, placing a soft peck on my mouth. "I love you. I love you so fucking much. I will make up for what I've done. I will prove to you that this is worth it. That we are worth it. I want you at my side. In my bed. In my life. Forever, baby."

My eyes welled. "You...you want that? You want to spend your life with me?"

"Yes, Piper. I told you that at the hospital and I'll continue telling you." He linked our fingers and kissed my knuckles. "I promise to show you that we are meant to be. That we've always been meant to be. Your name is on my bank account. You have access to everything I own, Piper. What's mine is yours. Literally."

He spun us around and slid from my body. Wrapping his hand around his cock, he pumped until he became hard. Until he grew. For me.

"I am yours, Piper. All of me. Every inch. Every piece."

I pushed my hands beneath his shirt, pulling it up his torso.

He pulled off the shirt, revealing his tanned torso to my feasting eyes. A bandage sat on his shoulder and another on his lower abdomen. He would have scars and they would constantly remind us for the rest of our lives of how he almost died.

We had so much to work through. We probably always would. Jail messed Jaron up. Brynlee being taken, messed us both up. But our love for each other would conquer all of the heartache life had thrown at us. It made us stronger apart and even stronger together.

"Remind me," I whispered at the same time he sunk back into my body.

I sighed, spreading my legs even wider and taking his slow thrusts.

With his hand in mine, he consumed me completely.

"Jaron." I ran my hands up his back. "I promise."

He lifted his head, staring down at me, his hips stopping. "Really?"

I nodded. "But you hurt me. You broke my heart." It had been the first time I voiced my feelings since he came home from the hospital. "Don't leave me. Ever again. If you need to go, take us with you. We are a team, Jaron. Don't forget that."

He leaned his forehead against mine. "I don't deserve you, Piper. But I will spend my days showing you how much I love you. How much I need you. How deeply in love with you I am."

"It's deeper than love. Isn't it?"

He kissed my nose and then my mouth. "It is." He released me and stripped the rest of the way. Kneeling back between my legs, he took my thoughts and feelings and made them his. He owned and consumed me, making me forget all of the pain.

A couple of hours later, we were still in bed and his hands were cupping my head as he thrust his cock between my lips.

I enjoyed tasting myself on him. It reminded me that I in fact belonged to him. It also reminded me of how far we had come.

My tongue slid along the veiny ridges of his thick length. It slipped into the slit in the tip.

He groaned, his fingers tightening on my head. "Baby."

I smiled around him. I loved when he became desperate and begged. It didn't happen often but turned me on every time it did.

Lowering my mouth, I took him down my throat. I gagged around him but kept going. I couldn't stop, knowing I needed to make him feel good. It made me wet the harder he became for me.

"Fucking hell." His hips bucked. "Your throat is so tight."

Releasing him, I kissed the tip and wrapped my hand around him. "You taste like me."

He grinned, his eyes darkening. "I bet you taste like me too."

A breathless laugh escaped me. "I'm sure I do."

"Let me taste."

Reaching between my legs, I slipped a finger inside of me before bringing it up to his mouth. I ran the wet tip along his lip.

His mouth parted, his tongue peeking out to lick along the soaked end of my finger. "Tasty."

It was dirty but it was needed, and it was ours.

THIRTY-FOUR

Piper

"HOLY FUCKING SHIT," MEADOW exclaimed. "Our parents told us some things, but I didn't know there was more to it than what they said."

I laughed lightly, shrugging.

I had just finished telling Gigi, Luna, and Meadow everything that had happened and why I had disappeared again after the last time I saw them at Gigi and Vince's place.

"I knew you two were struggling but I didn't know…" Luna shook her head. "Wow."

It had been a month since Jaron was shot and almost died. The next day after he was discharged, he went out and bought me a ring. He slipped the ring on my finger. I still gave him the same answer again and then he fucked me until I continued saying yes over and over.

We hadn't left the house since and spent most of our time as a family. The only time we did end up leaving, was for my doctor's appointment. Our unborn baby was strong and healthy, thankfully the stress of what happened had not caused any issues.

"I know." I sighed. "I'm sorry. For everything. For not keeping in touch when Jaron was in jail. For not letting you know Brynlee as much as you should. I'm sorry for being a bad friend."

"You are not a bad friend." Gigi moved from her spot and sat beside me on the couch.

The girls had come over to my place while Jaron brought Brynlee for a playdate with Luna and Zach's son, Benjamin. It was nice for Jaron to get reacquainted with his cousin, Zach, and I suggested that we do it more often.

"You've had it hard." Gigi grabbed my hand, holding it tight in hers. "I can't imagine what you've been through, but I knew that you would come back around whenever you were ready."

"She's right," Meadow said. "We all knew that. It's why we never pushed. We often talked about how worried we were, but Shade reassured me that Cyrus and Sammy constantly looked out for you. It made me feel a little bit better."

"I love you girls," I sniffled. "So much. I couldn't ask for better friends."

"We love you too." Luna moved to the spot on the other side of me. "Now we can all get married, so the guys can stop brooding."

We laughed.

"I should have waited for Jaron to be home. For you." Meadow moved to the spot in front of me and knelt at my feet. "I'm sorry we didn't."

"No." I pulled my hand from Gigi's and hugged her sister. "I get it. You and Shade lost..." I cleared my throat. "Anyway, I understand."

"I'm just glad you were there." Meadow pulled back. "Shade told me that he's heading over to Luna's place with Andrew."

Gigi laughed. "Vince is there too with Hannah."

"Oooo, all the dads with the babies." Luna tapped her chin. "Why do I find that hot?"

Another round of laughter erupted through us.

"Maybe we should go save them," Meadow suggested, stifling another laugh.

"Nah." Gigi leaned her head against my shoulder. "Not yet."

While we continued catching up, I couldn't help but realize how right this was. Jaron and I were happy and finally moving forward. We didn't take life for granted anymore and took each day as a blessing. We made sure to say I love you and constantly gave Brynlee and our unborn baby, all the love we could. It was the little things. Jaron had gotten into the habit of picking me up a bouquet of red roses every Friday. I made sure to pick off a single petal from each bouquet he had purchased and slid the petal between pages in a journal.

He still had his moments where he became moody and withdrawn but with every little second that passed, I helped him through it. His nightmares were few and far between but whenever he had one, I consoled him back to sleep.

Later that evening after the girls had left, I was making dinner. The girls and I had promised to meet up again and soon, while the guys had their playdates with the kids.

The sound of the front door opening, sent a shiver racing through my body.

I stepped out of the kitchen and went to the hall. Jaron's head turned, a slow smirk spreading on his face when his dark eyes met mine.

"Hey, Wifey," he said, his voice rough and gravely.

I giggled at the new term of endearment he had given me once he slipped the engagement ring on my finger. "How was your playdate?"

"Good. We're going to do it again next month to give you girls a break." Jaron came up to me and placed Brynn in my arms. "I would like a playdate with you later once Brynn goes to bed."

I laughed, smacking his shoulder playfully. "I don't think you'll have any issues convincing me." I winked, placing Brynn in her highchair.

"I don't think so either." Heavy arms wrapped around my middle, pulling me back. Jaron kissed the side of my neck before turning me around. "You good?"

"I am." I hugged my arms around his hard middle. "Are you?"

Jaron pulled out of my grip and grabbed my hands. He placed a soft peck on the ring on my finger. "I couldn't be better."

(Jaron)

Once Brynlee was put to bed, I was on Piper. She never even had a chance to shut the door to our daughter's bedroom before I had her up against the wall and my mouth fused to hers.

She gave as good as she got.

A few hours later when we were curled up in bed and I could still feel the scratch marks on my back.

While she slept peacefully beside me, I checked my phone.

My dad told me I could take over and be the president of Hell's Harlem. After everything that had happened recently, he told me to take my time and to go to him whenever I was ready.

Price was still nowhere to be found. I wasn't sure why, but a moment of peace settled over me. I knew that he would be caught. Eventually. I also knew that it wouldn't be me who did it. Someone else would take him out and I just hoped that I would be there to watch him fall.

My eyes flicked to the leather cut hanging over the back of the chair in the corner of the bedroom. Although the room was dark, the moonlight had cast an eerie glow around the vest. It was like the universe was saying that it's time.

I kissed the top of Piper's head, letting out a deep sigh.

I realized something in that moment.

Being president was something I was never ready for. Life always got in the way and prevented me from taking over the club.

Now that my daughter was safe, Piper was in my arms, and our unborn baby was healthy and growing inside of her...

I was ready.

EPILOGUE

JARON

"YOU READY, SON?" MY dad asked, holding a knife in his hand.

It had been over five months since I was shot and almost lost my life. Zach and Luna had finally gotten married. Piper was entering her third trimester with our second baby. I had heard through her that Cyrus had met someone. She only told me that the woman was nice and was someone who worked at the center. She didn't know much more than that but warned him in the meantime to be careful. I knew he would tell us more whenever he was ready. But I did notice that he was happier. Sammy was still grumpy, but I wasn't ready for a fight, so I never questioned him on his shit.

I had also approached Candace. I needed to make sure there were no further issues for Piper and I.

"Jaron." Candace's wide eyes looked up from her computer. "I wasn't expecting to see you."

"I need to make sure that you know that it's over between us. For good."

"I…" Her mouth opened and closed like a fish before a hard sigh left her. *"Yeah, I know. I knew that a long time ago. Even before you got out of jail. You could have called though instead of showing up here."*

"I'll be here often with my crew, I need to make sure that there aren't going to be any issues for Piper and me." I was tying up loose ends before Piper and I made things official between us.

"You won't have any issues," Candace said softly.

"Good." Instead of waiting for her to respond, I left her office and made my way out of the club.

Heading home, I made my way to the one and only woman who had ever captured my heart. The only one I wanted to spend my life with.

"Jaron?" Dad clapped my shoulder. "We can wait if you aren't."

"I'm ready," I told him.

"You sure?" he asked, raising an eyebrow.

I nodded, blowing out a slow breath and taking the knife from him. My eyes shifted to Piper who was standing between Cyrus and Sammy.

I love you, she mouthed, cupping her swollen stomach.

My body stirred at the sight of her. *I love you more.*

She grinned, shaking her head.

Taking another deep breath, I started cutting off the vice president patch from my leather cut. When it was removed completely, it had felt like the world had shifted.

"Did you choose?" Dad asked, low enough so only I could hear.

I nodded, grabbed the small patch, and went up to Cyrus. "We've been through a lot together. You fight me when I need it and have my back without me even having to ask. You keep me in line, voice your thoughts but still stick by me even if you don't agree with my choices."

Cyrus's jaw clenched, his throat working hard as he swallowed.

"I love you and Sammy like brothers. You took care of my girls when I couldn't." I glanced at Sammy.

He shifted on his feet, wrapping an arm around Piper's shoulders.

If it was anyone else who touched her, I would have killed them already but not him or his brother. I trusted them with her life and prayed that they found the happiness they both deserved.

"I can never repay you for what you've done for us." I looked back at Cyrus. "I want you to be my vice president."

His eyes widened a touch. His head whipped around.

Sammy returned the look, a wide grin spreading on his face. "Don't look at me. Wasn't my idea."

Piper laughed.

"But..." Cyrus cleared his throat. "You good?"

Sammy rolled his eyes. "I don't want to be vice president, C. I'd rather be the enforcer anyway. Means I can get bloody."

Laughter sounded around the room.

"You sure?" Cyrus asked me.

"I wouldn't want anyone else. Not even fuckhead over here," I nodded toward Sammy.

"Rude," Sammy grumbled.

I chuckled. "Seriously though, Cyrus. You deserve it and I need you at my side. Both of you."

Cyrus took the patch from between my fingers. "I'd be honored to be your VP."

A round of cheers and hollers sounded around the room.

Cyrus and I ignored them and sewed the patches on our leather cuts. When we were done, he pulled me into his arms. "I love you, brother."

"I love you too." I clapped his back, squeezing him.

"Let me in here." Sammy wrapped his arms around our shoulders.

My mom sniffled and muttered softly with the rest of the ladies.

Lifting my head, I found Piper standing beside us. Grabbing her hand, I pulled her into our little huddle.

She laughed lightly.

Along with my daughter and unborn baby, these three were my life. I would do anything for them, and I knew they would do the same for me.

It was a good day to be a biker but an even better day to be with the ones I loved.

My family.

THE END

The Next Generation Series:
https://www.aboutjmwalker.com/next-generation-series

ACKNOWLEDGEMENTS

We are now 6 books into The Next Generation Series!! I feel like with each book that releases, the crazy only gets worse and worse. But it's SO exciting and SO much fun to write!

First, I'd like to thank my team for their constant help on every book I write. I really couldn't do this without them!

Angie, Jennifer and Christina: You girls see my stories in the raw. You help me perfect each book. You tell me when to cut scenes or when to add them. I often find that you know these characters better than I do.

Joanne: Thank you for your editing expertise! I really couldn't do this without your help and I appreciate you more than I could ever say!

J.M.'s Jems: Best group ever!! You are my safe place.

Authors and bloggers: Thank you for your constant support and for cheering me on throughout my journey!

My readers: Best readers ever! Seriously. You all are amazing and I really couldn't do this without you. I thank you often for reading my stories but really, thanking you isn't enough because no words could ever describe how much I love and appreciate each and every one of you.

If you've read The Next Generation Series thus far, thank you! Also, a little warning: The books only get more intense from here.

JM

ABOUT

J.M. Walker is an Amazon bestselling author who also hit USA Today with Wanted: An Outlaw Anthology. She loves all things books, pigs and lip gloss. She is happily married to the man who inspires all of her Heroes and continues to make her weak in the knees every single day.

"Above all, be the HEROINE of your own life..." ~ Nora Ephron

Find me!

https://linktr.ee/authorjmwalker

Want more? Head on over to my website for my complete backlist!
https://www.aboutjmwalker.com/books